MW00619537

AMY FILLION

Broken and Breaking Free

Copyright © 2019 by Amy Fillion

All rights reserved. No part of this publication may be reproduced, stored or transmitted in any form or by any means, electronic, mechanical, photocopying, recording, scanning, or otherwise without written permission from the publisher. It is illegal to copy this book, post it to a website, or distribute it by any other means without permission.

This novel is entirely a work of fiction. The names, characters and incidents portrayed in it are the work of the author's imagination.

First edition

This book was professionally typeset on Reedsy.
Find out more at reedsy.com

For Memere

Contents

Acknowledgement

My sincerest thanks to my mother without whom this novel would not exist. I love you to the moon and back and back again.

Jason, you have been a rock. Your encouragement is unwavering, and for that, I am truly blessed.

Lila Wall and Heather Elmer, I thank you for the time and energy spent in reading my manuscript and helping me mold this story to be the best it can possibly be. Please know that I appreciate you immensely.

My thanks, also, to Mary Beth Constant. You are a truly amazing copy editor. I am humbled by your expertise. My book would not have come to fruition without you.

Dana Mathias, you blew me away with your book cover design. I was in the library when I received my cover proof and I'm not ashamed to admit that I teared up surrounded by other people. It's *that* good! Thank you for lending your artistic ability to my story.

My boys, I love you. You are my inspiration day in and day out. May you love your lives and what this world of ours has to offer. May you grow to embrace all of humanity. And through the years, don't forget that you're *never* too old to give your mother a hug!

ONE

Susan heard the shouting first.

She leaped from her bed and ran to close the door, careful steps on the balls of her feet. Nausea settled. She turned, small pajama-clad body readying itself for what would inevitably transpire within the next room. Already she could hear her brother's muffled protests, and she knew her father had unclasped the belt that held his pants to his slight frame.

A cry. She closed her eyes, lashes fluttering as she trembled. She crossed her arms upon her small chest, grasped her elbows with her hands. Her face scrunched, her nose pinched, and baby teeth ground together.

The tears were beginning now behind her pale lids, and as she slowly opened her eyes within her darkening room, they made their way onto her cheeks, upon her chin, finding their wet path to her heaving chest.

She ran to the side of her bed and released her elbows to swipe her cheeks with her fingers. Still, the tears came. Unbidden but silent. With small, trembling hands, she pulled back the comforter, revealing a white cotton sheet beckoning her a bit of comfort in which her weary body could retreat. She gratefully accepted.

She slid her naked toes under the blanket and lay on her left side facing the only window in her small room and a view of the setting

1

sun. Her head rested upon the pillow in its flower-print case as she brought her knees to her chest, and closed her eyes once again.

A recent memory found its way to her just then as she heard the gruff, deep voice of her father and the high, shrill wail that left the depths of her brother's soul.

Charlie was playing with Henry, throwing a baseball on the concrete road that was void of moving cars. Susan was on her bike next to Janet who lived in the small tan house to the left of theirs, which was at the corner of North Street and Pleasant Avenue. Janet and she were the same age in this spring of 1959, both five, cheeks and limbs indicative of the young.

She had inherited this bike from a neighbor down the street who had outgrown it a few years prior. It was a beautiful shade of cherry red. Although both she and Janet had difficulty maintaining their balance on their bicycles, they tried all the same. Even when she simply scooted along with her feet on the ground she felt an immense sense of pride and ownership.

Janet's brown eyes shone in the morning's sunlight as she smiled at her best friend. Her shoulder-length brunette hair was pulled into two ribboned pigtails just below the ears. Thick stockings warmed her legs under her checkered dress and a light brown sweater hugged her chest.

The girls continued to pedal, giggling as they'd trip up or need to rest their feet on the ground for added support to their wobbling bicycling attempts, the road's steady incline and many potholes and frost heaves the winter birthed only adding more difficulty to the task.

A sudden shattering of glass and a loud exclamation from her brother.

She halted her bicycle and abruptly turned around. Her clear blue eyes widened, pushing the long, sparse lashes upward, her tightly curled auburn hair a mass around her round face and small chin. Charlie and Henry had abandoned their game. Both still wore their gloves, but neither grasped the ball. Charlie's pale freckled face was contorted in a look of anger, and

2

then almost instantaneously she saw a look she knew all too well for her short five years. Fear. It exploded from his countenance, from his hunched shoulders and timid, shuffling steps as he walked toward the car.

Henry looked toward Charlie and then at the car's broken back window. A slight puff of unbelief left his mouth, and his lips formed a small uncertain smirk—a question—as he looked upon his friend. Charlie stared back, and Henry noticed a small tremble from his long, gangly nine-year-old frame, panicked trepidation in his green eyes.

The smirk faded.

The screen door slammed shut, and Father hastily stepped toward the boys, white undershirt tucked into slim pants, brown shirt unbuttoned and hanging loose at the sides, billowing with the force of his abrupt movements. His look was one of rage.

Mother was scurrying behind him, wiping her hands on her white apron. Her flower-printed dress brushed against her shins. Her feet were bare on the cold concrete as she stood on her toes, allowing her body to lean forward and look over her husband's shoulder at the car's back window. Curiosity now fulfilled, she hung back, turning her gaze to her son with a worried expression.

Susan stumbled from her bike and took a few timid steps toward her brother.

"What the hell did you do to my car, boy?" The look upon her father's face halted her movements.

"I'm sorry, sir. It was an accident. Henry and I, we... we were..." He didn't get any further. Her father forcefully slapped the back of Charlie's head and took hold of what short light brown hair he could to push his son to the ground. Charlie stumbled from the force and grunted as his hands instinctively broke his fall to the ground. Father yanked him to his feet by the back of his shirt, breaking the topmost button. Father didn't loosen his grasp and Charlie whimpered as he was hauled toward the house.

Mother wrung her fingers around the bottom of her apron. She felt little hands grasp her hips from behind, a little head rest upon her lower back. She turned around and stooped to embrace her daughter, knees on the pebbly concrete. She wiped the tears that were freely flowing from her daughter's eyes and then gently shook her head. A warning. She stood and took her daughter's small hand in hers as Charlie's cries reverberated. Together they slowly made their way to the front porch and through the door to the kitchen leaving a bewildered Henry and Janet behind.

Father had his belt in his hand. Dangling down his right leg, its presence was large and foreboding in the small room. Charlie faced his father, eyes wide, body trembling.

"You will pay for that window, boy. You will help me in the garage tomorrow and you'll go down the street to see if there's anything Mr. Biladeau needs from you. And you are not to see that boy Henry until this shit is done. Am I clear?" His voice was low, his words spoken slowly.

Mother, still holding her daughter's hand in hers, bent at the knee and leaned in to whisper gently in her ear: "Go to your room, darling. And close the door."

"Am. I. Clear?" Father was seething. He lifted his hand. The belt hung limply in the air.

"Ye—... ye—... yes, sir," Charlie shrieked with fright as his father vigorously turned his son's body and pushed him up against the wall, bringing the belt down upon his backside. "Yes, sir!" He was sobbing.

"What the fuck were you thinking, boy? I work hard to provide for this family. You ungrateful son of a bitch! You go and break my goddamn window!" His arm rose again, his pants fighting for hold on his narrow hips.

"I'm sorry, sir!" A loud exclamation. His arms stretched outward, bracing his body upon the wall as the belt seethed against his backside once again.

She couldn't move. Although silent, her body heaved from tears and terror. Her mother lifted her into her arms and ran out of the room. She put her head into the crook of Mother's neck and closed her eyes. She heard the door open and felt the bed touch her back as she was gently placed upon her soft blanket. She opened her eyes, imploring, and held her mother's intent blue gaze. She felt the dry palm that cupped her cheek. "Stay here."

Footsteps upon the creaking living room floor. Her mother's unassertive voice: "Gerald?"

"Shut up, woman!"

Shuffling. A scuffle. Something falling to the floor. Charlie's sobs. A yell. "Son of a bitch!" Her father.

No. She didn't want to remember. That time or any of the others. And as she lay there in her bed hearing Charlie and her father beyond the thin walls, she wanted to scream. She wanted to run.

"Shut the fuck up, boy!… Take it like a man, goddamn it!" Father was generous with his eruptions in these times of parental superiority.

She lay there in her nightdress, curls splayed upon the pillowcase as she listened to her brother in the neighboring room. Charlie's door shut a moment later, and her father's pounding footsteps sounded their advance to the kitchen.

Silence.

Her trembling body eventually found the sleep of the exhausted, her cheek resting in the cool wetness of her tears.

* * *

She awoke in the morning to a weighted presence on her bed, a hand gently tousling her curls. Her eyes protested opening, but open they did, and she found her brother looking down upon her. His deep green eyes were rimmed with the redness of a restless night's sleep, encompassed by a puffiness that gave them a hollow appearance.

"Charlie." She whispered his name as she reached to touch a fingertip to the skin below his eye. He sat there and smiled sadly down upon her.

"It's okay. It's my back that's sore." He lifted his shoulders and sighed in resignation. Her finger retreated but her eyes remained on his face.

"Mom's making pancakes and syrup. Your favorite. They're ready." Her body was slowly waking. Weary. "Okay." She smiled slightly.

"Susie T." She giggled as he tousled her hair once more. The nickname was his only, and it brought her joy when he used it, referencing Shirley Temple's hair, curls that Susan's perfectly mimicked. "Let's get you up and going." Charlie took her by the hand and guided her from the warm blankets. Together they quickly pulled the covers over the pillow in semblance of a properly made bed.

Her hand held tightly to his as they walked toward her bedroom door. While she was petite, he was tall for his nine years, despite his genetic predisposition to short stature. She squeezed his hand. He turned to look at her. "I love you, Charlie."

He inclined his head. "I love you, too, Susie."

Mother was already dressed when the children entered the kitchen, apron tied in back to save her dress from ruin. The smell of warm pancakes wafted through the room. She was pouring herself a cup of black coffee at the countertop. Father was at his place at the kitchen table with the Saturday morning paper held in hand, coffee before him, a cigarette billowing smoke from his mouth as he turned the page.

"Good morning, sleepy head." Mother's voice was soft, her smile genuine.

"Good morning, Mama," said Susan.

They walked to the table and sat down upon their chairs, Susan to her father's right, back facing the yellow wall, and Charlie directly across the table from Father.

Mother walked the few steps from the kitchen counter to the table, placing her coffee down. Breakfast, plates, and silverware were already set. Mother placed two pancakes on the plate that rested before Father. He uncrossed his legs and sat up straight, extinguishing his cigarette in the ashtray on the window ledge and folding his newspaper to place on the table. A daily routine. Mother forked a pancake onto both Susan's and Charlie's plates, smiling at each in turn, and sat directly across from Susan. She handed a bowl of strawberries to Father for him to partake of first. Strawberries were Susan's favorite, and as they didn't have them often, she could feel her mouth watering. When they had made their way around the table to her, she knew to leave a few in case Father's appetite determined he eat the rest.

Mother nodded her head, closed her eyes, and folded her hands together, elbows resting upon the chrome-and-vinyl table. The others followed suit.

"Bless us, O Lord, and the food upon this table that we are about to receive. Through Christ our Lord. Amen."

"Amen." Susan unfolded her hands and brought them back to her small lap. She waited for Father to pick up his fork and begin eating. Once he did so, she followed his lead and pierced a strawberry, bringing it to her mouth. She took an eager bite and smirked through her chewing, the combination of sweet and sour flavors bursting within. Charlie cut into his pancake, eyes downcast.

Father reached blindly and grabbed the handle of his coffee cup. He tipped it to his mouth. "Helen, I'm out of coffee."

"Oh, I am so sorry about that, Gerald. I was not aware. I will fill it up now for you." Mother stood and walked to the kitchen counter with the empty mug, returning it to its owner full and steaming. Father made no acknowledgment, merely continued working on the fluffy pancakes on his plate.

"Susan, are you going to see if Janet wants to play today? It is a beautiful day to be outside. And Charles, how about Henry? You are welcome to walk over to his house to see if he would like to come out."

Susan and Charlie began speaking simultaneously.

"Go ahead, Susie," Charlie said.

Susan looked to Mother. "Yeah. I want to play with Janet. Can I go over right after breakfast?"

"You certainly may," Mother said. "And Charles? What were you about to say?"

"Yes, ma'am. I was going to say yes, that I'd like to go to Henry's house. He said he'd be home when I saw him yesterday. We're going to play ball."

"What are you doing today, Mama?" Susan asked.

"Oh, well," she said, "Mrs. Levesque across the street has invited me over for tea and cookies and I have accepted. I did assume you children would be out with your friends for the day and your father is helping Mr. Biladeau down the street with a project in his home. I thought perhaps I would pack a picnic lunch for you and Charles, yes? That way you can head to the playground to eat if you would like. Of course"—she looked to Father—"Gerald, if you are done at Edmond's home, please come and get me from Maria's. I am happy to come back home to prepare a lunch for you." Father nodded his head and took a sip of his coffee.

"Are you still hungry?" Mother asked when she saw her children's plates were empty.

Susan shook her head as Charlie said, "No, ma'am."

"Well, then," Mother said in return, "let us clear the table, shall we?" The children helped to clear as Father lit a cigarette, lifted the newspaper, and crossed his legs.

"Thank you for your help, children," Mother said. "Go along now. You may get dressed and then go see if Janet and Henry would like to play for the day." She turned back to the kitchen sink and began filling it with hot, sudsy water, stealing a glance over her shoulder at her husband seated at the table, coffee in hand, taking a long, contented drag from his newly lit cigarette.

* * *

Sunday dawned. Susan awoke early: the sun was low in the sky, still making its way from its slumbering state. The house was quiet. Mother and Father were typically up before Susan, so she must have awakened early indeed.

She crept into the living room with the intention of turning on the television set but heard a muffled moan from her parents' bedroom that sounded like one of them was tormented. Her brow furrowed, and she inhaled a quickened breath as unease crept into the depths of her stomach. She slowly walked toward the wooden French doors of her parents' room. A creak. Quickening. A low grunt. She pushed on the left door steadily and opened it just well enough to allow a peek within.

Mother's bed was closest to the door. She lay supine, face tilted slightly to the right, eyes focused on the ceiling. Father had abandoned his own bed and was on top of his wife, a blanket draped upon his shoulders. His face looked bedeviled, eyes fully shut, nose crinkled, mouth slightly open in an agonizing grimace. What was wrong with him? And wasn't Mother worried? And oh, gosh, why was he moving that way?

A moment later, Father grunted and the motion ceased. He

collapsed to Mother's side, his head hitting the bedsheet. Susan didn't linger; she ran to her room and buried herself under her comforter, shaking with disquietude. She lay on her side, lifting her knees to her chin, wrapping her small arms around her shins and squeezing. She didn't move until she heard steps in the living room and the voices of Mother and Father beginning their day.

Susan slowly unwrapped her arms from around her legs and dared to exit her room, poking her head around the corner of her bedroom doorway to peer into the kitchen. She couldn't see the table from this viewpoint, but she could hear the talking and her parents didn't sound even the least bit affected. In fact, Father sounded very much like himself, cheerful even, if Father could be equated with cheerfulness.

Susan ventured through the doorway, tentative and unhurried. Father had seated himself at the table with his Sunday morning newspaper, cigarette smoking from his hand. Mother slouched, facing the window that overlooked North Street, and brought her cigarette to her mouth as she gazed absently at the world awakening. She turned at the sound of Susan's footsteps.

"Oh, good morning, darling." She corrected herself, sitting erect. "Come on over here and give your mother a good-morning hug." She smiled, but Susan wasn't fully convinced. It didn't reach her eyes.

She walked over and wrapped her arms around Mother's neck. Susan could smell the cigarette on her mother's breath, tar-like and putrid, even through the lavender scent she loved so well.

"How did you sleep?"

"Good."

"Well?" Mother winked, a tease to lighten the fact that she was correcting her daughter's grammar.

"I slept well," Susan conceded.

"I am pleased." She tucked a stray curl behind her daughter's ear. "You may go watch a Sunday morning program on the television if you would like, darling."

"I'm really hungry, Mama."

"Susan, you know that we do not eat on Sunday mornings. The Lord asks us to fast so that we may be more reverent when we attend Mass and, for your father, Charles, and myself, before we accept Communion. If our stomachs are hungry, then we can better understand the sacrifices of Christ; we are closer to Him this way."

"I know," Susan said with a sigh. "But I'm still hungry."

Mother chuckled. "I understand. But we are not going to eat until after church this morning."

"Okay." Susan walked back into the living room and turned the knob at the front of the TV set. Lassie, a show she adored, was on CBS. Charlie soon awoke and joined her on the green couch.

"Morning, Charlie," Susan said.

Charlie looked lethargically at his sister. "Good morning, Susie." He never was a morning person as far as Susan could tell.

She rested her head on his shoulder as they watched the remainder of the television show together.

"It is time to get ready for church," Mother said from the threshold of her bedroom. Charlie stood without complaint as Susan looked at Mother from her perch on the couch.

"Mama, you look pretty." Father entered the living room and sat in the seat his son had just vacated.

"Aww, thanks, Susan. That makes me smile. We will get you all dressed up in your Sunday dress, and you and I can be pretty together, yes?" She smiled, eyes dancing— a stark contrast from earlier that morning. Her voice was composed and soft. A sparkle. Her neck was bare to expose the fake pearls she'd received from their father years ago and which she wore to church every Sunday morning, then placing them gently back in her jewelry box atop her bedroom dresser when they returned home. Light blue church dress, one of three that

11

she alternated each Sunday, the best she owned.

"Would you like to wear your yellow dress to match your ribbon or your white dress with those little flowers on it? Although I suppose there are some yellow flowers there so your ribbon will match that one, too. I've washed them both."

"Oh, the white with flowers! *And* my yellow ribbon. Can you help me with my hair, Mama?" Her eyes expressed her eagerness.

"That's enough foolishness," her father said abruptly.

Mother and Susan didn't speak to that, but they both exchanged small knowing smirks before averting their eyes. Father never could appreciate a nice dress and a very special hair ribbon.

"Shall we?"

"Thanks, Mama!" Susan stepped from the small living room to the even smaller bedroom that she called her own, large enough only for her twin bed and a well-used dresser and nightstand. Mother helped her dress, and together they made their way to Mother and Father's bedroom. As they walked through, Susan hastened her steps, eager to pass the bed before the memories of that morning surfaced to engulf her mind.

Mother sat at her dressing table, clicking the knob on the small table lamp to brighten her features. Susan placed her small hand on her mother's shoulder. Mother ran her fingers through her thick, wavy hair and turned her face from one side to the other. She looked at Susan through the mirror and smiled, reaching for her tube of red lipstick. She applied this evenly and then placed it back down to pick up a pencil and begin with her eyes. Susan was always mesmerized at the transformation. Bright red lips. Beautiful, big blue eyes. Pale skin. Her mama was gorgeous.

Mother placed her hands in her lap, sat up straight, and turned to Susan with a slight smile as she began humming Paul Anka's "Put Your Head on my Shoulder." Susan reveled in the melody and the sweet sound of her mother's beautiful voice. Mother turned back to her tabletop, retrieved the perfume bottle, and applied a small amount to her neck with her fingertips. Placing the stopper back in the bottle top she turned her body toward her daughter, still humming softly, and leaned down to place her cheek upon Susan's tight curls. Susan breathed in the scent and reached her arms around her mother's waist.

"Are you ready, my Susan?"

"Yes, Mama."

"Then let us go! We'll see if your father and brother are waiting for us." She took hold of her daughter's hand, and together they walked back through the living room and into the kitchen, where Father and Charlie were sitting at the table in silence.

"Ready," Mother announced.

Father replied with a grumble, and both he and Charlie stood. On the porch they put their shoes on. Exiting through the screen door, they walked toward the waiting station wagon. It was a glorious Sunday morning, and Susan turned her face to the sun, closing her eyes and smiling before she climbed into the back of the car with Charlie. Father positioned himself in the driver's seat as Mother lit a cigarette for each of them. She handed one to Father, and he placed it in his mouth before starting the car and pulling out onto North Street, heading to St. John's.

They arrived at the church a mere five minutes later. Cutting the engine, Father pocketed the keys, and he and Mother extinguished their cigarettes. The family opened their respective doors and stepped out. Susan walked with quickened steps to take her mother's hand. Together they found their way with the rest of the crowd to the stone steps, climbing up. Father Denis held his back to the door, greeting families as they entered his domain.

"Good morning, Mr. and Mrs. Dubois." He nodded his head slightly, hands clasped in front of him. "Susan, Charles." He smiled, exposing his small and crooked teeth, pointed incisors. Father John was a tall middle-aged man and was rather menacing to the five-year-old Susan, who looked at the ground instead of in the piercing green eyes below his graying short-cropped, thick black hair.

"Good morning, Father Denis." Father shook his hand.

"A good morning to you, Father. Children?" Mother looked to both Susan and Charlie.

"Good morning, Father," Charlie said.

"Good morning, Father." Susan steeled herself for an upper glance before returning her gaze to her white Sunday Mary Janes. She grasped the back of her mother's dress as they entered the church, leaving Father Denis in their wake. Together they walked through the entryway into the nave, sounds from the outdoors almost immediately muffled as they crossed the threshold; Susan heard only the clicking of Mother's heels upon the wooden floor and rustling echoes as parishioners shuffled in their pews, soft voices rising to the rafters. Rainbows of color danced on the floor as people stepped forward, disturbing the muted hues emitted from the bright sunlight seeping through the stained glass windows.

Susan found she cared nothing for church. Father Denis spoke in a high-pitched, arrogant voice, and she always felt unsettled when she was around him, his head held high, white tab collar contrasting starkly with the midnight black of his shirt when he wasn't wearing the white robe that flowed past his knees. He simply wasn't a man she found easily approachable. Add to that the fact that she didn't understand Latin and it was no wonder she often closed her eyes and let her imagination run free as she tried so diligently to stifle her restlessness. Mass hadn't even started, and she was already thinking about what food would be waiting for her after church. Her stomach roiled with emptiness as her grandparents, aunt and uncle, and cousins arrived and surrounded her family, sitting upon the hard-backed benches in their pews. Charlie had already left to assemble with the other altar boys and change into clothes given to him entirely for the purpose of doing God's work by helping Father Denis. He would remain at the altar for the entirety of Mass, alternating between standing to retrieve something for the priest, and sitting on a bench against the wall. Susan had thought it looked like boring work to be up there with Father Denis in that baggy white robe he had to wear that reached just past the hips of his black trousers but Mother always beamed when she saw her son there, a swelling pride evident on her features.

She stood when others stood, was obedient to the tasks required of her.

She was pleased when Mother indicated it was time to leave, that they could wait outside until her brother arrived to meet them.

* * *

Sunday mornings after church were spent with extended family, and today Susan's mother and father were hosting. Father parked the car. Susan opened her door and stepped out upon the dirty pavement, her white strapped shoes distinctive against the grime, crunching on pebbles and dirt.

"Susan, Charles, please head inside and change out of your Sunday clothes. Everyone will be here shortly." A car turned onto North Street, and Susan recognized it as Memere and Pepere Richard's. She watched them park across the street. Her grandmother exited first, her right brown-clad foot slowly touching ground, exposing her stockinged shin. She swerved, and laboriously hoisted her short, stout body out of the car, pausing afterward to smooth her brown calf-length skirt over her ample hips and straighten her matching button-down jacket. She wore her short, gray-streaked hair pulled back from her pale, weathered face, which she now turned toward the house. Susan heard Pepere's door close and watched as he slowly made his way around the front of the car, his brown wooden cane aiding his limping left leg toward his wife. Susan had wondered why Pepere had a cane and was told a while back that Pepere was in the "Great War," whatever that meant, and had had an "accident" (Mother's word) sustained from a "goddamn Kraut piece of shit" (Father's words).

Although no taller than Father, whom Susan had grown to learn was not a tall man in the world of men, Pepere was quite a bit taller than his wife, who might have hit five feet if she wore heels. His tan suit framed his average build well. His hair was cropped short on his head, more gray these days than the light brown of his youth. It was balding in the front, a few thin wisps protruding through the pale skin. He turned toward the house, Memere at his heels. Susan looked at his eyes across the street. Blue, she knew, although she couldn't see their color from this distance. Wide on his face. The pupils and surrounding irises uncannily small within the white sclera lending an almost ghostly, sickly look.

Mother unclasped the few buttons at the back of Susan's dress and lightly tapped her on the bottom, a slight motion telling her to change for the afternoon. Mother began walking across the street toward her parents.

When dressed, Susan entered the small backyard. Father exited the house just behind her in a close-fitting white T-shirt and brown trousers and walked toward the cooler, where he extracted a glass bottle of beer and sat at the picnic table facing Memere and Pepere to begin a conversation. Susan turned and saw that Memere and Pepere Dubois—Father's parents this time—were making their way through the side yard carrying a platter of sweets. Susan stood on tiptoe when they approached. Cookies and cake slices!

"Susan." Memere looked down in acknowledgment, the slightest curve of her lips, a simulated smile of greeting. Her voice was deep and husky. Her beady brown eyes bored into Susan, disconcerting. She was wispy thin and tall; taller even than Pepere, who stood beside her. Severely curled reddish-brown hair topped her head and looked to Susan like a wig that perfectly framed her face and head in a circular pattern. Slight wrinkles nestled throughout her face, comfortable in their pale dwelling. A small flap of skin protruded from the tip of her chin down her neck, halting in the middle of her collarbone and wiggling slightly when she spoke.

Feeling reprimanded, Susan looked to the ground.

"Hi, Susan." Pepere stood beside his wife, holding her elbow with his hand as if she were too frail to find her way to the picnic table and chairs on her own. Almost completely bald with a few white wisps of hair at the temples and large blue eyes in a round, wrinkled face, Pepere smiled down at Susan as she lifted her eyes. She smiled back. Pepere always made her smile.

"We brought goodies." Pepere gestured to the platter in his wife's hands, and Susan hesitantly stole another glance before turning her gaze again to her grandfather, feeling Memere's reproachful eyes still upon her.

"Ah, I hear the other children." And he was right. Susan could hear them, too. Who could miss those giggles, those feet running into the yard from the street and the cars parked along the narrow road? Several of her cousins quickly made their way over, one almost swiping Charlie as he exited the kitchen door, done changing his clothes and ready to join the growing throng of family members.

"Wait up!" Eleanor was the same age as Susan was now, five. Ellie and her family attended a different church from St. John's, Susan knew, and she was so pleased that today her cousin was able to arrive at her house when she did; sometimes she didn't come until the Duboises had already been home for quite some time.

Eleanor gave up chase and pouted as she slowed to a walk, defeated. Ma Tante Alice—Ellie's baby sister propped on her hip—followed behind with Mon Oncle Paul. The baby squiggled, wanting to be let down, and Ma Tante obliged. She toddled toward her sister, feet bare in the grass.

Mother exited the house. "Alice." She gave her sister a kiss upon the cheek and Ma Tante, of a height with Mother, was able to embrace her easily to reciprocate the affection.

"Hi, Paul."

Paul smiled at Mother. Genuine. "Helen." He nodded his head in greeting. "I'll leave you two ladies to catch up." With a smile and a lingering glance at his wife, he began walking toward where Father, Memere, and Pepere were still conversing.

"You have got a good one there, Alice. I know I say it often, but it is no less true today than it was yesterday." One set of blue eyes looked into the other as Mother took her younger sister's hand and squeezed.

Ma Tante Alice grinned. "I sure do." She looked after her husband, who had sat down next to Father, shaking his hand in greeting.

Ellie was called into the house to change out of her dress. Susan found herself alone and walked in her mother's wake toward the adults at the picnic table. She lingered to the side as they conversed, her mother now having joined the family circle as Father started up the grill. She made her way to the yellow chrome-and-Formica rectangular-shaped folding table and stealthily swiped a few chips from the bowl. She was so hungry!

She turned her back on the adults. As she began to place the first chip in her mouth, she saw Elizabeth entering the side yard with her parents and her two-year-old brother. Susan quickly stuffed the remainder of the chips into her mouth, and with puffed cheeks, jogged toward her cousin. Ellie skipped toward the girls from the house with a large smile on her face.

Elizabeth's mother was Ma Tante Mary, Father's sister. Elizabeth's father, Mon Oncle Walter, was an exuberant man, tall and large with a boisterous personality. His hair was brown and so thick it stood on end when it was freshly barbered. He and his wife complemented each other nicely. He, tall and stout: she also brown-haired, but short and thin. Like Father, except Father's hair was red. Ma Tante Mary had a strong personality but was not unkind.

The girls ran off into the yard, leaving Elizabeth's smiling parents behind.

"You're it!" Susan tapped Elizabeth on the back of the shoulder, and she immediately ran off in the opposite direction as Elizabeth looked after her with a surprised expression, shoulder-length brown hair bouncing to the side as her head whipped in Susan's direction. Ellie squealed and began running away from Elizabeth and Susan both.

"Hey!" Elizabeth looked after her friends with a grin and began chasing Ellie, who was just a bit closer to her than Susan. Elizabeth, being six years old and rather tall, was a fast runner and caught up to Ellie quickly, tagging her on the back. Both girls laughed heartily. Knowing how fast Elizabeth was, Ellie ran after Susan. She grazed her hand on Susan's arm, and it was Susan's turn to chase.

And so it went until the girls tired and collapsed into a pile of giggling limbs onto the patchy grass.

"Come on. Let's get some food." Susan led her friends to the table.

Mother handed her a plate, and she scooped up some chips and macaroni salad. Mother placed a hot dog in a bun and handed it over to Susan, who put it on her plate and then squirted an immense amount of Heinz ketchup on top before joining both Elizabeth and Ellie on the grass. She put her plate down in front of her and sat down with her legs crossed.

She spilled ketchup down her chin and onto her shirt as she bit into her hot dog. Mother wouldn't be happy. She then remembered to lean forward so it would drip onto her plate. This was a constant reminder of Mother's, and Susan really did try to remember it. It's just that when she was with Elizabeth and Ellie, she forgot the manners Mother was attempting so hard to instill within her. She was just so excited and happy to be in their presence.

The girls finished the food on their plates. Susan ate every bite. It was the expectation in her home and now an ingrained habit. There were times Mother and Father had her remain at the kitchen table until she thoroughly finished even food she detested. Currently, cranberry sauce was an unwanted side dish. Recently she had found herself in front of this very substance, Father insisting she finish what Mother had spooned for her. This found Susan at the table for the following forty-five minutes taking extremely small bites of cranberry sauce, chasing each minuscule portion with a sip of milk from her glass. Each time that cranberry sauce reached the front of her tongue, she felt the slimy, slippery mass scoot around her mouth, and as the milk helped the sauce slip to the back of her throat, she'd gag. There were a couple of times it came back up and onto her plate, to cries of disgust from her exasperated father, who forced her to place it on her spoon once more. Forty-five minutes. But she did it. And she loathed the thought that the dark red substance would find its way back on her dinner plate sometime soon.

Between hopscotch, tag, jump rope, leapfrog, and talking to the boys and the adults, time passed quickly on this sunny June Sunday. Soon it was well into the early evening and company was getting ready to pack back into their cars and head to their prospective homes, all of which were within twenty minutes of Susan's. What a wonderful thing it was to have them nearby!

TWO

June quickly waned; spring gently melded into summer.

Emerson Park just up the road was frequented by Susan and Janet. Bikes were ridden incessantly, walks taken throughout the neighborhood, sprinklers erected and run through with squeals of laughter. Rainy days were no less appreciated. If no thunder was heard, no lighting seen, Susan would slip on her swimsuit and run barefoot onto the pavement of North Street to splash in puddles. On those days of true summer thunderstorms, when the luminous skies brought forth pounding thunder that rattled the little old house and lighting that illuminated the dark horizon with its zigzags, Mother, Charlie and Susan would erect a card table on the front porch and drag three kitchen chairs over. They would play war—Mother lending a little help to Susan at times—or slapjack while the rain pelted the roof, sprinkles of mist seeping through the screen to cool them, the earthy smell of rain on pavement and dirt wafting its way to envelop their senses.

July arrived, as did the humidity that so often accompanies it in New England. Susan and Charlie were both in their rooms packing a bag for their annual family camping trip. This was the one excursion the Dubois family took each year, and it was greatly anticipated by all, especially by Susan, who still experienced the wonder and excitement that children so often hold for even the smallest of pleasures. Ma

21

Tante Alice and Mon Oncle Paul would be spending the week in an adjacent campsite with their children, as would Ma Tante Mary and Mon Oncle Walter with theirs. Susan could not withhold or even tamp down her enthusiasm for the week to come.

When all bags were packed (Mother and Father had arranged the camping gear the few days prior), breakfast was had and the car loaded up. The Dubois family was on their way!

Susan's pillow was placed next to her on the car's back seat, as was Charlie's. He had a few G.I. Joes in his hand, and *Treasure Island* was resting on his lap. Charlie had an insatiable appetite for reading, and Susan was looking forward to the time— hopefully soon—in which she could read as well. Mother read to her often, and she so loved to nestle against her bosom, Mother's arm around her shoulder, her slight lavender scent adding to the pleasure of these moments of togetherness.

Father's spirits were always lifted during this week away from work and home, this week with family at the lake. It was a welcome change from his typical temperament. He started the car, and they were off.

Mother turned her head slightly to the left and gazed upon Father. The corners of her mouth lifted: her face softened. She reached and grasped his right hand, squeezing for a moment before letting go. Father looked at her and smiled. Charlie picked up his book from the seat and opened it to the bookmarked page and began reading. Susan opened her crayon box. She found a picture with an elephant on the page and began to color it in with a baby blue. Baby blue was, after all, her favorite color, and elephants were her favorite animal. The possibility of a baby blue elephant enthralled her.

A bend in the road and they had finally arrived. *Stuart's Campground* was written in large bold black letters upon a wooden sign in a median between two narrow dirt lanes. A small stone wall encircled a flower bed with rich summer hues of red and yellow. Father pulled into the right lane and followed the empty road slowly.

"C3, that's us," Father announced as he pulled in. Susan threw her belongings onto the seat next to her and opened her door in haste. In front of the car was their site. Small, yes, as campsites tend to be, but theirs for the week! Such bliss! There was an area where Father and Mother would erect the two tents. In front of that was a picnic table upon which they would eat their meals and the adults would play cards. There was a small firepit lined with stones, ashes from a previous family's use black and still upon the earth. To the front of the picnic table were several tall trees that helped to shade their site from the hot summer sun. And to Susan's delight, just through those trees was the sand of the beach and the inviting water of the lake.

She closed the door of the car and inhaled happily. A figure was running toward her. Elizabeth! The LaFleurs were already here!

"Hi, Susie!" Elizabeth was incredibly excited to see her younger cousin. She reached out and grabbed Susan's hands in hers. "We got here a little while ago. Look," she said, pointing toward their large tent. "Mama and Dad got a new tent for us this year. It's so big inside. And I even get my own room. All by myself. I even have my own sleeping bag and pillow, and Baby Doll is already on my bed sleeping and waiting for me to go to bed tonight." Baby Doll, Susan knew, was the doll Elizabeth had received for her third birthday, her favorite for almost four years now. Susan was the owner of only one doll, a raggedy old thing that was no larger than her forearm and made of cloth. She was missing a blue eye and never did have any hair. Her patchwork dress of browns and oranges had a rip up the right side. Her permanent dwelling had been the shelf at the top of Susan's closet for a while now.

"You wanna play? I've got a bunch of sand toys," Elizabeth said.

"Yeah! Mama, can I go to the beach to play with Elizabeth?" Susan called.

"Of course. Have so much fun, Susan."

Susan and Elizabeth both grasped their favorite choices in their arms from a container on Elizabeth's site—as much as they could hold—and walked toward the sand.

The girls gleefully built castles and starfish, an octopus and a large mound of sand that they claimed was the tallest mountain in the world—the aliens wanted to conquer it, but they would turn into superhero princesses and save the world. Eventually, they stomped on their large heap, thus defeating said aliens. Susan raised her arms in triumph while Elizabeth bent forward, face fierce, arms extended and palms fisted as if she were a bodybuilder showing her toned muscle definition to awed spectators.

"I'm hungry, Elizabeth. Want to go get a snack?" Toys abandoned in the sand, the girls walked back to their campsites.

* * *

By evening the Thomas family had arrived: Mon Oncle Paul and Ma Tante Alice with their four children. All belongings were unpacked: tents stood firm upon the ground. Susan skewered a hot dog and cooked it upon an open flame in the firepit. Dinners were relished by all at their individual sites, and then they congregated at the Thomases', where marshmallows were browned, some catching fire and burning black, and squished between two pieces of graham cracker to make s'mores that were devoured with delight by the children and adults alike. Susan asked for a second, cheeks sticky with the milky white goo of the marshmallow, melted chocolate streaking her lips.

Voices carried into the darkness of night. The moon's reflection could be seen glistening on the blackness of the water peeking through the trees. Two owls were echoing their cries in the still air. When Mother gathered Susan to her side and told her it was time to retire for the night, Susan wanted so desperately to refuse, but the yawn she was attempting to stifle was indication enough for Mother to grasp her hand and gently prod her to say her good-nights to her family. She led the way to the spigot, where she helped Susan to brush her teeth and then pulled the zipper from the bottom of the tent to the top, making an opening for Susan to follow through. As Susan yawned the exhaustion of a day well played, Mother helped her undress and put her nightgown on. Susan said her prayers, then slipped her body into her sleeping bag. Mother pulled the cover to Susan's neck and tucked the sides beneath her.

"Snug as a bug in a rug," she said, then kissed her daughter on the forehead. She lingered there for a moment on her knees, brushing Susan's curls off her cheek and tucking them behind her ear. She caressed her cheek, her chin, then kissed her forehead once again. "I love you, my sweet Susan Marie."

"I love you, too, Mama," she replied. "Nose kiss?"

Mother touched her nose to Susan's, then gently moved left to right over and over again, faster and faster until they both made a humming sound and air-kissed.

"Night, Mama."

"Good night, Susan." Mother stood and left the tent. Susan was sleeping just a moment later.

* * *

When Susan awoke in the morning, she opened her eyes to the sun seeping through the enclosed tent, the birds chirping in the trees, and the smell of eggs and bacon. She extricated herself from her sleeping bag and rose to her feet. She found her shoes near the tent door, put them on, then slowly exited onto the cool, slightly pebbled brown earth. The soft breeze of the awakening summer morning lightly blew upon her face, bringing with it a crisp sensation.

Father stood at the far end of the picnic table, his Coleman propane stove propped before him. Upon it were some small camping pots and skillets, the eggs and bacon frying within. Mother, already dressed for the day, was pulling paper plates and napkins from the large plastic bin and placing them upon the table as Susan approached.

"Good morning, sunshine," said Mother.

"Morning, Mama. Morning, Father," Susan replied.

Father looked up from the stove. "Good morning, Susan."

"Susan, would you please go wake your brother? Breakfast is almost ready."

When Charlie emerged, Mother greeted him with a ready smile. "Good morning, Charles."

"Good morning, ma'am." Charlie had a slight groggy sway to his gait as he neared the picnic table. He and Susan sat, and Mother placed a paper plate of food in front of them. Father looked at them both from his perch at the head of the table in front of the stove, raising his eyebrows.

"Thank you, ma'am," said Charlie.

"Yeah, thanks, Mama," Susan followed.

When the table was set, the family folded their hands, readying for the morning prayer. Mother thanked the Lord, and then Father picked his fork up from the table and began to eat.

"I'm fishing this morning with Paul and Walter," said Father as he forked a heap of eggs into his mouth.

"That should be nice for you, Gerald," Mother replied.

"Sure should," he said. "Charles, you want to come?" He looked at his son across the table.

26

"No, thank you, sir."

"The fresh air will do you good. And maybe we'll catch some big ones for dinner," he tried again.

"I'd like to stay here if you'll allow." Charlie gazed down at his food, pushing it across his plate with his fork.

Father looked thoughtful. "No, son. You should come along. It'll be good for you." His decision was the final say. Charlie didn't lift his eyes from his plate, but Susan saw him nod slightly in acknowledgment.

"Me, too, Father? Can I come, too? I want to fish," said Susan.

"You wouldn't rather stay here and keep your mother company? Leave the men to fish?"

"No, sir. I want to fish." Susan looked at Mother and gave her an apologetic grin.

Father gazed at Susan, at her anxious face. "No," he concluded. "You stay here and help your mother, play with your friends."

Susan looked down at her plate with a dejected expression. Father loved to fish and she only ever wanted to please him.

The family finished breakfast, and Mother stood to gather the paper plates and dispose of them in the large black trash bag that was tethered to the end of the picnic table.

"What do you think, Walter?" Father raised his voice to be heard at his brother-in-law's site. "Fishing time?"

Mon Oncle Walter called back, "I'm ready. Paul, too. Meet you at the lake."

"Heading over in just a minute," Father said. He turned to Charlie. "Go to the tent and change your clothes. Meet us at the lake where the canoes are."

"Yes, sir," said Charlie as he slowly walked to the tent. Susan followed.

When dressed, she crossed over to the LaFleur's site and found Elizabeth in front of a fire with her mother.

"Want to play? We can ask Ellie, too," Susan said.

"Okay."

The three friends passed the morning walking the campground, playing in the sand at the beach, and playing with toys on the picnic tables. By the time Father approached with Charlie in tow, she had almost forgotten her disappointment that Father hadn't permitted her to join them.

Father commenced gutting and cleaning the fish he had caught on a stack of newspapers upon the picnic table. When through, the table was cleared and the bloody newspapers discarded so the family could eat lunch. Susan regaled Mother with tales of playing that morning: Charlie ate in silence.

"Let's race," Elizabeth said. The girls were dressed in swimsuits after lunch and eager to enter the inviting water of the lake.

"Okay," Susan said.

Ellie agreed and together they stood in a line, bodies bent forward getting ready to shoot off.

"One," Elizabeth counted, "two... THREE! At that, their legs propelled their bodies forward and they ran into the water, splashing one another and themselves. Susan closed her eyes and shouted with happiness as water rose to meet her face. She plummeted under, bending her legs to allow the dunk and then shooting upward, breaking the water's surface, wiping her eyes clean and laughing with her cousins.

Susan's fingertips and toes were beginning to prune when the girls were joined by the rest of their family. Charlie ran in the wake of his cousins, looking back at his sister as he submerged his dry body into the dark water, smiling.

Father and Mother approached. Father's red-and-black-plaid suit was tight and short on his small frame. Susan adored Mother's suit. She'd had it for a few years now. It was a beautiful shade of emerald green. The straps were thick and tied into a knot at the back of her neck, supporting the weight of her hefty breasts, perking them upward. Her waistline was slim, and the suit tightly covered her curvaceous hips, ending just above mid-thigh.

Time elapsed quickly as enjoyment was felt by all.

"Susan, move aside," Father said. "Your mother and I have a quest!" He was looking over toward Mother on the shoreline, a glint in his blue eyes. He waded over, using his hands to scoop water as he moved. Susan followed behind.

"Come on," Father said when he reached Mother. His head jerked toward the water, the corner of his mouth lifted in a funny grin.

It took Mother a moment to piece out what Father was indicating. "No, Gerald!" she exclaimed.

"Yes!" Father countered, reaching for her hand and holding it in his, tugging her forward into the water.

"Gerald!" Mother protested. "We haven't done this for years! I simply cannot. I cannot!" Her voice rose as Father continued to drag her deeper into the water.

Mother attempted to extract herself from his grasp, but he was too strong. Eventually, she acquiesced to this silly demand of his, and he let go of her hand. She attempted to bolt back to the sand, but Father was quick on his feet and grabbed her around the waist, dragging her under the water. Mother emerged, wiping at her face, and Father laughed. Mother's eyes widened in surprise at having been plunged under, and then her shoulders began to shake with laughter.

"Gerald," she teased, "you are terrible!"

"Mmm-hmmm," he teased, and then kissed her neck. Mother giggled and attempted half-heartedly to pry him off.

They were soon joined by Mon Oncle Walter and Ma Tante Mary as well as Mon Oncle Paul and Ma Tante Alice, who were all well aware of Father's motives. Each woman climbed onto her husband's shoulders in the depths of the water with a bit of awkward difficulty. Once they were secure, the men walked toward one another, and the women gleefully began to reach out, grasping anything they could: arms, legs, hands. Father might have been of shorter stature and on the lean side, but he was strong. He held Mother to him with determination, especially alongside Mon Oncle Walter who had nearly eight inches on him as well as eighty-five pounds.

Ma Tante Alice lost balance first as both Mother and Ma Tante Mary pushed her backward. All three women were shrieking happily as Ma Tante Alice hit the water. Mother was the next to tumble from her husband's shoulders. When she bounced back up from hitting the water and wiped her eyes, she was grinning widely.

Susan didn't even realize that she was beaming as she watched the scene unfold before her. The smiles. The glee. The playfulness. Camping with her family was the highlight of her summer. This was why.

They splashed and played, talked and laughed as the sun descended in the brilliant blue sky. Susan found herself in the water and up upon the sand, digging and building. Sand chafed her skin in the folds of her swimsuit, but she paid no heed, simply went back to splashing and memory-making.

Evening emerged. It was easy to lose track of time during this one eventful and marvelous week of the year. Even though she and her family had snacked at the beach on chips and apples, Susan found her stomach was rumbling despite her attention being delightedly diverted elsewhere in play.

"Mama, when are we going to have dinner?" she asked.

Mother stopped chatting with Ma Tante Alice and gazed at her surroundings, at the sun low in the sky.

"Oh, goodness," she said. "Susan, you are right. Where has the time gone? I am hungry, too, now that I think about it," she admitted. She called over to Father, who was sitting in a camping chair at the back of the beach near the trees. Two picnic tables and a grill rested beside him. "Gerald, we need to have dinner. Would you like me to fry up the fish at the campsite, or would you like to use the grills here on the beach tonight?" she asked.

Father called back, "Let's do it here," and used his arms to help him stand from the chair.

Father called everyone over when the fish were hot and ready.

"Let's go!" said Elizabeth.

Susan jogged her way to the picnic tables where Mother handed both her and Charlie a towel. Susan tried to dry off as best she could but handed Mother her towel when she beckoned so Mother could finish the job.

She laid her wet towel in the sand. Elizabeth and Ellie joined her, and together they sat in a circle. Mother soon arrived with Susan's paper plate of fish and potato salad. She handed her a plastic fork.

The adults made themselves comfortable at the picnic tables. Laughter was heard: conversations were had.

"Mama, can I go back in the water?" Susan asked when she was through eating.

"Not right now, Susan," Mother said. "It is getting late. But you can play a bit with your cousins. Just run along and change into your nightdress first, yes?"

Once clean and changed, Susan joined her family back at the beach. A fire had been started and logs amassed, sending hot flames soaring upward. The sun was slowly making its final descent, leaving trails of pink and orange in its wake, the few clouds in the sky bursting with color, a final gift to commemorate this eventful, memorable day.

Father was sitting at the picnic table a while later with the rest of the adults in attendance. There was a pile of cards in the center of the table. Father grasped a beer in his hand, and a cigarette was dangling from his mouth as he peered at the cards held between his fingers, illuminated by several camping lanterns. Mother was taking a drag from her cigarette, and Ma Tante Mary had hers wafting smoke through a crack in the cards she was holding.

As the adults continued playing their game, the girls sat in the sand by the fire chatting to one another, reminiscing about the day and making plans for the next. Father got up from his perch on the picnic table's bench and pulled out another beer from a cooler that sat nearby. Susan heard a pop as the steel of the can was broken through with a church key.

"So I think we should go to the gathering place in the morning, don't you?" said Elizabeth to her cousins. She paused and looked at Susan. Susan was staring at her father, watching his movements. She turned her head and found Charlie by the water's edge with Ellie's brothers by his side.

"Susie?" said Elizabeth with exasperation. "Susie, are you even listening?"

Susan turned her head back, and Elizabeth saw a complex expression on her face. "You okay?" she asked.

"Yeah," Susan said. "What were you talking about?"

"I was just saying that maybe you can ask your parents if they'll let you come to the gathering place tomorrow morning when we all wake up. Maybe get a scone or muffin?"

"Oh. Um. I bet I can go to the gathering place with you but probably they won't give me money," she said. "We eat breakfast at the campsite."

"Oh. Well, you should come anyway. Maybe she'll let you get a hot chocolate?" Elizabeth ventured.

"Maybe," said Susan as she shrugged her shoulders.

Susan risked a look behind her and noticed that her father had tipped his beer can up and was downing the remains. She looked back at Charlie by the water again, then at her mother, who was gazing upon her husband with an expressionless face. The other adults were laughing at something one of them had said as Father got up and approached the cooler for another beer.

Susan turned back to Elizabeth and Ellie and smiled hesitantly, trying her best to remain in the conversation, but her anxiety was not to be quenched. Her stomach began to roil. She had been in a state of bliss as the day transpired, elated by the experiences and the feelings of togetherness and fulfillment. Now here she was, in just the turn of a moment, feeling nauseated. She folded her arms over her stomach and bent down, placing her elbows on her crossed knees in the sand.

"And how about we go to the playground tomorrow? Remember the playground from last year? It's kinda on the other side of the campground, but I bet we can go. Want to?" asked Elizabeth.

"I do," said Ellie.

"Sure." Maybe if she could just concentrate on what Elizabeth and Ellie were saying, then she could ignore the queasiness in her stomach.

A loud boom from the table. Mon Oncle Walter had apparently found something extremely amusing and had guffawed, banging his fists on the table as he exuberantly expressed his pleasure.

Susan turned. Father laughed. His cigarette had been extinguished, and he took another swig from his beer can. The other adults at the table appeared to be of good humor, no worried expressions. Laughter all around. Father slammed down his cards. "By God, Walter!" he exclaimed. "You son of a bitch. You got me." He laughed, and Mon Oncle Walter again bellowed his enthusiasm. Mother chuckled under her breath, a small smile on her face.

"And you," said Father as he finished his beer and plunked the can back down on the tabletop. "Come on over here."

Mother hesitated but slowly stood from the table and walked the step to stand behind her husband. Susan watched as Father put his hands on her hips, moved his legs out from under the table to rest on the back of the bench, and pulled her down onto his lap. Having changed out of her swimsuit, she was now wearing a pair of shorts and a flowered blouse, full breasts high with the push of her brassiere. Father was still in his swim trunks, chest bare. He slowly moved his hands from her wide hips onto her narrow waist. He was grinning and looking directly into her eyes as his right hand remained on her waist and his left continued to climb until he found the mound of her breast and placed the palm of his hand fully upon it, pressing down hard.

"Gerald!" Mother swatted his hand away with a stricken look of horror and embarrassment.

"Come on, Helen." Father looked around the table with a goofy grin, face splotchy and red from drink.

"But it is very inappropriate to do this in front of everyone. And Gerald," she added, "the children." She looked toward Susan and the girls by the fire, her voice low and muffled but still audible.

Father laughed. Ma Tante Mary took a drag from her cigarette and blew the smoke in the opposite direction of Father so she could ignore the situation. Ma Tante Alice looked about to cry. Even Mon Oncle Walter, expressive individual that he was, said nothing and simply stared at Father and Mother.

"Gerald, how about another game?" tried Mon Oncle Paul, speaking to Father's back. "Walter kicked our butt last time. How about we pay him back?" His soft voice was strained as he attempted to make light of the situation and distract Father.

Mother began to stand from Father's lap. "Oh, fuck it!" Father said and stood abruptly, pushing Mother off balance so she fell to the sand. Ma Tante Alice gasped as Mon Oncle Paul reached for her hand under the table. She looked at her husband in shocked silence, and Mon Oncle Paul gazed back with a reassuring smile, though the expression on his face was contradictory.

Father walked past Mother, who had quickly regained her senses and stood up, wiping sand from her bottom, eyes downcast and cheeks red. Father took another beer out of the cooler and opened it, taking a long, deep drink before sitting back at the table.

Mother feigned an expression of nonchalance, contrived to convince her family that all was well. "Goodness," she said. "I certainly am clumsy." Her lips lifted in a manufactured semblance of a smile. "Time has gotten away with me. The children really should be heading to bed." As Father continued to drink at the table and lit another cigarette, she called for Charlie first, quickly ushering him away from the beach and beckoning for him to go brush his teeth and head to bed.

"Susan. You, too, darling." She seemed flustered, which made Susan all the more anxious and willing to walk away from any further commotion that might transpire.

"Charles!" Father yelled after his son.

Charlie looked back. "Yes, sir?" he answered apprehensively.

"No good-night?" Father took a drag from his cigarette and blew the smoke out the corner of his mouth. "Where the hell are your manners?" He took another sip of his beer.

"Sorry, sir." Charlie began walking back to the picnic table.

"That is my fault, Gerald," Mother said. "I lost track of time and was so anxious to send the children to bed that I ushered Charles off so quickly. I am sure he would have said goodnight to you all otherwise." Mother tucked her auburn hair behind her ear and tried for a smile at her husband.

"He should—"

"But that certainly does not excuse bad manners. Charles?" She motioned for Charlie. "Susan?" She looked at her daughter. "Say good night to your father and to your aunts and uncles, please. And to your cousins as well." Mother held her children each by a shoulder.

"Good night, sir," Charlie said.

"Hmm." Father nodded.

"Good night." Charlie looked to all the adults at the table. There was a chorus of awkward acknowledgments, and Charlie turned and walked toward the campsite.

When it was Susan's turn, she looked to Father first. "Good night, Father," she said.

Father touched a finger to his lips—an indication that he'd like a good-night kiss—and leaned toward Susan. Susan walked forward and pursed her lips together tightly. She slowly bent and placed them upon her father's. The kiss was quick and Susan pulled back hurriedly. As she said good night to the rest of her family, she could still taste the metallic remains of the cigarette that had been in Father's mouth, the yeasty tang of beer. When Mother permitted her to go, Susan stepped lively, anxious to leave the night behind her.

* * *

The week progressed in a flurry. When vacation had come to a close, Susan was quite upset. She didn't want to leave. She felt elated by her time in the sun and water, uplifted and renewed.

The journey back home was uneventful. Charlie read from *Treasure Island*, and she colored while listening to music on the car's radio system.

Father parked the car in front of their garage. He told Charlie and Susan to help bring some of their belongings into the house. Charlie began walking toward the trunk and tripped over his untied shoelace, stumbling forward and bumping into Father.

"Jesus Christ, Charles. Watch where you're going!"

TWO

Vacation was over. They were home.

THREE

"Goodbye, my darlings," Mother said the evening of Susan's sixth birthday to her pajama-clad children. She kissed both Susan and Charlie on their heads. "Susan, I hope you had a wonderful birthday party today with family and friends. I love you so very much. Charles," she added, "you and Susan may watch a bit of TV, but I want you both in bed at the regular hour tonight. We have church tomorrow morning, and I want you well rested." Mother and Father were going dancing, something they did occasionally. Mother said it was how they met before she and Charlie were born.

"Well, Susie T," said Charlie once their parents had gone, "want to go watch some TV?" He reached for her hand and led her to the couch. Susan sat with her knees pulled toward her chest and her arms wrapped around her shins. Charlie was standing in front of the television set, fiddling with the knobs, the rabbit-ear antenna sticking from the top. There were only a few channels available on the TV, and Charlie soon settled on *The Donna Reed Show,* to which Susan had no complaints.

They sat in companionable silence for a while until "Charlie?"—Susan looked at her brother.

"Mmm?"

"Do you think Father will ever let us get a puppy?"

Charlie looked from the television set to his sister, eyebrows crinkled. "I definitely do *not* think Father will ever let us get a puppy."

"Why not?"

"He thinks they're too messy," Charlie said. "And he says that they're too loud when they bark and he doesn't like it when they smell."

"I really want a puppy, Charlie."

"Yeah, so do I," Charlie said. "But I asked him when I was younger, maybe your age even, and he said no. I think if we asked him again he'd just get angry with us."

Susan contemplated this. "Well, I'm gonna ask him," she decided.

"Yeah," said Charlie. "Good luck with that, Susie."

"Thank you," she replied, oblivious to his sarcasm.

They sat again without speaking, eyes trained on the television set.

When their show was over Charlie announced that it was time for bed.

"Aww, Charlie," said Susan. "Just a bit longer?"

"Nope," Charlie said. "Father would be really mad if he found out."

"But he won't find out," insisted Susan. "They're dancing."

"What if something happens, Susie? What if they come home early?" Charlie contemplated this and then shook his head. "No, I've got to get you to bed. And I need to go to bed, too," he decided.

"Okay," Susan sighed as she relented and began the short walk to her room. Charlie shut the TV off and followed. Susan knelt at her bedside to say a quick prayer and then lifted the covers of her neatly made bed and climbed in. Charlie pulled the covers to her chin as Mother often did, and began roughly tucking them under her body.

"Snug"— he feigned grunts as he pushed the blankets— "as a bug in a rug." Susan was cocooned within and was giggling almost uncontrollably. She loved it when Charlie did this.

"Night, Susie," Charlie said.

"Goodnight, Charlie," Susan said. "I love you."

Charlie looked down at his sister, blue eyes staring up at him, curls splayed around her head on the pillow, a look of adoration on her face. "Love you, too," he replied.

And he meant it.

FOUR

It was here. The first day of school had arrived! Susan awoke to the smell of French toast cooking and traipsed into the kitchen.

"Good morning, Susan," Mother said from the kitchen stove. "Are you so very excited for your first day of school?"

"Yes!" said Susan.

Father was in his usual spot at the kitchen table, morning cigarette in hand, newspaper open before him.

"Go wake your brother for me, Susan? It is his first day of school, too, and we want to get a good breakfast into the two of you."

Together, Susan and Charlie walked to the kitchen, where Mother had already placed a heaping plate of French toast in the center of the table with some orange juice in a pitcher. She was pulling down some plates and cups from the cupboards.

"Ah," she said, "good morning, sleepy head." She smiled at Charlie, who was walking toward her with a groggy frown. "Here." Mother handed Susan a stack of four plates and Charlie two of the four glasses. They walked together toward the table. When French toast had been placed on the plates and orange juice had been poured, Mother recited the morning breakfast prayer and they began to eat.

"So, what are you looking forward to the most on your first day of school, Susan?" she asked.

Susan had just taken a large bite of food and began talking through it.

Mother held up a finger indicating she should swallow her mouthful before answering the question. "Everything," she replied once she had done so.

"Everything?" Mother laughed. "Can you be more specific?"

"I'm glad I'll be in class with Janet and Betty." Betty Sanders was a girl Susan's age who had just moved to the end of North Street. "I hope I have nice teachers. And I want to learn to read so I can read books like Charlie does."

"You will definitely learn to read, Susan," Mother assured her, "just not all in one day. You have to be patient for that to come."

"I'm excited to walk to school with Charlie," Susan continued, "and Janet and Betty said they might walk with us, too. I think Betty is going to Janet's house and then they're supposed to come here. I don't remember. But I think so."

Mother's gaze turned to her son. "Charles," she said, "will you and Henry meet to walk as well?"

"Yes, ma'am," Charlie answered. "He's going to meet me at the corner of Brown."

"I would like for you to walk with your sister and her friends," Mother said. "At least for the first day. Make sure they remember the way and then in future you and Henry may walk ahead if you would like."

"Yes, ma'am."

"Well," said Mother, "I am certainly looking forward to hearing about your first day when you both come home this afternoon. Charles, please be sure to meet Susan after school so you can walk home together as well."

"Yes, ma'am."

They finished their breakfast, and then Mother, Susan, and Charlie cleared the table as Father left for work on the railroad. "Behave and respect your elders," he ordered as he walked out the open kitchen door. A moment later the sound of the car starting was heard by all and Father slipped away.

"Okay, children," Mother said, "go get dressed now. It is almost time to leave."

Susan dressed in her burgundy-and-white pleated skirt and white collared shirt and grabbed a ribbon from her top dresser drawer. She walked back to the kitchen, where Mother put down the dish she had been scrubbing and wiped her wet, soapy hands on her apron before tucking her daughter's shirt into her skirt. Mother pulled Susan's hair together and tightly tied the white ribbon to make a ponytail at the back of her head.

"There you go," Mother said. "Oh, Susan," she sighed. "You are getting so big." She knelt down on the floor and embraced her daughter heartily. When Susan was released, she saw that Mother's eyes had pooled with tears and the first was just beginning to fall upon her cheek and dribble off her chin. "First grade already. I can hardly believe it," she said. "And you, Charles—" She looked toward Charlie, who had just entered the kitchen. "Fifth grade and almost ten years old." She sighed, looking from Susan in her new uniform to Charlie beside her, tall and handsome, a child who was on the brink of becoming a young man.

A knock at the porch's screen door. "Just a moment, girls," Mother called. "Susan is on her way right now." She stood then, wiping the tears from her cheeks, and embraced her daughter one last time. She turned to Charlie and held his chin in her hands, tilting his head up to better look into his eyes. She smiled down, and although his gaze wavered with embarrassment, his heart leaped and he felt full as he and Susan picked their lunch boxes off the table and walked to the porch to put their shoes on.

"Hi," Susan said to her friends as she bounded out the door, Charlie following at a slower pace behind her.

"Hi," both Janet and Betty said simultaneously.

"I'm excited," Susan confided in her friends.

"Oh, me, too," said Janet.

"I'm excited, too," said Betty. "But I'm a little nervous," she admitted. "I've never been to school. And I don't know what to do."

"Oh, we've never been to school, either," said Janet. "But my mom told me that if I ever needed help, I could just ask a grown-up to help me and that's just what I'll do. But I don't think I'll need any help," she said.

Janet's confidence helped to alleviate the anxiety that Susan had suddenly felt when Betty admitted that she was nervous. Susan was so thrilled to be starting school that she hadn't really thought about anything she should be tense about, but now she had a lingering doubt in the back of her thoughts, and try as she might, she couldn't fully eliminate it.

The girls and Charlie turned right onto Pleasant Avenue from North Street. Charlie set the pace with the girls following behind, chatting as they walked. Henry's home was on Brown Avenue, parallel to North Street, with a steep incline like its counterpart. He met his best friend at the corner.

"Hi." Henry waved as Charlie and the girls approached.

"Hi." Charlie's smile widened and his shoulders relaxed a bit; he was clearly at ease and pleased to be with Henry now.

"Looking good, Susie," said Henry. He flicked her ponytail with his hand which made her wiggle but grin. "Your first day of school, huh?"

"Yep," said Susan.

"Well, I hope you like it."

"Thanks," she replied.

Together they walked the three-quarters of a mile down Pleasant Avenue—Charlie and Henry out front—until they came upon a large, well-manicured lawn on their left. A two-story brick building loomed before Susan. She had passed by St. Catherine's plenty of times, sure, but now this was real. Now she would actually be entering this building and remaining for the rest of the day. Her. Alone. Not with her parents or with Charlie. Her excitement morphed quickly into apprehension, and she felt slightly queasy in the pit of her stomach as she crossed the street with her companions.

Several nuns in full habit greeted the many children as they approached the large wooden double doors at the front of the school. "Good morning," said a pleasant, round-faced woman at the top of the stairs as she looked at Susan. "Ah, good morning, Charles," she said as she recognized the slightly freckled, lanky brown-haired boy beside her. "I do hope you had a nice summer."

"Good morning, Sister Mary Margaret," Charlie said. "I did have a good summer, thank you."

"I'm so pleased to hear that." She turned to Susan. "And this must be your sister," she said.

"Yes," Charlie confirmed. "This is my sister. This is Susan." Charlie was standing erect and speaking slowly and rather formally.

"It's very nice to meet you, Susan. Welcome to St. Catherine's. I hope you have a very nice first day of school."

"Thank you," said Susan quietly. She was nervous but comfortable in front of the warm smile that greeted her. Reading Charlie's body language, she could tell that, although formal, he was comfortable as well.

Charlie and Henry went through the large wooden double doors ahead of the girls. "Sister Mary Margaret is really nice," Charlie told Susan. "I hope you get her this year. I had her when I was in second grade, and she's been my favorite teacher so far. I know you're just in the first grade, but sometimes they switch the teachers up."

Susan was beginning to feel anxious again and didn't know what to say to Charlie, so she stood there and looked into the deep green eyes of the boy she loved most in the world. Charlie could sense the unease and took her hand in his. "Hey, Susie! You're going to have a great day," he said with enthusiasm.

"I hope so," Susan whispered.

"Okay," said Charlie. "You've got this, Susie." He squeezed her hand affectionately, and let go. "I want you to meet me after school, okay? Right near the stairs on the front lawn. We'll walk home together."

Susan nodded.

"First grade is usually right over there—" He pointed just ahead of them.

Charlie and Henry walked away through the throng of kids. Susan and her friends approached the door on their left that he had indicated might be their room. A sister was perched in the hallway with her back to the open door. She was stoic, standing erect with her hands clasped behind her back. Her countenance was cold and to Susan, she did not emit an aura of approachability.

"Do you think this is it?" she queried.

"I don't know," Janet said.

"Can you ask?"

Janet walked up to the sister, Susan and Betty lagging behind.

"Is this the first grade?" she asked.

"It is." If Janet was hoping to get a more substantial confirmation to her question, she would have to accept disappointment. She stood there for a moment, the sister gazing down at her, hands still clasped behind her back, black habit flowing to the floor. Her veil cascaded over her shoulders and came to rest below her chest, white wimple covering her neck and cheeks. Janet glanced at the cross dangling upon her bosom, the rosary at her hips, and turned to her friends.

"Okay, I guess we go in," she said, and walked over the threshold.

When Susan entered the room, the first thing she noticed was the lack of color. The walls were white, and with the large windows on the opposite side of the door facing the morning sun in the east, the light poured through, illuminating the space. There were individual desks in three rows facing a larger desk on the right side of the room. A rectangular chalkboard adorned the wall above the teacher's desk.

"Do we just sit down?" Susan was confused.

"Yeah, I guess so," said Janet. "Let's sit together over here." Janet led her friends to the first row of seats that faced the teacher's desk. She sat down in the chair at a desk closest to the windows. Susan sat behind her and Betty to Janet's right. There were a few children already seated in various chairs, and more children soon matriculated into the room. Janet and Betty were talking; Susan simply observed. She placed her metal lunch box on the floor.

Susan gazed out a large, sunny window at the side schoolyard. She saw grass and a couple of large maple trees but no play equipment. She was thinking that perhaps recess would be behind the building when she heard the door abruptly close and she turned in her seat. For the most part, the class had gone quiet, save a few giggling high-pitched voices. Sister looked around the room sternly, and the children behind those voices deemed it prudent to close their mouths.

She walked to the front of the room, stopping directly in front of her desk, and looked about. Susan sat erect, mouth dry.

"My name is Sister Mary Francis. You will call me Sister Mary Francis and not just Sister. I will be your teacher this year." She looked from child to child with dark brown eyes set close together in her round, lined face. Her deep, stern voice continued, "I expect obedience. You will not goof around in my class. You are to pay attention. We will review our classroom rules, and if you do not abide by these rules, there will be repercussions." She paused, mouth closed tightly. "When I speak to you, I expect you to answer directly. And when you confirm that you understand what I am saying, you are to reply with 'Yes, Sister Mary Francis.' Am I clear?"

A good portion of the class replied immediately with "Yes, Sister Mary Francis." Susan bit her lower lip with her teeth, wrung her hands in her lap. She felt molded to her chair, voice caught deep within the confines of her body.

"Now look behind you," said Sister Mary Francis.

The children obeyed, a collective rustling sound as skirts and slacks pivoted in their chairs.

"As you can see there are hooks on the wall," she continued. "I have placed your names on paper, one name above each hook. They are in alphabetical order by last name. If you cannot recognize your name, then I will help you, but I do expect you to recognize your full name by the end of the week." She paused to let this information settle in. "When I prompt you, you will stand up quietly from your chairs and form a line. You will then proceed to walk in this straight line to the back of the room and find your name. Put your belongings on your hook. This will be your space for the duration of the school year, and I expect you to visit this hook and place your belongings on it before you sit in your chairs at the start of the school day. I want only one row to walk to the back of the room at a time. Once that row has seated themselves back down, I will send the next row, and so on. Is this understood?"

"Yes, Sister Mary Francis." Again Susan was mute. She sent a quick prayer of thanksgiving that Mother had been working on letters with her at home and that she did, in fact, recognize her name, both first and last. She would have been mortified if she had to ask Sister Mary Francis for help.

Sister Mary Francis looked at the blond boy in his burgundy St. Catherine's cardigan sitting in the front seat closest to the door. She gently closed her eyes and gave a slight nod of her head. This boy as well as the other four children in his row turned toward the back of the room. The children found their hooks and placed their belongings on them.

Once all the children were seated again and looking at the front of the room, Sister Mary Francis turned to Betty in the middle row of seats. When she nodded her head, Betty lifted herself from her chair and formed a line with three other children. All the children, save one, soon found their desks again.

"Is there a problem?" asked Sister Mary Francis.

"Yes, Sister," said a small boy with black hair slicked back from his face.

"Sister Mary Francis." Her head was tilted down when she spoke to the boy, eyes thrust forward, mouth in a tight line.

"Yes, Sister Mary Francis," the boy corrected. His voice was high, and he ran his palm over the top of his head before clasping his hands together in front of him.

"And what is this problem?" she asked.

"I can't find my name. I have a nickname at home and I know how to spell that. Ma says my name is so long with so many letters that she wasn't going to bother teaching me it just yet, said she gave me the nickname *because* my name was so long with so many letters." The boy's cheeks were red with awkward embarrassment.

"You must be Michelangelo Bartolomucci," said Sister Mary Francis.

"Yes, Sister," said Michelangelo. "Sister Mary Francis," he hastily amended. "My parents call me Mikey."

"Well, here in my classroom, you will be called by your given name." Sister Mary Francis looked down at Michelangelo from her perch at the front of the room.

"Yes, Sister Mary Francis."

Sister Mary Francis walked slowly to the back of the room and motioned to the second peg from the left. Michelangelo mumbled a thanks and placed a light sweater and a lunch box on the hook. He followed Sister Mary Francis and sat in his desk chair as she proceeded once again to the front of the room. Michelangelo looked down at the hands in his lap, shoulders slouched.

When Sister Mary Francis nodded her head at Janet, Susan stood on wobbly legs. She turned with the other students in her row and filed toward the back of the class. Fortunately, most of the hooks were now taken, so she only had to look at the name cards that were not in use. She found her name rather quickly and placed her lunch box on her hook, walking hastily back to her desk to sit down.

"Sister Mary Francis?" said the blond boy in the first row.

"Yes, Mr...?"

"David Sanders," said the boy.

Betty's head whipped back to look at Janet and Susan, her eyes wide. "Sanders?" she whispered. She couldn't believe another classmate shared her last name and giggled under her breath to her friends.

"Ah, Mr. Sanders. What is it?"

"Thank you for putting the name cards at the hooks. It made it very easy to find mine."

Sister Mary Francis paused in contemplation of this statement. It was the first day of school, after all. Was this boy genuine in this thanksgiving, or was this a bit of foreshadowing—a troublemaker? She couldn't yet decide.

"You are welcome," she said in her slow, deep voice.

She turned to look at the other students. "Now, there is another Sanders in my classroom this year. Who is it?"

Betty raised her hand.

"I had questioned whether or not I had siblings in my classroom until I looked at parental information and saw that was not the case," she drawled. "And now to look upon you both, I see for certain you cannot be siblings. Neither is there a relation of any kind, if I am not mistaken. Is there?"

Susan looked at Betty's dark, almost black hair and medium

complexion and then at David Sanders with his towhead and pale white skin reminiscent of her own.

"No, Sister Mary Francis," said David. "I haven't ever seen that girl before."

Sister Mary Francis turned to Betty. "And what is your name?"

"My name is Betty Sanders, Sister Mary Francis." Betty's voice was small but confident.

"Now I would like to go around the room. I want you all to tell me your full name. I pride myself on having an exceptionally good memory and expect I will have memorized your names by the end of the day." Her lips lifted in a tight-lipped smile that did not reach her eyes.

She looked at Janet and nodded her head.

"My name is Janet Boucher, Sister Mary Francis." Janet's voice was loud and clear.

When Sister Mary Francis looked to Susan, she knew it was her turn, but she felt paralyzed. It was just her name. She'd known her own darn name for as long as she could remember, for goodness' sake. *Just tell the sister your name!* she thought. She sat there staring at Sister Mary Francis, her entire body rigid and on the cusp of shaking. After a moment she was able to open her mouth slightly, but the words wouldn't emerge. She sat there wracked with fear. She could feel thirteen pairs of children's eyes on her, and she began to burn, heat flooding into her cheeks.

Sister Mary Francis's cool indifference didn't last long. When Susan wouldn't oblige her by speaking, she clenched her jaw and pulled her shoulders back even farther. She picked up a book from her desk and walked over to where Susan had begun to tremble in her chair, looking up at her teacher with petrified blue eyes.

"I thought I had made it clear that in my classroom, you are to speak when you are spoken to." She peered down at Susan.

Susan grasped the edges of her desk tightly in her small hands. She opened her mouth to speak and found that she had no breath to do so. She looked pleadingly at her teacher, who gazed back contemptuously.

"What is your name?" she seethed.

Susan's jaw pushed forward as she attempted to speak, to extract something. Anything!

Janet leaned back and clasped Susan's hand in her own. "Her name is Susan Dubois, Sister Mary Francis."

Sister Mary Francis's eyes left Susan momentarily. "I was not asking you," she said in her slow, proud manner.

Susan's stare held Janet's beseechingly. Janet squeezed her hand, gave her a determined look, and nodded slightly in encouragement. Susan opened her mouth.

"M—…m—…my name is…My name is Susan Dubois," she stammered.

"Well, Susan Dubois, I will have you know that I am not to be trifled with. When I ask you a question, you are to answer it straightaway. Do I make myself clear?" she asked.

Susan nodded her head vigorously, pleadingly.

"Do I make myself clear?" The sister's voice rose.

"Y—…y—…yes." Susan breathed.

Sister Mary Francis stood hovering over Susan with exasperation. She lifted the hardcover book she was clutching in her hand and hit Susan on the top of the head with it.

A slight grunt of humiliated surprise and shame escaped Susan's lips.

"Yes, Sister Mary Francis," the sister corrected. "Do as I say and mind your elders, Susan Dubois, and we shall have no problems." She turned her back on Susan and slowly walked to her desk.

"Now, we will start again." She looked at the girl in back of Susan.

"What is your name?"

Susan felt like she was drowning. She was aware of nothing but the throbbing on her head, the heat that had extended from her cheeks and spread to her forehead, her ears. Her mortification felt like fever. She didn't hear the name of the girl who was so close behind her. She didn't hear Janet's whisper of concern. She didn't even see Betty's distressed eyes upon her. But she did feel the tears trickling down her cheeks and watched as they landed in a puddle on the top of her new school desk.

* * *

The smell of fresh-baked chocolate chip cookies filled the air. Mother, having heard the screen door slam, walked into the kitchen from where she had been cleaning in the living room, a large and expectant smile upon her face. She halted and her smile faltered as she saw her daughter. Some of Susan's hair had come out of her ribbon and was dangling down the sides of her splotchy red face. Where she had expected a smile and a declaration of bliss on this first day of school, she found instead a daughter who was hurt and miserable.

"Oh, Susan!" she exclaimed. "Darling, what happened?"

Mother knelt and took Susan's hands in hers as Charlie stood behind his sister in the kitchen. Susan told Mother about the book. "I was afraid, Mama. I don't know why, but I was scared. And you know how I get sometimes. When I get scared or even if I feel shy inside, I just can't talk, no matter how hard I try. And I tried. I really did. Of course I know my own name! But I couldn't do it. I tried but I couldn't get the words out. And Sister Mary Francis didn't like that one bit. And she let me know. And she let all the other kids at school know, too. And now they probably all think I'm stupid and maybe they'll be laughing at me." Fresh tears welled in her eyes.

"Susan Marie, you stop that right now," Mother demanded. "Your classmates do not think you are stupid. Did one person laugh at you today?" She looked at her daughter, and when Susan didn't reply, she asked again, "Did they? Did even one person laugh at you today?"

"No, Mama," Susan said.

"No. I am sure they did not. Susan, what Sister Mary Francis did to you was certainly not a kind thing to do. I wonder if perhaps there was a misunderstanding and she thought you were being smart and disrespectful toward her?"

Susan shook her head. "I don't know, Mama. But I wasn't. I just couldn't talk."

"Yes, I know, darling." Mother sighed. "Oh, dear. Honestly, I remember Sister Mary Francis well. Did you know she was a teacher back when I went to St. Catherine's?" She looked at her daughter, whose tears were still trickling.

Susan shook her head.

"Well, she was. Of course she was younger then. New to the school, I believe. And I had her one year as a teacher. I remember very well this time she had asked a math question and of course she chose me to answer it even though my hand was not up in the air. Oh, she liked to do that a lot, pick on a student who was trying to hide in their seat. And I was one of those students. Give me an English question any day and I could probably have told you the answer. But math? That was not an area of strength for me and she knew it. I could not answer her question, and she had me walk to the front of the room and stick out my hand. That is when she took a ruler from the chalkboard and rapped my hand with it." She looked to her daughter and wiped the tears from her cheeks. "I remember feeling so very embarrassed. And I remember thinking it was all my fault, that I should have known the answer to that question. But do you know what, my Susan?" She paused.

"No," said Susan, tears slowly drying.

"I know now that it was not my fault at all. We all have our strengths and we all have our weaknesses. Math was not a strength for me and it never has been. Not even now. And I am a grown-up." She winked at her daughter, and Susan gave a slight grin in return.

"Now, Sister Mary Francis was not kind to you today, but she is your elder and she is your teacher as well as a nun. We both know that nuns spread the word of God and do His bidding. So we need to mind her choices. Try your very best to be a brave girl when you are at school, Susan. And please know that there are so many kind and caring teachers at St. Catherine's." She lifted her bottom from the heels of her feet and knelt on her knees, pulling Susan to her bosom. "Are you feeling a little better?" she asked as she let go.

"Yes, Mama," said Susan, wiping the last of her tears from the corners of her eyes and giving her mother a slight smile.

Mother looked to Charlie. "And how was your first day of school today, Charles?" she asked.

"I had a good day at school"—he lifted his eyebrows—"and I'm thinking I should be very happy I never had Sister Mary Francis as a teacher. But you've got this, Susan! You show her and everyone else that you're not stupid. Just think of me doing this the next time she scares you." He began wiggling his body back and forth, side to side, putting his arms in the air and crossing his eyes as he danced. Susan giggled. Charlie sure did make her laugh.

"Okay, my sillies," Mother said. "How about some chocolate chip cookies?"

FIVE

Susan awoke the next morning and made her way to the kitchen and breakfast.

When the children were ready for school and heading out the door, Mother kissed Charlie on the forehead. "Have a wonderful day, Charles."

"Thanks, Ma."

"And you, too, Susan," she said. She bent down and embraced her daughter, lingering a bit longer than she typically did. "Chin up, my dear. Go into this day believing it is going to be a good one."

"Yes, Mama," Susan said. She didn't smile, but neither was she teary-eyed.

The kids met Janet and Betty in front of their house and Henry on the sidewalk at the corner of Pleasant and Brown. As they began to cross the street, Susan's stomach clenched and her legs felt weak as if they might give out at any moment and drop her body to the ground right then and there. Charlie could sense her hesitation, and he took her hand in his, leading the way. Once safe on the other side of the road, he looked down at his sister.

"Susie, you've got this. I'm telling you, you've got this," he encouraged.

"I know," she said. She didn't really, but she didn't know what else to say at the moment.

"Come on, we'll walk you to your room." Charlie looked to Henry, who nodded in confirmation. Together they led Susan up the stairs and to the large wooden double doors, where once again the amiable young face of Sister Mary Margaret greeted them. She smiled right down at Susan, almost as if she were the only person there. For a brief moment Susan didn't feel Charlie's hand in hers or Henry's presence by her side or even her friends following behind. She didn't think of Sister Mary Francis waiting impatiently for her just over the threshold. She looked at Sister Mary Margaret and her genuine smile, and her body relaxed. Although this respite lasted only a moment, Susan would not forget the way Sister Mary Margaret had made her feel, even for years to come. It might have been just a smile, but for Susan it was a smile at the exact time it was desperately needed, and she heartily accepted it.

Charlie gently pulled her forth, and she entered the school. Her body went rigid once again, but her legs walked of their own accord, and she followed her brother toward her classroom door, lingering off to the left in the near distance.

"Love you, Susie T." Charlie winked, ridiculously bringing the left side of his mouth up toward his closed left eye, teeth biting down on his exposed tongue.

At this she laughed. Gosh, she loved her brother!

He tossed her ponytail into the air and then walked off down the hallway with Henry. Janet and Betty both entered the classroom, and Susan hesitantly followed suit. Her teacher stood in front of her desk watching them. They immediately placed their lunch boxes on their assigned hooks and sat down in the same chairs as yesterday.

Once all students were seated, Sister Mary Francis began. "Good morning, boys and girls," she said monotonously.

A chorus of young voices greeted her: "Good morning, Sister Mary Francis."

"Now that we have a day in our past, I trust that you all have an idea of what is expected of you this year in school."

"Yes, Sister Mary Francis."

"Good," she said. "Now let us start with attendance, shall we? Let us see if I do remember all of your names, as I expect I shall." Her deep voice hit Susan and she tensed in her chair.

"Let us start on this side of the room today." Sister Mary Francis looked at the blond-haired boy in the first row of seats by the door. "Good morning, David Sanders."

"Good morning, Sister Mary Francis." David was erect in his chair, hands clasped together on top of his desk, eyes eager.

Sister Mary Francis went up the first row and did indeed remember each child's name. She then began on the middle row with Betty and moved up that row before looking at Janet.

"Janet Boucher, yes?" said Sister Mary Francis.

"Yes, Sister Mary Francis."

"Ah, good," she said. Then, looking at Susan, "And you are Susan Dubois." She lifted her eyebrows, the lines of her face pulled in a frown.

"Y—...yes, Sister Mary Francis." She had done it! She had done it! Her voice hadn't betrayed her!

"Mmm-hmmm," Sister Mary Francis mumbled. She turned to the girl behind Susan. It was over. At least for now, it was over and she was okay. She allowed herself to slump slightly in her chair with relief.

The rest of the morning ran smoothly. When dismissed for lunch, Susan, Janet, and Betty walked to the cafeteria. They found a table and sat down. Susan was just opening her plaid-patterned, metal lunch box when she looked up to see David Sanders walking with Michelangelo Bartolomucci. He smiled when he caught her eye and walked over to her table.

"Can we sit with you?" David asked.

"Yes," said Susan.

David and Michelangelo both sat down next to Betty. Susan and Janet were across the table.

"Hello, relative," David joked to Betty.

She giggled. "Hello, relative," she said in turn.

"So you're Betty, right?" he asked.

"Yep," she said. "And this is Janet and this is Susie."

"Well, I'm David," he said. "And I'm hungry." He opened his lunch box and took out a large sandwich and a thermos.

"Sister Mary Francis calls me Michelangelo but I really like Mikey. So maybe don't call me Michelangelo?"

"Okay," Janet said. Susan nodded, and Betty took a bite of a cracker.

David had half his sandwich in hand and took a large bite. While he chewed he said, "Did you know that the red-tailed hawk eats rodents? And it also eats other birds." He paused to swallow and continued, "And the male red-tailed hawk flies around the sky in circles. Around and around. And he glides with his wings out. And he circles around in the sky because he's telling all the other hawks, 'Hey, this is my territory so don't come here,' and male – that means "boy" – red-tailed hawks stay with the girl for their whole life." He took another bite of his sandwich. "And did you know that owls are really cool? They can almost turn their heads all around. I mean they can turn their heads to look behind them and they don't even need to move their bodies at all. For real. And do you know why owls have really big eyes? I'm sure you've seen a picture of an owl before, right? Do you know why they have really big eyes?" He swallowed his second bite and didn't wait for an answer. "They have really big eyes because they can't move their eyes like us. They have to move their heads to see. For real. But did you know that owls can't see things that are really close to them? Only things that are far away. And owls can see little mouses and things on the ground at night really good and they fly on down and grab them up and they have really big claws." He looked around the table at the girls and Mikey.

"Neat," Mikey said.

The girls chewed their lunches and looked at David, whose expression indicated he had more to impart.

"My favorite owl is the barn owl. I know there are lots and lots of kinds of owls, but we went hiking this summer and I even saw a barn owl. So now it's my favorite type of owl. What's your favorite type of owl?"

The children continued to look at David, but nobody swooped in to answer straightaway. After a few moments Janet said, "I don't think I have a favorite type of owl, but I sometimes hear them. Mostly when I'm at my grandma and grandpa's house. They live where there are lots of woods. I don't think I've ever seen one, though. I don't know."

Susan decided to contribute and said, "I hear them sometimes when I go camping in the summer. I only know because Father told me when he heard them across the lake and he made me and Charlie listen. But I don't think I've ever seen one before, either."

"Is Charlie your brother?" David asked.

"Yeah. He goes to school here, too. He's in the fifth grade, though."

"Do you have any other brothers or sisters?" David took an orange out of his lunch box.

"No."

"I don't, either. It's just me. And I have a mom and a dad, and my grandmom lives with us now. Granddad died last year, so my mom said Grandmom needed help, so now she's living with us. But I like having her with us. She's real nice."

"I don't have any brothers or sisters," Janet volunteered. Susan and Betty knew that she didn't have a father, either, but Janet wasn't willing to share this piece of her life so readily.

"Me, neither," said Betty.

"Oh, I have lots," said Mikey.

"Lots?" Janet asked.

"Yep. There's me, but I have three older brothers and I have a younger sister and a younger brother. My mom is always saying that she and my sister is outnumbered, that there's too much...What's that word? Too much testerine?" He shrugged his shoulders. "Something about having lots of boys at home. And she always says we're too wild. But she laughs when she says it. Francesco is only a year older than me, so me and him do lots of things together. Lorenzo is mean sometimes. He's older and he thinks he knows everything and thinks that I don't know anything and tells me I'm a baby sometimes."

"I have a brother," said Susan. "But he doesn't tell me I'm a baby."

"Yeah, Charlie. You said," David replied, not unkindly.

"Oh, yeah," said Susan. "Sometimes I repeat myself."

"You like Charlie?" asked Mikey.

"Charlie is the best brother," Susan said. After a pause she asked the boys, "Do you have a dog?"

"No," said Mikey.

"We do," said David. "Daisy. She's a little poodle. She's Grandmom's dog, so she lives with us now because Grandmom lives with us now. She puts pink bows in her hair and makes her look all funny. And she barks a lot and it hurts my ears. When I watch TV, she sits on the couch with me and puts her head in my lap and I like that. Do you have a dog?"

"No. Not yet. I'm gonna ask Mama, though. I really want a puppy. I would like a poodle puppy. I don't think bows in their hair makes them look funny. I'd put bows in my puppy's hair if I could. And brush her hair. And if a puppy could sleep in bed with me, that would make me really happy. I'm gonna ask Mama and maybe I can get a puppy for Christmas and name her Lucy."

"Maybe," said David.

The kids chatted for the remainder of lunch, and when they were dismissed, they took their lunch boxes out to the lawn with them for recess.

The afternoon proved uneventful and for this Susan was especially grateful. She met her brother in front of the school at the end of the day with a smile on her face and a lightness to her step. When Charlie saw his sister's expression, he smiled brightly.

"Better day today?" he asked.

"Yeah. It was a good day. And we made new friends," she said as she looked to both Janet and Betty for confirmation. They nodded their heads, knowing instinctively that Susan was referring to David and Mikey.

"So good," Charlie said.

The five of them crossed the street to the sidewalk on their way home. As they began walking along Pleasant Avenue, Charlie's posture became rigid and he tensed up beside Henry.

"Loser." Susan looked to Charlie's left and saw Tommy Walters standing there with two other boys. Tommy was a grade above Charlie—sixth—and he lived somewhere around them, though she knew not where exactly. When she and Charlie saw him along the streets or at Emerson Park on occasion, she was very uncomfortable. He had a way of looking at her with those dark brown eyes and bushy eyebrows that put her in a state of unease.

His friends chuckled at the abuse, which motivated Tommy into furthering his maltreatment of Charlie.

"My father says he knew your father back when they went to school together. He says your family don't even have a pot to piss in." He started walking alongside Charlie. "What is that, huh? A hand-me-down uniform?" He plucked at Charlie's sleeve. Susan faltered and fell behind.

"Leave him alone, Tommy," Henry intervened. "You're being a dick." While Charlie's shoulders were slumped forward and his eyes downcast, Henry stood erect and moved from Charlie's right side to his left, putting himself in between his friend and the instigator.

"'Dick', huh? Big word," Tommy said.

"Piss off," said Henry, obviously upset. He stopped walking and stood firm. Charlie felt the momentum had waned and stopped as well, looking from Henry to Tommy. Henry's jaw was clenched, and Tommy took a step back toward his friends.

Tommy grunted, then spit on the sidewalk. "See ya later, loser." He looked to Charlie as he walked back toward the school, friends in tow and snickering.

"Why do you let him treat you like that?" Henry turned toward his best friend.

Charlie shrugged his shoulders, face contorted in an expression of pained discomfiture and apprehension.

"Ah," said Henry amiably as he put his arm around Charlie's shoulders and pulled him forth so they were walking once again, "let's go."

Susan felt a hand grasp onto hers and turned to see Janet by her side. Betty laced her hand through Susan's free arm, and together the three girls trailed behind the boys. They didn't let go until they reached Susan's house.

SIX

The following few months were predominantly happy ones for Susan. Charlie turned ten in September shortly after fifth grade had begun. Janet and Betty met her each day to walk to school. Charlie and Henry met the girls when school was out to walk them home even though it wasn't expected they should do so. Weekends were spent playing on the streets and at Emerson Park with friends.

Fall hit and then winter. When the snow began to fall, Susan would bundle up in her snow clothes and head out the door, returning with rosy cheeks and a cold runny nose, the smell of frosty wet air and snow lifting from her jacket to permeate the air.

Snow she loved. In the backyard she'd make snowmen with Charlie and even have snowball fights when friends were over to play. She'd lie on the ground and spread her arms and legs and push them up and down to make snow angels.

One particularly nice winter day Henry, Janet, and Betty were all over. They had taken the snow shovel out of the garage and used it to pack snow into a large mound. With help from Henry and meticulous care on Charlie's part and a lot of fails and laughs from the girls, they were able to form a snow igloo in the yard. Susan was thrilled to learn that she, Janet, and Betty could all fit inside at the same time. Mother came out in her coat and a pair of boots, camera in hand, to bring them mugs of hot cocoa with marshmallows. With mittened hands, Susan held onto her mug with both palms, sat in the snow, and sipped the warm, chocolate deliciousness, leaving a brown, frothy stain on her upper lip.

Susan was elated the day she and her family loaded into the station wagon and set off to a local farm that was selling Christmas trees. She was all bundled up in her winter gear, hat on her head, scarf around her neck, jacket zipped to her chin. Her breath spiraled from her mouth in the frigid air. Her nose had begun to run and froze to the bottom of her nostrils before it could drip down her upper lip, which was perfectly fine with her; she didn't have to wipe with the back of her mittened fingers this way. Father had made a big show of going around all the rows, looking at the trees and sizing them up. Mother, Susan, and Charlie followed him around until he finally pulled a small tree from the rack and declared his choice.

"I love it, Gerald," Mother said.

Father's shoulders pulled back and his chin rose as his family surrounded him. Susan smiled blissfully on that cold winter's day as an attendant snapped a picture of her family with their camera in front of the tree that Father held upright.

Father secured the tree in the stand at home in the corner of the living room and let the branches settle for a couple of days. Once it had been in the home for only a small amount of time, Susan could smell the strong piney scent when she entered the room. Oh, how she loved that smell!

Decorating was always a family affair, and Susan was thrilled when the time came. Father had returned from work, and dinner had been eaten. Susan and Charlie gathered by the tree in the living room and Mother put a record on the small wooden record player. Kay Starr's "The Man With the Bag" began its up-tempo beat, and Susan swayed her hips as she waited for the boxes of decorations that Father had gone to the garage to unearth. When he returned, he placed them on the couch and exposed the Styrofoam-and-satin balls of reds, greens, and blues as well as the string of colored blinking lights and sparkly silver tinsel. He stood and surveyed the tree, hands on hips. There was a small portion on the right side that was lacking on branches and the trunk could be seen a minute amount. He grabbed his drill and drilled a hole in the side of the tree's trunk, sawed off a branch from a portion of the tree that had an excess, and stuck that branch in the small drilled hole to fill the space. He did this three times before stepping back, contented. He then constructed the train track under the tree and placed the train on top; it was a Christmas decoration that Father held with pride as it signified his work on the railroad. He wrapped the lights around the tree next, and Susan danced over to the box of ornaments while Dean Martin's voice proclaimed that they should "let it snow! let it snow! let it snow!"

They hung the ornaments on the tree. The tinsel followed, and when all was complete, Susan admired their work. It was so beautiful, those twinkly lights and the tinsel that was so lightweight it danced when you walked past! She clasped her hands together under her chin, bounced on the tips of her slippered toes, and grinned.

It was now Christmas Eve 1959. The day had been spent making chocolate chip cookies for Santa; they were rumored to be his favorite, so Mother said. In the evening they sat in front of the television to watch *It's a Wonderful Life* together, a Christmas Eve ritual. When the movie ended, she said good night to Father and Charlie and followed her mother into her room.

Slumber finally found her. She slept lightly but well. When she woke in the morning, the sun hadn't risen and the sky was still dark, the waning crescent moon distributing a diminutive glow to the earth.

She crawled out of her warm bed and slowly opened her door, peeking her head out into the living room. An eerie quiet enveloped her, and only a small portion of moonlight seeped through the window on the wall, but it was enough for Susan to see that Santa had paid them a visit. There were wrapped boxes under her Christmas tree! She opened her door fully now and ran to investigate, falling on her knees when she arrived at her destination. She touched a gift, lifted her hand, touched another. She inspected the tags affixed to the packages with ribbon and recognized her name on a few. She bounded to her feet and ran to her brother's room, opening the door and crashing onto his bed.

"Charlie," she said enthusiastically. "Charlie, wake up." Her knees on the bed, she leaned over her brother's body and pushed down on his back with her hands. "Wake up, Charlie. Santa was here!"

Charlie mumbled and then slowly opened his eyes.

"Santa came, Charlie. Wake up."

Charlie blinked his eyes forcefully and sat up, propping himself with his arms. "I'm coming," he said. Susan didn't wait for him to get out of bed before she ran out the door and into her parents' bedroom.

"Mama! Mama!" Susan shook her awake. "He came. Santa came!"

Mother was awake now and smiled at her daughter's enthusiasm. "Is that right?" she said sleepily.

"Yeah!" Susan said. "Yeah, he came. Come on!" She tugged on her mother's sleeve, and Mother groggily lifted the blankets from her legs. She leaned toward Father's bed.

"Gerald," she said. "It is time."

Susan turned on the living room light, ran back to the Christmas tree, and eagerly awaited her parents' arrival. Charlie was the first to meet her. Mother and Father soon followed. Father approached the stockings that were propped up against the wall beneath the window and distributed them to his family, taking his last and sitting beside his wife on the couch.

The stockings were small but full and Susan took no time in sitting with crossed legs on the floor and delving into hers. Mother and Father were slower to finish their stockings, and Susan tried her very best to wait patiently for them to conclude. Father stood from the couch and walked over to the tree, lifting a gift from the floor.

"What does this say?" he asked Susan as he tipped the small gift to her level so she could see the tag on the top.

"That's my name!" she squealed. She bounced up and down as she grabbed it from his hands. Father handed a gift over to Charlie as Susan tore into the red-and-white wrapping, pictures of Santa and his red toy sack dismissed as she dug toward the actual item lying beneath. A copy of *Harry the Dirty Dog* greeted her. "Oh, Mama," she said. "Santa got me a new book!" She held onto it with both hands and smiled brightly as Mother looked back.

"Well, you're always telling us you want a dog. Now you've got one." Father chuckled at his own joke, but Susan didn't think it was funny at all. She was thrilled to have a brand-new book in her possession, but it wasn't nearly the same as a real live puppy, now, was it? She frowned and looked down at her book, some of the pleasure in its acquisition having vanished.

Father handed her a new gift, and her displeasure dissipated. She tore at the paper, revealing a rectangular cardboard box with a plastic window. She peered in and saw that Santa had brought her a hairbrush. She hugged it to her chest and smiled at her parents.

Both Susan and Charlie opened a few more gifts from Santa Claus. The children were stunned to have received so many wonderful presents, and the delight shone on their faces.

Mother stood from the couch and walked to the Christmas tree, lifting from beneath it a large square package as well as a considerably smaller one in the shape of a rectangle. She handed the smaller package to Father first, and he opened it. Mother had gotten him a new pair of brown slippers.

"Yours are getting so old and worn, Gerald. I thought you may like some new ones. And I asked around and apparently these are some of the best ones you can buy right now. They are supposed to be rather comfortable, you see." She paused, looking down at Father seated on the couch. "Do you like them?"

"I do," Father said, "but you know how often I wear my slippers, Helen. I like the ones I have now." Annoyed, he placed them back in the shoebox, which he set on the floor beside him. He lit a cigarette, inhaled sharply. He exhaled as Mother handed him the second gift, this one apparently heavier than the first.

"I really hope you like this one, Gerald." Her smile was wary but her body stood erect portraying an air of confident excitement and expectation. She folded her hands in front of her and rested her chin upon them as she watched Father open her gift.

The paper fell to the ground at his feet. He gazed at the gift upon his lap, cigarette dangling between his closed lips.

"It's our wedding photo, Gerald. The one we have always loved. Do you remember what you said to me the very moment before that picture was taken?" She watched as Father took the cigarette out of his mouth and rested it between his fingers, looking down at the large picture before him nestled within a beautiful wooden frame. "You whispered in my ear that I was your wife, that I was yours. Do you remember that? I was so happy that day, Gerald. And that is what I had in my mind as I smiled for the camera. Those words. I thought it would be very nice to have that photo of us decorating our wall. We can take this one down," she said as she pointed at the wall above the couch on which a photo of a landscape was hanging, "and put this new one in its place. And we can look at this photo of us every time we are here in our home together, where we have made our family. And we can remember that day. We can remember how in love we were." She smiled down at Father, tears glistening in her eyes. "Do you like it?"

"It's a nice picture, Helen," Father said monotonously. He rested it against the side of the couch and took another inhalation of his cigarette.

Mother nodded. "I'm pleased you like it," she said in a soft, dejected voice. She sat down next to Father, wiping a tear that had fallen from her eye. She crossed her ankles and smiled tightly at her children.

Charlie intervened. "I made you both something at school," he said. He walked to Mother, handing her a package that was wrapped quite well, especially considering the fact that ten-year-old fingers had been nimble enough to do the work. Mother took the package from her son, smiling appreciatively. She unwrapped her gift.

"Oh, Charles," she said in wonderment, "this is so beautiful." Charlie had made her a journal. She held it aloft. Sheets of small paper were bound between a hand-designed cover made of thin stained wood, three holes having been drilled on the side. Twine had been placed through each hole to secure the paper with a knot. *1959* was etched into the middle of the wood on the front of the journal. "It is truly wonderful, darling, thank you." Mother stood from her seat on the couch and hugged Charlie tightly. Charlie beamed back at her, heart full.

"Sir." Charlie handed Father his gift. Father opened it to reveal a hand-carved wooden cribbage board.

"Charles Donald," Mother breathed. "You made that?"

"Yes, ma'am."

"Charles, it's splendid. You are a very talented young man." Mother gently brushed her fingers over the small holes on the top of the board.

"Well done, son," Father said. "Your mother's right. You did a good job here. This makes me proud."

"Thank you, sir," Charlie said, biting his lower lip and nodding slightly.

"Mama," Susan interrupted, "I made you something, too."

"Did you, Susan?"

"Yes!" Susan ran to her bedroom, where she had hidden her parents' gift under her bed, gleeful that she had a secret to keep. She returned and stood in front of Mother. She had wrapped her gift at school, and although her wrapping job was nowhere as neat as Charlie's, she was proud of the work she had done. Mother slowly removed the paper off the gift to reveal a small box. When she opened this, she found a folded sheet of thick paper. Susan had made her a juvenile picture of Jesus's birth with circular blue scribbles and straight one-dimensional legs for sheep, stick-figure people and angels, and horizontal lines for a manger. In the sky was a yellow burst of a star, and on the upper right-hand corner, Susan had placed her name in large red crayoned letters. She stood before her mother, beaming with pride.

"Very nice work, Susan," Mother said. "I especially like the sheep you have drawn."

"Thanks, Mama," Susan said joyfully. Mother leaned forward and embraced her daughter.

"I think I am going to place this picture right at my bedside, Susan," Mother said. "That way I can see it when I go to bed at night, and I can see it when I wake up in the morning, and it will truly remind me what Christmas is all about: Christ and family.

"Well," Mother said as she placed her picture back in the box and rested it gently beside her on the couch, "I suppose you are wondering what those last two gifts under the Christmas tree are, yes?" Her eyes twinkled with amusement.

"Yes!" Susan shouted. Charlie smiled and pivoted toward the tree as Mother lifted a large rectangular package.

"This one is for you, Charles. It is from your father and me. Merry Christmas." She presented him with the gift and he took hold of it

71

eagerly.

"Aww, thanks so much, Mom!" He exclaimed once the present was open. He looked at Father sitting on the couch. "Father," he said," thank you."

Father nodded and Mother beamed at her son's reaction. Charlie held the open package in his hands and looked admiringly down upon it. A pogo stick. He had asked for this, and Mother and Father had gotten it for him. He was elated, eager to actually have the opportunity to use it.

Mother turned to Susan. "Would you like your gift now, Susan?" she asked.

"Yes!"

Mother handed Susan a wrapped rectangular package large enough that she couldn't fully encircle her arms around it and tall enough that she stood to make the unwrapping easier. She tore at it with gusto. The first thing to appear under the wrapping paper was a face, a doll's face! Susan squealed, utterly delighted. She pulled the rest of the paper off the front of the box and jumped up and down, her cheeks beginning to ache with the pressure of her smiles.

"Oh, Mama! Mama, Mama! Mama, you got me a doll! My very own doll!" Susan danced on the balls of her feet as she looked at her mother. "Thank you, thank you! Mama, Father, thank you! Can you help me open her?"

Mother opened the box and unearthed the doll resting inside. "Now you will have to think of a name for her, Susan," she said.

"Oh," Susan said. "I already know that. I'm going to call her Shelly." Shelly was now completely out of the box, and Susan grabbed her from Mother's hands and held her tightly to her chest, rocking from side to side, a look of pure bliss upon her face.

"Oh, thank you, thank you, thank you!" She continued to sway, alternately closing her eyes tightly—Shelly within her embrace—and holding her at arm's length so she could look at her. Shelly was beautiful with her hard plastic face and blue eyes. She had long eyelashes and small red lips. Her golden hair was shoulder-length and wavy, and she wore a pale yellow short-sleeved dress with white trim on the collar. White booties adorned her feet, and a pink baby bottle was in her right hand. Susan didn't believe she could have been more perfect. What a wondrous thing that Shelly was just for her!

Mother looked adoringly at her children, content.

A loud thunder of a clap from Father as he stood from the couch. "We're not done," he proclaimed. "Helen, you'll have to come to the garage for your gift."

"The garage?" Mother said hesitantly. "Whyever the garage, Gerald?"

He didn't answer, and he didn't look behind him to see if his family was following. Mother looked at Susan and Charlie, hesitated, then smiled and began to walk after Father, quickening her pace to catch up.

Susan and Charlie walked in Mother's wake, and together they reached the porch to slip on their shoes and then hastened to the side of the garage, where Father had just entered, having trudged through the snow in his slippers to the paint-chipped white door. He pulled the chain on the ceiling light and the inside of the garage was illuminated. Father walked a few steps farther into the garage, and there toward the middle next to his tool bench stood a sight that halted Mother unexpectedly, forcing Susan to trip over her own feet and bump into her back.

"Gerald!" It was a drawn-out breath full of incredulity and disbelief. Susan looked to Mother and saw her eyes glisten over, her hand covering her mouth. "Gerald," she said. "This is too much. We simply cannot afford this!"

Susan looked beyond her mother. "What is it?" she asked.

"Oh, Susan," Mother said. "Your father got us a washing machine. One to replace our current one that you have seen me scrub and crank our clothes with. I cannot believe this." Mother spoke softly and slowly, fingers hovering over her bottom lip.

"Gerald, I do not even know what to say right now other than thank you. This is so wonderful. Truly wonderful." She stepped toward the machine and ran her hand over the smooth white top and round knobs. "Oh, Gerald." She looked at her husband with adoration. He clasped his hands behind his back and stood proud at the machine's side. She walked to him and kissed him on the cheek.

Susan and Charlie looked at each other perplexed. A washing machine didn't nearly compare to Shelly and a pogo stick. They backtracked out of the garage and back into the kitchen of their warm house, where they found the comfort of the living room in all its Christmas-morning splendor.

* * *

The children were left to their own devices for the next hour while Mother and Father prepared for the day. Susan enjoyed playing with Shelly. She fed her with the pink baby bottle and brushed her hair with her new hairbrush – it might have been intended for Susan herself, but she could find no better use for it at the moment than to beautify Shelly.

Mother entered the room and told Susan and Charlie that it was time to get dressed and ready for a full day of activity.

Breakfast was eaten, and then the family placed their coats and boots on. Father exited the house first with the car keys in hand, and Mother followed behind with a casserole dish and a dessert platter. Father approached the driver-side door and pulled on the handle with a gloved hand. Susan heard a crunching as the ice on the handle broke and an airy pop as the door was pried open, the ice along the edges cracking. Father stepped into the car, his long, thick brown coat hanging down as he descended. Her exhalations of breath curling up toward the sky in cold puffs of white, Susan stepped inside with Shelly. Father started the car, and they sat there idling on the concrete while it warmed up well enough for the ice to melt off the windshield.

Memere and Pepere Dubois lived across town, about a fifteen-minute drive from North Street. Susan spent the entire car ride talking to Shelly in a maternal voice using the word "darling" whenever it seemed fit to do so. From her seat in the front of the car, Mother smiled to herself at her daughter's choice of words. When they arrived at Memere and Pepere's, Shelly had been coddled and most assuredly had a full stomach of milk.

They pulled into the driveway to the left of the house just in front of the single-car garage. As theirs was the first car parked, Susan deduced that they were also the first to arrive. This disappointed her as she was looking forward to playing with Elizabeth and showing her Shelly and she welcomed Elizabeth's presence when she was around Memere, who discomfited her greatly with her stark comments and her disapproving looks.

Susan turned her gaze to the house: a small tan one-story home in which her father and Ma Tante Mary had spent their childhood days. They slowly made their way across the driveway and to the side of the house where the door stood awaiting their arrival. Charlie stepped through first, and Susan attempted to make her presence undetected by standing behind him.

The side door led directly into the kitchen. Memere was standing in front of the stove, stirring something inside a large pot. She turned her head to look behind her when she heard her son and his family enter but said nothing, just attended once more to the task at hand.

Pepere stood at the doorway.

"Welcome, welcome," he said jovially. Susan peeked her head around Charlie's back and saw a smile on her grandfather's features, his blue eyes bright in his round white face, his lashes almost translucent in their paleness. She looked upon his shiny, bald head with his wisps of white hair that stuck up around his ears and smiled, lowering her gaze to the floor.

"And how are you, Susan?" Apparently willing herself to become an apparition didn't actually make her invisible after all. But seeing as this was Pepere speaking and not Memere, she was comforted.

"Okay," she said. "Look, Pepere," she added, "I got a doll from Mama and Father." She held Shelly in front of her shyly so Pepere could admire her new gift.

"I bet you were happy to get that doll," he said. His high cheekbones were rosy in their elevation.

"I was," she affirmed. "I was so happy." She looked down at her new doll cradled lovingly in her arms.

"Well, come in, come in." Pepere moved backward and motioned with his arms that his family was welcome. Susan hung her jacket on the coat hook and kicked her wet boots off at the door. As Mother moved into the kitchen to place the casserole dish on the counter, Susan and the others sat on the couches in the living area. Mother began helping Memere, and Pepere stood before Father on the couch and began a conversation as Father lit a cigarette. Charlie had brought a book inside and opened it up to read as Susan gave Shelly another feeding, stroking her hair and ignoring the chatter next to her.

The side door opened and Mon Oncle Walter poked his head through, hand resting on the knob. His smile was wide, and his hair stood on end in its trademark, disheveled fashion. One large booted foot stomped onto the kitchen floor. "Hello, hello," his deep voice boomed. "Merry Christmas." He pushed the door wide, and the rest of his massive, soaring body came forth as he ducked to enter the house, large dessert container in hand. Elizabeth stepped into the warmth behind him, followed by her mother and younger brother.

Elizabeth had taken her coat and shoes off at the door and joined Susan now at the couch. "You got a doll, too!" she exclaimed.

"I did," Susan said. "Isn't she beautiful? Mama and Father got her for me for Christmas. And look, she has her very own bottle. And she's a good eater. She drinks her milk fast. And she's such a good baby. Aren't you, Shelly?" She rocked her baby back and forth in her arms. "What's your baby's name?"

"I named her Elizabeth." Her cousin took the seat between Susan and Father.

"You named your doll Elizabeth?" Susan giggled. "But that's your name."

"I know. But she's my doll, so I just named her Elizabeth."

Susan and Elizabeth played with their dolls while Ma Tante Mary walked toward the kitchen to help her mother and sister-in-law with Christmas food preparations. Father and Pepere approached a table on a small wall between the kitchen and living room. Father inspected the various types of liquor and alcohol and settled upon the bottle of Old Forester whiskey, pouring himself a generous glass. He took a large sip and swallowed, looking down at the amber liquid as he swished it around.

Soon the room was filled with the scent of cranberries and baked apples, turkey and gravy. Dinner was ready! Susan made her way to the kitchen and sat at a folding table resting against Memere and Pepere's kitchen table to make additional room for the larger crowd gathered.

Memere began the dinner prayer when all were seated. Once her husky voice was through, she held her pious head high, pulling taut the flap of wobbly skin that ran from chin to neck.

Conversation slowly and quietly began as Memere sat regally in her chair. Even after a hearty and delicious Christmas breakfast at home, Susan's mouth began to salivate as all the appetizing smells filled her nostrils and packed her plate. What a meal. Oh, how she loved Christmas!

Although Memere and Father remained rather silent around the table, the voices of others were gay and delighted. And Mother was so wonderful for she hadn't placed any of that abhorrent cranberry sauce on Susan's plate. Susan forked a piece of turkey and placed it in her mouth, chewing merrily as the juices dribbled on her tongue and down her throat.

"Susan." Across the table, Memere was grimacing. "This is the second time now that I have looked at you and you have had your mouth open. I care not to see the food rolling around in your mouth."

Susan immediately felt the warmth of blood pooling in her cheeks, and she ceased her chewing, balled-up turkey now lying dormant in the pocket of her cheek. Her hand rested against the edge of her plate, fork still clutched within her little fingers. In her embarrassment, she looked down upon her food.

"And I care not that you disrespect me by looking away. Haven't your parents taught you that you are to look in one's eyes when they are talking to you?" Susan felt the redness of her cheeks spread to her neck and forehead as she slowly raised her eyes to her grandmother's, turkey still held in her mouth as she dared not move.

"Oh, I'm sure she's not—" Pepere began to speak in his granddaughter's defense, but ceased abruptly when Memere, sitting erect in her chair, looked at him with an expression of annoyance, eyebrows lifting toward her rounded, curly hairline.

"Excuse us, Blanche," Mother interjected and looked over at Susan with a small smile on her worried face. "We are working on table manners, right, darling?"

Susan was petrified and said nothing in response.

"Shut your mouth, Helen," Father seethed, "before you embarrass yourself." He turned to Susan with an expression that conveyed his distaste and displeasure at having been chastised by his mother. Mother's smile faltered, and she looked at her husband with surprise and hurt but said nothing in her defense, merely looked from Father to her plate and forked food around to hide her humiliation.

"This turkey is amazing," Mon Oncle Walter said, his voice loud and clear. "My compliments to you, Blanche." He held his fork up high and nodded his head her way. She gave a small, stiff nod in return, and the stifling atmosphere slowly dissipated.

Conversations sluggishly returned to the table as the family finished their meals, although Susan remained silent. When everyone had finished, Mon Oncle complimented the food once again and then retired to the couch with Father and a bottle of beer. Father had poured himself another full glass of whiskey and lit an after-dinner cigarette as soon as he sat.

When the table was clean and the dishes were washed and dried, Memere presented herself to the family and announced that they could partake of dessert. Ma Tante had made Christmas cookies and a Jell-O mold. Homemade eggnog sat in a pitcher upon the table. Susan relished every last bite of her dessert and drink and was excused from the table to play.

"Let's go play in the spare bedroom," suggested Elizabeth. They walked down the hallway and Elizabeth turned the knob. The girls walked in. It was a small room and rarely used. There was a twin-sized bed with a brown quilt on top. Elizabeth closed the door behind Susan and the girls sat on the bed and began feeding their dolls.

"You know, my friend Mary said that we have nipples. Right here" Elizabeth pointed to her chest. "She said that nipples feed babies when a mama has one. She said the baby puts its mouth on the nipple and sucks milk. Mary knows. She has a baby sister and her mama feeds her from her nipple and not a bottle like all the babies I've seen."

Susan didn't know how to respond. She had seen what Elizabeth was now calling nipples on her own body while bathing, but Mother had always taught her not to question her body; she said that bodies were extremely private and we were never to touch ourselves other than to wash with soap and water in the tub. She took this at face value, and curiosity had not yet taken hold.

"When I was with Mary," Elizabeth continued, "we played doctor. You know how you go to the doctor to get a checkup, and they check your heart and stuff? Mary said that when her mama had the baby it came out of her vagina. Do you know what that is?"

Susan shook her head, and Elizabeth stood a bit straighter, proud that she was able to inform her younger cousin about something of which Susan was ignorant but that she, Elizabeth, knew.

"It's where you pee," she said. "There's a hole. And the baby comes out of the hole. Mary knows because her mama told her this and then she told me. We're girls, so we have vaginas. She said that boys don't have babies so they don't have vaginas. She said that her mama told her that boys have a penis. I remember that word because I thought it was a funny word. Don't you?"

Susan lifted her shoulders in a shrug. She didn't know what to think, but she did know this conversation was leaving her feeling quite uncomfortable. Her mother's words of warning seemed to hover around the room.

"My baby has a vagina. It's right here." Elizabeth lifted her baby's dress and pulled her legs up to reveal nothing more than a bare bottom. "Well, it would be there if she was a real baby. Does your baby have a vagina?"

Susan slowly lifted Shelly's dress and then her legs, booties pointing to the ceiling. Her head shook back and forth vigorously as she lowered Shelly's legs and smoothed her dress back down.

"Well, we have vaginas." Elizabeth paused in contemplation. "We should play doctor like me and Mary did. You can look at my nipples and I can look at yours. Want to play?"

Susan's words choked in her throat, so she shook her head again, eyes widening with her refusal.

"Okay." Elizabeth lifted her shoulders and the corner of her mouth simultaneously, brushing off the suggestion rather quickly.

"Susan." Her mother's voice calling from the hallway. She scooted off the bed and opened the bedroom door, spotting her mother just to her left. "Ah, Susan. It is time for us to go now. Say goodbye to Elizabeth and come on out, please."

Susan was extremely relieved for the interruption and waved to Elizabeth hastily. Elizabeth waved back.

Susan said her goodbyes and gave thanks to the rest of her family before stealing away to the door to put her shoes on and grab her coat from the coatrack in the corner.

The family walked to their car in the cold, the sky darkening now that it was later in the afternoon. Father started the car and backed out of the driveway, Susan shivering in her seat behind him.

Memere and Pepere Richard's home wasn't far away, a ten-minute drive at most. Father pulled the car into the driveway and parked behind a red Chevrolet that Susan knew to be that of her cousin Ellie and her family.

Susan exited their car and walked to the front door, taking the three brick steps to the entrance. Mother had prepared a dessert to share with all in attendance and held the container under her arm as she turned the knob to enter. Charlie carried a bag of gifts.

"Hello?" she said in a singsong voice.

"Oh, Helen, you're here." It was Ma Tante Alice who saw her sister first and walked over to greet her. The front door opened directly into the living room, and it was here that Susan took off her boots, a bit wet from a dusting of snow.

"So glad to see you, Helen." Memere joined her daughters and hugged Mother hello.

"Oh, Mom," Mother said. "We are getting your floor all wet with snow."

"Oh, fiddlesticks," Memere said. "I don't care about that one bit. I'll just clean the house when everyone is gone, won't I?"

Mother smiled and walked farther into the living room, where Pepere was sitting on a couch nestled under a central window at the left of the room. She leaned down and kissed her father on the cheek. "Hi, Dad."

"Helen." He looked at his daughter, white sclera quite large in comparison to the tiny portion of blue. If he had eyebrows, Susan couldn't see them. Pepere leaned his right hand on his cane and grunted as he lifted his frail, lean body out of its seat. "Gerald," Pepere said in greeting.

"Good to see you, John." Father held his gaze respectfully and firmly shook his hand. Pepere slowly lowered himself back onto the couch. "Leg giving you some trouble today?"

"Goddamn leg is always giving me trouble," he grumbled. "I feel like I'm eighty, for Christ's sake. Just gets worse each year, and the cold don't seem to help none. I feel like a damned cripple."

"Come now," Memere said, "the others are in the kitchen." She motioned behind her. Susan and Charlie followed. Memere held back a moment to allow Charlie to catch up with her and then placed her chubby arm around his shoulders. "And look at you, Charles," she said, an awed expression on her face. "You are just as tall as I am now, aren't you? Well, you just need to stop growing, or I'm going to start feeling like a shrimp, won't I?" She laughed at her own joke, which made Charlie smirk. "Ah," Memere said, "I'm just so happy to have you all here."

They walked through the entryway to the kitchen. Ellie and Mon Oncle Paul were sitting at the table with Ellie's older brothers playing old maid.

"They're here," Mon Oncle Paul announced over his hand of cards, although his family could clearly see that the Dubois family had arrived.

"Susie!" Ellie jumped from her seat, cards having been discarded on the tabletop as her cousin walked into the room. In her excitement to see Susan, she wrapped her arms around her shoulders in a strong hug. Shelly pressed against Susan's body and jabbed into her ribs.

"Oof," she grunted.

Ellie pulled back. "Oh, sorry," she said abashedly.

"That's okay," Susan said. "I'm happy to see you, too."

"Come on," Ellie said as she motioned to the table. "Want to play?"

Susan enjoyed a game of old maid and had begun a second when Memere said it was time to end so she could set the table for supper.

"I need a damn drink," Pepere grumbled as he entered the kitchen. He looked at Father beside him. "Want one?"

"Hmm."

Pepere walked to the refrigerator at the right of the kitchen and opened it. Reaching in, he extracted a can of Budweiser and handed it off to Father, who grabbed the church key from a small drawer. He lifted the small piece of pressed metal to his can and pierced the top at one side, turned the can and pierced a second hole. Handing the church key off to Pepere, he reached above to grab two large glasses from a cabinet and poured his beer into one.

Mother hesitantly approached her husband as he took his first sip. "Remember, Gerald, that you had a couple of drinks at your parents' house." She placed the palm of her hand on his back and smiled warily.

"Mind your own damn business, woman." His voice was hoarse

and low. He took another large gulp of the frothy liquid, not looking once at his wife.

"Everything set for dinner?" Pepere asked his daughter.

"It is."

Adults sat at the large kitchen table, and the children made themselves comfortable upon chairs at a folding table erected beside the kitchen counters. Plates in front of owners, a prayer of thanksgiving given, the family began to eat. When they were through, the girls went to play in the living room.

"Who wants presents?" Memere was walking into the room from the kitchen, Mother and Ma Tante following behind, speaking in hushed whispers, heads bowed together. Susan wondered what it was they were secretive about, but then again, it could be almost anything with Mother and Ma Tante Alice. Mother was often at her most jovial when she was with her sister.

"Okay, okay," Memere said. "Shall we? Let's see here." Memere squatted on her stout legs and began passing out gifts to the children first and then to the adults. They all began opening their presents once they were handed off, so a bit of chaotic exuberance filled the room.

Soon, all gifts were open, and paper littered the floor. The children began to play as the adults conversed on the couches.

Memere clapped her hands together loudly to get the room's attention. "How about some dessert. You'd like that, wouldn't you?" she asked the children.

"Yes!" The girls jumped up and ran to the kitchen.

Memere walked through the doorway just after the girls and continued on to the kitchen countertop, where the desserts had been waiting. Pepere called to her from the living room.

"Bring mine over here, Gloria. I feel like shit and ain't gettin' up."

Memere cut into both pies and portioned out a slice of each onto two plates and brought them to her husband and son-in-law in the living room while Mother took over at the counter to dish out slices of pie to the children.

Father entered the kitchen and extracted another beer from the refrigerator. Susan looked up. Father's eyes were glassy, his cheeks red. Mother approached him warily, put her hand upon his back, and whispered in his ear. Father lifted his elbow and rammed it into Mother's right breast as best he could while attempting to pour the liquid fully from one device into another without a slip and spill.

Mother started, a slight yelp unconsciously leaping from her lips. She backed away from Father and walked to the plate of pie she had left on the countertop. Father placed the empty beer can beside the sink and walked back to Pepere in the living room.

Susan stole a glance at her mother now at the table. Her cheeks were red, her eyes downcast as she ate her dessert. Whispering ensued between the adults, and Susan strained to eavesdrop.

"Helen..." Ma Tante placed her hand over Mother's beside her. "Listen, Dad has always been one for drinking, we all know that. And he sure can be an ass to Mom..."

"Alice!" Although Memere was speaking in a whisper, her voice was high-pitched with alarm in response to her younger daughter's audacity in speaking so freely about their father in her presence.

"Okay, Mom," Ma Tante said, "you may not like to hear it, but it's true. Dad is an ass to you. And he's an ass to us. He has his good moments, for sure, but he's ornery as hell, especially when he's drinking." She looked at her mother's scrunched-up face. "But my point is"— she looked back at her sister, squeezing her hand—"as much as Dad can be an ass to us all, he'd never hurt us, Helen. Never. His tongue is sharp, but he hasn't ever lifted a hand." Ma Tante was attempting to keep her voice at a whisper but was becoming emotional and finding it hard to maintain a composed tone. "We've all seen what

Gerald has done to you, Helen. We just saw him elbow you for no apparent reason, for Christ's sake!"

"Alice!" Memere gasped again and stole a glance at her son-in-law who sat beside his wife, but Ma Tante paid no heed and went on.

"At Stuart's this past summer, he practically pushed you right to the ground. And there have been other instances, too. Damn it, Helen, I'm afraid for you. If he's done these things to you in our presence, what the hell does he do to you at home? And the children? Helen, does he hurt the children?" Ma Tante looked at Mother imploringly, but Mother's gaze remained on the bite of pie resting on the fork in her hand.

"Please tell me he hasn't touched the children, Helen!" Ma Tante's voice was rising. Mother whipped her head to look at her sister.

"The children, Alice. They are right there. Please, please be quiet."

"They're all talking over there. They're not listening to a word we say. And it needs to be said, Helen." She leaned in, attempting to lock eyes, but Mother looked back down at her fork, tears running down her cheeks.

"He can't hurt you like this, Helen. I haven't actually seen him slap you or punch you or... I don't know...For Christ's sake, though, Helen, I know he's doing more!"

"Alice, that's enough now. Your language is quite inappropriate, isn't it?"

"Mom," Ma Tante said, "you know I love you very much and I certainly mean no disrespect, but I could care less about my language right now. Maybe my language is as it is because I'm insanely pissed off." She looked back at her sister. "You are my best friend, Helen, and I feel stuck. I feel useless." She shook her head slowly, and a tear made its way from her eye to her cheek. "I don't live in your home and I don't know the entirety of what goes on inside your walls, but I need you to know that I'm scared for you. And for the kids. You don't need to say anything right now, here at this table to me or to Mom, but you do need to know that I am here for you. If he's hurting you, Helen, if he's hurting the kids, then please let us help. In some way, Helen, let us help you."

Mother turned back to her sister. "He's my husband, Alice."

"Which is exactly why he shouldn't be treating you the way he does."

"Which is exactly why I need to allow him to treat me in any manner he deems necessary."

"What kind of horseshit, fucked-up thinking is that?" Ma Tante's eyes widened greatly, and she looked at Mother with astonishment and disgust.

"It's what is right," Memere chimed in. "Alice, you know that. It's right in the Bible. Ephesians chapter 5, verses 22 to 24. 'Wives, be subject to your husbands, as to the Lord. For the husband is the head of the wife as Christ is the head of the church, his body, and is himself its Savior. As the church is subject to Christ, so let wives also be subject in everything to their husbands.' And Father Denis has spoken so. He is her husband. And it can't be all that bad, now can it?"

Ma Tante was fuming. "Yeah, Ma, I know what the Bible says. You took me to that same stupid church from the moment I was growing inside of you. We were there as much as we were in this damn house!" Memere looked affronted as Ma Tante went on. "And I can recite Bible verses as well as you, I'm sure," she scoffed. "You're forgetting those Ephesians verses that follow. 'Husbands, love your wives, as Christ loved the church and gave himself up for her -' What has Helen ever done to deserve his wrath, can you answer me that? She's the most calm, loving person I have ever known. What the hell has she done? Oh, but it doesn't end there. 'Even so husbands should love their wives as their own bodies. He who loves his wife loves himself.' Well, now, does Gerald love himself so little that he has to take it out on his own wife? The wife he promised to love through good times and bad? Yeah, I was there. I remember the vows. I remember the love. What in God's name happened?"

By this time the voices at the children's table had quieted, and all eyes were on Ma Tante, who was looking at her mother with a steel expression of utter disgust. When she looked back at her sister beside her and noticed the shaking of her shoulders and the tears pouring from her eyes, her countenance immediately softened. "Oh, Helen, I'm so sorry. I'm so insensitive." Tears fell from her own eyes to dampen her pale cheeks. "Helen, it's only that I care so much for you. I love you so, so very much. I want you to be happy and I want you to lead a loved life. Damn it, Helen! Please look at me."

Mother refused to oblige, or perhaps she just couldn't bring herself to do so however much she willed. Ma Tante leaned forward and embraced her sister tightly. Mother melted into her sister's arms, emotions vocalized as sobs as Memere cried from the chair across from hers and Mon Oncle Paul sat erect, stunned.

"What the fuck is going on?" Mother whipped her head toward the doorway and found Father standing there in pure rage. His face was extremely red, his lips were pursed, and his hands were fisted at his sides.

Mon Oncle Paul stood from his chair, walked toward Father. He placed his hand upon Father's shoulder. "Gerald, why don't you and I head back into the living room for a while?" He attempted to steer Father away from the women, but Father was resolute and unmoveable.

"Get your fat ass up. We're going home." Voice low, gruff.

Mother's face was now ashen as she wiped the tears from her cheeks and slowly stood from the table. She turned and walked carefully toward her husband in the doorway. Ma Tante Alice followed.

"Gerald, maybe Helen can stay with us tonight? I miss her greatly and would appreciate the extra time with her."

"Are you daft, woman?" Father countered. He turned back toward Mother as Mon Oncle's face contorted with anger at his brother-in-law's outburst. "I said it's time to go." Father spoke through clenched teeth.

"Helen," Ma Tante pulled at her sister's arm.

Mother spun. She flung her arms around Ma Tante's neck in a tight embrace. "Alice, you need to step away. You have made this ten times worse." Her hushed voice broke. "I love you dearly, but I must go home, and I must go now. Please, Alice. I will be fine. You will see. He is just angry right now. We should not have spoken about him so negatively. Truly, I will be fine. He is my husband. I love him very much and I know he does love me." She let go of her sister and looked her in the eye. Her gaze held love and fear and pleading.

Ma Tante nodded her head, wiping a tear. Charlie stood from his chair, and Susan followed his lead, clenching her stomach as it flipped. Her chin quivered as she walked with her family to the front door.

Mother looked at her family after placing her coat and boots on, Christmas gifts forgotten on the living room floor. Memere, Ma Tante, and Mon Oncle were just before her, concerned and disquieted. Pepere was nursing a beer on the couch.

"Mom, thank you for having us," Mother said. She looked at her mother and nodded her head. "Dad, thank you," she called over to her father, who grunted in response. She looked first at Mon Oncle and then to her sister and gave a wary smile. "I love you, Alice," she said. "I will call you tomorrow. Merry Christmas to you and..." Her voice cut off as any patience Father might have had for the moment ceased and he grabbed her arm and pulled her through the entryway and out into the blustery night air.

The wind caught Susan off guard as she followed her mother and father to the car, the cold nipping at her nose, her cheeks. Father opened the passenger door and shoved Mother inside. As he walked around the front of the car, Susan and Charlie quickened their steps, opened their creaking ice-cold doors, and hustled inside the dark interior to sit down before they could incense Father with the audacity of forcing him to wait. Father tucked the back of his coat beneath him and sat, placing the key in the ignition even before the door was closed. He backed out of the driveway and peeled onto the road.

"Gerald!" Mother exclaimed as she held onto the side of the door to catch her balance.

In the back seat, Charlie began to shake, and Susan let out a yelp as her body was thrust toward the center of the car, Shelly landing with a thud to the floor.

"Shut the fuck up, all of you!" Father bellowed. Susan wrapped her arms around her little body and began to silently weep as Father swerved through the cold, dark streets of town. She felt a hand on her arm and turned to find Charlie looking at her beseechingly, worry in his deep green eyes.

"Okay?" he mouthed. All she could do in response was give a small uncertain nod. She felt her stomach jerk and thought she might be sick right there in the car, but tried her very best to hold off as she knew that would throw Father right over the edge.

A squeal of tires and the car was parked in front of their garage. Father took hold of Mother's arm and dragged her to the porch.

"Get in the fucking house!" He opened the kitchen door and shoved her through. Susan and Charlie followed behind, boots and coats still on. Charlie was shaking, and Susan began to hysterically cry, arms raised and palms fisted at her temples as she shut her eyes tightly and sobbed.

Mother was on the floor, where she had landed on her hip after losing her balance to Father's push. His eyes were bulging in his red, outraged face. "Shut the fuck up!" he screamed at his daughter. "Get the hell out of here!" He pushed Susan toward the living room. She squealed with complete and utter terror as she felt his hands on her back. Father turned to Charlie, who stood frozen in the doorway. "I told you to get the fuck out of here!" he boomed and palmed Charlie in the back of the head, forcing it to whip forward. Charlie gave a sudden grunt as the air he had been holding back in fearful anticipation was let forth with the force of the blow. His right foot stepped forward but wasn't fast enough for Father. He was pushed forcibly from behind and his knees hit the floor, the palms of his hands instinctively flying down in an attempt to break the fall. He scurried to stand, willing himself to move as fast as he possibly could, begging his body to extricate itself from the room and the clutch of his father's madness.

Once again, he wasn't fast enough.

Charlie was scrambling on all fours when he felt Father's boot hit his bottom with such force that it thrust Charlie forward to land on his stomach, hands failing to save his chin from impacting the floor. As he tried to catch his breath, he pushed his torso up with extended arms and inhaled sharply as Father's hand grasped his coat and propelled him forward, Charlie's elbows hitting the floor in response to the powerful thrust. He clambered and crawled to the living room.

Susan stood glued to the living room floor as Charlie lifted himself onto his feet. He ran to her and they clung together, Susan heaving and Charlie dry-eyed but holding his bleeding chin, his arms shaking profusely as he attempted to stay the dripping blood. They both looked on as Father backhanded Mother on the cheek, her head thrashing to the side.

A scream burst forth from Susan as she saw her mother's head twist, saw her hand reach to her cheek, saw the look of terror on her face.

Father turned to glare at his children standing in the living room and yelled, "I told you to get the fuck out! You want me to beat your ass?" He reached under his brown coat and began to unclasp the belt on his narrow hips. Motivated by this motion, Charlie took hold of Susan's hand and pulled her the few steps into his room, slamming the door behind them.

He stood with his back against the door, chest heaving as Susan grabbed her auburn curls and pulled, face contorted, eyes shut tight. "Charlie." Her voice was weak and scraggly. Charlie walked toward his sister and gently led her to his bed, where he helped her to sit upon its edge, one hand still clutching his chin. He grabbed for a wad of tissues on his bedside table and thrust them on the gash as he sat next to Susan. She pawed at him, face burrowed in his chest, tears meshing with the spots of blood that had stained the top of his coat. Charlie rested his cheek upon the soft curls at the top of his sister's head, both bodies shaking as they listened to the obscenities from the kitchen.

"You need to learn to shut your fat, fucking mouth." Father's voice echoed forcefully through the house, wobbly and hoarse from booze.

"Gerald!" Mother protested.

"I told you to shut the fuck up!" Susan and Charlie jumped in each other's arms as they heard a sudden and loud thump and a high-pitched yelp. "This'll teach you to talk shit about me, huh?" Another thwack. "Merry fucking Christmas to me!"

Shuffling. Dragging footsteps in the living room. Slamming of the bedroom door.

A minute later, a headboard thrashing upon the thin wall.

Susan lost control of her senses. She melted into Charlie's chest and stopped shaking as her body spent its energy. Charlie gently laid her down on his bed and draped his arm around her shoulder, lying down on his side and pulling her toward him. Only when Susan's protective instincts had taken over, allowing her to fall asleep in his sheltering embrace, was Charlie able to cry his first tear.

SEVEN

Round-faced Sister Mary Margaret smiled warmly and looked out upon the children seated at their desks in her second grade classroom at St. Catherine's at the dawn of a new school day in January 1961.

Susan sat in the first row of seats in the middle of the classroom, flanked by Janet, Betty, Mikey, and David. She gazed upon her much-adored teacher after half a year of second grade had transpired.

"Today is such a special day, children," Sister Mary Margaret announced. "Do you know why?"

David's hand shot into the air, his torso erect in his chair.

"David," Sister Mary Margaret permitted.

"Kennedy is president today," David answered as he lowered his hand onto the wooden top of his desk. "Pa says he's a Catholic and that's what this world needs right now, what with everything going on. I don't really know what that means, entirely, but I know my pa wigged out when he won against Nixon. And my grandmom loves him; says he's dreamy." David rolled his eyes.

"Quite right, David," Sister Mary Margaret said, voice soft but lively. "Today is the day that Mr. John Fitzgerald Kennedy will swear on the Bible that he will do his best for our people, the people of what country, boys and girls?"

"The United States of America!" Her classroom was united in their boisterous response.

"That's right. Today he will swear on the Bible that he will do his best for all the people of the United States of America, and he will give a speech, one which I am very anxious to hear myself, I must admit." She smiled brightly at the students attentively listening to her at the head of the room. "Today will mark the first official day of his presidency. And guess what?" She looked around the room. She didn't expect any hands to rise in the air due to the rhetorical nature of her question, but she greatly enjoyed leaving her children in suspense and so paused for a moment longer, intensifying their anticipation. "We have the opportunity to watch his inauguration today," she said. "We'll head to the library just around 12:30 this afternoon, directly after your lunch period, where we'll get to watch our own Mr. Kennedy become the thirty-fifth president of the United States." She clapped her hands below her chin and smiled at the children.

A few claps from various bodies around the room: others simply smiled at the prospect of breaking up the monotony of the school day.

The children continued with their morning lessons and were soon dismissed for lunch. Susan grabbed her lunch box and merrily bounded with her friends to the cafeteria.

When they arrived, Susan, Betty, and David sat while Janet and Mikey worked their way to the lunch line.

Susan's bottom had just settled on the cold seat when her body was propelled forward and her chest bumped into the edge of the table. She looked over her shoulder, stunned at the sudden interruption, to find a classmate leering at her through long blond lashes. "Oh, sorry," she said sardonically, "didn't see you there, Susan." Her closed, full lips turned up in the pretense of a smile. "Maybe that's because you're such a shrimp," she added haughtily. She turned on her heel, blond ponytail whipping to the side as she jerked her head away from Susan, long child's legs strutting.

Susan turned back to her friends at the table and situated herself on the chair, embarrassed.

"Oh, that Mercedes Doyle just makes me mad," Janet said as she approached the table with her metal tray of lunch food. "She just thinks she's so much better than everyone else. Don't mind her. She's just lame." Susan had always admired her friend's ability to brush matters off so readily, but she still felt the burn of her hot cheeks as she peered into her lunch box and the contents that Mother had packed for her that morning. "Don't let her push you around, Susie. She's just a big meanie."

Susan looked to where Mercedes Doyle was now sitting with Barbara Metcalf and Sandy Speckles, two girls a year older than Susan herself. She was smiling as she chatted with her friends. She frowned and turned back to the table. Mikey had now joined them with his tray of pizza and fries. Susan could smell the deliciousness as he plunked the metal tray down on the tabletop.

"Yeah," David chimed in. "For real, Susie. Just ignore her."

She continued to eat as David furthered the conversation from that morning about John F. Kennedy. "You know, too, that he's the youngest president ever? My mom told me that. She said he's forty-three. Well, I think that's what she said. For real, though—forty-three?" he said in astonishment. "That's old. Super old. And he's the youngest president ever?" He took a bite of cracker. "He was also in the navy. The navy is where they fight on ships for wars. I wouldn't like to be on a ship. Or a submarine. I really wouldn't want to be on a submarine. I think it would be scary. But he was in the navy. And Pa says he got an award for it, which is wild, if you ask me. Oh, and he wrote a book, too." He spoke quickly in his excitement, and Susan marveled as she often did at her friend's capacity for storing information. David was just amazingly adept at learning. She wouldn't be surprised at all if he was the president of the United States when he was forty-three years old.

For real.

Susan finished her lunch and continued conversing with her friends until her class was told it was time to head into the library to watch Kennedy's inauguration.

"Aww," David sighed. "I didn't finish my lunch again. Mom's going to be mad. She's always telling me to stop talking so much and just eat." He stuffed the uneaten food back into his sack and stood from the table.

Susan and her friends lined up at the doorway to the cafeteria at which Sister Mary Margaret soon appeared.

They entered the library a bit noisily, still needing time to compose themselves after the freedom of lunchtime.

"Come in, come in," said the librarian sister rather testily. "And hush now. Have a seat. You'll have to squish together. Yes, just there. On the floor. Hush now," she repeated as Susan and her classmates sat on the floor before a small television propped on a moving metal table. Two other classrooms were already present.

Sister Mary Margaret clapped her hands, and the children looked toward the sound, voices quieting to a dull mumble until the last person quit entirely. "Thank you, children. Sister Agnes, I assume we're ready to begin the program?"

Sister Agnes turned the knob on the front of the television set. A quick static sound and then voices, the picture blurry at first and then appearing before them in black and white. She turned the volume up. "Can you all hear that now?"

"Yes, Sister Agnes," the children recited.

Before long, Susan saw John F. Kennedy approach a wooden podium. She recognized him immediately as Mother and Father had been carefully watching the presidential race on television, this being the first man whom they had both wholeheartedly endorsed. There were frequent smiles and celebratory gatherings around the neighborhood for the few days after the votes had been counted and the winner announced. Even Father had been in good spirits, which was something to celebrate in and of itself as far as Susan was concerned.

Music surrounded the people on the screen as a man in a black robe with white hair raised his right hand and Susan saw the president immediately imitate this indicated stance.

"Do you, John Fitzgerald Kennedy, solemnly swear..." he said. Susan heard murmurings from the crowd gathered at the inauguration, but the microphones on the podium produced loud and clear projections of the man's voice.

"I, John Fitzgerald Kennedy, do solemnly swear..." He pronounced it as if he were saying "swayah". My, but this was funny to Susan.

"That you will faithfully execute the office of President of the United States..." the white-haired man said.

"That I will faithfully execute the office of President of the United States..." Kennedy repeated.

"And will to the best of your ability..."

"And will to the best of my ability..."

"Preserve, protect, and defend the Constitution of the United States..."

"Preserve, protect, and defend the Constitution of the United States..." Kennedy said, right hand still raised to the level of his head.

"So help you God."

"So help me God."

Susan heard a great deal of cheering from the crowd as the white haired-man shook the hand of the new president. President Kennedy stood at the podium, unfolding what appeared to be some sort of folder.

The president began to speak. Susan's eyes glazed over as her mind went elsewhere. She didn't come to until her schoolmates' clapping surrounded her and the television was being turned off by Sister Agnes. She had practically missed the whole thing!

Susan and her classmates stood when Sister Mary Margaret asked them to do so and positioned themselves in a straight line at the door of the library so they could walk back to their classroom.

"Oh, Sister," Sister Mary Margaret said to Sister Agnes, "when he said that the rights of man come not from the state but by the hands of God. Did you hear that, Sister? My heart fluttered. God has been good on this day, has He not?"

"He certainly has, Sister Mary Margaret."

Susan's teacher beamed, her round face straining at the tight white edges of her coif.

"And when he said, 'If a free society cannot help the many who are poor, it cannot save the few who are rich,' he speaks the truth, does he not?" She didn't wait for an answer. Unable to curb her enthusiasm she went on. "Oh, but when he spoke of weapons, did I raise a prayer up to God, but even before I was finished did our president speak of peace. Peace, Sister. May God guide President Kennedy." She reached for Sister Agnes's hands and grasped them within both of hers.

"Yes," Sister Agnes said.

"And what was it he said?" Sister Mary Margaret's eyes looked to the ceiling as she attempted to recall the president's words to mind. "'Let us never negotiate out of fear, but let us never fear to negotiate.' What a beautiful way with words our president has. And what a strong sentiment that was. And, Sister, I think the part that resonated with me the most through that entire inspiring speech was when he said, 'Ask not what your country can do for you—ask what you can do for your country.' Is that also not the truth, Sister Agnes? It is in our hands. Us. With the help of God we have the power to make a change in this world for the better, and this new president of ours is encouraging us to do so. My heart is full on this day." She smiled brightly, eyes watering.

Sister Agnes smiled back—a closemouthed smile, but a smile nonetheless.

Sister Mary Margaret dropped her hands and turned to her patiently waiting class. "Okay, my children," she said, "it's time for us to go back to our lessons. What a wonderful thing we were all able to witness today. I can honestly say that I believe we have all had the privilege of witnessing history in the making." She paused, thoughtful. She shook her head as if clearing her thoughts with a large smile on her face and then walked to the beginning of the line and led her class back to their room.

EIGHT

The snow had melted and the school year would soon be through. It was Sunday, the fourteenth of May. Mother's Day.

Susan woke and rubbed her eyes. She sat up in bed and brushed the hair off her forehead and cheeks, lifted the blanket from her body, and scooted to the floor. She smelled the chocolate chip cookies baking even before she entered the kitchen.

She made her bed and propped Shelly upon the pillow, fixed her dress to cover her legs.

"I am making your favorite today, darling," Mother said as Susan entered the room. "A nice treat when church is through." She winked. "Oh, Susan," she sighed, momentarily ignoring the ironing she had before her, "I am so very, very proud of you. I could not imagine a better Mother's Day gift than you making your First Holy Communion. Oh, Gerald, aren't you proud of our daughter?" she said dreamily, looking to Father at the table.

"Yep," he said through his cigarette.

Susan looked at the headline of the newspaper in his hands. *"Best of U.S. Jungle Fighters Ordered Into South Viet Nam,"* it read. Although she was able to read the words, she was ignorant of their meaning and so dismissed it immediately and looked back to Mother.

"Susan, how are you feeling about today?"

"I'm excited to wear my dress. It's like being a princess, Mama. When I tried it on at the store, I felt so pretty. I can't wait to show Elizabeth."

"Yes, this I know," Mother laughed.

Mother helped Susan dress in her bedroom and then together they walked into Mother's room.

Mother extracted her cherished pearl necklace from her jewelry box on top of her dresser. She pulled back the chair at her vanity and sat. She turned the small lamp on and gazed at her reflection, placing the pearls around her neck to rest against the collar of her light gray dress. Soon she commenced the morning makeup ritual that Susan had been privy to so very many times for many years now, and that she still treasured.

Susan stood by Mother's side in her adored white Communion dress: short puffed sleeves and cascading veil. She watched as Mother began to place red lipstick on her full lips. She rubbed them together, humming at her reflection.

"Hmm hmm hmm hmm hmm hmmm hmmmmm." "Put Your Head On My Shoulder." Susan knew it well. Although Mother hummed and sang often—her voice was so angelic—and was heard to practice many other tunes, this was by far her favorite these past couple of years. Susan had memorized the song. As Mother hummed, Susan sang the words. Mother continued to hum as she put thick, black mascara on her long lashes, and as she finished surveying her work in the lit-up mirror, she turned to her daughter. Mother humming, daughter singing, they smiled at each other. On the last verse, they sang in unison.

As soon as the singing concluded and the last syllable lingered in the air, Mother leaned forward and placed her forehead to Susan's. When she pulled apart, they gazed into one another's eyes. Mother smiled warmly at her daughter. Susan was convinced her mother's eyes were sparkling like the stars in a cloudless night sky.

"Ready?" Mother asked.

"Ready." She took her mother's hand and was led out of the bedroom and into the kitchen. Father was seated at the table, inhaling the last of a cigarette before extinguishing the minute portion left over in the glass ashtray on the windowsill. He wore a white collared button-down shirt and brown tie with a matching brown suit jacket. His thin red hair was parted severely at the left side and combed over, stiff and shiny from his pomade. A few blood vessels had broken and left splatters of red to paint his pale white cheeks.

"Is Charles not here?" Mother asked. "He must still be in his room. Charles," she called over her shoulder, "it is time for us to go."

Mother walked over and stood on tiptoes to feel the top of the refrigerator. When her fingers pulled back, they returned with a small black-and-silver camera.

Charlie entered the room as Mother put the camera into her purse. Father stood from the table. Susan slipped her shoes on her knee-high-stockinged feet—shiny white flats with small bows at the top of the fastening strap—and took along a white cardigan sweater that Mother handed over in case there was a chill to the May air. Mother placed her brown faux-fur coat over her shoulders, and they walked out to the waiting car.

Arriving at St. John's, Susan saw a swarm of vehicles in the parking lot, several white-clad girls exiting and congregating at the bottom of the church steps, thin veils billowing with the light morning breeze. She exited the car once Father had parked, approached her mother, and grasped her hand.

"Susie, Susie!" She quickly turned her head to see Elizabeth running her way. She was here!

"Hi, Elizabeth," she said when Elizabeth had approached her side.

"Come on. Mama said we go over here." She took Susan's free hand

and pulled.

"Wait." Susan was hesitant to leave familiarity and comfort behind for the growing and, in her opinion, bustling crowd of people. When she came to church each Sunday morning, she was always with Mother. But now Elizabeth was attempting to whisk her away, and although she was elated to have Elizabeth to aid in her procession throughout this ceremony, she would much rather be with her mother. "Shouldn't we stay here?"

"No," Elizabeth said. "We go over there. By the stairs, see? Everyone is going."

Elizabeth's observations were correct. Susan saw a mass of pure white amidst a sea of browns and grays at the bottom of the church steps, the occasional bright red or blue splattered throughout. A few felt and tweed hats bobbed up as the men wearing them walked toward the other congregants gathered together in anticipation of the ceremony to take place for their children and grandchildren, nieces and nephews.

Susan looked up at Mother for encouragement.

"It is all right, darling. Run along." She gently pushed Susan toward her cousin.

Susan held tighter to Elizabeth's hand as she was led among the throng of people and cars in the parking lot and toward the bottom of the church steps. Elizabeth, being the extrovert she was, spied some girlfriends and approached them readily, a skip to her step. Susan lagged behind but refused to relinquish her hold on her cousin's hand until they came to a full stop.

Susan nestled beside Elizabeth, gazing at the girls surrounding them. Beside Elizabeth stood Mercedes Doyle, flanked by Barbara Metcalf and Sandy Speckles. Mercedes's silky blond hair was loose today, hanging down the sides of her face to rest upon her shoulders beneath her veil. Her eyebrows lifted as her brown eyes found Susan's, one side of her mouth elevating in a snicker. Elizabeth was speaking now beside her, but she didn't hear a word of it, uncomfortable as she was. Barbara Metcalf was looking directly at Elizabeth, a smile on her face, while Sandy Speckles's hazel eyes found Susan's through thick lenses in a purple frame. She smiled and, although Susan believed Sandy's smile to be genuine, she wasn't certain it was. Unsure how to proceed, she merely blushed and awkwardly averted her attention to her cousin, pretending to insert herself into the conversation, ignorant though she was of its content.

Eventually, all had arrived, and a sister Susan was not familiar with announced it was time for the children to line up and for the families to be seated indoors. Susan stood behind Elizabeth, while the boys' line formed to her right. Another sister—this one Susan knew to be Sister Therese—placed herself in the middle of the two lines of children and ensured they were straight and orderly and the children were quiet and still. Once she was satisfied, she turned around and spoke.

"Now remember," she said, "when you receive the body of Christ, you are not to let the bread touch your teeth. If you do, it is a sin."

Susan's heart skipped as she stood rooted to her spot in line.

She felt a slight push from behind and realized the line was moving. She followed Elizabeth's back up the stairs and into the foyer, then through the doors and into the nave, hands clasped in a steeple before her, fingertips reaching toward the sky.

The children's shoes echoed through the large room as they proceeded toward the first rows of seats that had been reserved solely for them. Susan looked to the vaulted ceiling momentarily and then searched out the room to see if her parents had sat where they typically sat for Sunday Mass. She succeeded in spotting them; Mother was wiping tears from her cheeks. Charlie wasn't with them; instead, Susan saw him ahead, standing near Father Denis, resplendent in his white altar boy robe.

She continued down the aisle, palms still touching, fingertips just below her chin as the pipe organ's notes echoed throughout the open space. When all had sat, Father Denis began Mass.

Susan looked down at her thumbs fidgeting in her frilly white lap. Her mind wandered for a time, but she sat erect in the pew. When Elizabeth stood on her left and another girl she did not know stood to her right, Susan came to and stood as well. She followed the girl out of the pew and into the aisle and lined up behind her. She looked ahead and saw that Communion was being given. Her stomach roiled and her body began to shudder slightly at the anticipation of any wrongdoing. Her eyes remained forward and she stepped slowly as the line progressed closer and closer toward Father Denis.

She wrung her hands together and gritted her teeth as her shiny white shoes scuffled along. One step closer. Her stomach twisted. She implored herself not to get sick right there in the middle of the aisle, in front of all these people, in front of Father Denis. On her perfectly beautiful white dress.

She was second in line now. She hiccuped, and a small amount of bile rose to her throat, the acidity burning as she swallowed it back down. Her eyes welled as she attempted to concentrate on what the girl in front of her was doing.

She could do this.

Could she do this?

The girl moved to the left, leaving Susan to stand in front of Father Denis. She felt his narrow green eyes boring into hers as she looked up at his face. Her hands were shaking.

Father Denis was holding a circular wafer aloft. She heard herself say "Amen" and opened her mouth. She felt the bread touch her tongue as an "Amen" sounded to her right, where a boy her age had just received Communion from a visiting priest. She walked to her left, following the footsteps of the girls who had gone before her. She closed her mouth and left the wafer to dissolve in the exact spot in which Father Denis had placed it. As it dissolved, she noticed that portions of the bread were incorporating into her saliva and expanding to the edges of her tongue. She was petrified the soggy morsels would reach her teeth, so she immediately swallowed the wafer down, a couple of tears trickling out her eyes at the notion that she might have committed an egregious sin.

She walked back to where she had been sitting to find the girl in front of her kneeling in prayer, hands reverently steepled.

Susan knelt down, placed the palms of her hands together, and closed her eyes tightly, praying to God that she had done this well, that she had pleased Him. Praying that He would help her proceed throughout the morning without fault.

She kept her eyes tightly shut as she recalled just a few days prior, when Mother had taken her to see Father Denis for her first confession. She had clung to her mother's hand, reluctant to let go. Father Denis intimidated Susan, and now she was to sit on the other side of a screen and confess to him all that she had done wrong, to stand in judgment before this person to whom she could utter nary a word to on a normal Sunday during Mass.

Mother and she had approached the confessional, Mother assuredly, heels echoing on the wooden floor, Susan with more trepidation. When they arrived, Susan held tighter to her mother's hand, nestled closer to her side.

"It is all right, Susan," Mother had said. "Father Denis is in there, and he is there only to help you." She bent at the waist, placing her face closer to her daughter's. She continued lightly: "You will just go in there and confess your sins, tell him what it is you have done wrong, and he will absolve you. He has the ability to forgive you, Susan. It is through Father Denis that we may speak with God, and it is through this Sacrament of Penance that we save ourselves from going to Hell. It truly is a wonderful thing." She gently pried Susan's hands off her own and squeezed before letting them go. "You will do a wonderful job, Susan, I am sure of it. Just speak to Father Denis as you speak to me. I will be sitting right over there when you are done." She motioned to a pew nearby. "Now go along." She gently prodded her forward.

Susan understood any efforts to extract herself from the situation were futile, so she steeled herself, took a deep but trembling breath, and pulled back the thick, velvety curtain to enter.

She noticed a small seat before her and a screen that separated her from Father Denis. She took a step inside the confessional on wobbly knees and caught herself on the seat with the palms of her hands before her legs buckled beneath her. She landed with a thud that sounded entirely too loud in the small enclosed quarters, when the only other sound she could detect was her own raging heartbeat.

Now to remember the words. What was it that Mother had told her to say? They had practiced this many times in preparation for her first confession, but her confidence waned, buried deep within the bowels of her being, encircled by her nerves and agitation.

"In the...in the name...name of the Father," she began, then realized she had forgotten to cross herself, "the Son, and the Holy Ghost." She brought her hand up vertically and then horizontally, stiffly but with conviction, desperately hoping the way in which she crossed herself would absolve her of any wrongdoing in initially forgetting to do so when she uttered her first word.

"Bless me, Father"— she choked back a sob—"for I...I have sinned." She paused, squeezing the seat tightly on either side of her small bottom. Her hands were beginning to ache, but she found it helped her concentrate and so she squeezed further still. "This is my first confession."

"Proceed, Susan," Father Denis said in his high-pitched voice. He knew who she was! Susan simply had to close her eyes to envision his countenance before her on the other side of the screen: weathered skin, narrow eyes, small crooked and yellowed teeth.

"I said 'damn' when I stubbed my toe on the kitchen table yesterday," she said. "And...and I got mad at my brother because he didn't want to play with me. And when Father helped me with a button that was tough, I could smell his cigarette breath and I had mean thoughts. I was thinking that it was gross and I wish Father wouldn't help me at all. I wanted him to leave me alone. And Mother asked me to help with the dishes and I usually do it and don't complain because I know I'm not supposed to complain and I'm supposed to do what Mother and Father tell me to do, but I really didn't want to help her because I was gonna go to Janet's house, so I gave her problems and she was disappointed. And Tommy Walters was really mean to Charlie last week, or maybe that's not when it was. I don't remember. But Tommy Walters was really mean to Charlie and I kept thinking that I wished he would leave Charlie alone and that maybe he should just move away and maybe somebody would be mean to him then instead of him being mean to Charlie." Once she had begun, Susan couldn't stop and she proceeded with haste. She felt the need to confess everything that she could think to confess: then perhaps she would be forgiven for her wrongdoings and wouldn't go to Hell, which she knew was a place of fire and the Devil where she would be tormented for all time. This petrified her to no end.

"My mother told me I couldn't have any more apple-cranberry cake after dinner, but when she wasn't looking I stole a bite even though I knew I wasn't supposed to. And I don't like Mercedes Doyle even though I know I'm supposed to love everyone. But I really don't like her. She's mean. And I know what a vagina is and I'm curious, but I know it's a sin to touch myself, so I never have. I promise. But I still think about it. And every day when I go to school and see Sister Mary Francis, I get scared. I know I'm supposed to love her and that I shouldn't be scared, but I am and I know that's a sin. And sometimes my mother makes me something for lunch that I really, really don't like and I throw it away even though I know I should never, ever throw food away, especially because she tells me often that we don't have a ton, but I'm scared that if I bring it home she'll make me eat it, so I throw it away, but I know that's a sin because I didn't listen to my mother." Susan paused, thinking, heart still beating heavily in her chest.

"That's it," she concluded.

A few moments passed, but to Susan it felt like an eternity as she sat her small body upon the hardened wooden seat of the confessional. What did he think? Was she truly that bad if he wasn't going to reply right away? Oh, God! Was it the vagina? *Oh, God, help me*, she thought. *Help me not to think about my vagina!*

Father Denis began to speak, and a minute portion of Susan's anxiety was lifted.

"Be sure to listen to your parents. Be kind and have pure thoughts about everyone around you. Do not be worrisome about your body, for your body is a vessel created by God and He has control over your well-being. Do not swear. May God give you guidance and peace. I absolve you of your sins. Go home and recite five Hail Marys and five Our Fathers. You may go."

Susan nearly leaped from her seat and exited the confessional, walking with quickened steps toward her mother.

"How did it go, darling?"

"Okay." Susan didn't know what else to say. How could she tell her mother that she had been terrified; Mother, who took pleasure in church services and penance?

"I would like to speak with Father Denis," Mother said. "You can wait here for me. Be sure to stay quiet."

Susan nodded and sat down, relieved now to have her first confession over and done with. If each confession gave her the anxiety this one did, she didn't know how she would spend the rest of her days here on earth without simply collapsing from heart failure.

Susan opened her eyes as she knelt now on the bench in her pew at First Holy Communion, happy to push the memories of her first confession to the back of her mind.

The ceremony proceeded uneventfully, Susan ignoring the majority of the continued Mass as she typically did on regular Sunday mornings. She was pleased to have Elizabeth's presence by her side.

When Mass came to an end, Susan was more than grateful to be released so she could find her mother. Once reunited, Susan and her mother made their way outdoors, where the sun greeted them heartily after the echoing rigidity of the church service. Mother found female friends with whom she conversed, reveling in their shared pleasure of the first Communion of God's children as well as in the Mass itself. Susan stood patiently at her side, small hand clasped within her mother's larger one.

Pictures were taken: smiling faces abounded. Men shook hands, clasped their boys' shoulders. Women conversed together, girls at their sides or off prattling with friends, white fabric proliferating as they congregated, the sun's strong rays creating a halo around their pious figures.

After the celebratory assembly, families began to disperse. The LaFleurs followed the Duboises in their station wagon back to Susan's home, where her parents were hosting a backyard barbecue, this Sunday's get-together holding more meaning than it typically did for both her and Elizabeth's families.

They arrived almost simultaneously, Father pulling up in front of their garage, Mon Oncle Walter parking their Buick on the street in front of the screened-in front porch. Susan and Elizabeth bounded out of their cars to greet each other once again.

"Susan Marie," Mother admonished as she exited the station wagon and turned her head to her daughter, "that is such a beautiful dress you are wearing and I certainly do not want it in ruin. I know you are excited to see Elizabeth again and to have other family members over to our home today, but I ask that you go inside and change into play clothes before you get your dress dirty." She lifted her eyebrows.

"Yes, Mama," Susan said. She took Elizabeth's hand and guided her toward the bedroom. Ma Tante Mary soon joined them with play clothes for Elizabeth. Once her clothes were off, her mother took her dress and left the room.

Susan sat on her bed—white dress still on—and looked at Elizabeth as she changed into a pair of straight blue pants and a thin blue-and-white-checkered sweater.

"Were you nervous?" she asked.

"What?" Elizabeth looked confused as she wiped the strands of hair from her face after pulling the sweater over her head.

"Were you nervous? Today?"

"You mean Communion? No. What was there to be nervous about?"

"Oh, I don't know," Susan looked down at the fingers twiddling in her lap. She paused for a moment and then looked back up at her cousin. "Not at all? What about when you got the bread; weren't you nervous that it would touch your teeth like Sister told us about?" She looked back down at her lap and continued in a whisper. "I was nervous," she admitted warily.

"You don't need to be nervous, Susie," Elizabeth said as she stood in front of her cousin. "It's just bread."

"Well, yeah," Susan countered, "but it turns into the body of Christ, doesn't it? And there was just so much to remember and I wanted to do it right and I didn't want to make Mama or Father mad and I really, really didn't want to make God mad because that would be a sin and—" She broke off as she questioned whether or not she wanted to relay the next secret. She took a deep breath, and her voice lowered an octave as she whispered again. "I don't want to go to Hell, Elizabeth. It scares me. A lot."

"You won't go to Hell."

"How do you know?"

"You just won't, silly. Why would you?"

Susan reflected on this statement with wonder at her cousin's absolute certainty. "I don't know," she admitted. "We're supposed to do so much right. And when God isn't happy with us, He can put us in Hell, can't He?"

Elizabeth looked down at Susan with a slight grimace. "Well, I guess so. But my daddy says that He forgives. Isn't that why we had to do penance? If He forgives us, then why would we go to Hell?"

"I don't know," Susan admitted. Another pause and then, "Elizabeth?"

"Yeah?"

"What if He doesn't forgive us?"

"Oh, He will," she said flippantly.

"But how do you know?"

"I just know."

"But *how?*"

"I don't know. I just do. I'm going to Heaven. Mom says we go to church to be closer to God. Isn't that what He wants? And if He forgives us, then we're going to Heaven, aren't we?"

"I guess so."

"I don't want to talk about this anymore. It's stupid. I want to go outside and play games. Mom brought cake and I'm really hungry and want hamburgers and I know your dad is gonna make them. I'm going out. You coming?"

"Yeah," Susan said with a sigh. "I'm coming."

NINE

S usan and her classmates clapped their hands and cheered as the last day of fourth grade came to an end. She walked to the wall adjacent to the classroom door and picked up her lunch box.

"Have a wonderful summer, Susan," Sister Annette said at the doorway as Susan and her friends were exiting. Susan thought herself quite fortunate to have been taught fourth grade by Sister Annette, who, like Sister Mary Margaret, was young, kind, and considerate. Although mathematics had proven to be an area of weakness for Susan throughout her fourth grade year, Sister Annette had been patient as she toiled and had instilled within Susan an even deeper love of literature, reading, and writing.

This being Charlie's last day at St. Catherine's (he would be attending St. Joseph's High School in the fall), Susan was eager to meet him on the front lawn so they could walk home together one last time. She, Janet, and Betty walked out of the classroom and down the corridor. They meandered with the bustling, excited crowd out the large wooden front door and into the sunlight of the June afternoon.

Charlie wasn't yet at the foot of the stairs, so the girls simply waited, Susan swinging her lunch box back and forth as she chatted with her friends. She startled and jumped in place as Charlie snuck up behind her, pushed her on the shoulder, and said "Boo!"

"Charlie!" Susan exclaimed as she hit him in the side with her lunch box. "You scared me." Charlie just snickered beside her. "Hi, Henry," she acknowledged her brother's best friend.

"Hi, Susan." Henry smiled, amused at the affectionate exchange before him.

"Ready?" Charlie asked. When Susan nodded her head, he led the way to the crosswalk.

"Hi, Charlie." Susan turned to find Mercedes Doyle smiling up at her brother, blond ponytail still bobbing from her exertions down the stairs and slight jog to where Charlie now stood. Barbara Metcalf and Sandy Speckles trailed behind.

Charlie lifted his eyebrows. "Hi," he said with uncertainty.

"So, what are you doing this summer? Will you be around?" Mercedes put her hand on her hip and started twisting the thick blond hair in her ponytail. Susan, the girls, and Henry all paused and attended to the conversation in progress, Henry looking rather amused, though she wasn't all that certain why he would be. She herself was rather confused and a bit uncomfortable.

"Um," Charlie replied hesitantly, "yeah, we'll be around. We go camping for a week in the summer, but other than that we stay home."

"Oh," Mercedes said, "well, that's nice. I hope to see you around then." She walked forward, not even checking behind her to see if Barbara and Sandy were following; she knew they would be.

Charlie turned to Henry, lifted his eyebrows again, and scrunched his nose. "What was that?" he asked.

"Ah, Charlie boy," Henry teased as he put his arm around his friend's shoulder and they began to walk farther toward the road. "I think she's a bit stoked about you, yeah? Didn't know you attracted them so young, though. Man, she's just a kid!" Henry began to laugh, which infected Charlie as well; Susan saw the smile on his face, his eyes gazing at his feet as he crossed the road.

At Brown Avenue, Henry said his goodbyes. He snickered at Charlie—a tribute to Mercedes Doyle—said farewell to Janet and Betty, and then tousled Susan's curly hair before veering to the left.

Susan said goodbye to her friends once they turned onto North Street.

"Oh, how was your last day of school?" Susan looked up and saw Mother at the porch's screen door, feet bare. She wiped her hands on her apron.

"Ooh, are you making something?" Susan asked.

"Why, of course I am, darling. After all, it is your last day of fourth grade, is it not? And your last day of eighth grade, Charles, which is still something I am having trouble believing. High school in September." She looked down affectionately at her children walking to the steps of the porch.

"What are you making?" Susan asked.

"A pineapple upside-down cake. I put extra pineapple on it. It's cooling just now and will be ready for you shortly. Now come on indoors and tell me all about your last day of school." Mother held the screen door aloft and happily ushered her children in.

"I can smell it, Mom. It smells so good." Susan put her lunch box on the kitchen table and walked over to the counter, leaning down over the cake and inhaling deeply. "Oh, I can't wait. You are just the best cook ever!"

Mother tittered. "Why thank you, darling," she said and gave a slight curtsy, lifting her blue housedress at the sides. Susan giggled, then brought her finger toward the cake, looked at her mother purposefully, and feigned a swipe at a pineapple slice that rested on top.

"You do not dare!" Mother laughed and threw her arms around Susan, holding her tightly and eliciting a guffaw from her daughter. Charlie crept behind Mother.

"Well, since you're busy with Susie, then I guess I can just—"

He pretended to take the pineapple that Susan had unsuccessfully procured for herself. Mother let go of Susan and playfully whacked her son's hand away from the cake. Charlie held his hand to his chest.

"Ow! That hurt!" he insisted, and then smiled and let out a snort of laughter at the shocked look on his mother's face.

"Oh, Charles Donald, you goose!" Mother said. She lightly slapped his forearm and then paused, looking intently up into his face. "How did you become so tall?" she asked. "And so handsome?" She lifted her hands and cupped his chin, the tips of her fingers spread upon his cheeks. "Oh, my Charles. Stop growing."

Charlie looked down at Mother, slightly abashed at the look of adoration in her blue eyes, at the affection she paid to his thirteen-year-old self.

"Okay," Mother said, "Susan and Charles, please take care of your school supplies and I will cut you both a generous slice of this cake here."

When Susan returned, her brother was just pulling back his chair at the kitchen table and Mother was walking over with a small plate in each hand, large slices of cake piled on top, forks resting to the side.

"You don't want a piece?" Charlie asked her.

"Not right now, no."

"I guess that just means there'll be more for us," Charlie joked.

"And your father," Mother said. "He does like my cakes just as well as you do."

Charlie said nothing in reply. Susan took her second bite and relished it.

"So Susan, tell me about your last day of school," Mother said.

Susan swallowed her bite. "I had a good day today. Sister Annette gave us extra time to play outside because it was the last day of school and she let me borrow two books for the summer as long as I give them back to her next year."

"Is that right? And which books did she let you borrow?"

"*A Wrinkle in Time* and *The Hundred and One Dalmatians*."

"How wonderful," Mother said. "You will have to tell me how you like them."

"Sure," Susan said.

"Charles, how was your last day of the eighth grade?"

"It went well. I don't think we had as much free time as Susan, though." He smiled over at his sister. "I think the majority of my class is headed over to St. Joseph's next year, so we spent time reviewing expectations for high school. Mostly just behaviors and stuff, respect for the sisters. Henry'll be going. Definitely happy about that. I'm kind of excited to see what it'll be like."

"You and Henry have been friends for such a long time, Charles. He certainly is your best friend, yes?"

"He is."

"And what it is about Henry that you like so much?"

Charlie finished swallowing his last bite of cake and placed his fork down on his plate. "Honestly, I like that he's not a jerk." Mother started at the use of this term that Susan had never heard before. "He's a great guy. We both love some of the same things—baseball, reading—and I'm comfortable around him. And he's good to Susie." He smiled over at his sister, who was tunneling the last of her cake into her mouth.

"Mmm-hmmm," she mumbled with a full mouth. She swallowed and continued, "Henry's cool. For a boy. He's not mean like that Tommy Walters is. Ugh! I don't like him one bit, Mom! He needs to leave Charlie alone!"

"Charles?" Mother looked inquiringly at her son. "What is this?"

"Never mind," Charlie said. "It's nothing."

"It's not nothing," Susan countered with a sneer. "Mama, he's just mean. Really mean. He just says stupid things to Charlie, and Charlie doesn't even do anything to him. But Henry sticks up for Charlie. He's not afraid." She licked her fork before placing it down on her plate.

"Charles, is this boy unkind to you?"

"Yeah"— Charlie's eyes gazed down at the table—"but don't worry about it, Ma. I'm fine."

"What does he say to you?

"Really, Ma, I'm fine. I don't want to talk about it."

"He called Charlie a loser one time," Susan countered.

"Charles, did he?"

Charlie tipped his head down to affirm.

"Is this all he has done to you, Charles? Call you names?"

"Pretty much."

"Pretty much?" Mother asked.

"Yeah. Really, Ma, it's okay. I'm fine."

"It upsets me that this boy is calling you names, Charles. Have you tried telling him that you do not like him doing this?"

Charlie looked up at his mother, aghast. "I'd tell him if I wanted a pounding."

"And you think this boy would hurt you?"

Charlie looked back down at the table.

"Charles?"

"Maybe."

"Well, perhaps you could talk to a sister at the school? Or," she said, "I could talk to his mother, Charles. Would you like me to do that?"

"No! Ma, really, really, I'm fine. It's just words. I'll ignore him."

Mother contemplated this for a moment and then said, "Well, all right. For now. But Charles, I want for you to tell me if this boy does anything else to you, yes?"

"Okay." He just wanted the conversation to come to an end.

"Well, all right then." Mother looked unconvinced, but she let the conversation fall.

* * *

"The twist, Mama! Let's do the twist!" Susan was bathed and in her nightdress, ready to watch TV with Charlie as Mother and Father went out dancing with Mr. and Mrs. Levesque from across the street. They did so much less these days, so Susan was pleased to see they'd be doing it tonight.

"The twist?"

"Yes! Oh, let's do it!"

Mother laughed at her daughter's ready eagerness and grasped her hands. Susan admired the V-necked, short-sleeved floral dress that Mother was wearing, her black heels adding a couple of inches to her otherwise short stature. Her string of large pearls shone from her neck.

Mother began rotating on the balls of her feet. Slowly. Side to side. Her hips swung, her arms swiveled as she held onto Susan's hands.

A little faster.

"Charlie, come on!" Susan called from over her shoulder in the kitchen. Charlie appeared on the threshold.

"Dance with us, Charlie," Susan said.

The left side of Charlie's mouth lifted in a smirk. He began twisting his torso from side to side, bending his knees and lowering his body. Up. Down. Side to side.

Susan let go of Mother's hands and reached for her brother. He took them, and together they continued in their merriment, Susan's auburn curls bouncing with her momentum, bare feet splayed on the linoleum floor.

Father entered the kitchen smelling strongly of ivory soap. His face was flushed from drink and the hot water of the shower.

"Oh, do join us, Gerald," Mother said as she extended both her arms toward her husband. Susan and Charlie continued to dance, both smiling brightly.

Father walked forward and took the proffered hands of his wife. Whether it was the whiskey, the fact that it was now the weekend, his time relaxing in the shower, or a combination of it all, Susan didn't know and frankly couldn't be bothered to care at this particular moment. The simple fact that his thin lips had lifted to reveal his small, slightly yellowed teeth was all she needed to know. Father was happy. Susan's already jovial spirits lifted further and she moved her body ever faster in her exuberance.

Father began moving his legs, his hips in time with Mother, and now all four of the Duboises were twisting in the small kitchen as the sun continued its steady decline in the sky.

"Good night, my darling." Mother kissed Susan's forehead shortly after the dancing concluded. Susan closed her eyes and inhaled her lavender scent.

"Night, Mama," she said.

"Good night, Charles." Mother raised her chin and kissed his cheek. Even when she was in heels, her son was now taller than she was.

"Good night, ma'am." Charlie looked toward Father. "Good night, sir."

Father nodded. Together he and Mother walked out to the car.

Charlie looked to his sister. "TV?"

"Yep."

Charlie turned the knob at the front of the television as Susan sat Indian style on the couch, her flowered nightdress straining at the knees. *Rawhide* had already begun, not Susan's favorite show but she knew that there wasn't any other program on at this time on a Friday night that interested her more than this one.

They watched in silence for a while. Her mind wandered in thought and contemplation.

"Charlie?" she asked, still looking at the television set before her.

"Yeah."

"Thinking about Tommy Walters makes me think of someone else." Charlie's green eyes gazed into hers.

"Mercedes Doyle has been mean to me, and I have no idea why. I've never done anything to her at all. I don't think I've ever done anything to anybody. I have Janet and Betty and I talk to them because they're my good friends, but I'm so shy, Charlie, that I don't really talk much to anyone else. Well, except for Mikey and David. They're my friends, too, but I really just see them at school. Why do you think she's mean?" Susan didn't wait for an answer before saying, "And what in the world was she doing talking to you today? I didn't know you were friends with her."

"I'm not."

"Then why was she talking to you like she was?"

"I don't know, Susie. I don't get girls."

"She's not shy."

"Nope. She certainly isn't shy."

"I wish I weren't so shy. I wish I had confidence."

"To me, there's a difference between confidence and being just outright stuck up. Mercedes Doyle thinks too highly of herself for all I know of her. I guess I don't know much about her, really, but I don't want to, either. Especially now that I know she's being a snobby queen to my little sister." He elbowed her amicably.

"I just don't get it, Charlie. Why would somebody not like you when you've never, ever done anything to them?"

"I don't know. Some people are just like that. I've met a few myself. Tommy Walters, right?" He smiled over at Susan. "I just try my best to ignore them, but it's hard, isn't it?"

"Yeah. I know Mom would tell us to ignore it. Or tell us to tell a teacher but that's just stupid. Who does that? I just want people to like me. I'm a nice person. Right?"

"The best. You remind me a lot of Mom. But I hope you grow up to lead a different life than she does."

"What do you mean?"

"Do you think Mom is really happy, Susie? Really? She hardly gets to do the things that she wants to do. She's constantly trying to make our father happy, but she never seems to do it. She just gets knocked around. And his drinking is getting worse. He does it more and more. He's happy one minute, like tonight, and then the next minute he goes off. It's like I'm listening for the ticking of a bomb trying to figure out when the ticking will stop and the bomb explodes and I can never figure it out. I just try not to get in his way. And I've seen other families. Henry's family? They're like, I don't know, like *Ozzie and Harriet* or something. They're just so happy. Normal. But Father—"

"He hurts you, too."

"He hurts me, too."

"It makes me sick to my stomach when he hurts you and Mom, Charlie. Sometimes I throw up in my mouth." Her lips turned up in a grimace at the thought of regurgitation, the acidic taste threatening to burn her mouth even as she now spoke in remembrance.

Charlie nodded at this. "It's your anxiety again."

"Whatever it is, I don't like it one bit," she said. "Hey, Charlie?"

"Yeah?"

"Why doesn't Father hurt me?" she asked, her voice small.

Charlie's eyes bore into hers. "I really don't know, Susie, but I thank God for it every day."

* * *

"Okay, Susie T, let's go." It was the following week. School was out and it was officially summer vacation. Janet and Betty were both unavailable, so Charlie had promised to take Susan to Emerson Park. It being a warm morning, Susan had slipped on a pair of shorts and a plaid-printed cotton T-shirt.

"Bye, Mom," Susan called when she and Charlie were putting on their shoes, the June morning breeze gently sifting through the large window screens of the porch.

"Goodbye, Susan, Charlie. Have a good morning and I'll see you for lunch."

"Thanks for taking me," Susan said to her brother as they made their way up the bumps and potholes of North Street.

"You're welcome."

They turned right at the corner of North and Emerson and crossed the street to enter at the chain-link fence.

"Push me on the swing?"

"Aww, Susie, aren't you a little old for me to still be pushing you?"

"No way! Push me, Charlie?"

A sigh and then, "Okay."

They walked past the sandbox, past the seesaws, and Susan sat herself down on the black seat of the swing, placing both hands tightly on the chains to brace herself for the push to come.

"Underdog!"

"You sure?" Charlie teased. "I'm good at those, you know. Might fall off the swing."

"No, I won't," Susan said. "Go high!"

"Okay," Charlie said. "You asked for it."

Susan felt his hands as they pressed the side of the swing at her hips and pulled back. She held tighter to the metal chain and concealed a squeal that wanted to explode with the anticipation of the butterflies

Charlie's push would elicit in her stomach.

Charlie pulled up and up. Susan's feet left the ground and dangled above. He pushed her forward and up into the air as his tall body ducked under the bottom of the seat, dodging her legs as he ran forth. She was giggling at the propulsion. Charlie surely didn't go easy with that push, and for that, she was gleefully thankful.

She slowly came to a stop.

"Again?"

Charlie laughed. "I figured you'd ask."

They continued to swing for a bit and walked around the park. They attempted the seesaws but found the difference of weight to be rather difficult and gave up quickly.

"Susie, I think I'm done. There's not a whole lot here for me anymore, and I'm kind of wanting to just get home. Okay?"

"Aww, Charlie," Susan said, "I'm having fun. Just a bit longer?"

"We've already been here for a long time. I took you in the first place, didn't I? Let's go home."

"Okay," Susan relented. "But will you take me back sometime soon?"

"Yeah," Charlie said with a smile, "I can take you back sometime soon."

They began to walk toward the exit. Susan was looking down at her sandaled feet, admiring the polish on her toenails, and didn't notice that Charlie had ceased to walk beside her until she was well ahead of him. She looked to her side and then over her shoulder. Charlie stood in place behind her and motioned for her to join him.

"What are you doing?" Susan asked as she approached.

"Susie, let's go back," he said anxiously. "We can get onto County Road and go home that way."

"Why in the world would we do that?" She took Charlie's hand and attempted to pull him forth, but he wouldn't budge. Instead, he tugged free and turned his back. Susan was perplexed at his sudden reaction, and in her annoyance she began to walk by herself toward the opening at Emerson Street and saw there, off in the near distance, Tommy Walters.

He was looking directly at her.

Comprehension halted her steps. Panic engulfed her. She turned around and saw Charlie's back as he hastily walked farther away.

"Charlie, Charlie, wait up," Susan called as she ran toward him. Charlie turned to face her, and although his steps slowed, he still moved steadily toward the back of the park. His body was rigid, his face contorted. Susan chanced a glance behind her and saw that Tommy Walters was near, one of his friends straggling behind.

"Where ya goin'?" Tommy Walters was there.

Right beside her.

Looking at her brother.

His friend sauntered up, wiping his nose with the back of his hand. He expunged a yellow wad from the back of his throat and spit it onto the green grass.

Charlie said nothing in return.

"Cat got your tongue?" Tommy Walters sniggered.

Still, Charlie said nothing, just stood erect, eyes wide and staring.

"Henry not here, huh? You two always together. What, you queer or somethin'?" His friend chortled, which gave Tommy Walters more confidence to move forward derisively. He crossed his thick arms over his chest and smiled, brown eyes malicious. His brown hair was combed back in a duck butt and was stiff with pomade, which immediately equated Tommy Walters with Father in Susan's mind. Not the duck butt— the hair at the back of Father's head was always short and combed straight—but the pomade. She imagined she could smell it just now and her stomach churned.

"Hey," Tommy Walters said, "I'm talkin' to you. You two queer?"

Charlie didn't reply.

126

"Guess he's just stupid." Tommy Walters looked to his friend, the side of his lip lifted in a sneer.

"You a candy-ass, too, ain't ya? Specially when your boyfriend Henry ain't around to fight your fights." He looked Charlie up and down. "Hey, Mitch, you know what toughens up a candy-ass, dontcha ya?"

"Mmm?"

"A good pounding, that's what." His smile was sinister.

"Yep, that'll do it," his friend confirmed.

"That what your candy-ass, pantywaist self need, Charles?" Tommy Walters mocked.

Susan couldn't move, couldn't speak. She was petrified. She looked at her brother, slightly trembling as he stood.

Charlie took a step backward, slight and slow, his eyes never leaving Tommy Walters. She didn't know how she moved, or when her mind had beckoned her body to do so, but unconsciously she took a step toward her brother, reaching for him, attempting to grasp onto anything she could get a hold of on his person, but she was propelled back by a strong force and landed on her bottom in the grass before she could succeed. Her hands found purchase on the ground, and she looked up to see that Tommy Walters had reached her brother first, the force she'd felt having been his shoulder as he thrust her out of the way.

Charlie might have been the taller of the two, but she knew her brother to be calm, kind, and unassertive. He had never been in a fight before, and she was well aware that he was terrified of Tommy Walters. She sat there and watched as Tommy Walters threw his right fist into Charlie's cheek, his left into his chest. Charlie heeled over, face distorted, mouth open in an attempt to draw in a breath. She pulled her knees into her chest, placed the palms of her hands on her cheeks. She wanted to scream, wanted to force Tommy Walters to stop hurting her brother, her Charlie. She wanted this to end. That feeling in the pit of her stomach, the feeling that she was going to be sick, emerged and held.

Tommy Walters had Charlie on the ground. Charlie's arms were covering his face, his legs bent, his knees to his chest as he lay on his side, attempting to protect himself.

Tommy Walters's friend was laughing.

Charlie was kicked. Again and again.

Then it was over.

"Guess you need to go home to your old lady," Tommy Walters said as he looked down at Charlie. "Wipe that blood off your face. Don't worry. I'll let everyone know I was right. You *are* a candy-ass." He flexed his fist and walked off, his friend following in his wake.

Susan couldn't move her body. Her palms were still on her cheeks, and only now did she realize that they were wet with her tears.

Charlie eventually sat up, hand on his chest. He touched his left cheek and looked at the blood on his hand as he pulled it back. His lip was split: his cheek was red and already sporting the emergence of a large bump. He looked to Susan, found her eyes. She finally let out the sob that had been encapsulated within.

Charlie stood on wobbly legs and walked the few steps over to his sister. Bending down, he let out an expression of pain before touching her shoulder. She looked up at him then and realized that he, too, had tears in his eyes. The combination of the pooling liquid and the green in his shirt made them look strikingly emerald.

Beautiful.

Charlie placed his hands under his sister's arms and gently helped her to stand. Together they walked home.

* * *

Susan entered the house to find Mother sitting at the kitchen table, cigarette in hand. Mother started at Susan's despondent look, the sagging of her shoulders, the dispirited way she held her body aloft. When Charlie entered behind her, Mother audibly gasped and dropped the cigarette onto her lap. She stood abruptly, patting at her dress, sending the cigarette dropping to the floor as ashes sprayed from its tip. She lifted the cigarette and swiftly placed it in the glass ashtray before hastening over to her son.

"What happened to you!" she exclaimed as she reached to touch Charlie's cheek. He winced from the pain the touch induced.

"Nothing," Charlie said.

"Nothing?" Mother was incredulous. "This is not nothing, Charles. Who did this to you?" She looked up at her son, and still he said nothing.

"Charles Donald, you will tell me who did this." Mother was stern now, where often she was gentle. Charlie knew she was flummoxed.

"Really, Ma, it's nothing. I'll be fine."

"You will be fine?" Mother said. "Fine?" Tears welled. "In God's name, Charles, tell me what happened to you." She was pleading now as she grasped onto his shirt, pulling him down. He bent forward at her pull, his face close to hers. She reached up again and gently laid her hand on his cheek, then his lip, tracing the tip of her finger along the split and then touching the few droplets of blood that had made their way onto his shirt.

Still, he said nothing.

Mother relented. She led him to the kitchen sink and began dabbing at her son's lip. She unexpectedly halted, letting her hand and the cloth drop to her side.

"Tommy Walters, yes?" she whispered. "That boy you and Susan were talking about last week."

"Ma, please," Charlie implored.

"Who is he, Charles? Where does he live? Who is his mother?"

"Never mind. I don't even know where he lives. He just goes to my school, that's all. He showed up at the park."

"And did this to you? But why?"

"I don't know," Charlie said meekly.

"He just hurt you like this for no reason?

"I suppose so. I promise you I didn't do anything."

Mother looked into his eyes, into the green depths that both revealed and concealed. After a moment she said, "I believe you."

Mother finished cleaning Charlie, then mixed the children some chocolate milk to drink at the kitchen table while she made some sandwiches for lunch.

Father arrived that night almost exactly at five o'clock. Mother was just finishing the dinner preparations. Susan was setting the table, and Charlie was in his bedroom reading.

"Hello, Gerald," Mother said as she forced a smile on her face, "and welcome home. I hope you had a good day at work today." She brought the large white dish of hot tuna-mushroom casserole over and placed it on top of a pot holder at the center of the table.

"Work was work," Father said.

"Well," Mother said, "we are glad to have you home. Susan, please let your brother know that dinner is ready." She looked at Susan anxiously.

Father looked up from his perch at the kitchen table as Susan entered with Charlie just behind her. His eyebrows lifted. "What the hell happened to you?"

"It's nothing, sir," Charlie said.

"The hell it's not," Father said. "Looks like someone used you as a punching bag. Who was it?"

Susan knew it was pointless not to answer and was certain Charlie could intuit the same.

"Tommy Walters, sir," he said, eyes downcast in the kitchen entryway.

"Tommy Walters, huh? That the son of Bert Walters?"

"I'm not sure, sir."

"Bet it is. He was a real ass in high school. Son's probably the same." He paused to look across the room at Charlie, from his lip to his cheek, which now was even redder and more highly raised. "How's he look? You get any good punches on him?"

Charlie hesitated and then mumbled, "No, sir."

"What was that? Didn't hear you."

Charlie lifted his eyes from the floor and looked at his father. "I said 'No, sir.'"

"Nothing? What the hell, boy? Kid takes a punch to you like that, you punch him back."

"Gerald!" Mother exclaimed.

Father's head jerked to the side where Mother was standing. "You can shut your trap, woman. Nobody's asking you. No son of mine is going to get his ass pummeled and have nothing to show for it but a bunch of cuts and bruises on himself. He needs to man up, goddamnit. Not stand there like a pansy." He looked his son up and down and grunted. Mother let out a soft moan as she placed her right palm on her stomach.

"Well, don't you just stand there like that. Come over and get your dinner."

Charlie and Susan both walked to the table and took their seats in silence.

"Helen, where's my whiskey? You know I want my whiskey."

"I do, Gerald, yes," Mother said. "Although I thought perhaps—"

"Get my damn whiskey." Father's voice was rising. Mother said nothing further as she walked back to the kitchen and the decanter of golden-hued whiskey idly waiting to be drunk, to engulf the senses of the man who drank it.

They ate mutely. The scraping of forks upon plates and jaws clicking as they chewed were the only sounds that echoed in the small space of the kitchen table.

TEN

"Down on your knees! Get down on your knees and pray to God!" Sister Agnes, St. Catherine's librarian, bustled into Susan's fifth grade classroom on the afternoon of November 22nd, 1963, and startled each and every one of its inhabitants with her gesticulations and booming ejaculations. Her face poked out of her white wimple, flushed and worried. "Get down! Get down!" she continued as her arms whipped up and down. "The president has been shot!"

If Susan had initially thought this was another bomb drill, this last sentence quickly rid her of the notion.

Susan's teacher, Sister Annette (Susan was so pleased to learn on the first day of school that her fourth grade teacher was now her fifth), placed the palm of her right hand on her heart. Her knees buckled under her weight, and she fell into her chair.

"Shot?" Sister Annette's voice was soft, uncertain.

"Yes! Oh, yes!" Sister Agnes confirmed. "President Kennedy has been shot. We must pray." Her eyes darted from her colleague to the hallway behind her. "I must spread word," she said as she left the doorway in a flurry, black habit swishing in her haste.

Susan and her classmates just stared in shocked silence at their teacher, whose hand still remained on her heart as she sat on her chair behind her desk.

"Pray," Sister Annette said in a low voice, and then, as cognizance returned, she said louder and more firmly, "Class, get on your knees and pray with me."

Susan left the comfort of her chair and hurried to her knees on the hard floor. She folded her hands in a steeple before her and nodded her head. She heard muffled voices around her, sobs. She ventured a look at Betty, who knelt beside her. Betty was quivering, lips moving, eyes closed. Janet was behind Betty and was looking directly at Susan, her countenance twisted in an appearance of terror, brunette strands that had swayed from her ponytail clinging to her face.

Shot? President Kennedy had been shot?

She remained on her knees for what seemed like an eternity until Sister Annette dismissed the class early to go home to their families. The hallway was a mass of movement. Some bodies moved expeditiously: others were slow and deliberate. Faces were red and splotchy, voices low and whispering.

Charlie and Henry weren't outside to meet her and walk her home; they were at St. Joseph's now. She, Janet, and Betty walked down the stone steps of St. Catherine's and crossed the front yard. Walking to the opposite side of the street, they began their trek home.

Susan linked her arm through Janet's. Betty saw this and filled the space on Susan's other side, grasping her hand. In this way, they approached Susan's house.

Susan kissed Janet's cheek and turned to kiss Betty before walking through the porch and into the house. She found Mother sitting with Mrs. Levesque in front of the television. Mrs. Levesque's long blond hair was falling out of her beehive, and she was wiping tears from her cheeks. Mother turned at Susan's approach; her eyes, too, were red and teary. She didn't ask why Susan was home early, simply motioned for her to sit and turned back to the television set. Walter Cronkite's face took up the screen before them, his black glasses thick around his eyes.

"From Dallas, Texas, the flash apparently official: President Kennedy died at one p.m. central standard time, two o'clock eastern standard time, some thirty-eight minutes ago."

Mother and Mrs. Levesque both inhaled sharply at this new information: Mrs. Levesque then sobbed distinctly, shoulders bobbing, body heaving. Mother's tears were silent. She didn't bother to lift a hand and wipe them away.

Cronkite continued after a pause and clearing of his throat: "Vice President Johnson has left the hospital in Dallas, but we do not know where he has proceeded; presumably, he will be taking the oath of office shortly and become the thirty-sixth president of the United States."

Mrs. Levesque reached for Mother's hand, and the two women clasped each other tightly. Susan sat by watching the scene unfold before her. The president? Dead?

Dead?

She couldn't seem to fully grasp the reality of the situation.

She stood from the couch and made her way to the kitchen, where she put on a fresh pot of Maxwell House. Mother almost always brewed coffee when they had any sort of company, and Susan assumed that coffee was something the women could use just now.

"Mom..." Susan peeked through the doorway to the living room. "I made you some coffee. Want some?"

Mother could only manage a nod.

Susan went back to the kitchen counter and poured two cups of steaming-hot coffee into mugs and placed them at the table. Mother and Mrs. Levesque sat down.

"Maria," Mother said forlornly, "would you like some sugar or some cream at all?"

"Thank you, Helen, yes," Mrs. Levesque said. "Both, please."

"I've got it, Mom," Susan said.

"Thanks, Susan." Mother lifted the cup of black coffee to her lips and took a small sip. When done, she cradled the mug in her hands and stared out the window.

"I'm having a hard time here, Helen," Mrs. Levesque began after a moment of silence. "This is just ugly. Terrible. It's truly unthinkable. President Kennedy was wonderful, wasn't he? He was doing so many great things for our country and we had hope for our future and then this has to go and happen. Some person or people had to take that all away, they had to end his life. And his poor wife and children."

"I understand all of what you are saying, Maria. Truly I do."

"What a terrible time," Mrs. Levesque continued. "What a shame. John Fitzgerald Kennedy, our president... dead."

Mother said nothing, merely nodded and held her cup of coffee aloft, suspending it in front of her for a moment before taking another small sip.

This was the scene in the Dubois kitchen when Charlie entered. "You've heard," he said.

"We heard," Mrs. Levesque said as Mother nodded her head.

Charlie touched Susan on the shoulder and walked around the table to embrace his mother. She cried into his chest as Mrs. Levesque took up her cup of coffee and allowed a trickle of tears to find their way down her cheeks once again. Susan sat stoic and dry-eyed, attempting to take it all in, to fully understand. She wanted to close her eyes and wish this all away, to rest her head on her pillow in the comfort of her own room, her own bed, and wake in the morning to a new day in which there were no worries, no heartache.

Eventually, Mrs. Levesque left to make her way across the street to her own home.

"I need to start on dinner," Mother announced. She stood from the table and gathered the two empty coffee cups.

"Mom, how can you think of dinner right now as if nothing has happened?" Charlie asked.

"Your father will expect dinner to be ready when he gets home from work."

"Damn it, Mom!" Charlie ejected. "Can't he understand for one night that you need to grieve? Can't he understand that not everything is about him and what he wants when he wants it?"

"Charles!" Mother stood shocked at the stance that her otherwise obliging son had just taken.

"I'm sorry, Ma. I shouldn't have yelled. Or sworn. I'm sorry. It's just that right now we shouldn't even be thinking about dinner. Too much has happened today."

"Yes," Mother said. "But your father will want his dinner, and it is my job to make it for him."

Charlie shook his head, ran his hand through his growing brown hair, and left the room.

Susan stood. "I'll help you, Mom."

A single nod from Mother in turn.

Dinner was almost ready when Father returned from work.

"Have you heard?" Mother asked him as he entered the house.

"Yes. I don't want to talk about it." He walked straight to the whiskey on the counter and poured himself a generous glass.

Susan set the table and Mother brought the food over. Susan went to retrieve Charlie from his room, and they all sat down at the table. Mother folded her hands, motioning that it was time to begin the evening dinner prayer.

"Bless us, O Lord, and this food that we are about to receive. Tonight I also ask that you watch over the Kennedy family as you take our president into your loving arms. In Christ we pray. Amen."

Father looked over at Mother and took a sip of his whiskey. Nothing more was said at the table that night.

When Father had finished his dinner and his second glass of whiskey, he stood from his chair, walked over to the counter, poured himself a third glass, and left the room. Susan heard the door to his bedroom close. She could not remember a time in which Father had not rested at the table after dinner with his drink and cigarette. She locked eyes with Mother, both of their faces displaying their feelings of worry.

Perhaps the times were changing.

ELEVEN

I n December 1965, Susan was twelve, Charlie sixteen. On a
cold Saturday afternoon, Janet had walked the short distance
from her house to Susan's, where Henry would pick them up—
Charlie included—in his parents' car so they could drive over to Main
Street and explore the stores with hopes of procuring some Christmas
gifts for family members. Susan was thrilled. What fun they would
have!

Charlie had begun his first job the year prior as a grocery bagger
at one of the local supermarkets. From school, he was able to walk
the mile to work, and Mother (who had recently obtained a driver's
license) at times would pick him up and often drove him on the
weekends, as the store was too far away for him to go by foot from
home. Working had brought Charlie money he otherwise would not
have obtained, and although he was a great saver and quite frugal,
Christmas had always been a very special, magical time for him and
Susan, and the notion of purchasing his own gifts for his family
pleased him greatly, even at the age of sixteen.

"Bundle up, it is cold out there," Mother said as she hugged Susan
goodbye. "And have fun. Here," she said as she stealthily handed
Susan three dollars, "for your lunch out. Make a day of today. You
are in good company, and it is Christmastime, after all."

"Mom," Charlie interjected, "I said I would treat myself and Susan to lunch."

"I know you did, Charles," Mother said, "but you work so hard, and today I want to be able to do something special for you and your sister." Mother was speaking in hushed tones.

"Where did you get it?" Charlie whispered back. Father was watching television in the living room, but the wall was thin and he feared his father learning about this private matter transpiring within his home.

"Never you mind," Mother said. "Let us just hope your father did not count the money in the emergency jar on top of the fridge, yes?" She winked at her son. "I am so happy you can both have a day like today. Now go and enjoy yourselves." She ushered them out the door. When Susan entered the porch, she placed her boots on and looked back at her mother hovering in the doorway to the kitchen. Although many other women Mother's age wore pants these days, Mother still favored her dresses, some of which were quite outdated but that she still adored. Her hair remained on the shorter side, thick still, parted at the side and swept over just as it had been for as long as Susan could remember. Her face, though; her face had changed. The corners of her eyes crinkled when she smiled, the wrinkles deeper and more pronounced, and her skin had begun to take on a more pallid color. Susan had heard talk in the last couple of years about the newfound health risks of cigarette smoking, but Mother and Father both refused to take note and remained avid smokers. Her waist was thin still, though her hips and thighs had become more rounded, thick. Susan detested Father's insistence on telling his wife that she had become fat, but knew to say anything in Mother's defense would be to tempt his wrath and his exploding temper, which seemed to flare more quickly as the months progressed.

To Susan, though, Mother remained beautiful.

Henry parked on Main Street, and the foursome exited the car.

They walked inside a local diner and sat in a corner booth by the window overlooking the street, Susan's pants slipping on the thick, smooth red-and-white seat as she moved closer to the window so Janet could rest beside her.

Susan grabbed one of the menus that were stacked to her right behind a napkin dispenser and handed it off to Janet as a young waitress in a white uniform and black apron approached the table with a small white pad of paper and a pen.

"Can I get you something to drink?" she asked.

"Just a water for me," Charlie said. "Susie, get something special if you want."

"Milkshake, please," Susan said with a large grin on her face. "Chocolate."

"Me, too," said Janet.

"And just a water for me," was Henry's answer.

The waitress left the table. "Thanks so much, Charlie," Susan said. "I haven't had a milkshake in forever; I feel like I can taste it now. And thanks for letting us come along. I know you wanted to be alone with Henry."

"No problem," Charlie said. "Henry's a good sport."

"Yep, that I am," Henry confirmed with a teasing smile.

"Can you believe that it's almost Christmas?" Janet said. "Almost an entirely new year. 1966," she said with a touch of awe. "This year's been a blast for me."

"Kind of for me, too," Susan said. "But not with Sister Gertrude. She's just as bad as Sister Mary Francis. She whacked Mikey with the ruler last week, and last month she made David stay after school to clean the room just for correcting her when she made a mistake about some sort of animal life cycle, and that was after she made him stand in the corner of the room facing the wall for a really long time. Remember that? He didn't mean any disrespect; that's just David.

He's so smart and he remembers everything. He told me that now he doesn't even want to raise his hand in class anymore. I don't like her one bit, and I hope next year we have Sister Annette or Sister Mary Margaret again."

"Yeah," Janet said, "Sister Gertrude's a bummer. Downright mean. What about you, Charlie? You like school?"

"Sometimes. We've got some nice teachers and then we've got some teachers I could do without. Kids are okay for the most part with a few exceptions. I like some of my classes and can't wait for others to be over with. Typical." He paused and looked over at his friend. "Henry likes it, though," he said with a smirk.

"I do. I agree that there are definitely some teachers that shouldn't be teaching, but I've always liked learning."

"Me, too," Susan said. "Except for math.

"Well," said Henry, "that's certainly something I can understand." He smiled her way, revealing a straight set of white teeth, the incisors just slightly longer than the teeth surrounding them. A nice smile, Susan decided. She hadn't really noticed before now.

"Know what you want to eat?" The waitress stood before them with an air of nonchalance.

Orders in hand, she turned her back on the table. She returned shortly with the waters and chocolate milkshakes, the food orders submitted to the kitchen.

"Oh, yum!" Susan said as the milkshake was placed on the shiny off-white table before her: a clear, heavy glass with a straw emerging from the middle.

"Drink up!" Janet said as she reached greedily for her straw and began to sip.

"It is hard to believe sometimes, though, isn't it?" Henry asked.

"What?" Charlie looked at his friend with confusion.

"That it's almost '66. So much has happened this year. Good and bad. Think of it: Voting Rights Act, Operation Rolling Thunder—my dad has a lot of opinions on that one, I can tell you—and…oh, the spacewalk. How boss is that? Second inauguration of Johnson, Martin Luther King Jr., the Beatles are still bitchin'. It's been a year."

The Beatles were a band that both Charlie and Henry idolized, much to the chagrin of Father, whom Susan had heard on numerous occasions refer to them as "goddamn hippies!"

"Henry enjoys current events," Charlie announced to the girls.

"Yeah, I can see that," said Janet. "I do a bit, too."

"I think it's important to know what's going on in the world." Susan nodded her head but withheld the fact that she felt she had enough to worry about in her everyday life, let alone with world news. So much of what she had recently heard through various sources—radio, TV, word of mouth—shed negativity on the world and its people, and this heightened her anxiety.

"Well, hello there, Mr. Hunk." Susan looked up from her milkshake to see an attractive teenage girl smiling down directly at Henry.

"Patty," Henry said, "what are you doing here?" He stood with a smile, put his arm around her shoulder, and kissed her on the cheek.

"I was just out with my parents. We decided to stop on in for some lunch," Patty said. She was on the shorter side, maybe just an inch or two taller than Susan herself, and seeing as Henry was on eye level with Charlie, she had to look up quite a bit to speak with him. Her thick dirty-blond hair was parted down the middle and dangled past her shoulders, her bangs grazing her eyebrows. Her long mascaraed eyelashes lifted with her gaze and almost brushed the top of her eyelids, but she otherwise looked devoid of any makeup save perhaps a small amount of nude lip color with a hint of light pink. She was quite beautiful.

"Well," said Henry, "I'm happy you did. A nice surprise for me." He and Patty spent the next few moments simply staring at each other, with rather goofy expressions on their faces, Susan thought.

Henry turned to the table. "Charlie, you know Patty."

Charlie nodded. "Hi, Patty."

"Hi, Charlie. Good to see you."

"Patty, this is Charlie's sister, Susie, and her friend Janet." He looked at the girls before him and then back to Patty. "And this is Patty, my girlfriend."

"Good to meet both of you," Patty said. "Charlie's quite the guy to have around. I can see why Henry likes him so much."

Beautiful *and* nice.

"Good to meet you, too," Janet said with a smile. Susan merely sat mute.

"I should go," Patty said to Henry. "Mom and Dad are waiting for me on the other side of the diner, but I saw you when we walked in the door and I just had to come and say hello."

"I'm glad you did." He squeezed her hand with a smile before she turned and walked away. When he sat back down, the smile hadn't left his face.

"How about you, Charlie?" Janet asked. "Any girlfriend we should know about?"

Charlie blushed red and looked down at the table. "Not for me."

"Charlie's waiting for the right girl," Henry teased.

Charlie simply smiled.

Their meals came soon thereafter, and they ate amicably together, talking of school and the upcoming Christmas holiday and what their prospective families were planning in celebration.

They finished eating, and before leaving the diner, Henry sought out Patty's table and walked over to say his goodbyes. Susan stood in the doorway with Janet and Charlie and watched as Patty smiled up at her brother's best friend. Henry bent at the waist to give her mother a warm hug and shook hands with her father. He turned and walked back to his friends.

Together they proceeded down Main Street to arrive at F. W. Woolworth Co. They entered and were accosted by a flurry of Christmas decorations in bright hues of blue, red, and green. Baskets, ribbons, bows, papers. Before them stood all anyone would need to decorate their home for the holidays.

"Meet us back here in an hour?" Charlie said.

"Okay."

Susan and Janet walked off in one direction, Charlie and Henry in another.

"Oh, bath salts," Susan said after they had perused for a while. "Mom would really like those. Although," she said as she rethought the sentiment, "she doesn't really ever take baths."

"Well, it was a good idea," Janet said.

"Perfume! Oh, I can get her the perfume she's always wearing. It smells so wonderful. Honestly, I wouldn't think it was really my mother at all if she wasn't wearing her perfume. Let's go." She led Janet toward the counter that housed all the various perfumes in the store.

Susan began rifling through the fragrance bottles displayed until she came upon a particular box. Lifting it in her hands she said, "I think this is it!" She gently pried the box open and pulled forth a glass bottle with a golden-hued top. The front label read *Yardley English Lavender*.

"Oh, yes!" Susan exclaimed. "This *is* it. Oh, my mom will be so happy!" She placed the bottle back in its box and closed the lid. "I'll just ask Charlie if he can help me buy it for her. It says two dollars; that's not too much, is it?"

"I don't know." Janet shrugged her shoulders.

Susan held the small box to her chest and smiled. "I really should get my father something, too, but I have no idea what to get him." She thought for a moment. "Let's go to the record section. He does listen to music. Maybe there's something there?"

"Okay," said Janet.

Susan was happy to see that both Charlie and Henry were also at the record department when she and Janet arrived.

"Hi, Charlie," she said as she approached him. "What do you have?"

Charlie handed off a record he had been holding under his arm. Frank Sinatra. "I thought we could get it for Mom and Father," Charlie said.

"Oh, yeah," Susan said. "Janet and I came here because I was thinking of records, too. Charlie, can this be from you *and* me?"

"Of course."

"And I found this." Susan offered him the bottle of perfume.

"Mom," Charlie said.

"Yes."

"Good idea, Susie," he said. "Let's get it."

"Thanks, Charlie! You're the best!"

The foursome continued their excursions throughout downtown, perusing various stores and making a few Christmas purchases as they found items that pleased them. As the sun was making its final descent in the sky to the west, they piled back into the Beaumonts' car. Henry parked in front of Susan and Charlie's home, and they, as well as Janet, exited the car.

The foursome said their goodbyes. Henry pulled back into the street, and Janet started up the small hill to her own home, a small package tucked under her coated arm.

"We've got to hide what we have," Susan said to her brother as they climbed the couple of steps to open the porch door. "This is really exciting, Charlie," she said. "Thank you again."

"You're welcome." Charlie smiled.

They took their boots off on the porch, and once inside, Susan hurried to her room to place the small box of cologne under some clothes in her dresser drawer. This was the very first time she would ever hand Mother something Christmas morning that had not been crafted by her own hands, and she was thrilled for the opportunity, even if it was procured with Charlie's money.

* * *

Janet knocked on the screen door early Monday morning to walk with Susan and Betty to St. Catherine's. Father had already left for work, Charlie for school.

"Bye, Mom," Susan said as she grabbed her lunch sack from the kitchen table.

"Bye, Susan. Have a wonderful day at school."

Susan opened the kitchen door and walked out onto the cold porch where she put her red winter boots on. Grasping onto the black handle of her red book bag in one hand, lunch sack in the other, she walked out into the snow as Janet held the screen door open for her. She looked up to the dark, cloudy sky and felt cold flakes melt on her warm cheeks.

"Let's catch some," Susan said as she began walking. She lifted her chin, opening her mouth to the descending snow.

"We're too old to catch snowflakes," Janet said.

"We're never too old to catch snowflakes," Susan countered. Janet just giggled as Betty followed Susan's lead.

"Get any?" Janet asked when they were through.

"Not really," Susan said.

"Neither did I," said Betty, her nearly black bangs now speckled white with snow, the lower portion of her bobbed hair visible under her orange woolen hat.

"You're both just silly," Janet said with a grin.

The afternoon progressed, the end of the day was approaching.

Susan shuffled in her classroom seat and detected an uncomfortable dampness in the center of her panties. Oh, no! Had she urinated slightly? She crossed one leg over the other and raised her hand.

"What is it, Susan?" Sister Gertrude said.

"Sister Gertrude, may I go to the girls' room?"

"You may not," Sister Gertrude said. "You know it's almost the end of the day, Susan, and you can wait until then."

Susan got back to her work, paused, tried to slide her body over to one side of her seat in an attempt to see if she had urinated past her skirt and onto her chair. No success; she simply couldn't move that far without standing up.

The clock ticked, one agonizing minute followed by another.

She uncrossed her legs, folded her thick, pleated skirt between her thighs.

Finally, the day's dismissal rang over the intercom.

Please, God, let me be okay.

The class scurried to grab their belongings and exit the classroom.

"Aren't you coming?" Janet was by her side.

"Yeah....yes, I'm coming."

Her friends surrounded her, and as she looked around and saw there was no one else close enough to inspect her chair or her person, she slowly rose and peeked at her seat. Nothing. *Oh, thank you, God!*

She brushed her hand down the back of her skirt stealthily. Nothing. She still felt a slight dampness between her legs, but perhaps only a small amount of urine had seeped its way out. That was thankfully something she could take care of when she got home.

Mikey and David parted ways with the girls, and Susan walked home with Janet and Betty, conscious of the moisture below. She said her goodbyes in front of her home and walked inside.

"Oh, hello, Susan," Mother said when she saw her. "I do hope you had a good day at school. Would you like a snack?" Susan was twelve now and fully capable of getting her own after-school snack, but Mother remained adamant in asking each day when Susan and Charlie arrived home from school. Today, Charlie was working at the supermarket and wouldn't be home until dinner, having procured a ride home with a coworker in advance.

"I think I'm all set for now, Mom, thanks." Susan had taken her boots and coat off on the porch. She laid her lunch sack down on the table and looked at her mother, book bag still in hand. "I need to go to the bathroom," she announced and scurried off.

The door to her bedroom was open. She threw her book bag on her bed and ran to the bathroom, shutting the door behind her. She lifted her checkered skirt and pulled her stockings and panties down to her knees. When she was sitting, she pulled her skirt farther up her thighs to peek at her panties and noticed a thick, very dark stain at the center.

This wasn't urine.

She panicked. It looked slightly like a sort of excrement, but she didn't believe it was. She stood and pulled the skirt down her stockinged legs and kicked it off. The stockings followed. She sat back down on the seat to wipe. When she looked at the white toilet paper in her hands she noticed a bit more of this dark, almost muted substance. Where was it coming from?

Susan began to sob as she pulled her panties over her feet and bunched them into a ball, clinging to them tightly in the palm of her hand.

"Oh, my goodness, Susan," Mother called from the other side of the closed bathroom door. "What in the world is wrong? May I come in?"

Susan couldn't answer; she just sat there, naked from the waist down, clutching her panties and shaking.

A creak of the door, a slit in which Mother peeked through. "Oh!" she exclaimed. "Why are your clothes off, Susan?" Mother's head turned to look away.

"I...I...Something's wrong with me." Susan's sob caught in her throat and she choked on her saliva.

"Okay," Mother said. "I'm coming in."

Mother opened the door fully and stepped inside the small bathroom.

"I...I..." Susan held forth the balled-up panties. Mother took them and let them unfold. She glanced at the substance on them—the cause of Susan's turmoil—and smiled.

"Why are you smiling? Oh, my gosh, Mom! Something's wrong with me and you're smiling?" Susan was truly flabbergasted and a bit affronted.

"Susan," Mother said, "nothing is wrong with you. Not at all. Darling, today you have become a woman."

"What?" Susan looked up at her mother with pure ignorance.

"Never you mind, darling," Mother said. "We should not speak much about such things. But nothing is wrong with you at all. This will happen to you about once a month well into your adulthood. It will not look much like this, though, once it happens to you again. It is blood and will look much more like blood does, very red. I will wash these," she said as she motioned to the panties in her fist. "You may go change, Susan, and then you and I will walk to the general store and I will show you what to do each time this happens to you. Let us do this quickly, though, so we can come back home and get dinner on the table before your father arrives from work. This is not something he needs to know about."

Susan was utterly confused and still a bit scared but was willing to follow her mother's lead in this matter of which she knew nothing.

Mother left the room, and she wiped at her tears. She stood from the toilet seat and placed her skirt back on. Carrying her stockings in the crook of her arm, she walked into her room and changed into a pair of green pants and a sweater and new panties. When she walked back into the kitchen, Mother was already in her jacket and hat. Susan wordlessly opened the kitchen door and walked out onto the porch, putting her boots and coat back on. Mother followed and closed the door behind her. Together they stepped onto North Street and walked up the snowy hill. They turned left and walked a half mile down Emerson Street until Greenfield and Sons General Store loomed before them. It looked rather forbidding to Susan now, where it never had in any of her prior days of shopping the aisles.

Mother entered first, the bell at the top of the door chiming their arrival, informing all present that Susan Dubois was here with Mother to procure something for a bleeding issue that had begun earlier that day.

Mortified, she followed Mother through the entryway.

She stole a glance around the room. She knew this was the general store in which Henry worked, and she let out a slight breath when he didn't appear before her.

Mother seemed to know exactly where she was headed, walking directly to a small aisle toward the left side of the store and stopping to stand before products lined up in the middle of a metal shelf.

"Here we are," she said as she pulled a box out of its resting place. *Kotex Regular Belted Pads.*

What?

Another box followed. *Sanitary Belt.*

And yet another. *Sanitary Apron.*

"Thank goodness there was still a bit of money in the emergency jar, yes?" Mother said, but not so much to Susan as for her own benefit.

"Okay, darling," Mother said, not taking her eyes off the three boxes

151

in her hands, "let us pay and go back home."

Susan followed Mother to the counter, where a young man stood behind a cash register. Susan truly wished she could close her eyes and simply vanish, arriving in the safety of her bedroom back in her home without another step being taken.

Mother made the transaction—Susan standing behind her—the only words used being a soft "thank you" as the young man handed her a brown paper bag, the necessary items held within.

The door chimed their exit.

Susan and Mother walked home in silence. When they arrived, they took off their boots and jackets and entered the warm air of the kitchen.

"Okay," Mother said. "Let us go to your bedroom. There will be more room there for me to show you how to use these than in the bathroom."

Mother emptied the contents of the bag onto Susan's made bed. "Okay," she said, her cheeks slightly pink with embarrassment, "when you notice that you have started bleeding—it is called menstruation"— here she cleared her throat— "then you will want to take one of these pads out." She opened the box before her and pulled forth a thick white cotton pad. There were long strands of fabric at either end of the cotton rectangle. "You will need to wear this belt under your panties." Mother opened the box that held the sanitary belt and offered it to Susan. She moved Susan's hands to show her how she should put the belt on and demonstrated how to place the pad within. "Then you will place your panties on." She opened the last box. "You will want to wear this apron under your clothes. This will ensure that any leaks do not go through."

Leaks? Susan thought immediately of her desk chair at school.

"Do you think you understand?" Mother asked her.

Susan nodded uncertainly.

"Okay then. You can put this one on now. You will want to change your pad every few hours, especially when you are bleeding a lot."

A lot of blood? Oh, dear Lord!

Mother left the bedroom, and Susan did as she was bid. When she began walking toward the door of her bedroom, she was nervous that she was waddling with the novel material wedged snuggly in a place she wasn't even supposed to think about.

Mother was in the kitchen beginning to prepare dinner. She smiled reassuringly at Susan. Susan gave a dubious smile back.

"Come on over," Mother said. "You can help me with the potatoes."

Darkness descended. Father arrived home while Susan and Mother were still cooking.

"Why isn't dinner done?" Wet boots still on, he sat in his chair.

"Oh," Mother said. "I am so sorry, Gerald. We fell behind this afternoon. We are almost through."

Father grunted his annoyance. Charlie entered the house not long after.

"Oh, hello, Charles," Mother said over her shoulder. "How was your time at school today? And at work?"

"I had a good day. Thanks, Ma." Charlie walked over and kissed her on the cheek. Turning to Susan, he tousled her hair.

"Ugh! Charlie, you know I don't like that anymore."

"What?" Charlie feigned ignorance. "You know you love it, Susie." He tousled her hair once again, and although it annoyed her, she couldn't help but smile.

Mother brought forth a dish of meatloaf and Susan the casserole dish of diced potatoes seasoned with parsley and butter to the already-set table.

The evening's dinner prayer finished, the family began to eat.

Mother looked down at her plate of food: Father took a sip of whiskey. He was already on his second glass. Susan looked over at this man who had sired her, this man whose blood she shared. His red hair had grown a bit sparse, and he still wore it combed to the side with pomade, only now she could see a small portion of his pale white scalp through the strands. His face was red and splotchy, and a good amount of blood vessels had burst on his cheeks. He remained to this day waiflike and gaunt, very small compared to a lot of grown men Susan had seen around town.

He lifted his glass and downed the rest of his whiskey. He pushed his empty glass over to his wife.

Charlie dropped his fork, the metal producing a clinking sound around the table.

"Got a problem there, son?" Father asked with a belittling manner.

Charlie dared to look Father straight in the eye, pursed his lips, then lowered his gaze. "No, sir," he seethed.

"What was that?"

"I said 'No, sir.'"

"You bet you did," Father said. As Mother hadn't yet filled his glass, he lifted it and handed it to her.

Charlie dropped his fork again.

"What the hell?" Father said, staring Charlie down.

"You don't need to treat her like that. If you want your whiskey, you can get it yourself," Charlie said, voice low, eyes downcast.

"What the hell you just say to me, boy?"

Charlie brought the palms of his hands to his cheeks and rubbed his face. He looked his father directly in the eye and said, "You can get your whiskey yourself. Mom deserves to have a nice dinner. Uninterrupted."

"Charles!" Mother exclaimed, fear creeping into her countenance.

"It's okay, Mom," Charlie said as Father simultaneously yelled, "Shut the hell up, woman!" and looked at his son across the table. "How dare you disrespect me like that, boy?"

Charlie sat erect in his chair. Susan could sense his perturbation, but he held firm, eyes holding onto Father's, daring, beckoning.

Father's chair scraped against the floor as he swiftly stood. He quickened his steps behind Mother to lunge at his son. He grabbed onto the collar of Charlie's supermarket shirt and firmly pulled him to his feet.

Charlie's fists were balled at his thighs, a grunt escaping his throat with the force of Father's haul.

Mother gasped. Susan shook. Neither dared intervene.

Charlie's arms went to protect his head as Father's fists hit their marks. Charlie suddenly jerked to his full height, much taller than Father himself, and pushed Father with extreme force, both hands to the chest. Father was propelled backward, falling to land on his bottom on the floor. He sat there stupefied for a moment, looking up at his son, who towered over him, jaw clenched, heaving heavy breaths. A small stream of blood ran from Charlie's temple to his cheek.

"Get out of my house." Words spoken slowly, deliberately, and with extreme malice. "Today I lost my son. You are nothing to me now. Never did please me, did you? And now this?" His eyes didn't leave Charlie's. "Get out."

"Gerald!" Mother was horrified. She stood from her chair, hands on her stomach. She looked as though she'd be sick. Susan's tears began.

Mother was quieted from just one threatening look from her husband. She slowly sat back down.

Charlie went to his bedroom, grabbed his school books, put a few changes of clothes into a bag, and then reentered the kitchen, where Father had lifted himself from the floor and was now smoking feverishly on another cigarette, gazing out the window while holding a full glass of whiskey. He refused to look at Charlie.

Mother's legs wouldn't listen to her desperate pleas to stand. She sat convulsing in her chair. Charlie walked over to her and kissed her on the cheek. A torrent of Mother's tears dropped to stain her blouse.

Susan stood. Charlie walked her way and then embraced her firmly. "I'll be at Henry's," he whispered. "Tell Mom when this asshole isn't around." He let go, looking down into her overflowing eyes. Another embrace and a whispered "I love you, Susie T." The term of endearment sent her over the precipice. She collapsed back into her chair, covered her eyes with the palms of her hands, and bawled.

Charlie left the house. Father only took his eyes from the window when the door slammed so he didn't have to look at the retreating figure of a young man whom he had only moments before called his son.

* * *

Bedtime.

Susan changed her sanitary pad in the bathroom and brushed her teeth. When she emerged, she found Mother sitting on the couch gazing at the blank screen of the television set, the glow from the moon the only illumination in the stuffy room.

Father was nowhere to be seen.

She walked forward and took her mother's hand. Mother gazed at her wretchedly, with a puffy red face. A tenebrous air enveloped her, weighed her down.

"I'm going to bed," Susan said.

"Don't forget your prayers." Mother's hand was limp in her own. Susan let it go and watched it flop to her side. Mother stared beyond her.

Susan sighed. She looked above Mother at the picture in the moonlight that her mother had given to her husband back on a Christmas morning many years ago. A photo of the two of them on their wedding day. Father was leaning into Mother. Mother was smiling shyly. Happily. Contentedly.

Susan stood there for a moment. As Mother stared at the blank television screen, she gazed at every minor detail in the photograph. She looked at the large, light headband upon Mother's head, the veil that cascaded down her shoulders and back. She studied the subtle silk dress that rose to the divot at the base of her throat. Pearly beaded buttons running down the length of her dress to her navel. Long, thick sleeves. She looked at her father, handsome and young. His hair slicked to the side but stylish. Fuller. His dark tuxedo and light pressed shirt. His solid-colored tie, dark against light in the black-and-white photograph of their younger days.

They look so happy.

Susan walked to her room in a stupor. She knelt at the side of her bed, folded her hands before her. Then she listlessly stood and climbed under her blanket. Tonight would mark the first time she would fall asleep without having said her prayers.

TWELVE

Susan couldn't concentrate in school the following day. She was cognizant of the fact that she was tempting the wrath of Sister Gertrude, but for the first time, she simply couldn't be bothered to care. Concern for her brother's well-being overwhelmed all other anxiety.

At the day's end, Janet and Betty walked her to the beginning of Brown Avenue.

"Tell us about your brother tomorrow," Janet said.

"I will," Susan promised.

Betty threw her arms around her friend and hugged her tightly.

Mrs. Beaumont answered her knock at the door. Susan walked in and found her brother on the large couch to her right facing the stairwell.

Mother was by his side.

Charlie stood and walked toward Susan. She lunged at him, jumped into his embrace. He held her aloft, his arms encircling her waist. Her tears wet his brown hair, which he'd been wearing longer lately. Yet another area of contention between him and Father.

"Charlie, I'm so glad to see you!" she exclaimed.

"Me, too, Susie." Charlie gently placed her feet back on the floor.

"Mom, you're here."

"Yes," Mother acknowledged. "I only just arrived a few minutes ago."

"I really wanted to see you," Susan said to her brother as he led the way back to the couch where Mother remained seated, ankles crossed and knees leaning to the side. "I need to know you're okay."

"I'm okay," Charlie assured her.

Susan reached to touch the side of his left eye. It was still a bit puffy and raised and was turning from red to a dark purple color. Susan knew the look well. There was a slight tear in the skin, this the source of the blood that had trickled down his cheek last night.

He winced when her finger grazed the sore.

"It hurts?" Susan asked, concerned.

"Yeah."

Mrs. Beaumont had arrived from the kitchen, a cup of hot coffee in her hand. She held it out to Mother, who brought it to her lips and sipped, then cradled the mug in the palms of her hands, resting it upon her lap.

"Charlie, I miss you. I know you've only been gone for a day, but I miss you. It's just not the same in the house without you there."

Charlie looked over at his sister and smiled dispiritedly. "I miss you, too, Susan. But this is better for me right now. I'm comfortable here. I really am. I'm happy here. I'm only concerned for you and Mom."

Susan reached over and threaded her arm through his. "Charlie, I just love you so much. And you're hurt and you're gone and you're not home with me and you're not around. I don't know what to do. I'm glad you're here, though. I'll come and see you whenever I can."

"So will I," Mother said. "Charles, I am so sorry this has happened to you. I'm not that strong. I'm just not that strong." Her shoulders began to shake, and she bowed her head to her chest as she cried.

When Mother's body had calmed, Charlie placed his fingers under her chin, gently lifting her face to look into his, mimicking the gesture she had often made toward him. Her blue eyes were watery and red, her lashes shining from the tears that clung.

"You are the strongest woman I have ever met." Charlie was unyielding in his conviction. He wiped a tear from his mother's cheek.

They spoke for a while longer, and then Charlie wrote down his most recent schedule at the supermarket. Susan promised to hide it in her closet so Father wouldn't discover their excursions to the Beaumonts'. They embraced, said their goodbyes, and Mother and Susan left the house.

* * *

It was Saturday. Christmas Day 1965. Susan typically woke from slumber on this particular holiday morning with such elation, such hope and anticipation, but today she remained in bed until Mother knocked lightly on her door and stepped inside.

"Susan, darling," she said. "It is getting late now. It is Christmas morning. Come out to the living room. We will open some gifts, and then I will make a nice Christmas breakfast for us all."

"Can I sleep for just a little bit longer?"

"Not today. Come on out."

Susan reluctantly climbed out of bed and followed Mother into the living room where Father was already sitting, dressed, on the green couch. *The Andy Williams Christmas Album* was playing "It's the Most Wonderful Time of the Year" on the family's record player, upbeat and optimistic. The irony didn't elude Susan, and she disagreed vehemently. This most certainly was not the most wonderful time of the year. Her brother was gone.

She sat on the floor in her pajamas. Mother, too, was still in her nightclothes.

Father stood and walked over to the Christmas tree, bending at the waist to inspect a strand of lights. He repositioned them to his liking and sat back down upon the couch to light a morning cigarette.

Susan opened a few gifts from Mother without much enthusiasm. She then watched her mother open the bottle of lavender cologne.

"Susan, this is wonderful," Mother said, "The First Noel" soft in the background. "Thank you very much."

Susan handed another wrapped gift to Mother. "It's for you both," she said.

"Gerald, would you like to open this one?" Mother asked.

Father placed the waning cigarette between his lips and unwrapped the thin square package, revealing the Frank Sinatra record Charlie had found at Woolworth's.

"Very nice," Father said between clenched lips, cigarette bobbing up and down.

"Oh, Susan, that is wonderful. Thank you. You certainly do know the kind of music we prefer to listen to."

"Charlie found it." She didn't know why she announced this. She simply felt compelled to do so. Somebody had to mention the absence of her brother.

Father grimaced and handed the album to Mother. She took it from him and rested it upon her lap, caressing the front cover.

"Helen, I'm hungry."

Mother set the album aside and stood. "I'll start breakfast."

* * *

Breakfast was a somber, rather silent affair. Mother attempted small talk but to no avail, receiving monosyllabic answers in reply to any question she asked. Susan helped her clear the table, and as Mother washed the dishes in the sink, she dried. Father sat at the table with his second cup of coffee and another cigarette, browsing through yesterday's newspaper. He still preferred his newspapers as a means of keeping up with the times: it had been a ritual since she was a small child, probably longer, and if anyone had difficulty with change, it was Father.

"Are you okay?" Susan eyed her mother's forlorn expression, her lethargic movements.

In extremely hushed tones she whispered, "I just cannot pretend. Not today. I want to see my son. My heart aches that at this very moment he is happy in another woman's home."

While we're here, Susan thought.

THIRTEEN

C hristmas passed. New Year's, too. January began, and Susan returned to school and Sister Gertrude's seventh grade classroom. She returned, also, to her friends.

"Come for a slumber party tonight," Janet said to Susan and Betty on their way home from school on a Friday afternoon.

"Oh," Betty said, "I'd love to. Let me just ask my mom. I'm sure she'll say yes."

"I don't know if I can, but I'd definitely like to," Susan said.

"Okay," Janet said. "Both of you ask your parents and then call me to let me know if you can come."

Susan and Betty assured her they would.

Susan walked into the house, but Mother was not in the kitchen. This perplexed Susan as Mother was often found in the kitchen when she knew Susan was due back from school. And she knew also that Charlie was working today, so she wouldn't be over at the Beaumonts'.

"Mom?" she called.

No answer.

Susan dropped her book bag and lunch sack and walked farther into the kitchen, then on through to the living room. Mother wasn't there.

Not in the bathroom.

Not in Charlie's room.

Susan opened the small French double doors to Mother and Father's room and crept inside. The curtains were drawn, and her eyes took time to adjust to the darkness within. Mother was sleeping.

She sat on the side of the bed and touched her mother's shoulder. "Mom?" When she didn't get an answer, she shook her gently. "Mom?" she asked again.

"Mmmm."

"Mom, are you okay? It's the middle of the day. I just got home from school."

"Oh, oh, yes. I am all right. I was just sleepy. I just needed some sleep."

"Would you like to get up, or are you not feeling well?"

"No, no," she said. "I am fine. I will get up." She began to rise, but her head hit the pillow once again. "Just so sleepy."

"That's okay, Mom."

"Your father." She was mumbling into the pillow. "Your father will want dinner."

"I can make dinner, Mom."

"Yes, yes," she said almost incoherently. "That's good." Her eyes were closed, the blanket pulled up to her chin.

Susan walked to her bedroom. She sat down on her bed and sighed. She picked up a copy of Lloyd Alexander's *The Black Cauldron* that she had borrowed from the library from her nightstand and riffled through the pages. Perhaps she could get a start on reading before the kitchen beckoned to her? She'd like nothing more than to lose herself in these pages and plummet into the world of Prydain.

When she next took a look at the little clock upon her nightstand, she was surprised to see that the time said 4:34. She should have known that she seldom had the ability to read just a few pages in a book.

Father stepped into the house almost exactly at 5:00. He halted as he saw Susan stirring soup upon the stove. "Where's your mother?"

"Not feeling well," Susan said.

Father started for the bedroom.

"Oh, no," Susan stopped him. "It's okay. Please, can we let her sleep? I've got this."

Her father looked at her skeptically, but as long as he got his dinner, he didn't so much care if it was his wife or his daughter who made it. He sat in his seat at the table. "Better be good," he said. "And I'll take my whiskey."

She had forgotten. She attempted to mask her irritability as she poured her father's drink.

Susan set the table for two and placed a steaming bowl of soup in front of her father. She helped herself back at the stove and sat down.

"Um," she said. "Should we pray?"

Father looked at her expectantly. She folded her hands before her, nodded her head, and closed her eyes.

"Bless us, Lord, for this food we are about to receive. In Christ's name we pray. Amen."

She opened her eyes and looked at her father, who had already taken up his spoon and begun to eat. She did the same. His eyes were on his bowl and then on his glass of whiskey; she assumed he didn't want to engage in small talk, which was all the better for her as she really didn't even know what to say.

The phone began to ring.

"Jesus Christ," Father said, annoyed, "who could that be?"

"Oh," Susan said as it dawned on her that she had never called Janet as she had promised. "I think that might be Janet."

"You'll have to call her back."

"Yes, sir."

The remainder of the meal was eaten in silence. Once Father had finished, Susan cleared his bowl and began on the dishes.

"Father?" she said, turning around to look at him.

"Mmm?"

"Janet was hoping that Betty and I could go for a slumber party tonight. At her home."

"Yeah?"

"May I go?" she asked with unease.

"Makes no matter to me. But you do those dishes. And if your mother still isn't feeling well in the morning, I want you here to make breakfast."

"Yes, sir." She turned back to the sink, a smile on her face. She was going to her first slumber party!

When all the dishes were done and the table and countertops were clean, Susan picked up the telephone receiver in the kitchen to call Janet as Father worked his way to the living room couch to watch TV.

Susan hung the phone up and walked to her room. She emerged a few minutes later with pajamas and a change of clothes stuffed inside her pillowcase along with the pillow and went to the bathroom to get her toothbrush. She put this, too, inside her pillowcase and then stopped to stand in the doorway to the kitchen.

"Father?"

"Mmm?" He didn't lift his eyes from the television set before him.

"I'm leaving now," she said. "For Janet's."

"Mmm," he mumbled.

"Okay, bye." She slipped her boots on when she got to the porch and left the house before Father could change his mind, not even bothering to put her coat on. Moments later she knocked on Janet's front door.

"EE!" Janet squealed. "You're here!"

Susan entered the warm house, took her boots off, and followed Janet to her bedroom, where Betty was sprawled out on the bed, dark strands of hair a mess upon a bright orange-and-yellow-flowered pillow.

"Hi, Susie," she said. "It took you so long. But Janet told me that your mom's not feeling well. Sorry."

"Thanks," Susan said, placing her pillow down on the floor and sitting on the bed. "What are you doing?" she asked as a means of diverting the conversation in a much more positive and encouraging direction.

"Honestly?" Janet asked.

"Of course," Susan said.

"We were talking about making out and who we'd want to do it with."

Susan blushed. "You were?"

"Mmm-hmmm," Betty said. "Who do you think is hunky, Susie?"

"I hadn't really thought about it."

"Sure you have," said Janet. "Who do you think?" she pressed.

"Really, I don't know." Admittedly, she had begun to notice boys, to think of them in a different light these past months, but it just wasn't a topic of conversation she was fully comfortable with, even with her coconspirators being her two best girlfriends.

"Well," said Janet, "I was talking about Dave Hubert."

"Dave Hubert?" Susan asked. "Really?"

"Really," Janet said. "He's dreamy. Just look at those eyes. They look like melting chocolate. I wish he'd stare at me with them."

This was news to Susan. This was a conversation that she, Janet, and Betty had never had together. Was it possible that Janet and Betty had spoken of such things when Susan was not around? She supposed it was. Perhaps they were simply ahead of the times and Susan was being left in the dust, a little girl still.

"And his hair," Janet continued. "Those dark curls. I think of how they'd feel sometimes if I touched them. Do you think they're all soft?"

"I think they'd be soft," Betty said.

Susan sat on the edge of the bed, silent.

"And Betty was talking about…" Janet looked at her friend teasingly. Both she and Betty turned their heads to Susan.

"What?" Susan asked. Where was this going?

"There's a boy that I think is super cute," Betty said. "But I don't know if I should tell you."

"Why wouldn't you tell me?" Susan asked, truly dumbfounded.

"Because of who it is," Betty said.

"She just doesn't want to make you uncomfortable," Janet offered.

Susan stared at Betty.

"Oh, okay," Betty said. Then, after a pause, "It's Charlie."

Susan was silent for a moment, letting this new information take hold. "You mean my brother Charlie?" she asked, shocked.

"Your brother," Janet said as she playfully pushed Susan's shoulder. "What do you think of that?"

Susan didn't know what to think or even what to say, just sat there with her mouth slightly open.

"Say something," Betty pleaded.

"I…" Susan said. "I'm just really surprised. My brother?" She crinkled her nose.

The girls laughed at her reaction.

"Yes, your brother," Betty said. "He's really handsome, Susie. Especially with those freckles on his cheeks—they're really cute. You probably just don't see it because he's your brother."

"Yeah," Susan agreed, "I guess not. But," she added, "my brother?" Janet and Betty both laughed again, and Susan found a smile.

"I've got another one," Janet said.

"Who is it?" asked Betty.

"Henry."

"Henry who?" asked Susan.

"Henry Beaumont, silly. I saw him the other day. I hadn't seen him around in a while. He's gotten so tall and he's so handsome."

"Yeah," said Betty. "I can see that."

"Henry?" Susan asked. "Henry's got a girlfriend."

"I'm not saying I'm going to break them up so I can go steady with him," Janet teased. "I'm just saying he's a hunk."

"Really?" Susan asked.

"Yeah! Really handsome. And nice, too. He said hi to me and he's got those hazelish eyes, but they've got yellow in them, too. And they're big and he's got these really long and thick eyelashes. And his nose. It's cute," Janet crooned. "And I think he might have muscles. You can kind of just tell."

Susan's eyes had gone wide.

"Who knows, maybe one day Susan will marry him? Her brother's best friend? How cool would that be?" If Betty's intention had been to make her good friend blush, then she had succeeded.

Janet saw the look upon Susan's face. "She's just joking. Although," she added, "it would be kind of perfect." She laughed at the color rising even brighter on Susan's face, then reached over Betty and grabbed a pillow.

"Hey!" Betty exclaimed just before the pillow hit her head. "Oof!"

Janet's giggles were contagious. Betty grabbed a pillow and returned the blow. Janet erupted in laughter. She hit Susan on the chest and sent her tumbling to the floor from her precarious position on the edge of the bed. Susan had stumbled right next to the pillow she had brought from home. She emptied her effects from the pillowcase and brought the pillow forcefully upon Janet's back.

"Hey!" Janet yelled as she continuously laughed with pleasure.

The conversation of just moments ago was left in the past as the girls swung their pillows around. The strands of Susan's curls became staticky and floated in the air, wild and carefree. Betty's dark cheeks were flushed with exertion, and Janet's teeth shone in her enormous smile.

Spent, they eventually lay together on the bed, staring at the ceiling.

"You're my best friends," Janet said. "Promise me we'll be friends forever."

"Friends forever," Susan and Betty said simultaneously.

FOURTEEN

J uly 20, 1969, had been a hot, humid day, the high reaching 81 degrees in Susan's small New Hampshire hometown. She began her day at church with her family and then headed to the local nursing home, at which she had recently procured a part-time summer position. She was almost sixteen, after all, and it was time she began to make her way in the world. Father had no objection to Susan's part-time work as long as she was home to help Mother with the chores around the house. Mother had dropped her off for a short shift as her parents weren't planning on spending time with family after church this day. Unfortunately, Susan's place of employment was not within walking distance, so Mother had to pick her up as well when her shift was through. Father had gone fishing, his companion retrieving him from the house once he returned from church that morning.

Charlie was nineteen now, twenty in a couple of months, and Susan thought he had matured into quite the handsome man. Together, after her shift was over, she and Mother stopped by to see him in the new home he shared with Henry, just about a mile and a half away. Their visit would have to be a quick one; Father would expect them home.

"Are you watching tonight?" Susan asked.

"Of course!" Charlie said. "How can I not? A moon landing?

Honestly never thought I'd see something like this with my own eyes, really. I'm shocked it can even be done, but it looks like they're going to make it. Incredible to me."

"It really is incredible," Susan said. "Airplanes are incredible enough, but for this big, huge spacecraft to actually leave Earth, go into space, and for a part of the craft to land on the moon?" She shook her head. "I can't wait. I just wish I were watching it with you."

"Why don't you? Father's known for a while now that you come and see me. He may not know about you, Mom, but he knows about you, Susie. Come and watch it with us. There's someone I want to introduce you to anyway."

"Thanks, Charlie, but I can't leave Mom."

"Of course you can," Mother said. "I will be so pleased to know that my two children can experience something as momentous as this together. I will watch it at home with your father."

"Mom, really? I can be there with you if you'd like me to be."

"No, no," Mother dismissed the sentiment. "Charles, as long as you can pick Susan up and take her home later tonight when all is through, then I would love nothing more than the two of you having this time together."

"Thanks, Mom," Susan said.

"Charles, I am so very happy to see you and to see that you are doing well. Susan, we must go home now. Your father will be wondering where we have gone off to. He knows what time I left the house to get you from work. I do not believe he is home just now from his fishing trip but he may try to call, nonetheless."

"I know," Susan said dejectedly. She didn't see her brother nearly as often as she would have liked. Not now that he worked full-time during the week. And with Father refusing her permission to use the telephone to call his house, it was rather hard to schedule meeting times together.

"I'll meet you outside the house at 3:30, Susie. That gives you all enough time, right, Mom?"

"That should be okay."

Susan and Mother exited the small home and walked to their waiting car, the same car the family had had when Susan was a small child, much more beaten and weathered from the years now than it had been back then.

Upon their arrival home, Susan walked next door to Janet's house, as she had promised the previous day she would visit.

Janet opened the door when Susan knocked. "Come on in," she said. "I love that dress on you, Susie." The past year had seen Janet mature into a young woman with a sense of style; her adoration for clothes and makeup were apparent in every choice she made in adorning herself, so Susan thought the comment ungenuine but polite as she was wearing quite a plain dress of blue and white. Janet, on the other hand, thrived on color. Her thin brunette hair was longer now, down past her shoulder blades, and she wore it loosely around her head. She wore a pair of navy-blue flare-legged polyester pants and a nylon shirt of swirling colors in bright red, blue, black, and yellow with a matching belt that she had tied tightly around her thin waist.

Susan stood in the doorway of Janet's house, looking upon her good friend and contemplating the fact that, based on appearance alone, they were such different creatures. Susan mirrored her mother with a smaller stature, thin waist, large breasts, thick thighs, and an unruly mass of tight auburn curls.

"Thanks," Susan said. "You look wonderful. As always." She smiled and walked in the door. "But aren't you hot?" She looked down at the thick pants her friend wore.

"I'm actually not. I was wearing a skirt earlier but took it off. I'd better not be coming down with something. Bobby and I are supposed to go out tomorrow night. He's taking me to some friend's house to meet some college kids. They've got a little weed. I bet Bobby'll get blitzed and they'll talk about Vietnam. He's wicked against the war, and he's been teaching me all sorts of things, Susie. Oh, come have something to drink, silly. We're just standing here talking."

Susan walked farther inside, and she and Janet entered the kitchen to get bottles of Coca-Cola from the deep yellow refrigerator.

Janet popped the caps off with a bottle opener she'd taken from the silverware drawer next to the fridge. "Cheers," she said, clinking bottles with Susan.

"Ah," Janet said after her first large swallow of the fizzy liquid, "now that's good."

"Sure is," Susan said as they walked into the living room and sat down on the Bouchers' new couch, a synthetic-velour wingback sofa, beige and brown floral designs set atop a background of mid-tone tan.

"So," Janet continued, "you know Bobby's brother is off fighting, right?" Susan nodded. "I know you don't listen to the news very often, but it's so important, Susie. I've heard so many stories about boys coming home completely messed up, and all for what? Nothing. We shouldn't be over there, Susie. I didn't see it, but Bobby was telling me about Cronkite back last year, wintertime; he went to Vietnam, you know. He was always telling people that he supported the war, but then he saw what was going on over there and it wasn't what Johnson was telling us was going on. And he changed his mind. He said the only way the war would end would be to negotiate. And to negotiate not as the winners of the war, either. He doesn't think it can be won. We shouldn't be there," she repeated. "So, yeah, we're getting together tomorrow night and I'll meet his friends. But not if I'm coming down with something, so hope for me." She smiled. They clinked glasses.

They passed slightly less than an hour together, Janet mostly talking of Bobby and Vietnam, Susan listening intently.

"I've got to go," Susan said. "I need to make sure Mom is all set with everything before I go to Charlie's."

Susan left and walked home, where she made herself a sandwich to appease her appetite since she hadn't eaten lunch and then, ensuring all was good with Mother, walked outside.

"Hop on in," Charlie said a few minutes later as he pulled up in his hunter green Austin Mini Cooper, a car he had bought used a couple of years ago to help him get to and from work.

Susan climbed into the passenger seat of the car, and they drove the few minutes to Charlie's home.

"Hi, Susan." It was Mrs. Beaumont. Susan hadn't realized the Beaumonts would be at the home Charlie and Henry shared this afternoon, but she welcomed the fact that they were.

"Hi, Mrs. Beaumont," she said.

"Susan, I really do think it's about time you called me Viola. We've known each other for years now, ever since you were a little girl, and I certainly don't think of you as being a little girl anymore. Viola, please."

"I'll try," Susan said. It had been instilled within her to treat her elders with the utmost respect, and to call Mrs. Beaumont by her Christian name would have been frowned upon in her household. But it was respectful, too, to adhere to her wishes. It would take some getting used to, and it was a source of discomfort, but she would try.

She walked farther into the room, closing the door behind her. Henry's bedroom door was to her right, her brother's just beyond that, with the television set on the wall between the two. The couch rested against the left-hand wall and faced the TV. The kitchen entryway stood ahead of Susan at the back of the house.

"Welcome, Susie." Henry walked merrily into the living room, a large grin on his face, his father by his side. Through the years she had noticed how comfortable and at ease Henry was with his father. She wished she had the same relationship with her own.

"Hi, Susan," Mr. Beaumont said.

"Hi, Henry, Mr. Beaumont."

Another figure entered the room. He was tall, though not as tall as either Charlie or Henry. His dark hair was thick, shorter on the sides and longer on top. His skin was tanned and blemish-free, his nose the perfect length and width for his high cheekbones and pronounced jaw. His eyes were the clearest shade of blue, striking a dramatic contrast with his dark hair, thick eyebrows, and plentiful eyelashes. His lips were pink and full. Susan was taken aback.

He was gorgeous.

"Susie, I want you to meet Gilbert." Charlie walked over to this newcomer and placed an arm around Gilbert's shoulder. "I think Gilbert's going to be around for a bit, and I want him to meet my best girl." He winked over at Susan.

"Nice to meet you, Susie." Gilbert extended his hand, but Susan was so affected by his presence that she couldn't manage to reciprocate. She willed herself to lift her arm, just to lift it a bit and he could take over, but her efforts were futile.

"Earth to Susan," Charlie said.

Susan broke from her reverie and found her voice. "Nice to meet you, too." Oh, my gosh, had her voice broken on the last word? Please, let her act cool. Please!

"Apparently my sister's shy in your presence, Gil," Charlie teased, and to Susan's absolute mortification, she felt her face pool with blood.

"Susie, want anything to eat?" Henry. Blessed Henry!

"Um," Susan managed, "sure."

"Right over here." Henry took her aside to a small table that had been erected to the side of the couch. "Mom made these." Henry

176

pointed to baked mushroom caps stuffed with cheese and finely diced pecans.

"Then I'll have to have some," Susan said. She felt very much back to her typical self here with Henry.

Susan took a paper plate and placed some of each offering upon it; she found that she was still hungry after the small sandwich she had eaten not long ago. Henry, by her side still, piled food upon a plate for himself as well.

"You're hungry," Susan teased.

"Always." Henry smiled down at her. He *was* a handsome man, wasn't he? No Gilbert, mind you, but quite handsome nonetheless.

The television set was on, the sound muted in the background with the conversations of the merry people taking precedence in the small space. "Everyday People" sung by Sly and the Family Stone was playing softly on the record player near the front door.

"Viola—" Susan still found the informal address uncomfortable—"these mushrooms are great."

"Oh, wait," Mr. Beaumont said, "Viola are we now? If you're Viola, then I'm James. It's always felt weird for me to be a Mr. Beaumont anyway. Mr. Beaumont is my father. And my father is old." James guffawed at his own joke.

"Listen up, everyone," Charlie announced, "it looks like they're making their way down." He turned the volume up on the television, and Henry took the needle off the record. Viola and James sat down on the couch, followed by Henry. Susan sat at Henry's feet on the floor, and Charlie and Gilbert sat beside her.

The television screen quickly went to a shot at Disneyland in California—too quick, really, for Susan to make much out other than the throng of congregated people and a tall structure in the background. The counter on the screen stated there were four and half minutes left until lunar landing. Four and a half minutes until a truly historical moment that Susan would experience along with countless others around the world.

Three and a half minutes.

Susan saw the surface of the moon, crater-filled.

"A go for landing, three thousand feet." The moment was near!

Two thousand feet.

Five hundred forty feet.

She had difficulty understanding the transmission, but saw now that there was a clear shot of the module descending. It appeared so close! And what was that ball in the background? Was that the sun? She made a mental note to ask Charlie later.

Seventy-five feet.

Sixty seconds.

"The *Eagle* has landed."

The room erupted in cheers.

"Hot diggity dog!" James whooped. "Never thought I'd see a day like this. On the damn moon, I tell ya! The moon!" His grin was wide, white teeth gleaming.

Viola had her hands clasped in front of her chin. "Whoo!" she exclaimed.

Charlie's arm was around Gilbert's shoulder. Henry was clapping him on the back.

Charlie turned left to look at his sister. "They made it," he said, smile enormous.

"They made it."

Susan and the rest of the party continued to express their awe and appreciation for this momentous event. She stood and picked a few more snacks from the side table to bring back to the floor with her as they watched some movement within the module.

Gilbert leaned forward and spoke in front of Charlie. "Susie, Charlie's told me so much about you. I'm really glad I'm finally meeting you."

Finally?

Susan's mouth was full of cracker and spread, so she smiled awkwardly as she chewed and swallowed. What a fantastic time for Gilbert to speak with her, catching her with her mouth stuffed. Nice!

She looked at his lips rather than attempting to gaze into his eyes; she feared if she did that, she wouldn't be able to look away.

"I'm glad to meet you, too." By golly, she had done it! She *could* speak.

"Only good things, Susie," Charlie said. "I don't think I'd ever be able to say anything bad about you."

"Oh, yeah," Gilbert affirmed, "only good things. He's told me about growing up with you. About your parents and about how wonderful you are."

What was it that Charlie had said about their father? How much did this Gilbert know?

Susan could only manage a smile.

"So, you're fifteen?" he asked.

"Sixteen next month. Charlie was born in September, so we were always celebrating just a few weeks away from each other."

"Yes, September sixth."

Susan nodded. He even knew Charlie's birthday?

"How old are you?" she asked.

"I'm twenty-one. My birthday's not until April, though.

Gosh, he was dreamy. She made the mistake of looking into his eyes and found herself momentarily mute.

"Going into eleventh at St. Joseph's?"

She nodded.

"I have a cousin going into twelfth. She goes to your church. Sandy Speckles?"

Whoa. Sandy Speckles was Gilbert's cousin? Sandy Speckles, the girl with glasses (although no longer purple) and a friend of Mercedes Doyle?

"She's your cousin?"

"She is." Gilbert smiled. "We're pretty close, actually. Her mother is my mother's sister, and they're the best of friends, always have been, so Sandy and I have practically grown up together. Great girl, Sandy."

Susan pondered that for a moment. "I don't really know her."

"I'm trying to convince Charlie to allow me and Henry to throw him a birthday party. I'll have Sandy come along."

"Okay," Susan said rather hesitantly.

Conversation continued to flow: spirits were high.

At around 10:40 that night Susan watched with her companions as Neil Armstrong slowly made his way out of an opening in the spacecraft and walked down a ladder.

She could see his feet, then his legs!

"So that's a foot on the moon, stepping down on the moon." It was Cronkite announcing.

She could see him now, the astronaut, walking slowly away from the craft, his large suit thick on his body.

A man on the moon! There was an actual, living man on the moon! They had done it!

"That's one small step for man... one giant leap for mankind." Cronkite didn't fully understand the last portion of Neil Armstrong's words, but Susan had. Oh, she had understood, and wasn't that the simple but amazing truth?

Cheers around her. Excitement. Awe. She sat on the floor in front of the television set and let a tear trickle down her cheek. That the human race was capable of such a feat was beyond her comprehension but completely inspiring. A man on the moon? What could we do next if we actually had a man walking on the moon at this very moment she sat between the walls of her brother's house? She, here in her small community; Armstrong, there on the surface of the moon. Possibilities were endless. The world, she thought for the first time in her life, truly was enormous, was it not? And what did it hold in store for her?

Charlie drove Susan back home not long after Armstrong set foot upon the moon's surface; she was quite tired after a very exhilarating day.

He idled in front of the house, the low thrum of the engine discernable in the quiet of the dark night.

"What a day, huh?"

"Yeah, it really was. I'm still kind of shocked."

"So am I," Charlie said. "Hey, Susie?"

"Yeah?"

"I'm glad you were there with us tonight."

"Me, too. Love you, Charlie," she said as she leaned over and kissed him on the cheek.

* * *

Henry and Gilbert had indeed convinced Charlie to have a birthday party, for here she was, Janet and Betty by her side, as she walked out to the small backyard of her brother's home. Charlie had told her to bring friends along, that he didn't want this day to be so much about him as just simply an excuse to get good people together to have a good time.

Creedence Clearwater Revival was playing, music loud enough to be heard over the hubbub of happy partygoers who had already arrived.

"Hey, look who's here," Charlie said as he spotted Susan and her friends. "It's the best sister in the world." Charlie was overzealous in manner, which led Susan to believe that his spirits were truly elevated today.

Charlie walked over to her, placed his arm around her shoulder. "Welcome, welcome," he said exuberantly.

"Thanks," Susan said. She laughed as she looked up into her brother's green eyes, corners crinkled with the force of his large smile.

Gilbert walked over. "Hi, Susie," he said. "I'm glad to see you again." Susan had in fact seen Gilbert several times since their first introduction; he had been at Charlie and Henry's house almost every time she'd been to visit, and with time she'd learned how to speak to him without hesitation or timidity. Once she was able to relax in his presence, she learned that she really did like him quite a lot and saw why Charlie was such good friends with him now.

"Hi, Gil," Susan said.

"Who are your friends?" he asked.

"This is Betty"— Susan motioned to the dark-haired girl by her side—"and this is Janet."

Gilbert shook hands with each girl and expressed pleasantries upon introduction.

"I see Ma Tante," Susan said. "I'm going to go say hello. See you both in a bit."

Susan began walking toward Ma Tante Alice. Charlie had maintained a close relationship with his mother's sister and her husband, and Susan felt no surprise whatsoever at their presence at his party. Janet and Betty followed by her side.

"You weren't kidding," Betty said. "Wow!"

"I know," Susan said. "But he's a really nice guy."

"I'm not thinking about him being a nice guy, Susie," Janet said, "I'm thinking about running my hands through that hair of his!"

Susan giggled and lifted her eyebrows. "I know!"

"You've got Bobby," Betty interjected. "I'm not taken. I'll take him anytime!"

The girls laughed as they approached Susan's aunt.

"So good to see you, Susan," Ma Tante said as she embraced her niece.

"You, too, Ma Tante. No Ellie?"

"Not today. Paul and I are actually here alone. We're going out to dinner afterward. A much-needed date."

Mon Oncle approached, two plastic cups filled with red liquid in his hands, one of which he offered to Ma Tante.

"That's right," he said. "Cheers to us." He and Ma Tante clinked cups.

"Sweet sixteen now, Susan," Ma Tante said. "Are you excited?"

"I kind of am," Susan admitted. "I know it was just another day and another year, but sixteen is kind of a big deal and I can't believe it, that I'm sixteen now."

"Neither can I," Ma Tante said. "It just means that I'm that much older."

"But beautiful," Mon Oncle said.

"Leave it to you, Paul," Ma Tante said, rolling her eyes. "Always the flatterer."

Ma Tante was getting older—this was fact—but where Mother's wrinkles were pronounced, her skin a pasty pallor, her aura one of defeat, Ma Tante was quite the opposite. Her skin was still very pale and she certainly had wrinkles, but they added sophistication as opposed to sickliness. Her hair was still luxuriant, not much gray added within the auburn, her presence still self-assured.

Susan and the girls spoke with Ma Tante and Mon Oncle for a while longer until she felt a tapping upon her shoulder. Gilbert stood by her side, Sandy Speckles next to him.

"May I interrupt?" he asked politely.

"Of course," Ma Tante said. "Paul and I were just going to get something to eat." She led her husband away.

"I know you've gone to church together—school, too. So Sandy tells me anyway. But I know that you don't know each other well, so I thought I'd make a sort of formal introduction. Susan, Sandy. Sandy, Susan." Susan smiled uncertainly but noticed that Sandy was doing much the same.

"Hi," Sandy said.

"Hi," said Susan.

"And these are Susan's friends," said Gilbert, "Betty and Janet. Did I get that right?"

"Sure did," Janet said.

"I'll leave you to it," Gilbert said. He turned and walked away.

Susan honestly didn't know what to say to this girl who stood before her. Luckily Janet was an extrovert, and where Susan was uncomfortable, she was not.

"So, what are you doing here?" she asked not unkindly. "How do you know Gilbert?

"Gilbert is my cousin," Sandy said demurely. "I see him all the time."

"Cousins?" Janet said. "Are all the girls crazy about him? He's a hunk for sure!"

Sandy visually relaxed at this comment and at Janet's playful tone. "Yeah," she said. "All the time. If we're out somewhere together—our families do dinner out a lot—then all the girls are staring at him. He may be my cousin, but even I can see he's a hunk." She giggled.

Susan smiled, though she was still a bit uncomfortable to be a part of this conversation.

"Well, you know," Betty interjected, "if Gilbert doesn't have a girlfriend, then he can look my way." She blushed at her own joke, but it made the girls laugh.

"Honestly, if he weren't my cousin, I'd be looking, too," Sandy said. There was a slight lull in the conversation, and Sandy looked to Susan. She took a deep breath and upon exhalation said, "Susan, I have to ask you something."

Susan immediately became apprehensive. Ask her something? But why? She gave a slight nod of the head.

"Did you tell Mercedes Doyle a couple years ago that she would never win over your brother? That she was ugly and not good enough?"

Susan was so incredibly taken aback that she couldn't utter a single word in her defense.

"What?" demanded Janet. "Susan would never say something like that. What kind of ditz does Mercedes Doyle have to be to spread a lie like that?"

"She told me and Barbara Metcalf that you said that. Back when she was trying to get your brother to ask her out. She's always liked boys, even when I still thought they had cooties, and she liked your brother most of all. Didn't you know?"

Susan vehemently shook her head.

Janet sniggered. "Really? Way back when we were little, I thought she had a baby crush on Charlie, looking at him with doe eyes and all, but I thought that was just a little-girl crush. She liked Charlie after that, too?"

Sandy nodded. "For a really long time. She's always kept so much from us—we could never go to her house, and she didn't tell us many secrets about herself or anything, but I knew she liked Charlie. She talked about him all the time. And I always thought you were so close to your brother. I thought maybe he said something to you."

"No!" Susan finally erupted. "I never knew this. I really didn't." She was shocked. Mercedes Doyle and her *brother*? "But... but why did she say those things about me? Why did she say that I called her ugly? I would never say that. I don't understand!" Susan's lip began to tremble. Even at sixteen, she had difficulty controlling her emotions.

"I don't know. But she's been different lately. I think I'm finally starting to realize that she never really appreciated me as a friend. She's never treated me very well, I suppose. And I've been thinking, you know, that if she's always been like this, then maybe the reason I haven't liked you very much was based on a lie?" She looked at Susan, uneasy, waiting for confirmation.

"I never said those things," Susan was adamant.

"I think I believe you," Sandy said sadly.

"You're damn right!" Janet exclaimed. "I might say something like that about Mercedes Doyle, but Susan never would."

"Susie, I think I need to say that I'm sorry. Back when we were younger, I wanted to be friends with you, but Mercedes always told me not to be and I followed her lead. And then we got a little older and she said that you had said those things about her and I couldn't believe that someone could be so mean and I really didn't like you one bit for it. These past few months I've been struggling a lot with it all. And then I have Gilbert tell me that he's got this really great friend and it's your brother and that he's met you and he really, really likes you and it just confused me even more. When he asked me to come today, I was so nervous. But I was also hoping that I'd bite the bullet, you know? That maybe I could talk to you. And then you were all just so nice to me right now. I didn't know if it was fake or if it was real, and I'm beginning to realize that it's all real and I've been wrong. I'm really sorry."

"You don't need to apologize. I didn't even know you were thinking these things," Susan said.

"Yeah, but I do need to apologize, don't I? Even if you didn't know, I did. And it was wrong."

"Well, thank you," Susan said with honesty. She admired Sandy for having such a quality, that she could admit to a wrong and remedy it. Perhaps Sandy Speckles was a girl she'd like to get to know after all?

"I suppose I should admit that I didn't want to see you here today. You've never done anything to me, Sandy, but Mercedes Doyle has, and I think I've judged you just for being her friend."

"I understand. I really do. I think maybe there's been a whole lot of judging going on when neither of us knew the full truth about each other." She paused for a moment, contemplating. "I'm not sure I should be telling you this, but I know you're all going to find out really soon anyway. Mercedes will be leaving St. Joseph's. She's knocked up and her parents are sending her away to have the baby."

Susan audibly gasped. "What!?" she demanded.

"Oh, whoa!" Janet said with a little snigger.

Betty's eyes widened.

"Yeah. She got pregnant this summer."

"Who's the father?" Janet asked.

Sandy crinkled her nose and bit her lower lip. After a slight hesitation she said, "It's Mr. Snow, the gym teacher."

"Holy shit, no way!" Janet exclaimed. "Mr. Snow? The guy who's in his thirties with a wife and two kids?"

"Yes," Sandy said. "Once this all gets out, I'm not sure he'll have a job. Or a wife."

Susan couldn't believe it. Pregnant? How had this happened? Mercedes Doyle would be incessantly teased, the topic of many a conversation throughout the school. She was being sent away by her own parents.

For the first time, Susan felt sorry for her.

She was saddened, too, for the wife and children of Mr. Snow.

She stood there rooted, the revelation settling. She remained horrified and found that her heart ached so suddenly for a young woman she never would have predicted would elicit such a strong feeling within her.

"Susie, I've got to—" Charlie halted when he saw the expression on her face. "What's wrong?"

"Oh, nothing, Charlie." Susan forced a smile and feigned nonchalance.

"Okay, then," he said. "I want you to see something. Come inside with me for a minute?"

"Sure." She excused herself from the conversation, which she knew would continue in her absence, and walked with her brother around the side of the house.

"Mercedes Doyle?" She looked at Charlie, incredulous.

"What?" Charlie's expression was that of confusion.

"She likes you, you know? Apparently she has for a while now."

"Oh," Charlie said. "That."

"What do you mean, 'that'? You knew?"

"Of course I knew," Charlie said. "She didn't take pains to hide it."

"How many times has she actually spoken to you? I saw it at church a few times, but really? How is this news to me? Why didn't you tell me?"

"I didn't think it was worth telling," Charlie said. "Mercedes Doyle is a girl who needs a lot of attention. She always has been. I'm not going to go around telling everybody I pass that she's interested in me. I think she has a lot that she needs to sort out, and I don't need to be the type of person that adds to her troubles."

"Well, I'm still standing here shocked," Susan admitted. "My brother. And Mercedes Doyle?" She grimaced.

"There was never, ever going to be a me and Mercedes Doyle. You can't wish something into fruition."

"No," Susan admitted. "No, I suppose not. But what I just found out... Charlie, I'm still trying to let it sink in."

They continued their way to the front of the house and entered through the door.

"Look what Gil got me," Charlie said. He walked to the couch, where he picked up a guitar.

"Charlie!" Susan exclaimed. "How did he afford this?"

"He said he's been saving up for a bit. He's in school, you know, so he doesn't have a whole lot, but he does work part-time. Isn't it bitchin'?"

Susan had never heard her brother use this terminology before, but she could concur that yes, it certainly was.

"I've been wanting to learn for a while now," Charlie said. "And Gil knew. Surprised me with it this morning."

"This morning?" Susan asked. "Did Gil come early?"

Charlie's smile faltered, and he lowered the guitar. "No, he didn't come early," he said, voice soft. "Gilbert lives here now."

"He does?" Susan asked. "But where does he sleep, Charlie? You've only got the two bedrooms."

"We share a room."

"Oh," Susan said. "Your room is so small, Charlie, he must be uncomfortable if he's on the floor," Susan chuckled at the thought. Poor Gilbert!

"Not on the floor." Charlie's face blanched.

"Not on the floor? Charlie, what do you—" Susan began. "Oh!" Her fingers went to her mouth. "With you?"

Charlie's head slowly descended in a nod, his eyes boring into his sister's.

"Charlie, I—" She couldn't find the right words. How could she when she truly didn't know how she felt?

"Say something."

"I just...I just don't understand." What to say? "How long?"

"How long has he been living here," Charlie asked, "or how long... have I known?" he whispered.

189

"Both."

"I've known since I was about twelve or thirteen that I was different than everyone else. Henry was the only person that ever knew this about me, and I didn't even tell him until I was about seventeen or so. Nobody else for the longest time. James and Viola know, and of course Gilbert, but really nobody else. I'm not sure his parents know; they haven't been to the house yet, and I don't think he's told them. It's just not something you tell. He's been living here just a week now. Please say something, Susie," he pleaded.

"I… I'm just having trouble understanding."

"So am I," Charlie said. "I've been having trouble understanding for years now! But this is who I am, Susie. I've tried to change it. I have. I can hide it from most people, but I can't hide it from you. You're too important to me." He hesitantly reached for her hand. When Susan didn't recoil, he took it in his own. "Please don't tell Mom."

"I won't," Susan promised.

Charlie's face was still devoid of color, and his eyes were welling with tears. "Do you hate me?" He looked miserably down at his sister, whose own eyes began to overflow with tears at this last heartbroken inquiry.

"No! Charlie, no." She took his free hand in her own and willingly let the tears fall. "I could never hate you, Charlie." She paused. "The Charlie I know," she said, "my brother? He's the best man I know. Always has been. I could never hate you. Never."

Charlie's shoulders began to heave as he let go all the emotions, the agony, he had been holding within. "Thank you," he sobbed. "Thank you."

Susan released his hands and reached up, placed her palms upon his face. "Look at me," she demanded. "I could never hate you. I love you so much, Charlie. So much!"

Charlie's eyes were reddening, the color in his cheeks intensifying.

"I love you, too. It's always been me and you, hasn't it, Susie?"

"And always will be," she promised.

They eventually wiped their eyes, gave each other a few minutes to compose themselves, and returned to the backyard and Charlie's twentieth birthday party. Susan walked directly to Janet and Betty, still conversing with Sandy Speckles, smiles on their faces. Janet was gesticulating wildly. Charlie veered toward Gilbert near the food table and whispered in his ear. Gilbert's smile promptly faded, and he turned to seek out Susan. He caught her eye and she smiled, gave a small wave of acknowledgment and reassurance. He smiled in turn, lifted his hand to wave back.

"Don't you think so, Susie?" Janet asked, breaking her from this harmonious interaction with her brother's... *boyfriend.*

"Think so what?" Susan asked.

"You haven't been listening to a thing we've been saying, have you?" Janet asked, humor in her voice.

Susan shook her head. "I just...gosh, really I'm just overwhelmed with everything. Mercedes Doyle is pregnant. I just have trouble processing things sometimes."

Janet scrutinized her friend's countenance for a moment. "You know I love you, right?" she began.

"Yeees," Susan said hesitantly, unsure of what was to follow. These words from Janet's mouth often preceded something she thought Susan might not want to hear or would take offense to.

"I think you've been in a bubble. A church bubble. You've been told certain things are true, and you haven't questioned those truths, have you? I love you so much, Susie, but you don't know much about the world. You're very naive. Innocent."

Susan stood before her friend, extremely hurt. She ached to take Janet's criticism constructively but found she was so taken aback by her words that she could do nothing but stand there, mouth agape.

And yet, if she was being honest with herself, even she was beginning to believe that these words just spoken rang true. Perhaps she was naive. Perhaps she really didn't know much about the world in which she lived in. The people she knew lived right beside her, went to school with her. She had a small group of friends, and she preferred to have it remain so. She wasn't interested in current events, although she was beginning to believe that it might be of some importance to be knowledgeable about what was going on in the world, especially with the war off in Vietnam, men fighting even as she stood there with her friends on a beautiful September afternoon in the safe environment of her brother's home.

"You okay?" Janet asked. "You mad at me?"

Susan shook her head slowly.

Janet leaped and embraced her friend forcefully. Susan wrapped her arms around Janet's back and held on.

"I do love you, Susie."

"I love you, too," Susan said.

She was thankful for the blunt observations of her friend, even if still slightly wounded.

She was just so damn confused.

FIFTEEN

G ilbert and Henry were exempt from the Vietnam draft as they were in school. Charlie was not.

On this Monday evening in December, Susan sat on the brown carpeted floor in Charlie's living room, Gilbert and Henry on either side of her brother on the couch. She wished Mother could be here as well.

Eight o'clock marked the start of the live broadcast on CBS. Susan had driven herself to her brother's house with Father's car (she'd acquired her licence just a month prior), and upon her arrival, Henry had asked if he could get her something to eat or drink. She refused. Her stomach was roiling so much she didn't think she'd have the ability to keep anything down.

Three men—all in suits and wearing glasses—stood in front of a microphone. A clear, cylindrical container housing numerous blue capsules rested in front of them. People were introduced, explanations given, but Susan wasn't listening to any of it. She was anxiously anticipating the pull of the first draft birth date.

Please God, don't let it be Charlie's.

The middle man walked a few steps to the clear container and reached in, extracting one blue capsule and handing it off to a man sitting at a desk. He opened it, unwound the paper within.

"September—" he read and paused momentarily. A pause that

was long enough to elicit an abundance of panic within Susan. "Fourteenth."

One down.

One out of 366.

Henry squirmed in his seat.

Susan couldn't move. She rested her chin on bent knees, wrapped her arms tightly around her shins.

Another man approached the cylinder, pulled forth a blue capsule, and handed it to the waiting palm of the seated man at the desk.

"April twenty-fourth."

Not Charlie.

"December thirtieth."

Another pause. Vast. Immense when you're waiting to see if your brother was going to be drafted to fight a war he didn't believe in.

"February fourteenth."

"October eighteenth."

Thank you, God!

"September—" Oh, dear Lord. September? Please not Charlie. Not her brother! "Sixth."

She stopped breathing.

A gasp from behind.

Was that Henry? Gilbert? Could it have been Charlie himself as he heard his birth date being called forth?

She looked over her shoulder at her brother. His face had blanched.

Gilbert reached out and took Charlie's hand. They sat there together staring at the screen as more and more birth dates were pulled forth. Henry looked down at Susan. She placed her hand on his knee. His palm reached to cover it.

The four of them sat there for quite some time. Silent tears were shed: hands were held. Love and fear permeated the room.

"Well, I guess that's that," Charlie eventually said.

What do you say in return? What words of wisdom, words of reassurance, could you possibly say to a young man whose life had taken a drastically appalling turn just moments before?

"I don't want you to go," Susan said after several more minutes of silence.

"I know you don't," Charlie said. "But I have to now. I have to go and fight a war in a place I've never been for a cause I don't believe in. At this point I can only hope that we smarten up and pull out before I get there."

Susan laid her hand on Charlie's thigh. "I don't want you to go," she repeated. Any other choice of words she might have used to convey her emotions or to allay his fear eluded her entirely.

He took her hand in his, rested it on his upper leg.

"*I* don't want to go. This scares the shit out of me."

* * *

"Knock, knock?" Susan opened Charlie's front door and stepped inside with a bag of gifts. Today they were to celebrate their last Christmas together before Charlie was to report for duty.

"Come in!" It was Henry who walked to the door first, opening it more fully to allow her access.

"It's so cold!" She shivered as she entered the warmth of their home, taking her boots off at the heels and placing her bag down.

"Here," Henry said, "let me take your coat."

"Thanks." Susan shimmied it off, and Henry brought it to the coatrack to the right of the door.

"Hi there, little sis," Charlie said as he entered the living room from the small kitchen at the back of the house.

"Well, hello there, big brother," she teased in turn. He leaned down and kissed her cheek.

"Hi, Susie," Gilbert said from the doorway to the kitchen. "Glad to see you."

"Glad to see you, too, Gil. Always am." Susan smiled heartily.

The foursome chatted gaily, snacked on chips and cookies for a while.

"Henry, let's get that player going. This is our Christmas celebration together, damn it! Let's celebrate!" Charlie leaped from the couch and pulled Susan to her feet while Henry went to the record player and Gilbert stood by.

Susan recognized the music instantly. "Charlie!" she squealed. "You got the record?"

"Sure did," Charlie said. "Just for you, Susie T. I know you love the Archies, especially 'Sugar, Sugar.'"

Susan started shaking her hips, Charlie threw his hands toward the ceiling. Gilbert sidled next to Charlie, and Henry shimmied his way over to Susan in the center of the living room floor.

Henry took hold of Susan's hands and together they danced, smiles immense, spirits soaring.

In this room, with these three men, Susan was at her most comfortable. She began to sing along.

Her hips continued to swing from side to side, her auburn curls bounced from her shoulders. She looked at the pure bliss on Charlie's face as he and Gilbert danced, at the twinkling of his green eyes, at the look of adoration Gilbert bestowed upon her brother.

She felt nothing but contentment in this moment.

Her gaze turned to Henry in front of her. She noticed the way his right lip curled slightly higher than his left. She noticed the breadth of his shoulders, the sharpness of his nose. She noticed also how his incisors were ever so slightly longer than the rest of his white teeth, and she found it to be—did she dare admit this to herself?—alluring.

She looked into his eyes as she continued to dance, continued to smile joyously, and found there in the depths of hazel and yellow a look she had never noticed before, a look that she couldn't identify.

He took her by the hand and swung her around in a circular motion. His left palm grasped her right: his right hand found purchase on her upper back. She placed her hand on his shoulder, and he danced her around the room.

A hysterical laugh, openmouthed, cheeks pulled taut as she tripped over her own feet, and Henry caught her in his arms before she fell.

They stood there for a moment, both laughing heartily as Susan righted herself. Henry swung her around the room with dramatic enthusiasm once again. Susan felt happy. Free.

The dancing came to a crescendo, and the foursome collapsed upon the couch and the floor in exhaustion. Sweat was tricking from Charlie's brow.

"Susie," he said after a lapse of a few minutes, "I got you something."

"And I'll take it," she said. She was by no means a greedy individual, but if Charlie was to gift her something, then she immediately knew it would be of some sentimental importance to her.

He leaned over the left side of the couch and lifted a Christmas bag from the floor. He handed it to her with a large grin.

She saw several sheets of blue and red tissue paper that she pulled out and discarded beside her on the floor. She placed her hand inside the bag and pulled forth a small wooden frame. She gazed upon its center, a photo of her and Charlie at Stuart's Campground.

"That's from '59. Ten years ago. It's been years since we've been back, but boy, did we make some good memories, yeah?"

She and Charlie were on the beach facing the camera, their backs to the water, swimsuits and bodies wet and dripping. They had their arms around each other, smiles on their faces. Susan looked like she was just about to erupt in laughter; Charlie must have been telling her a joke.

A tear landed upon the glass, smearing the face of the little girl she once was.

"You okay?" Charlie leaned forward on the couch.

She lifted her chin to face him. "I love it," she said. "Where did you get it?"

"I had Mom's help."

"I'll have it for always," she promised.

She composed herself and walked to the front door, where she had left her bag of Christmas gifts. "I got a little something for all of you." She walked back and sat on the floor, opened the bag. She handed Charlie his gift. "I hope you like it," she said.

Charlie unwrapped the shiny green paper surrounding the small gift. He lifted an embroidered blue handkerchief with the initials *C* and *S* stitched into the center in burgundy, his favorite color.

"Susie, did you do this yourself?"

"I did." She smiled bashfully.

"It's very nice. You did a great job. I'm going to take this with me when I leave. It'll be my good-luck charm," he said.

Susan leaned in to kiss his cheek.

The rest of the gifts were distributed, opened. They ate a deliciously cooked (by Henry mostly) meal of turkey, potatoes, rolls, and green beans, and finished it all off with a dessert of fruitcake that had been baked and provided by Henry's mother, Viola.

When through, they sat around the kitchen table cradling cups of after-dessert coffee, talking well into the night.

Eventually they made their way back into the living room, where Henry put a record on and they conversed further. Susan vowed to store each moment within her memory, thoughts to extract someday when she needed a smile or two.

"Are you spending Christmas Day with your parents?" Susan asked

Henry, who was sitting beside her on the couch while Gilbert and Charlie were deep in conversation on the floor beside them.

"I will be, yes. My mother looks forward to it each year, especially since I've been out of the house. And honestly, I really like being with them. I know not everyone appreciates their parents but I've got some pretty great ones."

"You really do," Susan affirmed. Her gaze was down in her lap when she saw his hand slowly reach for hers and cover it with his own. She looked up. He wasn't smiling; he was just gazing at her. She felt her cheeks flush in response.

"Yes!" Charlie's voice was loud and eager enough to demand her attention and break free of Henry's hand.

"Next weekend," Charlie said, "ice-skating, the four of us, on the pond?"

"It's been such a long time," Susan chuckled, "that I'm not sure I'd be able to do it."

"What do you say?" asked Charlie.

"I'm in," Henry said.

"Me, too," said Susan.

A short time later Susan was stifling a yawn when she realized she needed to return home. "I've got to go," she announced.

"Yeah," Charlie said, "it's getting late. I'll walk you—"

"No, let me," Henry interjected swiftly.

Charlie sat back down on the couch and looked quizzically at his friend. Then he slowly crossed his arms over his chest, leaned back, and grinned. "By all means," he said playfully.

"Bye, Susie."

"Later, Gil."

Henry retrieved her coat and helped her put it on. She held the bag Charlie had gifted her with the framed photo of the two of them in her hand as she and Henry both put their boots on and he walked her outside. He opened the car door for her and she climbed in.

"Susie?"

"Yeah?"

"How about a movie?"

"Oh, sure. It's been a little while since I've gone to the movies. Betty just saw *Hello, Dolly!* and said she really liked it. But do you think Charlie and Gil would want to see that one? We can always see something else instead."

"No." Henry shook his head and smirked. "You've misunderstood. I mean, do you want to go to the movies with me? Just me."

"Just you?" Susan looked up at him from her seat in the car and felt the blood rush into her face, felt her stomach lurch.

"Yes, just me."

"Oh," she said. "Okay."

"And yes, we can see *Hello, Dolly!* if you'd like. But there's just one thing." One thing? Susan felt rather apprehensive at the notion of a possible stipulation. "We'll need to get popcorn. Lots of popcorn. And Starburst. I can't have a movie without Starburst." He looked down at her and smiled. That lip. It curved when he was making light of a situation, didn't it?

She gazed down at her lap. "Okay. Popcorn and Starburst."

He gently laid a finger on her chin and beckoned her to look up. "How about after we go ice-skating?"

"Okay," she said, face hot.

"I'm looking forward to it, Susie."

"Me, too."

"See you then," he said and closed her door. When he walked away and into the house, she sat idle in the car for a few moments to catch her breath. Did she just agree to a date with Henry Beaumont?

* * *

"Henry Beaumont!" Betty ejaculated. "Eek!" She flung her arms around Susan and hugged her close. Susan couldn't help but smile.

"How did this happen?" Janet asked. "How is this the first we've heard about any of this?" She was in Janet's bedroom the following afternoon surrounded by her two best girlfriends, expressions of pure elation evident upon their faces. She had been desperate to tell them the good news, and now that she had, she was filled with a thrill, an excitement for the prospect of spending time alone with Henry Beaumont. During Mass today, while tuning out Father Denis (something she had found herself doing often these days), she had thought about Henry. She had convinced herself that she wasn't going to fret, that she would attempt to calm her nerves throughout this next week. She had a tendency to overthink matters, and she vowed she would quiet her misgivings.

"Well," Janet said, "don't just stand there with doe eyes! Tell us what happened!"

"It was just yesterday," Susan began, "I was over at Charlie's. We had a great time, really. It was getting late and I needed to go home, so I said goodbye. Henry said he'd walk me out and he did. He walked me all the way to the car and he even opened the door for me. I sat down and was about to leave and then he just... he just asked me."

"No," Janet said. "That's not good enough! What exactly did he say?" She bit her lower lip in anticipation.

"I think he said something like 'How about a movie?' and I thought he was talking about all of us, Charlie and Gilbert and him and me. But then he said that I misunderstood him, that he wanted to go to the movies with just me. I didn't even know what to say! I was so nervous."

"You obviously said yes!" Betty exclaimed.

"I did." Susan smiled.

201

"But when did this all happen?" asked Janet. "I didn't even know you liked Henry in that way."

"I don't think I really knew, either, until he asked me to the movies. And then it was all just... different."

Betty squealed, hugging Susan with so much force they fell back onto the bed giggling.

Janet jumped up to stand on the bed and began to bounce. "You're going on a date with Henry Beaumont," she shouted. "Oh, hey," she said, and stopped her bouncing, a mischievous smile upon her face. "I bet he's a good kisser."

Susan's eyes widened, her face flushed considerably.

"Your face is as red as your hair!" Janet exclaimed. "You were probably thinking the same thing."

Susan looked down at her lap, embarrassed. She had actually not been thinking the same thing; in fact she was too caught up in how she would act (what was she supposed to do!?) that she hadn't thought about him kissing her.

Oh, goodness!

"Oh, Janet, stop teasing the girl," Betty said playfully in her friend's defense. Susan looked up and gave a small, thankful smile. "But really, Susan, if I were you I would totally think about kissing Henry Beaumont!" The girls all giggled. Susan, to save herself from any further embarrassment, took up the pillow closest to her side and knocked Janet's legs with it.

Thus ensued another of the girls' enthusiastic pillow fights.

* * *

Saturday arrived. Though she attempted to pacify her anxiety, Susan had spent the entire week toying with various scenarios of how today would progress. Charlie was going to pick her up with Henry and Gilbert and was due any moment now. She kept peeking out the kitchen window to see if they had arrived.

She had agonized over what to wear, something that she hadn't really ever bothered with prior to today. Sure, she wanted to look good when she left the house, but she had never before wanted to look good for a specific person. She found this newfound predicament rather irritating.

Eventually, she chose a pair of straight pants in a shade of deep red. She liked the way her black-and-gray striped blouse looked with the pants, so she kept that on. She concluded that she'd put her thick gray wool sweater on as well. She didn't want to be cold when ice-skating outside.

She pulled her coat tighter around her middle, bouncing on the balls of her feet as she looked out the window.

There they were!

She opened the kitchen door, but before she could hasten her steps to the car, Mother called from behind. "Have a wonderful time, Susan. I will be thinking of you."

"Thanks, Mom."

As she walked toward the car waiting for her on the side of the road, Henry opened his door and stood. "Hi," he greeted her.

"Hi," she said, the word a bit timid in its execution.

"Ready to have some fun?" he asked as he held the passenger door open for her.

"I am." Henry climbed in first as the car only had two doors. He situated himself in the back seat next to Gilbert. Susan sat herself in the front passenger seat.

"And we're off," Charlie announced as he began to drive away from the house, his head almost hitting the roof of the small car.

The pond was only a fifteen-minute drive from Susan's home. They turned into a parking lot and Charlie cut the car's ignition. They exited the car and walked over to a small building. This pond was town-owned and maintained, so there was no snow evident on the ice. Susan saw quite a few skaters, some rather fast and agile on their feet, others losing their balance and falling clumsily to the ground. There were young couples skating hand in hand, mothers aiding their wobbly-legged children, fathers taking photographs. Susan thought upon the times when she was much younger, when she and her family had ventured over to the pond to skate themselves. It had been many years since they had been back.

They entered the small building, Henry holding the door open for them all. Henry clutched his skates by their blades; he had told Susan on their way over to the pond that he still skated with his parents on occasion. Susan liked this image very much, an even deeper insight into the relationship he had with his mother and father.

"Can I help you?" the young man behind the counter asked as they approached.

"Yes," Charlie said. "We'll need some skates, please."

"Size?"

"I'm a twelve," he said.

"Seven, please," Susan told the attendant.

"And I'm an eleven," Gilbert said.

The young man went to various cubbies behind him and extracted the appropriate-sized skates for them all, handing them over the counter. Charlie and Gilbert paid for their rentals, Henry offered to pay for Susan's, which she accepted modestly.

Charlie led the way to some wooden benches off to the right side of the establishment, where they all took their boots off and donned their skates.

"Do they fit?" Henry asked Susan as he was tying his last lace.

"They seem to." She stood. She had forgotten how awkward skates felt on her feet, how tight and stiff they were on her ankles, and how she couldn't bend her knees well at all when walking, but she managed to walk over to the door with the rest of her party and out into the cold. They brought their boots with them, placed them among the rest of the assorted footwear along the edge of the pond where you entered and exited the ice.

"Let's do this." Henry held onto her mittened hand with his gloved one and gently pulled her onto the ice. She wobbled instantaneously, her curls flying upward under her colorful woolen knitted hat. Henry's legs bent to brace her under the arm and lift her back into position.

"Thanks," she said as he righted her.

"How long has it been since you've skated?" he asked.

"It's been a really long time. Charlie and I used to come with our parents a bit when we were younger, but we stopped coming for some reason and I've never been back. The opportunity just never came up and it wasn't something I had thought of suggesting. My friends don't really skate, I don't think, and with my parents not doing it anymore, and Charlie out of the house for so long now..."

"I understand," Henry said. "But are you glad we came today?"

"I am," she said as she slid her right skate forward. "I'm a little shaky, aren't I?" She laughed.

"Yeah"— Henry smirked—"you are. But you'll get used to it again."

Charlie and Gilbert passed them by, both lighter on their feet than Susan. Gil turned, began skating backward, and waved at them. Henry gave him the bird through his leather-gloved hand, which made Susan's eyes widen and all four of them laugh before Gilbert faced forward again, increasing his momentum.

"Show-off," Henry teased.

"But he's good," Susan said.

"That he is."

Why had Susan been anxious about this day? Had she forgotten how comfortable she had always been with Henry?

A child skated in front of them, lost her balance, and fell to the ice. Henry had to stumble to a halt rather quickly so as not to trip over her supine body on the ground.

"Tough break there," he said heartily.

"Ouch," the little girl said as she sat and rubbed her thigh.

"You okay?"

"Yeah."

Henry reached down and helped the girl to her feet. She got a hold with her skate and took off once again.

"So, Susan," Henry said, "how are you liking school this year? Halfway through eleventh. Senior next year."

"I am, yeah. I'm liking it all right. I like that we have a different teacher for most subjects, unlike St. Catherine's. St. Catherine's was just so small. I think that was really good for me when I was younger. I remember my very first day of school. I was so nervous and I was so happy that I had you and Charlie and my friends to walk with. I didn't know who my teacher would be, I didn't know who I'd make friends with, I didn't really know any of the other kids but a few. I just didn't know what to expect, and that's always been something that I've struggled with." She smiled up at Henry as they continued to skate side by side. "I do like that several schools pool into St. Joseph's, though. It's offered me a little more, and while I might not like one teacher or one subject, I might like others. I hate math. Hate it. I've never been good at it. Something I apparently share with my mother. I had a teacher that hit me on the side of the head with an eraser once for not knowing how to do a geometry equation she had written on the chalkboard."

"Ouch," Henry said.

"Yeah. It hurt a bit because she got my ear, but really I was just mortified. I cried. Nothing new there, though. I'm emotional. But you already knew that." She smiled.

"I do," Henry chuckled. "But I like that. It's honest and raw. Admirable." He squeezed Susan's hand.

She looked up into his hazel eyes, the long lashes surrounding them. His cheeks were red from cold, his breath wafting through the air.

"Thank you," she said as she slowed her speed. She was a bit taken aback by his honesty and forthrightness.

They came to a stop, skaters passing on either side.

"You're welcome," he said. "But I'm only saying what I see. I don't think you have a mean bone in your body, Susan, and I've known a lot of people. I like surrounding myself with like-minded individuals, with people that are true and kind, and while I know you well as being Charlie's sister, I'd like to know you even better as just Susan Dubois."

He left her speechless. What kind of man actually spoke in such a manner? She just stood there in the cold afternoon air and gazed into his eyes.

"Come on," he said, and he pulled her forward. "Let's go fast!"

The moment broken, she shrieked as she lost her balance and pitched forward, toe picks clinging for purchase. She tumbled clumsily to the ice.

Sitting on her bottom, she started laughing hysterically. Henry skated over, placed his hands on his thighs in a squat above her, and chuckled at her reaction.

When her laughter eventually subsided, Henry extended his arms and helped her to her feet. She accepted and struggled to stand; she found it much more difficult to find her balance on the ice than on the frozen earth at the entrance of the pond.

"I think I need a little more practice," she said.

"Yep, you sure do," Henry jested.

Susan gave him a mock grimace and began to glide forward on the ice, pleased when Henry took her hand into his once again.

Henry continued to shift his gaze between Susan and the path before him, attentive and interested as they spoke. Susan wasn't typically the center of attention, but with Henry she didn't feel discomfited at all. On the contrary, he was making her feel that she could continue speaking and—dare she believe—that she could open herself up to him without fearing scrutiny.

"You know, it's kind of strange to think that I've known you for so long. It's almost like you and my brother go hand in hand." She grinned his way.

"Your brother's the best guy I know. Well, maybe not the best because my dad's right up there with him. Charlie's struggled a lot through the years, but he's always come out strong. I honestly don't know how a kid who's been through what he's been through can be the kind of guy he is. He's always thinking of other people, and he tries to have a good attitude about life even when I think maybe I would have broken down. I really hope you're okay with my saying this, Susie, but I would have bugged out of your house way before he did, and he only did because your father kicked him out. Maybe it's just because I grew up where I did. I hope you don't think I'm being disrespectful here, but the shit your brother's been through? I'd be a different guy." He shook his head then in contemplation. "But your brother? Your brother is strong, and cool, and... well... he's a great guy. And the way he's been with you? I think I knew way back when we were small that he took you under his wing. And even back then when most boys were playing ball and cared only about themselves, had no worries, your brother was enduring some crazy shit and loving you all the more for it." He shook his head again.

"He really is a great guy," Susan said.

"He sure is."

Charlie sidled up to them, put his arm around Henry's shoulders, and said, "Gil and I are going back to the lodge to get some hot cocoa. Join us?"

Henry looked to Susan, who smiled and nodded her head.

"Let's go," he said.

They continued on their circular path, going with the flow of the other skaters on the ice, and made their way to the lodge. Susan was reminded once again how very different the sensation was when you transitioned from ice to land on skates. She found she was wobbling like a penguin.

The heat accosted her when she walked through the door of the lodge, a pleasant and welcoming feeling after the nipping bitterness of the cold, crisp winter air outside. Her chin had begun to stiffen, and she had been finding it more difficult to speak. Now the warmth of the indoors was beginning to thaw her out, which generated a running, sniffling nose. She wiped it on the back of her coat sleeve, ensuring Henry's gaze was elsewhere before she did so. She'd have to find a tissue!

To the left of the desk was a small counter on which rested several Styrofoam cups, a bowl of mini marshmallows, and a large cylindrical container with a spout.

"Ladies first," Gilbert said with a wink of an eye, lashes so long and thick they touched his upper cheek. He might be her brother's boyfriend, but she could still appreciate his beauty! Damn!

"Thanks, Gil," Susan said. She took her mittens off and set them aside, unstacked a cup, and lifted the spout to pour some steaming dark brown cocoa into it. She grasped a tiny spoon from the bowl of mini marshmallows and scooped two spoonfuls on top.

"Ah," Henry said jovially, "look at this." He, too, procured a cup for himself, but instead of pouring the cocoa in, first he spooned himself some marshmallows. The cocoa came next. "It melts the marshmallows a bit faster so they're soft and mushy. I like them like that. All we're missing is some whipped cream."

"You're such a geek," Charlie teased.

"And proud of it," Henry quipped.

"Inside or outside?" Gilbert asked once their cups were full and they had paid a quarter into a donation box on the countertop.

They looked around the lodge, found no seats available, and decided to head back out.

There were several benches scattered around the pond. They sat upon the cold metal of a bench to their left. It was just large enough for the four of them to seat themselves together.

Susan held her cup between her mittened hands and took a microscopic sip, testing the heat of her cocoa to ensure she wouldn't burn her tongue.

Charlie sipped his beside her on the bench, lowered it to his lap, and looked at his sister. "Having fun?" he asked.

"I am."

Charlie gazed fleetingly beyond Susan to Henry. Eyes contacting Susan's quickly again, he smiled mischievously.

"I'm glad," he said, wrapping his long arm around her narrow shoulders and pulling her toward his chest in a quick and playful embrace.

The foursome sipped their cocoa, which soon cooled off considerably in the frigidity of the early-afternoon air. Susan made small talk on occasion, but she much preferred listening to the boys' playful bantering with each other, the ease in which they held themselves. She felt dwarfed on the bench between Henry and Charlie, her small stature more pronounced with the men that surrounded her.

She felt safe. Happy.

Cocoa now drunk, Susan told Henry that she was going to rest on the bench while the men continued to skate.

"Want some company?"

"Thanks, but go with Charlie and Gil. I've been slowing you down. Go ahead," she encouraged him, "have fun. I'll watch."

Henry placed a foot on the ice and skated backward momentarily to wave goodbye. Flipping himself around with ease, he sped off to join his friends.

The boys skated for a while longer, and Susan remained comfortable on her perch on the bench, although a little cold. When they approached her and asked if she was ready to head out, she affirmed she was. She skated back onto the ice to ease her transition to the lodge, and once inside (after grabbing her boots), she took her skates off and wiggled her toes, feeling much less restricted and uncomfortable. Boots all on, skates returned to the counter, they walked to the car.

Charlie drove back to the home he shared with Gilbert and Henry, and they all warmed up inside with a light dinner and some music.

"Suze, you ready to go?" Henry asked.

Suze?

Nobody had ever called her Suze before.

She found she liked it.

Susan nodded shyly and stood from the comfort of the couch.

This was it. She was going to be alone with Henry!

She rubbed her hands down the length of her sweater and followed Henry to the door.

He helped her arms through her jacket, then put his own brown coat on while she pulled her woolen hat over her unruly hair. Donning her boots and a small yellow canvas tote, she was ready.

Although a bit nervous, she saw the genuine smile on Henry's face, seeping even into his hazel eyes, and was able to relax slightly as he opened the door. He held it open for her and she walked through the threshold and into the biting cold of this dark, winter night.

Henry shut the door behind him and sped to surpass Susan's steps as she walked toward his car. Opening the door for her, he motioned for her to step inside. She shivered as she sat, the confines of the car not much warmer than the open air outside.

"Brrr," Henry said as he plunked himself into his seat and turned the key in the ignition. "Let's warm this baby up."

He put the car in reverse and slowly backed out of the small driveway and into the street, beginning to talk almost instantly. He held the conversation easily as he drove them to the theater, something Susan was very grateful for as she sat beside him.

Alone.

They arrived at the theater and walked to the ticket window, glass enclosing the person inside and sheltering them from the elements.

"Two, please," Henry said. *"Hello, Dolly!"*

"Three dollars."

Henry handed the money over to him and grasped the tickets offered in return.

"Great," he turned to Susan. "Popcorn, here we come!"

"And Starburst," Susan smiled.

"You've got that right."

They walked inside to the refreshment stand and waited patiently behind a young blond man and a girl with straight brown hair parted in the middle and flowing freely. His arm was around her shoulder, and she was blowing large bubbles with a thick wad of pink gum.

A date, Susan thought to herself. *That's me right now.*

"Two popcorns, please," Henry said when it was their turn to order. "Some Starburst and two small..." He looked over at Susan. "What do you like to drink?"

"I like Coca-Cola and Sprite. And I like Dr Pepper, too."

"Looks like they have them all. Any preference?"

"Sprite?"

"Sprite it is," Henry said. He looked back at the attendant. "We'll get two small Sprites. And…" Turning back to Susan, he asked, "would you like anything else?"

"No," she said. "The popcorn should be plenty for me."

"Guess that's it," Henry said as he handed cash over the counter.

When all was procured, he transferred a Sprite and popcorn over to Susan.

"Thanks, Henry," Susan said.

"Not a problem."

Walking into the theater, they sat themselves in a middle row.

The movie began. Some popcorn was eaten, soda drunk. When they were both done with their popcorn, Henry placed the boxes on the floor at their feet and opened his package of Starburst, removing the top one—pink—and extending it to Susan as an offering.

She took it from his hand and opened the wrapping, placing the sugared square on her tongue.

Henry took one for himself and placed the rest of the candy on the chair. He extended his arm behind Susan, resting his hand on her shoulder. "This okay?" he asked.

Susan nodded, heart beating rapidly in response.

She looked in front and to the right; a young couple was making out. To her left, there were a few boys throwing popcorn at the backs of their friends' heads.

Henry's hand remained on her shoulder.

Her heart continued to beat.

When the movie ended, Susan wasn't sure she'd be able to effectively answer any questions put to her about its content.

Henry picked the boxes up off the floor; Susan, her empty soda cup. They walked to the door and discarded their trash in an overflowing receptacle before walking into the night.

"What did you think?"

"Hmm?" Susan asked.

"The movie. Did you like it?"

"Oh, yeah," Susan said. "I liked the movie. Did you?"

"I actually did like it. I have to admit that I wasn't sure I would, but usually I'll give something a try and it was the movie you wanted to see so I was more than willing, but I thought they cast it well. Love Louis Armstrong. I was happy he was in it."

Susan smiled, feeling suddenly more at ease. She was annoyed that her emotions had varied so greatly over the course of the evening.

Henry held the car door open for her, and she sat down, tugging her coat closer to her body to keep the heat in, arms wrapped tightly around her chest.

The conversation on the way home was light but steady. Henry pulled to the front of Susan's home and idled the car.

"I'm really glad you came out with me tonight, Susie," he said.

"So am I. Thanks for inviting me."

"Look," Henry continued, "Gil, Charlie, and I are headed over to my folks' house tomorrow, late afternoon, for dinner. Would you like to come along?"

"I'll need to ask my parents' permission, but if they allow me to, I'd love that."

"Great. Why don't you ring us up tomorrow morning then?"

"Sure," Susan said.

"Then I'll talk to you tomorrow morning."

Susan took this as her cue to exit the car. She opened the door and stood. "Thanks for tonight, Henry," she said.

"You're welcome. I enjoyed it. Hopefully I'll see you tomorrow." He smiled, eyes crinkling at the corners.

"I hope so, too." She shut the door and turned her back to the car, walking up the few steps to the front porch and entering the house.

She looked back before she shut the kitchen door and saw Henry was still on the side of the road.

Susan waved and Henry waved in return before pulling away.

She shut the door behind her in the dark, silent kitchen, leaned her body back, and smiled.

* * *

Church was the last place Susan wanted to be the next morning, but church was where she was bidden, and obey she would. Father Denis's high voice echoed through the nave, but Susan's thoughts were elsewhere. She was eager to get home.

There was a knock on her bedroom door that afternoon.

"Come in," she called.

Mother opened the door a crack and poked her head through the opening. "I think you may have lost track of time, Susan," she said. "Henry is at the front door."

"Oh, my goodness!" she exclaimed. She quickly shut her book and placed it on her nightstand.

She followed her mother to the kitchen, where Henry was seated in the chair that Charlie had once occupied. Father was across the table from him, nursing a beer.

"Been a long time," Father slurred.

How much had he had to drink?

"Yes, sir," Henry said, "it has." He feigned a smile.

"Helen here says you're taking Susan to dinner." He placed a cigarette between his lips and lit a match.

"I'm taking her to my parents' house, where we'll have dinner." He didn't mention that Charlie would be there.

"Ahh," Father said with an exhalation of smoke. "Got me a new toy, Henry boy. A new toy." Susan fidgeted with her fingers behind her back. *Please stop talking,* she pleaded silently. "Got me a, well…

come and look." He put his palms down on the tabletop and hefted himself to a standing position, cigarette dangling from his mouth, legs wobbly.

Henry followed him to the living room, Susan's eyes apologetic as he passed her. She and Mother trailed behind Henry and walked to where Father stood before the newly erected Christmas tree. It was decorated in exactly the same manner as it always had been. A few gifts were under the branches.

"Look at that, will you?" Father said. He was gazing with adoration upon a new model train, sleek and shiny in black and red. It rested upon a black track that Father had constructed on the floor around the tree.

"Nice, ish-int she?" Father placed his hand on the window sill to right his unsteady self.

"She is, sir."

"Gerald, darling," Mother interjected, "Susan should really be going now."

"Yeah, yeah," her husband replied, annoyed.

"It's a great train, sir," Henry assured him with a palm to his shoulder. "Really."

Father grinned.

Susan clasped onto Henry's hand and gently pulled him toward the door. He followed willingly. She put her coat and boots on and quickly picked up an apple pie she had made and placed to rest upon the kitchen table. She walked under Henry's outstretched arm holding the door open.

"Have a wonderful time," Mother said. Father remained in the living room.

"Thanks," Susan said.

Henry closed the door behind him on the porch. Susan sighed heavily.

"I am so sorry, Henry. He gets like that when he's drinking and he's only been drinking more and more."

"Susie, I've known your father since I was a little boy. I'm not surprised. And you don't need to apologize for him."

"No, I suppose I don't. He should apologize for himself." Her voice was forceful as Henry opened the car door for her to enter.

"But he won't," Henry said. "And you need to know that this is who your father is. You can distance yourself as much as you'd like from him, Susan. You are *not* your father. Don't apologize for him again. If anything, I should say that I'm sorry to you."

"What in the world for?" Susan was astonished.

"Sorry that he treats you that way, treats your mother that way. Sorry for the shitty way he treated Charlie as well." He shut Susan's door and walked in front of the car. When he sat in the driver's seat, Susan turned her body toward his. She placed her hand on his shoulder.

"Thank you, Henry," she said. She could still see the agitation on his face.

He looked her in the eye.

"Thank you. Just thank you."

* * *

Susan had been amiably chatting with her brother, Gilbert, and Henry in the living room of Henry's parents' home when Viola announced it was time for dinner.

Susan followed Henry. Just to the left of the front door was the entryway to the dining room. She walked through and saw the table set up with six place settings, each with a large white plate trimmed with golden flowers, petals of pink and purple stemming out and toward the center. There were china cups of the same pattern as well as bowls. Cloth napkins were to the left of the plates, silverware resting on top.

Viola and James took the two place settings at either end of the table. Charlie and Gilbert sat facing the wall that abutted the living room, Susan and Henry sat facing the windows to the outdoors.

"Viola, these plates are gorgeous," Susan said as she lightly ran her finger around the rim.

"Oh, thanks, sweetie," she said. "This was my mother's china back from the early 1920s; it's what I grew up with when we would have company over. She gave it to me before she passed a couple of years ago, and it makes me so happy to have it, brings back a lot of memories. And I love that I'm now able to create some of my own when I use it."

"Leave it to Viola," James teased. "Always so sentimental."

"Why yes, I am," Viola said as she sat erect in her chair. "You should be used to that now, James." She stuck her nose in the air with faux haughtiness.

"James and Viola," Charlie said from in front of Susan, "this all looks and smells so delicious. Thanks again for having us over tonight."

"It wouldn't be Christmastime without you, Charlie," Viola said.

"And we're glad to add Gilbert and Susan to our table this year," James added.

"That we are." Viola raised her glass of red wine. "Cheers to all of us. Cheers to our family."

A chorus of "Cheers!" went around the table as all glasses were lifted.

James cut the roast and dished some out to each extended plate, and platters of food went around the table: cherry tomatoes in garlic with green beans, bread rolls, roasted potatoes and mushrooms in a steaming broth, applesauce and boiled cranberries with sugar and cloves.

Susan looked down at her plate and was amazed at the amount she had given herself. She wasn't sure she'd be able to eat it all!

"Once again, you have outdone yourselves," Henry said. "So much food."

"See now, that's our trademark," James said enthusiastically. "Left-overs!"

"Oh, hey," James said, "Susan did you know that your neighbor down the street, Edmond Biladeau, will be in a nursing home at the beginning of next week?"

Susan put her fork down on her plate. "No, I didn't know that at all."

"Yes," James continued, "I was talking to him just yesterday, and apparently he just can't maintain his house any longer; he's old. He's—what, the old man's got to be in his mid- to late eighties by now. Having trouble walking these days. Wife's been gone for many years and his kids don't live around here, or at least I don't think they're close. Susan, I think he's going into the facility you work for. I bet you're certain to see him."

"I guess I will," she said. All in all Susan enjoyed working at the nursing home. Some people she had met she enjoyed speaking with, hearing stories from the olden days. Other people were just plain curmudgeonly, if she was being honest. One of her duties was to help the residents with their bathroom needs. Would this entail her helping Mr. Biladeau if he required aid? She hadn't yet had a resident whom she had known before their placement into the home, and the anonymity helped to ease her transition in this role. If Mr. Biladeau needed her aid in helping him to—what? To take a bath? Wipe his bottom? Oh, gosh!

She blushed right there at the table.

She remembered just then when she had seen her first penis. Mr.

Albert Waterworth was a ninety-six-year-old man who had lost a great deal of his bodily control. A nurse at the residence was bathing Mr. Waterworth when Susan had knocked on the door to his room with fresh linens so she could make up his bed. When she heard the nurse beckon her in, she obliged. She saw a very naked Mr. Waterworth in the warm water of the tub, small penis bobbing, and she dropped the linens and gasped. She had very quickly averted her eyes, regained control of her senses, and scooped up the linens. She stripped the dirty bedsheets hurriedly, made the bed anew and practically ran out the door in her haste to exit.

She had since adapted to seeing many naked bodies of the older population at the nursing home, but to have Mr. Biladeau there? Oh, goodness…! She looked down at her plate and blushed an even deeper shade of scarlet.

Dinner was finished, and Susan helped Viola to clear the table. Viola began on the dishes and Susan took up a hand towel to help dry them when they were done, but James took it from her hands before the first plate was handed over. "I've got this," he said. "You go on over back to the table. Enjoy your time."

"Are you sure? I really don't mind helping at all."

"I'm sure."

Susan hesitantly walked back into the dining room and sat down next to Henry. James? Doing the dishes? Susan was mystified.

Viola poked her head around the door frame from the kitchen. "How about some coffee or tea while these dishes are being washed? Then we can have some of that apple pie Susie brought over."

They sat chatting and sipping the warm liquids. Susan felt purely blissful around the table with this particular company.

They retired to the living room after dessert, the couches lending more comfort for them to continue their conversing. Susan looked at the clock on the wall and marveled at how quickly time had progressed.

"I need to head home," she said apologetically.

"Oh, what a shame," Viola said. "But of course we understand. I just love having you all here. It gets quiet in the house with just this old man for company." She pointed her thumb at her husband.

James gave his wife a phony grimace.

My, how Susan loved their antics.

"We're staying just a bit longer," Charlie said. "A hug for your big brother?"

Susan walked over to Charlie and hugged him fiercely. She had not forgotten that this was the last Christmas she would have with him before his deployment to Vietnam.

"Bye, Gil," Susan said.

"Bye." Gilbert stood and kissed Susan on the cheek.

"Thank you so much for tonight," Susan said, "and for having me over."

"It was our pleasure," Viola said.

"Thanks for coming," said James. "I hope you won't be a stranger and you'll come back soon."

"I'd like that," she said wholeheartedly.

Henry guided her to the front door and helped her with her jacket and the newly washed pie pan. He held his hand on the small of Susan's back as he led her to his car. She found she liked this very much.

They arrived at Susan's home only a minute later as Henry's childhood home was only a block away. He parked in front of her porch.

"I'm so glad you came tonight," he said.

"I really am, too," she admitted. "Henry, I really like your parents."

Henry chuckled at this. "Yeah, they're something, aren't they? I'll keep them," he jested. "And Susie?"

"Hmm?"

"I really like you, too." His voice went deeper, softer.

"I like you, too, Henry." She felt her hands begin to tremble, an extreme prickling sensation in the depths of her stomach. She looked at her lap.

Henry touched her chin with his finger, lifted her head to look into her eyes. "Suze?"

She didn't answer, just sat there studying him, his hazel eyes, thick lashes.

"Can I kiss you?"

Her stomach flipped.

This was it! She was going to have her first kiss.

His finger still on her chin, she nodded ever so slightly.

His palm moved to her cheek, and he slowly leaned toward her, gently running his fingers to find the curls at the back of her neck. He closed his eyes when he was close to her face and gently touched her lips with his own, soft and warm.

Her eyes remained open. She was so nervous she didn't know what she was supposed to do. As he pulled back and his lashes fluttered to reveal the yellow specks within the hazel of his eyes in the porch light, he smiled.

"I've been wanting to do that for a little while," he admitted. "Susie?"

"Yeah?" Her voice was soft, a butterfly in the wind.

"I'm not sure if we'll see each other before Christmas Day. If not, then Merry Christmas."

"Merry Christmas, Henry."

"I'll call you?"

She nodded with a smile.

Henry reached to her forehead and delicately tucked a stray curl behind her ear.

"Good night."

"Good night," Susan said and opened the door of the car. She closed it and walked up the stairs and onto her front porch. When she was at the kitchen door, she turned back and gave a slight wave of her hand, to which Henry returned. She closed the door on the cold December night, leaned against the wood, and placed her fingers upon her smiling lips.

SIXTEEN

Charlie chose to leave quietly; he didn't need a sizeable reminder that he was headed to Vietnam. He said his goodbyes to those he loved. He was content, here, at this moment in his home, with his boyfriend, best friend, and sister. That was enough.

The record player was going, music carrying the background as the four friends talked, laughed, reminisced. Susan held onto every precious moment she had with her brother before it was time for Gilbert to drive him away.

She and Mother had visited just yesterday afternoon once Susan had arrived home from school. Susan was so pleased that Mother had the opportunity to say goodbye to Charlie, but her heart ached now that she was here with her brother and Mother was not. She had left her mother home with Father, who had begun drinking early that morning. He was aware of Charlie's circumstances but stubbornly refused to impart any thoughts or feelings. In fact, Father still angered when Charlie's name was mentioned in his house.

"It's time," Gilbert said quietly as he took Charlie's hand in his own.

Charlie placed his guitar on the couch—he had been strumming the strings to occupy his hands as well as his mind as this time drew near.

Susan had been desperately attempting to hide her anxiety, was laughing and joking throughout the morning with her brother, was trying to breathe in his presence beside her. And yet as Charlie began to stand from the couch, she lost her bearings. She rose quickly and flung her arms around him.

Her brother wiped the tears from her face with his thumbs, looked his sister in the eye, and leaned down to kiss her forehead, much the same way Mother still did upon occasion. He placed his large palms on either side of her head, curls seeping through the gaps of his fingers, and placed her small head upon his chest to rest as he held her close.

Susan eventually pulled away and breathed deeply in, inhaling the breath her brother had just expelled into her own lungs.

"Love you, Susie T."

"I love you so much, Charlie," Susan said.

Charlie turned to Henry and embraced him. "See you when I get back."

"Sooner rather than later, I hope."

Gilbert placed the palm of his hand on Charlie's back and gently led him to the door.

Henry's hand slid into hers as they stood by the couch in the living room he shared with Charlie and Gilbert, the living room that had become a second home to Susan.

"I'll be back," Charlie said at the doorway with a wink, a facade of bravery. An attempt to conceal the breaking of his heart at leaving the ones he loved most dearly in the world.

Susan cried freely, making no attempt to wipe her tears away.

Henry's grasp tightened on her hand. "We'll be here when you get back," he said.

And with that, Charlie closed the door behind him.

Susan went to the window, watched him step into Gilbert's car and drive away.

Her knees buckled beneath her, and she fell to the ground, hands on the windowsill now above her, head lolling between her arms, tears falling to the carpeted floor.

Henry walked to her, bent, and lifted her easily in his arms, taking her back to the couch, where he placed her gently down. He sat by her side and embraced her, let her expunge the devastation within until she was left spent.

* * *

January 3, 1970

Susie T -

I haven't even left yet. I look around and I'm reminded that we're all so young, really. We're all just kids. This isn't where I want to be. I wish I were home with Gilbert. I wish I was playing my guitar while the four of us were together in our house. Being here reminds me of what I have and what I'd be losing if I don't make it home to you all. But you know what? I think I'm deciding right here and now that I refuse to write about my time over in Vietnam. Instead, I'm going to write about our happy times. I'd much rather think about those, wouldn't you?

I can't write home, so I'm sending your letters to my house. Henry can hand them over. And I'm writing to Mom, too. Can you be sure she gets my letters without our father finding out?

Love you, Susie,

Charlie

* * *

Charlie had been gone for a couple of weeks when Henry invited Susan over for dinner. Gilbert was going to be out of the house, and he wanted to cook for her, which she found incredibly endearing.

"Henry?" She opened the front door and walked inside.

"In the kitchen," he called back.

"I smell pasta," she said hungrily as she walked to the back of the house.

"Spaghetti and my own homemade sauce. Well, not my own; it's my mom's. I grew up on this stuff. You'll love it." He held a wooden spoon out to her, red sauce steaming. She walked over and took a small bite, hot on her tongue.

"Oh, that is good," she said.

"Told you." He dipped the spoon back into the sauce and stirred.

"I smell garlic, too."

"Bread's in the oven."

Susan walked to the oven and opened it a crack to peer inside. French garlic bread with mozzarella cheese bubbling on the top, edges crisping to a light brown. She inhaled deeply before closing the oven door.

"This is pretty much done," Henry announced.

Susan set the table, and Henry brought the food over.

"Henry, it all looks so good," she said eagerly. "I haven't had much to eat today, so I'm really hungry."

"Good!" Henry said. "I made way too much food for just the two of us. I guess I've learned that from my parents." He laughed.

"Leftovers," Susan teased.

"You've got that right. You'll just have to come over to be with me again."

"I won't complain about that." Susan surprised herself with the boldness of her comment; she was becoming increasingly comfortable with Henry as the days progressed.

"Neither will I," Henry said. He slid his arms around her small waist and leaned down. Susan lifted her head, and as Henry's lips touched hers, she closed her eyes. They lingered there momentarily and then he pulled away. Hands still on her waist, he looked at her intently. She didn't waver.

Henry's sauce was delicious, and Susan made a mental note to thank Viola not only for the recipe but also for teaching her son to prepare it so well. She was pleased to be the recipient of such thoughtful, familial intercourse; pleased to be on the receiving end of a home-cooked meal as opposed to being one of the women in the house fixing it.

They ate, conversed.

"Henry?"

"Mmm?"

"So..." She hesitated.

Henry looked at her, the corner of his mouth lifting in a grin. "What is it?"

"Ah," she sighed. "Okay, I'm just going to ask." She paused for a moment before continuing. "Whatever happened to Patty?"

"Patty?" Henry frowned. "You mean Patty Lundveg, the girl I dated back when I was sixteen?"

Susan nodded.

"Where did that come from?"

"I've just been thinking and I'm curious about other girls you've dated. I met Patty that one time, remember?"

"I don't."

"We were at the diner? Christmas shopping?"

"Oh, yeah!" Henry said. "How in the world do you remember that?

It was a long time ago, Susie."

"I think I remember because I was surprised. Charlie had never dated a girl before and I didn't have older friends and none of my friends dated. I was only twelve. I had girlfriends who had crushes, but nothing came of those then, so I think I remember because there you were, my brother's best friend, with your arm around a pretty girl. I remember you looked really happy. And I remember the way she looked at you."

"Yeah, Patty," Henry said. "She was a great gal. Really nice. She was my first real girlfriend, actually."

"So what happened with her?"

"She and her family moved out of town. We both knew things wouldn't work out after that, so we broke things off."

"I see," Susan said. "Do you think you'd still be with her if she hadn't moved away?"

"I don't really know," Henry admitted. "Mom has told me since I was really small that things just fall into place if you let them. She says that you need to just step back and let life take its course. God talks to you if you just listen; He's got a lot of ways to get through. It's our job to let Him. When you've been told something since you were really small, it sets in, you know? You really start believing it. As an adult now, I question a lot of things I've seen and been through, and I've definitely concluded that my mom is right with this one. So the way I see it: Patty moved away, we made the decision to end things, and that's the way it was supposed to go. Does that make sense?"

"I think so. But it's hard for me to just let go."

"I think it would be for me, too, if I had been brought up to believe some of the things you have. I believe in God, Susie. I do. Very much. But the God I was raised to know is a loving God and not one to fear. We've just had very different childhoods, and I think that has molded us into different people. But we work well together, you and I."

Susan smiled broadly and took a bite of bread.

When they had both finished dinner, they remained at the table, greatly enjoying further conversation.

"I need to go," Susan said a while later. "Mom is expecting me home."

"I understand."

Henry walked her to the door and helped her with her jacket. He turned her around, palms remaining at the back of her shoulders. Susan stood on tiptoe and brought her face to his, kissing him quickly. "Thanks for dinner, Henry."

"You're welcome," Henry said. He leaned down and kissed her more slowly, passionately.

She could get used to this.

* * *

March 2, 1970

Susie,

Rough day here toward the end of my stint at basic training. I won't go into details. Can't. But it makes me want to sit down right now to write to you all. I've got to. Got to get my mind off all this shit.

Henry and you both talk about each other pretty often, and let me tell you that it's one of the only things that I can hold onto right now. Never did I think this would happen, my best friend and my little sister. And thank you for including Gilbert so much in all you do. How'd I get so lucky to have you all?

Saw some sort of squirrel the other day and it made me think about that time that damn squirrel got into the house. Do you remember that? The old man was sitting at the table with his damn paper and cigarette and Mom saw it run in from the side door that was left open. There it was right in the middle of the kitchen floor. Mom wasn't wearing any socks or shoes; must have been spring or summer because I remember her in one of those thin dresses of hers with one of her aprons on. She saw that damn squirrel and screamed louder than I had ever heard her scream. Do you remember how fast she stood on top of her kitchen chair? I don't think I had ever seen her move that fast before. And there the old man was, giving her shit for freaking out. But did he do anything about it? Bet you can guess the answer to that. That pisses me off but not the point of my story. Boy, did we have a laugh that day. You heard the commotion and came running from your room. I was already in the kitchen, so I got to see this all unfold. And it was you, Susie. It was you that thought of getting the broom and trying to shoo it out the door. You weren't that old, I don't think. Seven? Eight? I was laughing my head off, you were shooing the damn squirrel, and Mom was still on top of her chair. And you did it! You got it out. Don't know how you did it so easily, really. Must be a squirrel charmer. Ha! Mom didn't come down from the chair for minutes after you got that squirrel back outside. You've got to remind her of this story, Susie!

Love you,

Charlie

SEVENTEEN

Winter rapidly progressed and spring arrived, glorious and welcoming. Flowers bloomed: rain fell. Susan could smell the rebirth in the air.

She entered the nursing home at which she was employed and reported to her boss for the day's schedule. Saturday in the later morning hours, bingo commenced to get the residents out of their beds and moving. First on her list was Mrs. Tremblay. She smiled; she was certainly bound to start the day positively with Mrs. Tremblay.

She folded the sheet of paper and placed it in the square pocket of her white uniform before stepping into the hallway from the nurses' station. She advanced down the white-walled hall and knocked on the open door of a room on the right-hand side.

"Hello, Mrs. Tremblay," she said as she closed the door behind her and edged toward the sleeping woman's bed. Her eyes fluttered open, and she looked somnolently in the direction of Susan's face. Her eyes adjusted to the interruption and she smiled warmly.

"Oh, Susan, dearie, it's you." Her voice was hoarse from disuse, though soft and kind. She struggled to lift the upper portion of her body, elbows depressing the bedsheets beneath her.

"Let me help you, Mrs. Tremblay." Susan placed her arms under the old woman's shoulders and helped lean her body forward so she was resting her weight on Susan's chest. Once she was propped up,

Susan fluffed her pillows against the brown headrest and scooted Mrs. Tremblay's frail body backward so she was in a sitting position. "How does that feel?"

"Very good, dearie, very good. Thank you, kindly."

"You're welcome."

"Now," said Mrs. Tremblay, "let's start where we left off, shall we? Tell me more about your young man."

Susan grinned.

"Ooh..." Mrs. Tremblay crooned with enthusiasm. "I know that look, I do. I had that look once upon a time when Mr. Tremblay and I were young, God rest his soul." She spoke slowly, a bright smile on her face, wrinkled lips creasing with the motion. A small cough into the crook of her arm and then, "He was a looker, he was. Black hair like midnight. And these brown eyes that could make a woman lose herself. I lost myself, I did. Married him when I was just seventeen, did I ever tell you that?" She looked wistfully beyond Susan, lost within the past. "Oh, well," she sighed. "That was a long time ago, it was, dearie. Oh, but what a man my Georgie was. He gave me eight children, did I ever tell you that? Eight children. My youngest died when she was just a baby, poor angel. And my girl followed her when she was ten years old. She would have been a looker; had the same black hair as my Georgie." Mrs. Tremblay paused to catch her breath for a moment and then continued: "Oldest boy died just a few years ago. Cancer, they said. But my other kids come visit me. Fills my heart. And grandkids, you know. And even great-grandkids. I hope you and your young man can be as lucky in love as me and Georgie were." She patted Susan's small hand with her own extremely wrinkled one, large blue veins protruding through the papery-white skin. "I sure am blessed."

"I love your stories, Mrs. Tremblay," Susan said as she held the old woman's hand. Mrs. Tremblay was prone to repeating herself often, but Susan didn't mind in the least; in fact, she rather enjoyed these bouts of reminiscence, took pleasure in the fact that Mrs. Tremblay chose her as a confidante.

She smiled at Mrs. Tremblay, the wisps of white hair upon her mottled head swaying with the soft breeze elicited from the small moving fan resting upon the top of her wooden dresser.

"Okay," Susan said, "what do you think about some bingo? I can take you down to the rec room if you'd like."

"I think I would like that very much, dearie."

"Wonderful. Then we'll just have to get you dressed. Here," she said as she began lowering Mrs. Tremblay's legs to the floor, "let me help you. Do you have to go to the bathroom first?"

"No, love," Mrs. Tremblay said, "that young nurse as was here before helped me to the bathroom. I was just resting my eyes when you came in, is all."

"Okay, then," Susan said with a smile.

Mrs. Tremblay lifted her emaciated arms into the air. Susan pulled her nightdress over her torso, taking care not to nick her nose when she lifted it off her body. Mrs. Tremblay's naked breasts hung loose, wizened upon her chest, her skin wrinkled and worn, soft as fine satin. Susan had taken a while to habituate to seeing the geriatric population unclothed, natural, and placing their trust in her care. Never was she to touch her own body; this she had been taught, but she had been taught also that it was a woman's work, a woman's responsibility, to care for the elderly population, and this was simply one portion of her responsibilities to them. She had eventually become accustomed to executing these responsibilities with the utmost of care and consideration, with love and tenderness. For the elderly population here at the home, their naked figures were simply... well... bodies.

"Now, let's see what we've got in your drawers." Susan walked over to the dresser beside the bed and opened the middle drawer, pulling forth a flowered short-sleeved dress that looked much too big for Mrs. Tremblay's physique. "How about this one?" She held it up for the older woman to see.

"That one's just fine." Susan gently slipped it onto her companion's body, lifting her to her feet so the dress would flow to her knees. Mrs. Tremblay stood slightly hunched, holding tightly to Susan's forearms.

"Would you like your slippers, Mrs. Tremblay?"

"I would, thank you." Susan ensured Mrs. Tremblay could stand unassisted before removing her hands from her body and scooting her slippers to rest beside her feet. She allowed the woman to grasp her arms once again to aid her balance as she stepped her feet into the oversized shoes. "Now, those always do feel good," Mrs. Tremblay said.

"Okay, if you're sure you don't need to use the restroom, then I can walk you down now."

"I'm okay for now. I do wish I could walk, dearie, but I suppose a chair really would help me today."

Susan steadied her partner, then walked to the corner of the room for the wheelchair. She helped lower Mrs. Tremblay into it and wheeled her the rest of the way to the facility's recreation room, where bingo had already begun.

"Hi there, Doris," Mrs. Tremblay said as Susan approached a table.

"Hi, Irma," Doris replied.

"I've got the nice one here," Mrs. Tremblay said to her friend as Susan lowered herself into an open chair beside her. Mrs. Tremblay reached over and patted her kindly on the forearm.

"What you say?" Doris raised her voice.

"Nice one," Mrs. Tremblay yelled as she motioned to Susan beside her.

"Oh, yeah, yeah," Doris said.

"Good morning, Paul," Mrs. Tremblay said to the elderly gentleman across the table.

Paul grumbled in return.

"Well, he's not in a very good mood, now, is he?" Mrs. Tremblay leaned over to her friend conspiratorially.

"Huh?" Doris asked.

Mrs. Tremblay gave her a wave of the hand. "Never you mind," she said, abandoning the conversation.

"Here's a card, Mrs. Tremblay, and some playing chips. I know you've got this, so I'm going to see if anyone else needs any help right now and I'll be back to check on you in just a bit, okay?"

"That's okay, dearie."

Susan stood from her chair and was beginning to walk away from the table when she was accosted by a co-worker in a nurse's hat and uniform.

"Susan," she said, "I need your help."

"Oh, sure."

"Mr. Biladeau over in room 133. He's soiled his bed. I need you to strip the bed, make it, and bathe him."

"Oh," Susan said dejectedly. "Okay."

She approached Mrs. Tremblay a moment later. "Mrs. Tremblay?"

"Oh, hello. Back again so soon?"

"I actually need to help another resident. Will you be okay here for a while?"

"I do enjoy my bingo, don't I? I'll be just fine, my dear. You go on ahead."

Susan walked apprehensively down the long corridor until she reached an intersection and veered to the left. Here she found the room in which Mr. Biladeau resided. She knocked on the door and stepped inside to find another worker aiding Mr. Biladeau from his supine position on the bed.

"Oh," Susan said. "Are you helping here? I was told to come."

"No, no," the woman said. "I'm needed in 117, was just starting until you came by."

"Okay," Susan said and fully stepped into the room. The smell permeated throughout the small area, the open window lending no respite from the pungent odor. Susan stifled a grimace, plastered a smile upon her face.

"Hi, Mr. Biladeau, I hear I could be of some use."

"Ah, I don't need any help," the old man said as he flung his arm in the air. "Accident is all. I can wash myself up." His voice was gravelly, guttural. He attempted to rise from the bed, but his legs buckled beneath him, sending him back to land on his soiled bottom.

"Here," Susan said as she briskly stepped forward, "let me help, please, Mr. Biladeau." She held him under the shoulders and lifted him to a standing position. The stench overwhelmed her, and yet she couldn't stand by while this man she had known her entire life—even if not well—struggled to maintain his dignity.

All reservations left her at that moment.

"That's my cue," the other employee said. She walked out the door leaving the pair in her wake.

"Tellin' you I can do it," Mr. Biladeau grunted as he bore the full weight of his body on his feet.

"I know you can do it, Mr. Biladeau," Susan said, "but sometimes, even when we can do things, it's good to accept a bit of help." She wasn't sure where her confidence had materialized from, but standing with this man now, she felt nothing but affection and pity.

"Sucks to get old," he grumbled.

Susan said nothing in return, merely guided him to the bathroom, where she ran the warm water from the spigot and let the tub fill. She helped Mr. Biladeau strip from his soiled clothes and placed them, bunched up, within a towel to be taken to the laundry. She warmed a large cloth with water and began sponging his bare back, gently, efficiently. She wrung it out in the sink and sponged the worst of the excrement from his bare bottom before sympathetically helping him into the warm bathtub.

She grimaced at the smell pervading her senses but willed it away, attending instead to this man in his time of need, this man who had led a long life in control of his own body and now sat in a steaming bath drawn by a young woman who had lived down the street from him for years. Mr. Biladeau was a man who didn't want to admit defeat, who believed he would always have his pride to fall back on.

He looked up at Susan with his big blue eyes. Tears pooled at the corners.

Susan brought a fresh, clean cloth down into the warm water, grabbed a bar of soap in the palm of her hand, and scrubbed the two together, friction amassing soapy suds. Looking into Mr. Biladeau's eyes, she tenderly began to rub the cloth upon his chest, then his shoulders.

She smiled at the old man in front of her as he trembled slightly at her affectionate touch. She scooted on her knees to face his back, his shoulders slouched as he sat in the bathtub. She moved the cloth around in circles, dipped it into the water, moved it again.

Mr. Biladeau bent his head forward, tears dripping down to merge with the water below, salt commingling with soap suds, with the remainder of his own bowels that had failed him so miserably.

Susan ran the cloth back on Mr. Biladeau's shoulders and slid her knees against the hard, white floor, white pantyhose leaving too small a barrier to grant a bit of comfort. She paid no mind. Instead, Susan lifted Mr. Biladeau's head with the tip of her finger, just as Henry at times did to her. He looked her in the eye, nose scrunching upward in an attempt to mask his agony.

Susan smiled. Large, broad, and genuine.

Humane.

"How are you feeling, Mr. Biladeau?"

"Name's Edmond. Might as well call me Edmond."

"Well, then, Edmond," Susan said, "how are you feeling?"

"Bit better. Bit better."

If she were disgusted by him, by his degenerate body, then she hid it well, for here before him was a young woman who forced his shoulders back just a bit with the fondness in her gaze, with the endearment in her eyes.

* * *

May 3, 1970

Susie,

Closed my eyes last night trying to get some sleep and thought of home. Thought of you and Gilbert and Henry. Thought of Mom. She just seems more and more broken to me these days. Not just from her letters, but as the years have gone by. I have no idea how someone like her ended up with someone like our old man, but here we are, I suppose.

I remember when we were younger. Mom was in the kitchen doing the dishes after dinner. Dress, bare feet. Kind of how I remember her, really. She was humming something to herself, maybe Paul Anka. She did always love him, didn't she? So there she was, humming and scrubbing and swaying her hips from side to side, as if doing those dishes made her happy, you know? You and I were right behind her and she didn't even know. She must have been off in her own world not to notice because you were giggling

239

like crazy, and even though you had your hand over your mouth and were trying to be quiet I was surprised she didn't turn around and hit you with that dish towel she had over her shoulder like she usually did. Always with a smile, though, remember? The old man walked in the door then from the living room and saw us making fun of Mom. He gave us this nasty look, but then he smiled! I remember going from being really nervous to suddenly being some sort of coconspirator as he quietly walked up behind Mom and scared the shit out of her when he wrapped his arms around her waist. She dropped something into the sink and water splashed everywhere, and Father, instead of getting pissed, laughed. He laughed. And she laughed. And then there they were, dancing in the kitchen to some kind of imaginary record in their heads. I remember standing there as a kid not knowing what was going on, but probably with a stupid grin on my face.

I don't have many good memories of the old man, that's for sure. But this I have. Makes me think that once upon a time they had to have been happy. Once upon a time, maybe he had something in him that she fell in love with.

Love you, Susie. Go give Henry a kiss. Ha! (Are you blushing?)

Charlie

* * *

"How was work?" Betty asked. She and Susan were at Janet's house for one of their slumber parties and were resting on Janet's bed.

"Just fine. I had a good day today."

"Glad to hear it," Betty said.

Susan had made the conscious decision not to divulge her interactions with Edmond Biladeau that morning. She could harbor this secret within her to help maintain the old man's pride.

The girls conversed for a while and then Susan excused herself to go to the bathroom. Once there, she lowered her panties and noticed that she had begun her period. Wiping herself after urinating, she lifted her panties and pants and walked back into Janet's bedroom.

"Janet?" Susan asked quietly. Should she just walk over to her home and grab the necessary items? No, she'd ask Janet if she had something she could use; she didn't want Father asking any questions if she unexpectedly turned up at the house now that it was the middle of the night.

"Ah," Susan said hesitantly. "Do you have a pad?"

"A pad? Oh, a pad," she said, now understanding the predicament her friend was in.

"No, don't use them. But I have a tampon. Want one of those?"

"I've never used one," she admitted.

"Oh, they're easy. I'll get you one."

Susan followed Janet back to the bathroom. Janet opened the cabinet door under the sink and placed a small box of tampons on the countertop. "See you in a bit," Janet said, leaving Susan alone in the small bathroom.

Susan began to panic. She knew of tampons; she had seen them on the shelves right there beside the pads that she purchased. Surely using one was normal, easy. If women inserted tampons daily, then certainly she had the ability to do so as well.

She opened the top of the box and peered inside. She pulled out a folded sheet of directions. She looked at the drawings provided, read the instructions.

She pulled her pants and panties down once again, resting them around her ankles and sat on the toilet. She spread her legs. Grasping the edge of the tampon, she lowered it and brought it between the darkened space near her upper thighs. She took her left hand and touched herself.

She began to sweat.

Mother had warned her never, ever to touch herself in this most private of places.

It was a sin, after all.

She explored with the tips of her fingers, trying to find a hole.

She began to shake.

Bringing the tampon closer to her body, she poked it around, hoping it would insert itself where it was needed.

Her breathing became deeper, more strained. Faster.

Her eyes rolled, her vision blackened, and there, on the top of Janet's toilet seat, Susan fainted straightaway, landing with a thud to the pink floor below.

* * *

May 17, 1970

Susie,

Remember that time when we went to Emerson and I stepped in that huge pile of dog shit? You were what? Maybe seven? I don't know. Younger anyway. You grabbed a stick from the ground and told me to use that. I stood there in the middle of the park trying to get that damn shit off my shoe and I just couldn't get it all off. We walked home hoping the old man wasn't there and you ran ahead of me and told Mom what had happened. She came out of the house and laughed hysterically. We went to the side yard and she grabbed the hose and just doused my shoe with the water. Then she lifted the hose and soaked me. You started laughing your little head off, so she turned the hose on you. You should have seen your face! So funny! Then she squirted you right in your open mouth. I'm laughing right now just remembering that look on your face.

See? These are the things we need to think about right now. These are the things I'm holding on to.

Love you, little sis,

Charlie

EIGHTEEN

The following year was a whirlwind of activity.

Eleventh grade came to a close. Although Henry had to work quite a bit at Greenfield and Sons—the local general store—to help pay his college expenses, Susan still saw him often and found she was completely and utterly smitten and in love with this man who was so unlike any man she had ever met, save her brother and Gilbert.

She split her time between Henry, home, work, and her girlfriends, becoming more intimate with Sandy Speckles as the days progressed. She found her to be quite the kindred spirit and was so pleased that she had been proven wrong in her unfounded prejudice that Sandy Speckles couldn't be a very kind person if she was such close friends with Mercedes Doyle.

Mercedes Doyle hadn't returned to St. Joseph's, and Sandy had no further information on her whereabouts. Although Mercedes wasn't the friendliest of people toward Susan, she still felt empathetic toward her plight in life and wondered if she was well.

August arrived, and Susan turned seventeen. Henry baked her a large chocolate cake that was heartily devoured.

Christmas was spent between her home (Henry joined her, which eased her discomfort in the presence of her father, whose drinking had become a more pressing issue even than it had been in previous years—just the week prior he hit the side of the garage coming home from a bar he frequented, smashing the right headlight and denting the side) the Beaumonts', and Henry and Gilbert's house.

The only person desperately missed was Charlie.

New Year's Day passed. Snow fell in droves, then melted with the warm, bright rays of the spring sun.

May arrived, and with it came Susan's senior prom. Henry and she would be attending. Janet and Bobby were still a couple and would be joining them. Betty was dating a young man by the name of Walter Wentworth, a man with hair every bit as dark as hers and a large nose on a narrow face. Walter was gentle and kind and held Betty dear.

Susan felt such contentment as she dressed in her bedroom now, unzipping the zipper at the back of her dress and stepping inside.

A knock at the door. "Susan, are you decent? May I come in?"

"Yes," she called back.

Mother opened the door, stepped in, and closed the door behind her. She walked toward her daughter and helped her zip the last of the zipper she couldn't quite reach, turned her around by the shoulder and held her at arm's length. Tears welled in her eyes.

"You are so beautiful."

"Mom, you need to stop because if you don't, then I'm going to cry."

She looked at her mother then, at her changed appearance. Her hair was much thinner on the top of her head, with a great deal of gray commingling with the auburn that was once so rich and pronounced. Her skin was a bit saggy, wrinkled, with a ghastly color of—if Susan were being honest with herself—*decay*.

But her eyes. Her eyes were still the same crystal blue they had ever been. A blue that took you to the depths of her soul, her trials and tribulations, but also revealed the kind spirit that had never been vanquished.

Susan remembered then the day that Mother had bought her the dress she wore right now.

It had only been a few weeks ago, a Saturday afternoon. Father had left the house, although neither Mother nor Susan knew where he had ventured. They could predict from experience that he was probably at the local bar or fishing. Or the local bar after fishing.

"Ready?" Mother asked.

"For what?" Susan was quite confused.

"To go buy you a prom dress, darling."

"Mom! Father would never let you spend the money. I was just going to borrow a dress of Betty's since most of what I get at the nursing home is pooled into the family."

"I know that," Mother said. "But you only get one prom, do you not? And I would like to do everything in my power to make this night special for you. Let us go out. Right now," she said with enthusiasm. "Let us get you the most beautiful dress we can find!"

"Mom," Susan said, "how in the world are we going to do that?"

Mother held her hand up and opened her palm, several bills unfolding.

"Mom!"

"Shhh…" Mother said as if Father were just in the other room. "It will be our little secret."

"But won't Father find out? Isn't he usually pretty stringent with money and finances?"

"Oh, fiddlesticks," Mother said. Susan smiled at the term her grandmother often used, now echoed down a generation through her mother. "I will take care of your father. If he ever finds out." She winked.

Susan was aghast. With the exception of visiting Charlie and a dollar here and there, Mother never defied her husband. *Never.* Yet here she was, doing just that. And for her.

How long had Mother been planning this excursion?

"So," Mother said, "are you ready, darling?"

"Yes!"

With Charlie gone, Susan had been borrowing his car, so transportation was a nonissue.

When they entered the dress section at the department store, Susan was overwhelmed with the mass of various choices. When you're content in simply borrowing a used dress from a good friend and you're suddenly flooded with possibilities in which you could drown, it's truly a wonder.

She looked at Mother by her side.

She would remember this moment always.

"Oh, Susan, darling," Mother said as she lifted a dress with thin spaghetti straps and frills upon the bosom, a white dress with small red polka dots and a small strip of red ribbon marking the waistline. The bottom of the dress ended in frills mimicking that on the bosom. Mother held it aloft for Susan to see. "I know you like polka dots."

"I really do. But the straps? I don't think I can do that with my chest." Darn these large breasts of hers! They certainly did make it more difficult to find well-fitting clothes. And oh, that dress...

"This one is pretty." Susan had found a dress of light pink, short-sleeved with a V-neck. There was a ribbon that would fall between her breasts, perhaps masking their enormity a bit. The waist was tapered, which she appreciated as she did have a small waist. Perhaps this would fit well?

"Well, then, you will have to try it on," Mother said.

Susan took it off the rack.

"How about this, Susan?" Mother called a moment later from another rack. "Darling, come here."

Susan walked over. Mother was holding a wispy dress of pale yellow. It was sleeveless and the bodice puffed out in a great amount of lace.

"Ugh," Susan said, "I don't think I want to look like a birthday cake."

Mother laughed. Though once a twinkling sound as if a spoon were being gently clicked upon a glass, Mother's laugh was now hoarse. Quite possibly because she no longer heard it often, Susan still thought it one of the most beautiful sounds in the world.

"Well, all right then," Mother grinned as she put the dress back.

Susan inhaled a breath as she spotted a baby blue dress. "Oh, Mom! Look at this!" Pink dress dangling from the crook of her arm, she held the newly found garment to her body and looked up at her mother.

"Oh, Susan, that is beautiful. And I know how much you adore the baby blue color. Shall you try it on?"

"Definitely!" Susan looked back at the dress. "I think right now."

Mother chuckled at her daughter's enthusiasm. "Well, all right then," she said. They arrived at the dressing area, and Susan entered a small room.

"Will you try on the pink dress as well?" Mother called.

"Maybe," Susan said, "but it's just this blue one. It's gorgeous. Trying it on now." A pause and then, "Mom?"

"Yes?"

"I can't get the end of this zipper."

"Okay. Let me in, darling."

Susan unlatched the lock on the door and allowed Mother entrance.

"Oh, Susan!" Mother placed a hand over her lips as she gazed upon her daughter.

"I know!" Susan's voice was near to squealing. "Help?" She turned her back on her mother and felt the zipper being lifted to the base of her neck. She looked at herself in the mirror of the dressing room, lifting the soft blue material at her thighs and gently swaying her hips from side to side.

"Oh, darling, this is the one."

Susan was beaming at her reflection in the mirror. She adored this dress. The long sleeves were sheer and her pale skin peered through.

The neckline was high. A satin ribbon rested directly under her chest in an empire waistline, the body of her dress falling straight and slightly shimmery to the floor.

"I love it!" Susan said. "Mom, I love it!" She clasped her hands in front of her chin and bobbed her body in excitement. "Maybe I should try the pink one on? It can't be this easy, can it?"

"Well," Mother said, "how do you feel? What do you think?"

"I think this one is the one. I love it!"

"Then it is the one, darling. Let us get it." Mother's palms found Susan's cheeks. She leaned over and kissed her daughter on the forehead.

Now, standing in her bedroom, Mother gazing adoringly at her, Susan felt elated.

"Okay, okay," Mother said. "I will stop." She fanned her wet eyes. "You are just so beautiful, darling, and this is such a happy moment for me. I love you so much, Susan Marie."

"I love you, too, Mom."

They walked out Susan's bedroom door and into the living room where they sat down upon the weathered green couch.

"Stay here when Henry arrives," Mother said. "I want to see the expression on his face when he sees you."

"Mom," Susan said, "isn't that a little silly?"

"Nonsense. That is not silly at all. Just look at yourself, Susan. Henry is going to be so surprised to see you. Oh," she said as she held her daughter's hand, "I cannot wait until he is here!"

Susan giggled. "Mom, you're kind of acting like a little girl."

"And so I am," she admitted. "I kind of feel like a little girl, and what a good feeling that is." She laughed and touched her forehead to her daughter's.

A knock at the kitchen door.

"Oh, he is here," Mother said eagerly. "Susan, stay here until I call you in."

Susan sat on the couch, scrunching the fabric on her thighs as her mother walked into the kitchen.

"Henry, welcome. We are so pleased you are here. Just you wait until you see Susan!"

"Hi, Mrs. Dubois. I'm sure she looks great."

"Okay, Susan," Mother called. "You may come in."

Susan stood from the couch and slowly walked the few steps to the entryway. Henry would have looked handsome enough had Susan only had his countenance to look upon, for he did wear the largest grin, showing those white teeth she loved so much. His eyes scanned her hair, her face, her dress with a look of astonishment as she walked bashfully toward him. "Wow," he exclaimed. "Susie, you look wonderful."

"Thank you," she said, butterflies coursing within. She felt her cheeks flush slightly at the way he was looking at her so appreciatively. "You look so handsome, Henry," she said. "I've never seen you in a tux before, I don't think."

"Aww," Henry said. "Thanks. Feeling pretty good, I have to say." He grasped the lapels of his jacket and tugged them forward.

Mother began taking photographs of the couple while Father sat silently at the table and Susan looked at Henry. His jacket was white with a thin black trim around the edges of the lapel. Black pants. White dress shirt under the jacket with a light blue bow tie.

Henry presented Susan with a simple wrist corsage of white and baby blue, and Susan gifted Henry a white rose boutonniere.

Susan turned to her mother. "We should be going," she said.

"Okay, okay." She ushered them through the door. She stood on tiptoe and kissed Henry on the cheek. "Thank you for being such a wonderful young man to my daughter," she whispered in his ear before lowering her heels to the linoleum floor. Turning to Susan, she kissed her on the forehead and tucked one of many stray curls behind her ear. "I love you, Susan," she said. "Very much. Now you go on and have yourself a wonderful time. You will have to tell me all about it tomorrow morning."

"I will," Susan promised.

"Bye, Father," Susan called. To his credit, Father turned his head and looked at Susan.

"Bye."

"Goodbye, sir," Henry said. "I'll have her home after prom."

"Yes, yes," Father brushed him off, "very good. Bye."

Susan and Henry walked onto the porch and out the door toward Henry's waiting car.

"You really do look beautiful," Henry said as they both sat in their seats and he started the ignition. He paused to look at her once again, leaned over, and kissed her slowly.

They stopped at the nursing home first. When Susan got out of the car, she felt rather embarrassed; here she was in this beautiful dress and not in her white uniform, stockings, and shoes.

A whistle from the nurses' station. It was Clara, a middle-aged woman whom Susan sometimes worked with and appreciated greatly. "My, my..." she said. "Aren't we lookin' all fancy tonight."

Susan gave a meek smile and approached the counter. "Prom tonight. Mrs. Tremblay and a few others were hoping to see us before we left," she said, "so here we are."

"So here you are," Clara repeated. "And lookin' beautiful if I do say so myself."

"Thanks, Clara." She turned to Henry. "This is Henry."

"Ah, yes," Clara said, "so this is your man, huh? Nice to meet you, Henry," she said, extending her hand for him to shake. "Clara."

"It's nice to meet you as well, Clara."

"Well, ain't he a handsome one," she said to Susan with a wink of an eye.

Susan looked up at Henry. "I think so," she agreed.

They walked down the hallway and entered Mrs. Tremblay's room. She was sitting up in bed, white wisps of hair combed back, a mass of makeup on her face.

"Oh, my goodness, Mrs. Tremblay, look at you!"

"Hello, dearie," she said, "I should say the same about you. You came to visit after all. How wonderful."

"Mrs. Tremblay, are you going somewhere?"

"Oh, no," she said, shaking her head. "No. I'm not going anywhere."

"I've never seen you with makeup on."

"One is never too old to make an effort, are they?" Mrs. Tremblay said with a coy smile.

"Well," Susan said, "I suppose not. You look wonderful."

"Why, thank you, dearie. Now turn around, turn around. I want to see you in that dress of yours."

Susan obliged.

"Just gorgeous," Mrs. Tremblay said. "And that hair. Look at those curls. What I wouldn't do to have hair like yours." She touched the thin wisps atop her mottled head. "Ah, well." She sighed dreamily. "I suppose this will have to do, won't it?"

"You're beautiful," Susan said wholeheartedly.

"Thank you, my dear," Mrs. Tremblay smiled. She extended both her arthritic hands toward Henry. "This must be your beau."

Henry walked forward and took her hands in his. "Henry's the name."

"Well, hello, Henry," Mrs. Tremblay said. "My son's name was Henry, did I ever tell you that?" She turned to Susan, who shook her head. "Yes, Henry he was; the cancer got him, God rest his soul." Her look was wistful as Henry held her small, wrinkled hands in his large palms, his bottom resting on the edge of her bed. Susan looked at the man before her, tender interactions with this woman she had grown to love dearly, and she felt an instantaneous surge of tenderness and devotion.

"Oh, I do hope you will have a wonderful evening," Mrs. Tremblay said, looking at Susan and then at Henry. She released her hands from his grasp and patted his cheeks. "You treat her well, you do," she said. Turning to Susan, "I know you'll be a good girl, dearie. I know some girls aren't these days. Now, you save your maidenhead, mind you. Wait until this handsome young man marries you."

Susan gasped audibly. "Mrs. Tremblay!" She was utterly shocked at the advice offered from the old woman and blushed profusely in response.

"Oh, my, my... "Mrs. Tremblay said. And surprising Susan further still, her friend chuckled and then began to laugh louder until she was holding her slight belly, eyes closed, mouth open. "Oh, your face, dearie," she snorted, "your face." Tears trickled down her withered cheeks. "I haven't laughed this hard in a long time," she said.

"Well, I'm glad I can be the cause of your laughter," Susan said. Henry looked from Susan to Mrs. Tremblay and began to laugh out loud.

"I like you," he said to Mrs. Tremblay.

"Well, I like you, too, young man," she said in return, patting his cheek once again.

Susan and Henry soon left Mrs. Tremblay's room to visit a few other residents down the corridor.

Exiting a room a while later and closing the door behind her, Susan looked down the white hallway and saw the backs of two figures walking slowly, and with a bit of difficulty, hand in hand.

She grabbed onto Henry's jacket sleeve. "Oh, my goodness, Henry," she said, "that's Mrs. Tremblay and Mr. Biladeau."

"Well, look at that," Henry said, a smile on his face.

Clara approached. "They're sweethearts now," she said. "Ain't that somethin'?"

"I'll say," Henry said.

"It sure is something," Susan said as she looked at the two elderly residents walking away from her. Mr. Biladeau dropped Mrs. Tremblay's slight hand and instead placed it in the crook of his elbow, leading her down the hallway to the recreation room.

"Oh, my heart," Susan said.

"Well," said Henry, "a good place for us to take our leave and head to prom?"

Susan nodded. "Let's go."

* * *

"I've got a surprise for you tonight," Henry said conspiratorially.

"Oh, you have, have you?"

"Mmm. And you're going to love it."

A surprise? She was eager to uncover this secret of his.

"You're here!" Betty had spotted Susan and Henry as they walked into the hotel ballroom, the venue for this year's senior prom. Susan was slightly overwhelmed with the throng of people and the hearty noises of merrymaking.

"We're here," Susan confirmed.

"Come on! Come dance with us." Betty pulled Susan to the dance floor, where Janet and Bobby had their hands in the air—Mikey and David beside them with their dates, David having arrived with Sandy Speckles—bodies moving to the beat of the band's music. Betty began dancing with Walter as Henry took Susan's hand in his own and twirled her.

Her nerves soon eased, then dissipated entirely as Henry led her around. She laughed with Henry, with her friends, danced until her feet were beginning to get sore. She was relieved when the band announced it was time to sit for dinner.

The circular white cloth-covered tables were set to hold six people, a number that pleased Susan greatly as this elicited the opportunity to sit with Janet and Betty and their dates.

"Here, here," Janet motioned for David and Sandy to sit at a table directly beside theirs with Mikey and his date, whom Susan had learned on the dance floor was in actuality his cousin.

"So, Janet," Henry began, "Susan tells me that you and Bobby are leaving next month. Still on?"

"It's still on," Janet confirmed. "Isn't that right, Bobby?"

"Sure is. Me and my boys have been traveling a bit, odd jobs here and there. We've got a great van and sometimes just sleep in that. Manny's girl is coming with us when Janet does. It'll be a groovy time and it'll get us out of here." He tucked his shoulder-length hair behind one ear.

"Are you that eager to leave?" Henry asked.

"Hell, yeah!"

"Why is that?"

"Nothing happens here, ever. Me and Janet, we're gonna make something of ourselves, make a good life. A life of our choosing. And we get to see the country while we're at it, meet new people."

"Well, I certainly hope you enjoy yourselves."

"Thanks, Henry," Janet said. "I can't wait to leave. With a few exceptions, we're surrounded here by nothing but the same. French Canadians whose kids meet other French kids, who then marry within the confines of this sleepy little town. I want more. Need more."

Henry nodded and took a sip from his water glass.

"And what about you, Betty?"

"After graduation, I think I may go work for my father's friend. He said there may be secretarial work over at his office, and I think that might be a good opportunity for me, at least for a little while." She looked over at Walter, who smiled in return.

"David's going to end up at NASA or something like that," Susan said. "He's always just been so smart."

"I heard that." David turned in his chair to look at his friend from the adjoining table.

"Well, it's true, isn't it?"

"I suppose it is," David said, having always been forthright in his responses. "School first, though. I'm headed to Dartmouth," he said for Henry's benefit.

"Yes, Susan told me," Henry said. "Congratulations, man, that's great."

"Thanks," David said.

"And what about you?" Henry contorted his body further to look at Mikey.

"Not sure yet," Mikey said, "but I'll figure it out."

Henry nodded. "Well, best of luck."

"Thanks."

Henry turned back to the table just as dinner plates were being presented.

Susan's stomach began to rumble. When your dinner was ready at five each day for as long as you could remember, your body often acclimated to that schedule. It was now past seven in the evening. She was hungry.

Susan ate heartily, extremely pleased to be in the presence of Henry and her friends.

When dinner was through, the band began to play once again.

"Let's go," Henry said as he extended his hand to Susan. She took it, stood from her chair, and let him lead her to the dance floor. She and her friends gyrated, swayed. She was in such a pure state of contentedness, she didn't want her time to end.

A slower song began to play, and Henry pulled Susan close. She rested her head upon his chest. She closed her eyes and breathed in.

She wasn't sure this night could possibly be any more wonderful.

"May I cut in?"

A voice over her shoulder.

Susan opened her eyes and turned around.

"Charlie!" she screamed. "Charlie!" She jumped into his arms, and he caught her deftly, hugging her with such force she struggled to breathe.

She was sobbing now, clinging onto the back of his shoulders with her arms, her soft cheek against his shaven one. Her shoulders were shuddering with the force of her bawling, tipping his hat askew.

Squeals from behind her. Commotion.

Charlie gently brought his sister's toes back to the floor and released her. Janet and Betty both hugged Charlie, one on either side.

"You're home," Janet said.

"I'm home." His voice sounded almost foreign to Susan just now, she hadn't heard it in such a long time.

It was mellifluous.

Henry walked forth, the two men embracing heartily. Henry looked into his friend's eyes, his hands still resting on the shoulders of Charlie's dark green uniform.

"Good to have you back, my friend," he said.

"Thanks for keeping it secret."

"Wait," Susan interjected, "you knew about this? You knew he was coming home and you didn't tell me?" She couldn't decide if she was upset or impressed.

"Sure did," Henry said, arms crossed over his chest, a devious smile on his face.

"But when? How?" Susan looked at her brother again. She touched his forearm. Was this a hallucination? Was her brother truly standing there before her?

But wait—

A cane?

"Charlie?" she said hesitantly as she looked at the cane he held in his left hand.

"Yeah," he said, following her gaze. "That's why I'm home."

"Charlie, what happened? Are you okay?" She was surrounded by her friends, Henry at her side, worried expressions abounded.

"Shot. Three times. Bum leg now. I have to walk with this thing." He held the cane aloft. "I'm told it'll get better with time, though." He looked at his sister. "I'm okay, Susie, really. I'm home."

"You're home." She almost couldn't believe the words as she said them, even as she was looking upon her brother right there in front of her in the flesh.

"You're home," she repeated as she wrapped her arms around his back, rested her cheek against his chest, breathed him in.

She lifted her head. "Does Mom know?"

Charlie shook his head. "Not yet. I was hoping you could invite her to brunch tomorrow morning."

"I can do that," Susan assured him.

"Keep it secret?"

Susan nodded, hoping she could wait that long.

Charlie looked down at his sister tenderly. "I've missed you."

"I've missed you so much!" She paused, looked at him. "Wait! Gilbert!"

"He picked me up from the airport."

"Oh, yes," Susan said. "I suppose he would have." She giggled.

The band picked up the pace.

"Time to dance," Henry announced.

Charlie smiled. He placed the majority of his weight on his right leg and swayed back and forth, the best he could muster under his current circumstances. His family and friends danced around him, with him, for him.

Through the night.

* * *

Although drowsy from her excursions the prior evening, Susan woke early Saturday morning and met Mother in the kitchen. Father was still in their bedroom; he slept later on Saturday mornings these days.

"Good morning, Susan," Mother said cheerily from her seat at the kitchen table. Her hands were cradling a cup of coffee. "I was not expecting you up so soon."

"Oh, well," Susan said feigning nonchalance. "I just wanted to tell you about last night."

"And I would very much like to hear about it. Here—" She motioned to the vacant seat by her side. "Sit next to me."

Susan sat and stretched her arms over her head. While she did indeed wish to relay the night's events to her mother, what she wanted more desperately was to divulge the knowledge she was endeavoring so mightily to hold within.

"Tell me every little detail," Mother said eagerly. "Did you have a good time?"

"Honestly, Mom," Susan said, "it was magical."

She told her mother about her time with Henry, with her friends. She told her about dancing, the band, the dinner, all the while privy to a secret of such magnitude she couldn't wait to see how thoroughly Mother would be affected when this secret was finally unfolded.

"Oh, my goodness, Susan," Mother said happily, "it really does seem like you had a magical time. I am so pleased."

Susan smiled, paused. "Mom?"

"Hmm?" she said through a sip of coffee.

"Henry has invited both of us to brunch this morning. We can go, right?"

"I will just run it by your father, but that would be lovely. And how nice of Henry."

"We have a little something for you."

"You do?" Mother's eyebrows lifted.

Susan nodded her head.

"Your father will expect breakfast when he wakes up. Was there a specific time Henry would like us over?"

"No," Susan said. "I'll just call when we're on our way."

"Well, okay, then," Mother said. Susan lifted herself from the seat at the table before she divulged the surprise.

She returned to her bedroom to dress for the day, then followed with a couple of chapters from her current novel. She felt incredibly anxious. *What is taking Father so long?* She thought to herself.

When she heard sleepy, stumbling footsteps emerge from the bedroom, Susan bounded from her bed and attempted to compose herself before following Father to the kitchen.

Breakfast didn't take long to cook, and soon the three of them were seated at the kitchen table eating their meal. Mother and Susan had smaller portions upon their plates, saving room for Henry's.

"Gerald?"

"Mmm?"

"Henry has invited me and Susan over for a brunch. Would you mind terribly if we went after the dishes were done?"

"Didn't want me?" Father grumbled.

"Oh, well…" Mother was unsure how to answer.

"I think Henry assumed you'd either have plans already or would maybe like to be by yourself instead of with us. We'll be talking a whole lot. But I'm sure he'd love for you to come if you'd like." Susan held her breath and desperately hoped Father wouldn't accept the invitation.

"No," Father said. "Don't want to go. Got somewhere to be anyway."

"Oh, okay," Susan said, attempting to mask her relief.

When breakfast was done, Mother and Susan washed the few dishes that had been used, cleaned the table, and got ready to leave the house. Susan made a quick call to Henry to let him know they were on their way.

"It is such a beautiful day, Gerald, that Susan and I are going to walk." Father chose to ignore her, but Mother knew he heard. "Bye, Gerald." She closed the kitchen door behind her, and she and Susan walked outside, stifling their giggles at having left the house alone.

"Oh, but I am happy we are out," Mother said as they made their way to the corner of North and Emerson.

"So am I," Susan said. She took her mother's arm in hers.

They turned left on Emerson and soon passed the general store on their right. Walking a bit farther, they turned right onto Pine Street—Henry, Charlie, and Gilbert's road. Their home was situated halfway down the street and on their left. A total of approximately a mile and a half from the Duboises'.

When they arrived at the house, Susan knocked upon the door, waiting for it to be answered as opposed to walking straight in as she typically did; she didn't want Charlie to be right there in the living room for Mother to see.

It was Henry who opened the door for them. "Good morning, Mrs. Dubois," he said.

"It is a good morning, Henry. Thank you for having us over. Especially for inviting me along. That was very kind of you."

"You are very welcome," Henry said pleasantly, a large grin on his face.

"It smells good in here," Mother said as she stepped inside.

"We've got some coffee cake in the oven."

"Lovely," Mother said.

"Here, please sit down," Henry motioned to the brown couch against the wall at the left of the room. "Can I get you anything to drink? Coffee, tea, water?"

"Thank you kindly, Henry. I just had some coffee at home, but a glass of water would be very nice."

"Coming up." He smiled at Susan before walking into the kitchen.

Susan began chatting with her mother, attempting to distract her from the kitchen area in case she had any inclination of going inside. Mother's head was turned toward Susan on the couch, and therefore not directed at Charlie when he entered the living room, a glass of water in his hands.

"Well, here you are," he said, "one glass of water."

Mother's head whipped to the side. "Oh!" Her fingers went to her lips. She began to tremble. She stood from the couch and walked to her son, slow at first and then faster. "Charles!" She reached for his face, cupping his cheeks in her palms. She released him and then fiercely flung herself into his arms, the water in the glass spilling over its sides as she clung to his shirt and showered kisses upon his lowered face.

Henry took the glass from his friend's hand and brought it back to the kitchen. Mother was sobbing. "My Charles! Oh! Oh!" More kissing, more grasping of his shirt. "How are you here? When did you get here? Oh, Charles!"

Charlie was laughing: Susan was crying at her seat upon the couch. Henry and Gilbert were beaming at the display of love before them.

Charlie lost his balance through the force of his mother's movements, and it was then that she discovered the cane in his left hand.

"Charles?"

Charlie explained to his mother about the wounds in his left thigh and calf, about his time in the hospital and his discharge from the army, and, thus, his journey back home.

"Oh," Mother said, "but you are home with us, darling. Home and safe from harm's way. Thank you, dear Lord God above!"

* * *

Susan was able to spend some time at Charlie's house with her loved ones for a while before heading back home to dress for work.

When she arrived at the nursing home, she was eager to visit Mrs. Tremblay to tell her about the previous night with Henry and her friends and to relay to her the great fortune of having Charlie back home.

She walked in through the front doors of the facility and straight to the nurses' station, where Carla was manning the front desk.

"Oh, my goodness, Carla," Susan said by way of greeting, "did you even go home last night?"

"Sure did," Carla said, "but had to get my behind back here bright and early this morning," she said.

She looked at Susan momentarily, then dropped her gaze.

"Carla? What is it?" Susan was immediately concerned.

"Ah, baby girl," Carla said. "I'm so sorry. It's Mrs. Tremblay. She passed away in her sleep just last night."

Susan was so utterly shocked she just stood there stupefied, looking at her friend, unsure of what to say. Her mouth opened; nothing emerged.

Carla walked out from behind the nurses' station and took Susan by the hands. "I'm so sorry, baby girl," she said. "You okay?"

"Mrs... Mrs. Tremblay?"

"Yeah. I'm afraid so."

"Mrs. Tremblay?" Susan began to cry, the tears falling upon her white dress.

Carla nodded, then embraced her young friend.

Susan let the older woman hold her. The tears eventually dissipated, and Carla stood back. "One thing that sucks about this job, that's for sure," she said. "We sure do have some nasty patients, but then you get one like Mrs. Tremblay."

Susan wiped the tears from her cheeks, attempted to compose herself.

"I was here just last night," she said.

"I know." Carla's voice was sympathetic.

"I'm sorry, Carla. I know we've lost a lot of patients in the time I've been here, but I've never been hit this hard."

Susan brushed the palms of her hands down her dress, stood tall. "Do you think I can go visit Mr. Biladeau before I start my day?"

"I don't see why not."

"Thanks, Carla."

Susan began her way down the hallway, paused in front of Mr. Biladeau's doorway. His door was ajar, and she saw him there, sitting on his bed. She knocked on the wall and his head slowly lifted her way.

Susan smiled sorrowfully and walked toward him. She sat down upon the bed's edge.

"You heard?" he asked.

"I just did."

"We lost a good one there."

Susan nodded, sandwiched his hand within both of hers. "It won't be the same here without her, will it?"

"Can't be. She was a light. I may not understand much about this world, what that I've been in it for more than eighty-seven years even, but I know this: some people are better suited for Heaven than for being here."

Susan pondered this, gave a slight smile.

"If I've learned anything in this life of mine, I've learned that people come in for a reason and they go out for a reason. They come to you when you need them. Might not know why that is, but they do. You need them. Irma came into mine to remind me what it was like to be happy. Haven't felt that way in a long time. Don't know why I didn't meet her sooner. Maybe God didn't see me fit, maybe he had other plans for me—I don't know. Never will, I suppose. But you know what I think?"

"What's that?"

"He sent her to me so I could die having loved again."

Susan held his hand tighter between her own, rested her head upon his shoulder.

Edmond Biladeau patted her curls with his free hand. "Growing old sure does suck."

NINETEEN

June dawned, and with it came Susan's high school graduation. She stood in her bedroom now, donning her white graduation gown, square hat pinned to the top of her head, curls shooting around the sides.

High school was essentially over, and she was eager to learn what fate had in store for her. Charlie was home now. She had Gilbert, Henry, and her mother. She had her friends and her work at the nursing home. Her life was falling into place.

The graduation was to take place in the gymnasium, so this was where the throng of people were directed when Susan arrived at St. Joseph's. Dodge, Ford, Toyota, BMW: they were all there scattered among the parking spaces in their reds, greens, whites, and oranges. Susan opened her door to the sunny day and stepped out of her family's rusted, ramshackle car.

Inside the gymnasium she found Janet, Betty, David, and Mikey—all of whom had arrived before her—among the masses of white and hunter green, St. Joseph's school colors.

"Look at us," Betty remarked.

"Thought this day would never come," Janet said, a scowl on her face.

"I'm kind of sad it's here," Mikey admitted.

"Are you really?" Janet asked him.

"I am. School was just something I took for granted every day. Just got up and came to school. I still don't have plans for after graduation. I'll figure it out, I know, but I liked just coming to school every day. Now it just means I need to grow up. Ugh."

Susan chuckled at her friend's honest remarks.

"I'm glad it's here," she said, "but at the same time, it's bittersweet to me. I got to see you all every day and now I won't."

"Oh, we'll still see each other," Betty said with the conviction of the young.

"I know we will," said Susan, "but not nearly as often. We'll all be starting our lives, really. I think it will be harder for us all to get together."

"We'll make time," David offered.

Susan smiled at her friend. "How about this summer? I'm sure Charlie and Henry will let us use their yard. A backyard barbecue, anyone?"

"I'll be gone," Janet said.

"Oh," Susan said regretfully, "I knew that. I think I just forgot for a minute there. Oh, now I'm getting kind of sad."

"Okay, time to stop," David said. "Today's supposed to be a happy day. For real!"

"David's right," Janet said. "Nothing sad today. Today we graduate! And we're together right now." The friends all smiled, embraced.

* * *

Mother left the house the next morning directly after breakfast for the grocery store, claiming she had forgotten a few ingredients that she needed in order to prepare that evening's dinner. Susan took this as her cue to grab her cardigan from her bedroom to warm her from any morning chill still in the June air, and begin her way to Henry's, as she had promised she'd head over before work. She held a bag in which she had folded her uniform and white shoes. She had already asked permission of her brother to use his car.

She walked onto Pine and approached the brown house to her left, noticing a curtain was pulled back and Charlie was peeking outside. He shut the curtain immediately and retreated.

Susan passed Gilbert's and Charlie's cars in the driveway (Henry's was parked on the street), and knocked on the front door, opening it shortly thereafter to step inside.

Sam Cooke's "Cupid" was playing on the record player to the left of the entryway—one of Susan's all-time favorite songs, sung by an artist whom both she and Henry appreciated greatly. Balloons were floating all around the small living room: a vase of roses was on the table to the right of the couch.

Susan was astonished. Was this Henry's idea of prolonging her graduation celebrations? He never did cease to amaze her, to make her feel loved and appreciated.

She smiled broadly.

"Henry?" she called. "Charlie? Gil?"

Charlie and Gilbert both walked out of the kitchen and toward Susan who had found herself in the middle of the living room floor surrounded by the hovering balloons.

"What's going on?" Susan asked.

"Nothing," Charlie answered, a sly grin on his face.

"Gil?"

Gilbert shook his head and crossed his arms over his chest.

Another figure in the doorway.

Susan turned her head to find Mother walking toward her.

"Mom?" Susan asked, bewildered. "What are you doing here? I

thought you were at the grocery store?" A pause. "What?"

"I told a little white lie," Mother said. "I parked the car down the street, darling." Mother stood as if she were walking on air; an aura of pure excitement permeated forth.

"I am so confused," Susan said.

Mother looked to Charlie and Gilbert. "Boys?"

Charlie and Gilbert followed Mother back into the kitchen, leaving Susan standing utterly perplexed on her own.

She looked around the room, at the vase of flowers, at the red, white, and pink balloons (she hadn't thought to question the choice of color). She listened to Sam Cooke's voice penetrate the air.

Henry walked in holding a single red rose in his hand.

"Hi, Susie," he said, taking her hand in his free one. "Sit with me?"

"Okay," Susan said. She remained addled. "Henry, I am so confused. What's my mom doing here? And she's acting funny. Why's she acting funny? And why the balloons if not for my graduation. What's going on?"

"Well," Henry said, "at least you've got one thing right. I asked you here today to celebrate you in a way."

"You did?" she asked. Pondering this, she looked back at Henry. "I'm still confused."

Henry chuckled. "Susie, I just love you so much."

Susan smiled. Should she laugh or be affronted that he received such pleasure in her naivete?

Henry was still clinging to Susan's hand. He lifted it now and placed it in his lap, scooting his hips closer to hers on the couch.

"Susie," he said, "I do love you. Very much." He paused before resuming. "I think that we all go through life learning each and every day, don't we? I think I *want* to learn every day. I think that's how we grow and how we can strive to be better people." His words were slow, voice deep.

Where is this going? Susan thought to herself.

"Here's the thing," Henry continued. "We may change. I think everybody does in a way. But when we have someone we love, someone that makes us want to be the best person we can be right by our sides, then we change for the better, we change together. Suze?" She looked up into his eyes. "I want you to be by my side. Forever."

Susan gasped, her eyes widening, tears beginning to form.

She was oblivious to the camera that was peeking out the side of the kitchen doorway.

"I'm not sure if I'm articulating myself well enough here. I guess I'm just saying that I love you. So much. I love the way I've seen you grow. I love the way you treat those around you. I love the way you love."

Tears were falling down Susan's cheeks, and she began to tremble.

"Marry me, Susie. Please say you will. Be by my side as we both grow old. Be by my side as we learn from each other?"

Susan flung her arms around his neck. "Yes, yes, yes, YES!"

"Whoa, hold up." Henry laughed as he extended the hand with the rose away from his body. "We don't want to destroy this. Here," he said, handing it to Susan, "look at the petals."

Susan took it from his hand and peered down. In the center of the rose was a ring. She pulled it out and held it between her thumb and forefinger. "Henry!" she exclaimed.

"I really hope you like it, Susie. It was my grandmother's ring passed down to my mom when she passed away."

"It's gorgeous!" Susan was still in shock that she was sitting there with Henry by her side having just been proposed to. She peered down at the ring, studying it closely. The band was of medium thickness and made of rose gold, a darker shade of gold than the small wedding band Mother wore. A circular diamond was at the ring's center surrounded by smaller diamonds set with gold. In fact, there was so much gold that it rather muted the shine of the diamonds themselves, but Susan thought the ring was lovely. No, more than lovely. As she was holding it just now, as emotions poured forth and she realized that this ring had been worn by a woman who had been dear to Henry, who had birthed the woman who had raised such a wonderful man, she found the ring to be simply incredible and she was honored to have it now.

"Here," Henry said as he took the ring. He placed her left hand in his and slipped the ring onto Susan's ring finger. "Oh, my gosh," he said, "does it actually fit?"

"I think it does!" Susan laughed.

"Umm," Henry said. "Providential?"

"I'd say so," Susan smiled.

"May we come in now?" It was Mother calling from the kitchen, exhilaration in her voice.

Henry laughed. "Yeah, come on in," he said behind his shoulder.

Mother came bounding into the room, a hop to her step as she approached her daughter. Susan stood from the couch and Mother embraced her mightily. "Oh, Susan," she said, "Susan, I am so very happy for you."

"Thanks, Mom. I can't believe you knew about this!"

"I sure did. Henry asked my permission, and he asked for your father's as well."

"He did?" Susan was amazed. It would have been common courtesy to ask Father's permission for her hand, but Father was not an easily approachable man. She would not have faulted Henry if he had forgone this tradition, yet it did leave her impressed.

"Let me see the ring, Susan," Mother said as she reached for Susan's hand. "Oh, how beautiful it is on you." Mother placed her fingers to her mouth and began to cry.

"Mom," Susan said, "you're going to make me cry again."

"Well, then we will cry together. It certainly is a happy day." Mother kissed her, then turned to her soon to be son-in-law. "Oh, Henry," she said placing the palms of her hands on his cheeks and patting gently.

Charlie and Gilbert expressed their congratulations, and they all passed the next half hour in merriment.

"Henry, I can't believe I have to go to work. Why'd you do this when I had to leave? I want to spend all day with you now."

"I thought the timing was perfect," Henry said. "And see? Now you have some exciting news to tell your friends at the home. And," he said as he held her close to his chest, "we can look forward to seeing each other maybe after work?" He kissed her gently.

"I think I can do that," Susan said teasingly.

"Susan, I will walk out with you," Mother said. "I suppose I really should get those groceries I told your father I needed. And perhaps I've run into a friend at the store to excuse my tardiness in arriving back home if your father is there?" she said with a wink.

Susan and Mother said their goodbyes and walked outdoors.

"I am so happy for you, Susan," Mother said again as she squeezed her hand and looked intently into her daughter's eyes. "So happy. He is a wonderful man and he will treat you well, no doubt. I think he is going to make you a very happy woman."

"Thanks, Mom. I really think so, too."

Mother began to walk farther up the street to retrieve Father's car, and Susan walked toward Charlie's, bag in hand. She'd dress once she got to the home. She sat a moment before starting the car, hand on heart, a feeling of pure joy within.

She brought her left hand to the steering wheel and looked adoringly at the ring she now wore.

Engaged! She was engaged!

TWENTY

A lapse of a week—Susan's last actual week at school before high school was officially over—and she found herself walking to the front door of the home Henry, Charlie, and Gilbert shared together once again on a Saturday afternoon after having worked at the nursing home that morning.

"Hello?" she called lightly as she opened the door and stepped foot inside. Gilbert sat—elbows on his knees—in the middle of the couch, flanked on either side by Charlie and Henry. He held an open letter in his hands.

"Why the somber faces?" Susan asked as she walked toward them. Gilbert raised his head, handed her the letter.

Order to Report for Armed Forces Physical Examination, it read. She knew what this letter entailed.

Gilbert was being drafted for Vietnam.

"You have to be kidding me," Susan said. "Charlie just got back. We just got Charlie back." She was near hysterical. "And now you have to go?" Her voice was raised as she thrust the letter back into Gilbert's hands. "This is crap!"

"Susie," Henry said as he rose from the couch and put his hand gently on her shoulder.

"No!" she yelled. "Don't 'Susie' me right now, Henry. I've had enough! What more are they going to take from us?" Her eyes were

273

dry, but she was fuming.

"It's bullshit," Charlie mumbled softly from the couch.

"What?" Susan turned toward him, fists clenched.

Charlie looked her in the eye and raised his voice.

"It's bullshit."

"You're darn right it is!" She took a deep breath, Henry squeezing her shoulder to help her calm down. "Gil," she asked, attempting to compose herself. "When did you get that?"

"Just today," Gilbert said. "When the mail came. Just about a half hour ago now maybe."

Susan buckled. She let her body fall to the floor, landing on her bottom. She pulled her knees to her chest, wrapped her arms around her shins and rocked back and forth. "Why'd you get it?" she asked.

Gilbert lowered his head forlornly. "Just my time, I suppose," he said. "Pity they did away with the graduate deferments, Henry. I don't want to be worried you'll be joining me where I'm going." He paused, looked at his friend. "Draft numbers have been lower these past months, though. Hopefully, you're set. I apparently have shit luck."

Henry looked at his friend with pity and heartache, while Susan looked at Henry with outright fear. The last thing her heart needed was for both Gilbert *and* Henry's lives to be in jeopardy.

Charlie said nothing, just sat to the right of Gilbert, face stoic.

"I'm sorry, Gil," Susan said. "I'm so sorry for the way I'm reacting. This is a time where you need us all and I'm having a fit." She stood and sat in the seat Henry had vacated, taking Gilbert's hand in hers. "I'm really sorry."

"It's okay, Susie," Gilbert said. "We've had the last half hour to process this. We've had our fits. It's your turn. Makes me feel loved." He bumped her gently with his shoulder, a dejected smile on his face.

"I do love you, Gil."

"We all do," Henry said as he sat on the floor.

"Charlie, I'm being so selfish," Susan said, looking beyond Gilbert to her brother. "Are you okay?"

Charlie sat with the backs of his hands on his thighs scrutinizing his palms. He began to quietly and slowly speak. "I've been there," he said. "I know what it's like. You see shit over there you'll never be able to erase." He paused, rested his head in his hands. "It changes you," he said as he ran his hands through his hair and looked at his boyfriend beside him. "It changes you."

Gilbert closed his eyes.

Breathed.

* * *

"Edmond, what's wrong?" Susan walked forward and sat next to her forlorn friend on the edge of his bed.

"Tough day," he said. "Feeling it today."

Susan placed the palm of her hand on Mr. Biladeau's shoulder. "Anything I can help with?"

"Wish I could say yes. It's just this body of mine. Don't think I'll be here much longer." He sighed again. "At least I've got my mind. Had a friend got the Alzheimer's. Now that's a shitty way to go. Might not have much in my life to be happy about right now, but I got a couple things. At least I know that. At least I got my mind." He paused and looked to Susan beside him. "Just a tough day today."

As a child, never did she imagine she'd become friendly with the old man down the street who rarely spoke or smiled, but sitting here now beside her friend, she knew she'd grown to care a great deal for him. He let her in a small amount and to this she grasped, refusing to relinquish her hold. Once Susan loved, she never surrendered.

275

"Hey," she said as she playfully nudged his shoulder, "there's a new resident down the hall. Mr. Baker. Perhaps you could invite him to bingo this morning? I could use some help to get him going here."

"Heard him last night," Mr. Biladeau said. "Ranting away. Threw something, I think. Heard the crash and a scream from a nurse."

"He hasn't been very friendly," Susan said.

Mr. Biladeau looked her in the eye, countenance forlorn. "He's a man at the end of his life. And he's here. He's not in the home that maybe he'd been in for the last fifty years or more. No wife here, no kids. Don't know his story and probably never will, but I know how he feels. We all deal with it differently. I'm trying to accept the end of my life but it's hard, Susan. It's really hard. Don't get discouraged. He needs you."

Susan had been privy to very few words from her neighbor throughout her almost eighteen years of life, but as he'd begun to open up to her these past months, she contemplated every sentence he uttered.

"Edmond?"

"Yeah?"

"I'm glad we've come together." Susan rested her head on the old man's bony shoulder.

"Mmm," he mumbled. His body went rigid at the display of affection and then relaxed.

"Me, too," he quietly said. He took his wrinkly, withered hand from where it had been resting by his side and patted Susan gently on her curls. "Me, too."

* * *

Gilbert passed his physical examination. Almost identical to his previously received notice, the official draft letter came shortly thereafter, demanding he report within ten days for induction. In no haste to leave, he savored every moment of his last ten days with Charlie.

Gilbert's parents requested the privilege of driving him to report for induction and, in turn, being the last of his loved ones to see him off. They were, Susan believed, still ignorant of his relationship with her brother, Charlie and he having purchased a second bed that had been crammed against the wall of their small bedroom to fool the unsuspecting, Mother included.

The household was altered significantly without him there. Charlie, still adapting to home life after his return from Vietnam a month and a half prior, plummeted into a depressive state that not even Susan or Henry could remedy at times.

She often wondered what demons her once very open brother struggled with on a daily basis, what traumas had reshaped his character and temperament so wholly.

Would Gilbert return home to them equally transformed?

TWENTY-ONE

Susan continued her work in the nursing home, Henry at the general store throughout the summer. Fall arrived, and with it, the beginning of graduate school for Henry, which demanded a great deal of his time even though the college was less than a half hour away from his home. Susan was fortunate enough to alter her work schedule to work weekdays only, leaving the weekends free to spend time with her fiancé.

The majority of the leaves had fallen from the trees by Thanksgiving Day. Henry was on vacation from school and accompanied Susan to both her grandparents' homes. She didn't spend nearly as much time with her extended family as she had done as a child, so she was pleased to have the opportunity but was thankful, too, when it was time to part.

Susan was already quite exhausted from the time spent with both sets of grandparents', but she desperately wanted to be with her brother and ended her Thanksgiving contented in his home, though Gilbert's absence was sorely felt.

The holiday came to a close, snow fell, and Christmas approached.

Now on this Christmas Day she and Henry were resting gratefully on Henry's couch, his arm across her shoulder after they spent the morning with Mother and Father at their home.

Father had begun drinking when he woke, a glass of whiskey in hand even as they were exchanging presents, juggling golden sips with deep inhalations of his cigarettes. Mother had been pleased to have both Susan and Henry present, and Susan felt quite guilty for leaving her mother once the afternoon was well under way, but she wanted, too, to be with Henry and Charlie, and though Mother said she was pleased Susan could spend the rest of this Christmas Day with others, Susan knew she was loath to have them leave her alone with only Father for company. They were due at Memere and Pepere Dubois's soon.

In just a short amount of time, Susan and Henry would marry, and then Susan would be living here, in Henry's home, sharing it with Charlie and Gilbert when he returned from the war. She feared what her mother might suffer living alone with Father.

"Charlie, you okay?" Susan asked her brother. She was sandwiched between Charlie and Henry on the couch. "You went off somewhere just now."

"I'm okay. Some days are better than others. I was just thinking I'm really glad to be home and with you both right now, but we're missing Gil, and today I'm having a really hard time with that."

"How about we raid the fridge?" Henry suggested.

Charlie gave a downcast smile. "Okay."

"Do you ever go grocery shopping?" Susan asked. "Look at this refrigerator. You boys are ridiculous. Um….yeah, I think you need me here, don't you? I'll fill this fridge up and get some food into you."

"Oh, we get food into ourselves." Henry said, "That's why there's nothing there."

"Gil has always done most of the shopping," Charlie offered quietly. "For some really warped reason, he enjoyed it. Henry and I both hate it, so you won't find us going until we're paper-thin with starvation."

Susan was so pleased to hear this semblance of a joke that she put her arm around her brother's waist and patted him on the chest. "Well, then, Gil and I can go together when I'm here, and we won't have any space left in this refrigerator for all the food we'll bring back. Just you wait and see," she said, "we'll fatten you up in no time."

Charlie gave her a downcast smile. She knew he was trying. She knew.

"Okay, you know what?" Susan said as both sets of eyes turned to her. "That Chinese place down on Warren Ave? I'm pretty sure they're open Christmas Day. Let's give them a call and we can eat there tonight. It'll get us out of the house, too."

"Sounds good to me," Henry said. "And tomorrow, when we visit my parents, Mom will give us food to take home." He smiled schemingly.

"Henry!" Susan gently hit him on the arm. "Well, I do suppose you'll need it," she admitted.

"They're open," she announced when she was done with the call. "Ready?"

"Yeah, let's go," Henry said.

"Charlie?"

"I'm ready."

And thus, the remainder of their Christmas Day was spent eating greasy Chinese food down the street.

Susan was delighted.

* * *

"Let's dig in!"

It was the following day, a Christmas celebration at James and Viola's. The food was on the table and the party had settled. James carved the turkey and forked slices over onto plates held aloft.

Conversation abounded and dinner was finished, stomachs full.

A knock at the door.

"Who in the world could that be?" James asked as he and Viola stood from the table, both grinning broadly.

Henry's chair slid backward as he, too, stood from the table and walked toward the door. Charlie remained seated, though the smirk on his face indicated to Susan that there was shared information in the house of which she was unaware.

"Oh, Frankie, how very nice to see you," Viola said cheerfully.

Susan gazed across the table at her brother, who lifted his eyebrows at her and smiled knowingly.

"What's that look for?" Susan asked.

Charlie merely lifted his head in the direction of the door, signaling for her to inquire where inquiry would elicit a response.

Susan stood and walked through the entryway from the dining room into the living room, the front door just to her right. A slight woman with dark blond hair parted in the middle, the ends bobbing outward upon her shoulders, held a small, scraggly puppy in her arms just inside the home, the door having closed behind her. "And you must be Susan," she said as Susan approached the door timidly.

Susan merely nodded.

"Well, then," she said, "Merry Christmas to you." She transferred the puppy into Susan's arms. Susan held the puppy under its bottom, its front paws upon her chest. Boy or girl she didn't know, but this puppy was adorable. Scraggly, wiry brown, tan, and red fur jutted every which way; large brown puppy eyes gazed at her from the comfort of her arms.

"I don't understand," Susan said as she looked at the woman. Frankie was it? She turned from face to face: Viola, James, Charlie, who had come to stand beside her, and Henry just before her. Henry, whose smile was wider than any other and whose eyes radiated love and happiness.

"Merry Christmas, Susie," he said as he slowly placed his arms around her shoulders, cocooning the puppy between them. "She's for you."

"Me? You mean… Henry, do you mean you got me a puppy?" A nod of Henry's head, and the smile upon his face confirmed this to be so. "A puppy?" Susan said, standing with the small bundle in her arms, tears beginning to well. "For me?" A break in her voice and the tears began to fall obscuring her vision.

"For you," Henry confirmed. "She'll stay with me and Charlie for now, and when you move in with us in June…"

Susan lacked the ability to convey her feelings into words. She stood there, holding the puppy tighter to her chest and crying. A puppy. For her. She wiped her eyes with her upper arms and looked at the faces surrounding her. "How?" she eventually managed to croak, laughing.

"This is Frankie," Viola said. "Henry came to me a while back and told me he was thinking of getting you a puppy for Christmas. I just so happened to know that Frankie's girl was having a litter and I made a phone call."

"Oh, Viola," Susan said, "thank you!"

"Sweetie, you are so very welcome."

"Henry, I just… I can't even…"

"You don't need to say anything, Suze. The look on your face tells me all I need to know." He leaned down and kissed his fiancée, then kissed the brown-furred head of their new puppy. "What are you going to name her?"

"I actually don't even need to think about a name," Susan admitted. "I've known ever since I was a little girl and asked Charlie if he thought our parents would ever let me get a puppy. Obviously, they didn't. But here she is now." She looked down at the newest addition to her family and kissed her wet black nose. "Her name is Lucy."

∗ ∗ ∗

A Saturday morning in February found Susan playing with Lucy on the living room floor of Charlie and Henry's home while her brother and fiancé played Scrabble on a TV tray propped up in front of them on the couch.

"'Exorcize,'" Charlie whooped. "That's the winner right there."

"Damn!" Henry exclaimed. "You're kicking my ass, man. Must be all that reading you do. I may read a lot, too, but maybe I need to catch up to you."

"Even if you did," Susan interjected, "you still wouldn't be able to beat him. He's a Scrabble master."

"Yeah," Henry agreed, "I know. My ass has been kicked way too many times by this guy right here."

Charlie held a firm smirk on his lips.

"How—" A knock on the door.

"I've got it," Henry said as he stood from his place on the couch. "Be right back."

Henry opened the door, and Susan saw a couple standing on the walkway just outside. A woman and a man perhaps in their late forties, early fifties. Both had dark hair, the man's waved and thick, the woman's also thick but perfectly straight to her shoulders. Both wore entirely somber expressions as they were welcomed into the home.

Charlie scrambled immediately to his feet when he saw who stood at the threshold of the doorway. He wobbled momentarily as he lost his balance. He no longer needed the aid of his cane but wasn't entirely back to his normal self, either.

"We're so sorry to bother you and sorry that we didn't call first. But," the man said, "we know you are Gilbert's best friends and you deserve to hear it from us in person and not over the phone." He stood erect, face stoic.

Charlie took a step forward, hesitant.

"It's Gilbert," the woman added. "They came yesterday. To tell us." Her voice cracked as she grasped onto her husband's sleeve.

Lucy tugged on the opposite end of a rope Susan held in her hand, growling to be played with. Susan dropped the toy and gently pushed Lucy aside as she stood from the floor and walked to her brother's side.

"Is he—?" Henry didn't finish.

Gilbert's parents both nodded their heads, his mother now openly weeping.

"Come in," Henry offered. "Please come in and sit down."

Gilbert's parents sat upon the couch. Susan sat next to his mother, Henry and Charlie on the floor in front of them.

"How?" Charlie's voice was soft, exceptionally wounded.

"Shot," Gilbert's mother said, tears flowing freely. Henry handed her a tissue from the side table next to the couch. She nodded her thanks.

"Apparently there was a raid. They were caught in the middle. Several casualties and Gilbert was one of them. They're flying his body home," his father informed them.

Susan sat there next to Gilbert's parents, watched his mother nod her head, wipe her tears, looked at his father as he sat erect and uncomfortable on the couch beside her. Flying his body home? Who was responsible for doing so? What man was to look upon the face of her brother's lover, breath gone? Still. He'd never move again. She'd never hear his voice. She would never see the smile upon her brother's face as he embraced his Gilbert. She would never again speak to him, laugh with him, touch his warm body in jest. He wouldn't be there with them when she married Henry. He wouldn't be there with them when she moved into his home. Only an echo would remain.

The puppy whined at her feet. She gently nudged Lucy away as the tears formed and fell upon her bosom.

Charlie sat on the floor, respectfully attempting to console Gilbert's parents with a light touch on the knee, a look.

Susan ached for her brother, sitting there unable to pour himself forth.

"I am so sorry," Henry said to Gilbert's parents.

"Thank you," his mother said. "You were both so good to him. All of you. I know you're Susan," she said as she looked to her left. "Gilbert talked about you."

Susan gave a doleful smile.

"We knew this was a possibility," his mother said, "that Gilbert wouldn't come home to us alive. But it hurts. It just hurts so much." She broke down then, sobbing as her shoulders slumped. Her husband put an uncomfortable hand on her shoulder. Susan saw a tear make its way down Henry's cheek.

"I'm sorry," Henry said apologetically, "I really just don't know what to say." He looked to Susan and Charlie. Charlie remained motionless on the floor at Susan's feet, his eyes trained on Gilbert's parents. Susan wanted so desperately to throw her arms around him, to embrace him, to rock him as he wept. She wanted to grant him the opportunity to grieve, to wail, to hurt.

Instead, he sat there respectfully, his emotions in check.

"I understand," Gilbert's mother said. "It's a shock to us all."

Gilbert's parents remained at their home for a few minutes longer before standing and making their exit.

Henry closed the door softly behind them and looked immediately to Charlie.

"Charlie," he said gently.

Susan reached for her brother, but he dodged her hand, shook his head vehemently. He walked to his room, closed the door behind him.

Susan and Henry looked at each other. He walked to her, took her in his arms.

Susan's tears were plentiful, her face becoming splotchy, her nose beginning to run. "How do we help him?" she asked.

"I don't know if we can right now, Suze. I really don't. Maybe we just leave him in there for now, for a minute anyway."

Susan nodded. "Okay," she agreed. "But I'm going in there soon, Henry. I have to see him." She looked up at her fiancé. "He's gone, Henry. I can't believe he's gone. How could this have happened? To Gilbert? To Charlie?"

"I don't know." Henry shook his head, held her closer. They walked to the couch, sat down together. Henry took Susan's hand and held it firmly within his own. No more words. Words were futile.

Susan placed her head upon Henry's shoulder and there they remained for an indeterminate amount of time, for time itself was fleeting just now.

The winter sun peaked in the sky, began to wane, and still they sat upon the couch. Only when Lucy began to whine did Henry stiffly lift his body and take her outside. Susan walked forlornly to Charlie's bedroom door, knocked gently.

No answer.

She turned the knob, cracked the door open.

Charlie sat upon the edge of Gilbert's small bed on the left side of the square room, looking out the single window before him. Hands were in his lap, shoulders stooped. His face was dry, pale.

The only movement Susan could discern was his steady breathing.

She sat next to him, the bed groaning softly with the new weight, though small, that it bore.

"Charlie?" Susan placed her hand on his arm.

He didn't move, didn't speak.

Susan stood and walked to face him straight on. "Charlie?

Charlie's eyes slowly moved to miserably glance into her own. It was momentary, as they flickered back to look out the window soon thereafter.

Susan placed a hand on his shoulder. "Charlie, is there anything I can do?"

Inhalation, exhalation. Steady, shallow.

Eventually, he spoke. "Alone." It was a croak, hoarse and cracked. "I need to be alone."

Susan wanted nothing more than to remain in that room with him. To hold him, comfort him in any way she possibly could, but she knew that she needed to respect his wishes, whatever they might be.

"We're here, Charlie. Please let us help you." She touched his shoulder and slowly left the room, closing the door behind her.

* * *

Gaumond Funeral Home stood twenty minutes away from Susan's house, residing on a well-traveled road a couple of towns over. There was a small parking lot to the left of the white three-story circa-1890s home in which the first floor had been converted into the funeral parlor, and as they had arrived a few minutes prior to the two o'clock viewing hour, Henry found a spot there to park his vehicle.

Susan exited the car with Mother by her side, smoothed her skirt worriedly. She pulled her jacket tighter around her torso and, folding her arms around her bosom, followed Henry to the steps of the front door.

Upon entrance she was immediately accosted by a putrid smell, what she would, in later years, learn to be embalming fluid interspersed with fresh flower arrangements and cigarette smoke. She swiftly placed her hand to her nose and then, not wanting to appear disrespectful, lowered it once more and continued into the foyer.

Footsteps to her left. Gilbert's mother appeared in the open doorway. "Please come in," she said.

Susan began walking forward behind Henry, her eyes downcast. She lifted them and halted instantaneously, Charlie catching himself behind her as her momentum ceased.

There were several chairs facing the wall to her right. Two windows immediately to her left allowed the afternoon sunlight to seep into the room, leaving mirrored halos upon the wooden floor, tiny dust particles floating in the stagnant air. Large flower arrangements were placed upon tables against the wall directly across from the doorway. In the corner of the room, to the right of the flowers and to the left of a small entryway into an adjacent room, lay Gilbert. The lower section of his dark wooden casket was closed, revealing only the upper portion of Gilbert's body. He was wearing a dark gray suit. She could see his profile, his still lips, his nose, his dark hair, shorter now than when he had left them. She saw his broad shoulders and his chest enclosed within the confines of the stark white silken material of the inner casket.

Her body refused to budge.

Henry placed a hand upon her shoulder. He leaned and whispered in her ear, "Are you okay?" She shook her head, tiny frenetic movements back and forth. Henry led her to sit upon a chair in the back row. She watched as Charlie slowly and methodically approached his lover. He ran his hands gradually from the base of the casket, down the side and along the shiny edges until it rested upon Gilbert's hand.

She watched as Henry approached her brother, watched as his hand rested on his shoulder. Charlie's back remained erect, his shoulders motionless. His head bent.

Mother stood beside Henry, her hand upon her bosom, tears dripping from her eyes.

Charlie slowly turned from Gilbert and faced his parents, who were both seated in the front row of chairs. He looked from one to the other, nodded his head.

She watched as he approached Gilbert's mother, the woman who had birthed the man he loved, and took her hand in his own, speaking his condolences. He turned to Gilbert's father and did the same, then to the older couple who sat at his father's side.

Dry-eyed.

Stoic.

Expressionless.

Numb.

He walked toward the back of the room and through the doorway, to the foyer and out the front door into the sunlight of the cold winter afternoon.

She didn't follow.

Henry sat down in the chair next to Susan, sighing heavily as he positioned himself. Susan saw his Adam's apple bob as he took a large swallow and then a deep breath, attempting to compose his body, his emotions.

Her nostrils were beginning to acclimate to the malodorous air as a few more people entered the funeral home to pay their respects to the deceased and his parents. Susan watched as they slowly walked to the front of the room.

"I don't think I can do it," she whispered.

"Do what?"

"I don't know if I can go see him." Henry looked over at her, waited. "But he would want me to, you think? Is it incredibly disrespectful for me not to go up there? I'm so scared, Henry."

Henry took her hand. "If you don't want to go up there, then don't," he said. "I don't think anyone here would judge you if you didn't go up to look at him. There are other ways of saying goodbye."

Susan looked at Gilbert's parents. "But I should go say something to them, shouldn't I? Isn't that the right thing to do?"

"I think you need to decide on your own what the right thing is," Henry said.

Feet to her right. Susan turned and saw Sandy Speckles enter the room. She nodded miserably at Susan. Henry's parents followed. They sorrowfully smiled at Henry and Susan and walked to the casket in the corner.

"Henry, I think I need to do this, no matter how scared I am."

"Do you want me to go with you?"

She shook her head. "Your parents are there right now, and besides," she said, "I think it's something I need to do on my own."

"Okay," he said. "I'm right here."

Susan took her hand out of his and walked behind the last row of chairs and down the aisle to the foot of Gilbert's casket.

She felt herself shake in fear and trepidation.

James parted and went to introduce himself to Gilbert's parents and convey his condolences. Viola followed.

Susan was alone.

She crept a few steps farther until she was standing at Gilbert's hidden thighs. A few more steps and she met his chest, the chest that was riddled with bullet holes she would never view. She looked upon his ashen face. His lips were pursed tightly, an unnatural shade of pink, the creases evident in the skin. She looked at the closed lids of his eyes, still. The long lashes that in life had been so uncommonly beautiful, thick and lustrous around his blue eyes, were now closed and caked, resting perfectly motionless and matted upon his cheek.

His dark hair was short but was otherwise the only thing about Gilbert that looked like... Gilbert.

Susan saw his large right hand resting upon his left, both set near his navel. She reached out. Slowly. Fingers shaking, she gently brushed his skin, pulled back. She looked upon his face once again, then back at his hand. Reached.

Her fingers grazed and then, summoning her bravery, she rested her palm on his skin, fingers gently rubbing. This wasn't Gilbert at all. His skin felt rubbery to her touch. She pondered the fact that no blood coursed within his veins any longer, no breath filled his empty lungs.

"Bye, Gil," she whispered.

One last look upon his face, one last touch of his hand, and she turned her back on her dear friend.

"I am so sorry," she said to Gilbert's parents, looking from his mother to his father. "So, so sorry."

"Thank you, Susan," his mother said.

Susan walked up the aisle, past the towering flower arrangements and back to her fiancé.

"Can we go?"

Henry nodded and stood. Mother stood as well, having seated herself next to Henry, and followed them out the door and to the car, where Charlie was gazing passively out the window.

The car ride back to Susan's house was silent. Henry parked the car, idled.

"Thank you for the ride, Henry," Mother said.

"Of course, Mrs. Dubois."

"Mom, I'll be right in," said Susan.

Mother turned to Charlie in the back seat. "I'm so sorry, Charles," she said. "I know Gilbert was a dear friend of yours."

Charlie nodded, acknowledging her words.

"A dear friend to you all," Mother said as she looked from Charlie to Susan and then rested upon Henry beside her. "I know how hard it is to lose a loved one," Mother went on, "but please try and remember that Gilbert is with the Lord now." She opened her door, walked outside into the cold.

Charlie watched her enter the porch before scoffing, "That's not what we need to hear, Mom, but hey—thanks a bunch."

Susan looked at her brother sympathetically. "Are you working tomorrow?"

Charlie shook his head. "I took time off."

"Good," she said. "Then I'll see you tomorrow after my shift." She leaned over, took him in her arms. Though he didn't embrace her back, neither did he pull away. She perceived it as a slight victory.

She opened her door, stepped outside. She walked to Henry's window and motioned for him to turn it down. She leaned in and kissed him gently. "Please watch over him tonight," she whispered. "Do you think he'll go back tomorrow afternoon to see him again?"

"I don't know," Henry whispered in her ear as he smoothed stray curls that had fallen out of her thick braid. "Viewing hours again tomorrow, two to four, funeral on Friday morning."

"Yes," Susan said. "I won't be going back tomorrow, but pick me up on Friday? Mom, too?"

"Of course." He kissed her on the cheek and she pulled away, walked inside her house and to her mother.

* * *

Susan finished her day at work and drove to her brother's house. Even though Gilbert's car now belonged to his parents, she was using it with their permission to get herself to and from work; had been since Gilbert had left for Vietnam, just as she had used her brother's car when he had left. Henry was in class, and she was pleased to have the time alone with Charlie.

"How are you doing today?" she asked when she arrived.

"Shitty."

"Visiting hours are now. I wasn't sure if you'd be home."

"I'm not going back. I don't need to see him like that. I don't need to remember him like that."

"I understand," Susan said empathetically.

"This is such bullshit, Susie. I'm angry. I don't know why this had to happen. Not to Gil." He paused for a moment, looked at his sister imploringly. "Don't do that to me."

Susan's expression was that of confusion. "What do you mean?"

"Don't do that to me. You need to make me a promise, Susie, right here, right now, that you won't have me in a damn casket, dead, frozen, the blood sucked out of me. You won't have me on display for everyone to stare at. That's not the last image I want you to see, for Henry to see. For anyone to see. I don't want to be remembered looking like that. I want to be remembered for me, who I am right now, who I've been and who I will be. When I die, Susie, promise me that you won't do that to me."

Susan was astonished, so many thoughts running through her mind from only this one sentiment. "Charlie, you're not going to die. Well, not for a really long time anyway. And who's to say you'll die before me? And Charlie, even if you do, I don't know anything else. Charlie, I'm so confused right now. This is the first time I've been through this. I don't know anything else."

"You've been in that house too long," Charlie said, disgust evident on his face, in his voice. "Susie, I know our parents are staunch Catholics. Mostly everyone you've been around is, I suppose, but I refuse to believe that's the only way. I believe in God. I do. But I can't believe that God allows our father to do what he did, that He encourages it. I can't believe in a God who... well, never mind. I just can't do it. I believe in God, but I have to believe that I'll get to Heaven being the person I am, even if I don't go to church anymore, even if I don't confess my sins, because how can it be a sin for me to use a cuss word but not a sin for Father to pummel the shit out of me, out of his wife? And I've struggled for years, Susie. Years. I loved Gilbert. With my entire being, I loved him. And now he's gone and I can't help but question whether God has taken him away from me because of who we were. Together."

"No, Charlie, NO! You can't think that!"

"See, that's just the thing. I've struggled. From when I was a boy, a teenager, now a man grown. I loved Gilbert, and love should be the very thing that allows us to feel the goodness of God, right? No matter who you love. And yet, as much as I feel convinced that this is the truth, we've been taught, you and I, for our entire lives that this is an egregious sin. Hideous. And based on those teachings, I'm headed to Hell. No matter what kind of person I am, Susie. To commit this unforgivable sin, I'm going to Hell. So, there you have it. My heart needs to believe that I'm leading a good life, that I'm a good person and that my love for Gilbert was justified, was true. Was right. And yet deep down inside, what we've been told is bubbling up to the surface, and it's haunting me and it's because of this that I can't help but wonder if he was taken away from me because I loved him."

Susan reached over and placed her hand on top of her brother's as they sat on the couch—such a central fixture in this house, the couch where they had laughed with Henry and Gilbert—and cried.

"I don't even know what to say, Charlie," Susan began, "I'm just so confused. About everything. I feel like we're taught one thing but see another. Does that make sense? It makes everything such a contradiction. I'm not going to lie to you. That day when you told me that you and Gilbert were together—we were right here in this room, remember?—that day I was shocked. I couldn't believe it. Because everything I had ever been taught told me that for two men to love each other in that way was wrong and a sin, like you said now. I was scared for you, if I'm telling the truth. Scared. Because of Mother and Father and our grandparents and because of Father Denis."

"Father Denis," Charlie scoffed, "don't get me started."

"See, that's what I'm trying to say, I think." Susan continued, "I was scared for you Charlie, but then I got to know Gilbert more and more and I'm here all the time and I saw the two of you together. Charlie, your love was real. I know this. *Know* it. I saw it with my own eyes. And I've grown to believe that your love was just two people here on earth. Not a man and a man—though of course you were—but two *people*. Does that make sense?" She looked into her brother's eyes. "It took me a while, I'll admit that to you. And I'm so sorry for that Charlie, but I'm learning. Sitting here with you now, I know God didn't take him away from you because of your relationship with him. I can't believe that. If anything, He teaches us to love, right? And the two of you loved each other more than most other couples I've known in my life so far."

Charlie took a deep inhalation in, filling his lungs. He held it there momentarily before exhaling audibly, forcefully. "I just can't believe he's gone," he said. He rested his face in the palms of his hands, rubbed his skin harshly. "Susie, I can't get his image out of my mind. For all this time I've had this beautiful man before me, this beautiful, kind man that I could touch and hold and who wanted to touch and hold me back. And man, did that feel good. And now? Now I try to remember that face, I try to remember and hold onto all the good times we've had together, but all I see when I close my eyes is how I saw him yesterday. In his casket. Dead. Not looking like himself at all. And I'm afraid that when I close my eyes that's what I'm always going to see. That image of the man I love instead of the smile, and his eyes, and the way he looked at me with them. Nope. I'm gonna remember his face in that goddamn casket. I feel like my memories have been taken away from me." He looked over at his sister imploringly. "So I've got to ask you once again, please don't do that to me. To yourself. When I die, cremate me. Please. Please cremate me. Don't put me in a casket and have me just lying there for two full days. Don't have people come and look at me like that. Don't prolong it. I'll be dead already. I don't need two days for people to realize that. Just cremate me, hold a small gathering. And for Christ's sake, don't make it so somber. Jesus Christ! Don't our lives, our memories deserve more than that? More than prayers and people crying, and Mom saying I'm with the Lord and in a better place?" He ran his hands through his brown hair agitatedly. "I don't know. Maybe I'm not making sense anymore. I'm not making sense to myself. I've had so much to think about these past few days and I can't get anything straight." He looked at his sister again. "I'm so sorry, Susie. I'm just having a lot of trouble and my mind is kind of fucked up."

"You don't need to apologize to me, Charlie. I can only imagine what you're going through right now. I just love you so much, Charlie. I really do. And I hate to see you hurting."

"Yeah, well…"

"When is Henry supposed to be home?"

"Said he'd be back around 4:30."

"Good," Susan said, "then he'll be back any minute now. Let me stay here with you until he gets home."

"Think I'm gonna do something to myself?" Charlie teased, though his countenance looked pained.

"No, I don't think that," Susan said, taken aback. "Not at all, Charlie. We need each other right now. Why be alone when you can have someone here with you?"

"Okay," Charlie said, "I'm sorry. That was really unfair of me. I'm just... I'm just all messed up."

"I understand," Susan said, her voice soothing, calm. "Hey, Charlie?"

"Yeah?"

"I love you."

Charlie smiled sadly. "I love you, too."

* * *

The funeral was set for ten o'clock the following morning. Susan had taken the day off work and Henry was missing a class. Father was at work, which made it quite easy for Henry to pick her and Mother up from the house.

He and Charlie arrived at 8:30. It would take them approximately twenty minutes to make the drive to the funeral home. Both men were to be pallbearers, carrying Gilbert's casket.

Henry handed Susan the keys to his car as she would need them after the Mass, and Susan and Mother parted ways with both Charlie and Henry in the parking lot and drove to the church. Though not St. John's, this church looked similar, emitted the same aura. Susan took hold of her mother's hand, and together they moved forward. There was a young man in the entryway to the nave. He handed them each a folded sheet of white paper. Susan looked down upon hers to find Gilbert's name printed in a large font on the front, his birth date and date of death below.

As they were still quite early, there were not many people present and they had their choice of seats. Walking forward, they rested upon a pew in the middle right side of the nave.

People began to gather, some whispering, others entirely quiet save for shoes upon the wooden floor or clothes scuffling. They were joined by Betty, Walter, and Sandy Speckles. James and Viola, too.

Eventually, the organ began to play. The priest walked forward into the aisle from the front door. Henry and Charlie (limping slightly without the aid of his cane) were joined by other men, young and old, bearing the weight of the casket down the aisle. Slowly. The priest was sprinkling it with holy water as he walked. When they arrived at the end of the aisle, the casket was placed down gently, elevated, and the men walked to the left side of the nave and sat in the second and third rows of pews.

The priest stepped up onto the altar with those assisting him, knelt in reverence, and kissed the altar. He slowly walked to the left and stood within the wooden pulpit. He paused to look out at the congregation, then spoke into the microphone before him. "Let us pray." He bowed his head and Susan followed his lead. "Almighty God, to whom mercy and forgiveness belong, hear our prayers on behalf of your servant Gilbert, whom you have called out of this world; and because he put his hope and trust in you. Command that he be carried safely home to Heaven and come to enjoy your eternal reward. We ask this through our Lord Jesus Christ, your Son, who lives and reigns with you and the Holy Ghost, one God, forever and ever. Amen."

"Amen," Susan mumbled in response.

"Now we invite Emily up for our first reading," the priest announced, his voice reverberating through the church.

Susan watched as Gilbert's mother rose from her perch in the first pew. She walked toward the pulpit and stood before the microphone, the priest having seated himself upon red velvet in a large chair against the wall to the left.

Emily cleared her throat, placed the palms of her hands upon the wood before her and spoke. Though her words were slightly choked, they were clear and easily defined.

She had composed herself well and, when through, stepped down from the pulpit and walked back to seat herself next to her husband in the front row, Gilbert's deceased body lying still in his closed casket just to her right. Her husband's arm rested on her shoulders as she bowed her head and laid it upon his chest.

A second reading was recited at the pulpit, and then the priest regained his place once again and read the gospel. Susan wasn't listening to his words. Instead, she surveyed the room, the people here for Gilbert. The atmosphere surrounding her was such a somber affair. Tears from some, pursed lips from others, closed eyes from a person or two.

When Gilbert's father was called up to the pulpit, Susan merely watched him stand and walk toward the priest. She didn't listen as he spoke, lost as she was in her own thoughts.

Mother sat beside her now reciting the Lord's Prayer in unison with other congregants. She did so with gusto and conviction.

A tear fell upon Susan's cheek.

She let it dribble to her chest.

The priest presented the body and blood of Christ, lifting them toward Heaven as he spoke his route words in a monotonous voice. She knew that she would be expected to receive Communion in just a few minutes, and receive it she would, though she was hesitant just now to do so.

She stood when her row was prompted to walk the aisle and up to the priest, who was now standing near Gilbert, holding the host aloft for believers. The priest placed the bread on her tongue and she let it disintegrate. She walked to her left and accepted the cup of wine, then proceeded along the outside of the pews and back to her seat. Mother joined her a moment later.

A song, a prayer, a hymn, and the Mass was through. Gilbert's father approached the pulpit and invited all in attendance to his home for refreshments and remembrance of his son. Charlie and Henry joined the other pallbearers and lifted the casket upon their shoulders. They walked forward down the aisle, and out the open doors into the February morning.

Whispering ensued. One row and then another began walking outdoors, Mass agendas in hand. The cold halted Susan momentarily when she stepped outside. She pulled her jacket tighter around her body and followed Mother to the car, passing the hearse in front of the church as Gilbert was being loaded in.

After saying goodbye to friends, Susan and Mother climbed into Henry's car.

Charlie and Henry were to drive with other pallbearers behind the hearse to help bring Gilbert back to the funeral home. For now, his body would remain out of the ground until spring conditions were more conducive to digging the hole that he would forever rest within. Mother and Susan walked to Henry's car, and Susan extracted the keys Henry had handed over. She started the car and inched her way into the line of vehicles that began to amass.

She drove back to the funeral home and met her brother and fiancé. Both men wore grave expressions as they made their way toward her.

Susan handed the keys over to Henry.

"Thanks," he said.

She stood on the balls of her feet and kissed him lightly on the cheek before sitting behind him in the back seat of the car.

Henry drove to Gilbert's parents' house. They had chosen to pay their respects once again, if only for a brief visit in the home where Gilbert grew up.

"Ready?" Henry asked as he turned the key in the ignition.

"I suppose," Susan said from the back seat.

"Oh, my heart," Mother said. "How Gilbert's parents must be hurting right now. I can only imagine how much pain they are in."

Charlie looked out the window at the home that would welcome

him inside. Welcome him as a friend of Gilbert's.
Nothing more.

TWENTY-TWO

Spring blossomed. June arrived, and with it a reprieve from school for Henry. One year more and he'd be a graduate, holding a master's in education. He had already procured the promise of a position at the college that he attended thanks to the connections he had made, as well as the hard work, motivation, and natural intelligence he conveyed to those on higher rungs of the educational hierarchy than he.

Charlie had been promoted to manager at the supermarket but struggled to appreciate the honor. For him, work was done and done to the best of his ability, but he found no pleasure in his job these days. He struggled to find a good deal of pleasure in much of anything at all.

In an attempt to get Charlie out of the house and regaining a bit of delight in the little things this town of theirs had to offer, Susan and Henry took him roller-skating at the local rink. Susan was incredibly gratified by Charlie's enthusiasm on the floor, by his laughter and playful bantering.

They sat now, on the floor of Charlie and Henry's living room, exactly one week before Henry and Susan were to be married. Dorito chip crumbs littered the carpet, and glass bottles of Tab stood on the stand to the left of the couch. Cards in hand, Susan was defeating both Henry and Charlie in a game of rummy.

"Take that!" Susan exclaimed as she slammed her cards down on the floor. "Ha!"

"Oooh, she got you there," Charlie said to his friend.

"Yeah, she did," Henry said. "Again."

"Luck," Charlie said.

"No luck about it," Susan jested. "All skill."

A knock at the door.

Lucy barked her high-pitched announcement in case the knock hadn't been detected by her family.

"Got it," Henry said as he stood from the floor, Lucy on his heels.

"Hi," a voice said from the doorway. "Are you Charlie?"

"I'm not, but who's asking?" Henry said, not unkindly.

"I'm so sorry to bother you. I know it's a bit of a surprise. I was hoping you'd be home. My name is Norm. I served with Gilbert over in Vietnam. I only just got back last week. I made this promise to him, you see..."

As soon as Charlie heard Gilbert's name, he scrambled from the floor and stood in front of the young man still in the entryway.

"Come in," he said hastily.

"I'm sure you have a lot of questions and I'm so sorry to just be showing up here at your house. See, I live in New Hampshire, too, went to school just south of here near the Mass. border. When Gilbert and I were thrown together in the same squad, well, those are your men, you know? You get to know each other. Gilbert was a mighty good guy, that's for sure. Didn't talk much about his life back home, but he did talk about his best friends. Specifically told me about a Charlie. I'm guessin' that's you."

Charlie nodded and offered Norm a seat.

"Can I get you something to drink?" Susan asked.

"No, thank you, I'm good."

Susan looked at this young man from his head to his feet, discreetly so as not to make him feel uncomfortable. There didn't appear to be anything defective in his physical functioning that could have sent him home, but she sure wasn't about to ask him such a personal question.

"He spoke about his parents, Gilbert did, but not a lot. Talked about you, Charlie, and about a Henry and a Susan. Guessin' that's you two?"

"It is," Henry said.

"Made me memorize your address, though it wasn't all that hard to do. Helped that I live in New Hampshire. That's what got us off on the right, the fact that we were both from New Hampshire, such a small state. The odds of that happenin' weren't all that good, I don't think. But there we were. Made me promise if he went that I would find you, come tell you, no matter how it happened. He wanted you to know." Norm cleared his throat, shifted in his seat a bit. "Is it okay I'm here right now?"

"Shit, yes!" Charlie exclaimed. "What the hell happened? We heard from his parents that it was a raid of some sort, that Gilbert got shot, but that's all we were left with."

"Funny he didn't want me headin' to his folk's house, but this is where he told me to go. Made it mighty clear, that."

Charlie nodded, eyes intently staring at Norm in anticipation of the information he'd soon relay.

"It was a raid. See, over there in "Nam, it's a damn jungle in places. Gilbert said you served, man."

Again, Charlie nodded but said nothing in response.

"They came out of nowhere. Bullets. I heard them first, a whooshing, really, right through all that green. I should have known what was going on right away. The second it started. I'd heard it enough. But I stood there, just watched as the kid next to me collapsed. Jack. Gilbert, he was behind me. He had more sense than

I did. He pushed me to the ground. Real hard. I hit my nose and lost my sight, what with all the tears that were comin' from the force of the blow. And I was gushing blood. I remember I blinked a few times—hard—tried to set myself straight. I saw Gilbert throw another kid to the ground and then he fell. At first, I thought he was hit, but then I saw him over another guy; I think he was checkin' to see if he was still alive. I don't know for sure. He turned his head and I saw his face, his chest, and that's when I knew he got hit. Saw it happen." Norm choked back a sob. "I tell ya, I saw a lot of men die over there. Surprised I wasn't one of 'em. Still can't believe I'm home." He shook his head in disbelief. "But here I am. And you know what? I think Gilbert probably saved my life that day. And any other kid he threw to the ground before he pushed me. You ask me, Gilbert's a hero."

All three listeners had free-flowing tears as Norm was telling them Gilbert's story.

"I tell ya, you have this idea in your head before you go to war. Whatever it may be, it doesn't turn out to be what you thought it would. Nobody deserves to die like that. Nobody. Some kids think they'll go on over to Vietnam and be like Gilbert: selfless, flingin' kids to the ground with no care for themselves. The truth? Most of us are scared as shit. You got a bullet and it just whizzed past your head, you could feel the damn thing, hear it in your ear, but it missed you? Next time that happens, you don't go pushing kids down, you freeze. Freeze or hide or cover yourself. Man, I even pissed myself the first time we were raided on. Still can't believe I'm here." He shook his head again. "I really hope I haven't told you too much," Norm said. "I hope I'm not ramblin'. I just really need you to know that I'm not lying. Swear it. Gilbert saved my life that day. I'm convinced he did."

Eventually Henry was the first to respond, wiping a tear from his cheek. "We all knew how wonderful Gilbert was, but now? It's like looking at his death in a whole new way."

"Thank you so much for coming here," Susan said to Norm.

"I'm glad I could do this for you," he said. "Oh!" He pulled something from the pocket of his brown corduroy pants, held it in the palm of his hand.

"Charlie, he gave me this; specifically asked me to give it to you if he didn't make it and I did." He held his hand out.

Charlie picked the item off his palm, held it in his fingers. Tears were now streaming down his cheeks, and he wiped them with the sleeve of his shirt in an attempt to view the item more thoroughly.

"His dog tag," he said.

"Yeah," Norm said. "Made me promise. I'm just glad I made it home to give to you."

"Thank you," Charlie said sincerely. He looked into Norm's brown eyes. "Thank you." He let the silver chain dangle through his fingers, ran his thumb over the engraving of Gilbert's name.

"Would you like to stay for dinner, Norm?" Susan asked.

"No. Thank you, though. I should get back home. Mom and Pop haven't wanted me out of their sight since I got back." He chuckled. "I guess I can understand that. Made it through my two years, but two years is a long time."

"Thank you again," Henry said. "We really appreciate this very much."

"You're welcome," Norm said as he rose from the couch.

They walked him to the door, giving thanks once again for his visit. Henry closed the door behind him. "Well, I'll be damned," he said, appreciatively. He looked at Charlie beside him. "Gilbert was a hero. I don't think any of us can deny that."

Charlie shook his head. "I have no doubt in my mind whatsoever that all of what Norm just told us is the truth. I needed that." He looked at Henry and then to Susan. "I need to shut myself in my room. I'm okay," he assured them, "I just want to be alone with this for a bit."

He lifted Gilbert's dog tag slightly. "And I just need to think."

"Okay," Henry said. "We'll be here, though."

"I know you will be," Charlie said and gave them both a dim smile before heading in the direction of his bedroom.

"Thank God Norm came here today to tell us about Gilbert," Susan said, full of wonder.

"Thank God for Gilbert himself," Henry said as he looked in the direction of the door that Norm had just left through, heading back to the family that had waited anxiously for their son to return home. Alive.

* * *

The following Friday was the day before Susan's wedding to Henry. She had taken time off work, and she and Mother had spent the day together looking at Susan's dress and veil, reminiscing upon Susan's childhood. Mother had popped Orville Redenbacher's popcorn on the stovetop, and they ate it now watching *Jeopardy!*.

"My," Mother said, "I sure do think Art Fleming is handsome."

"You do?" Susan asked through a mouthful of popcorn.

"I do," Mother said, gazing at the television. Art Fleming looked back at her in black and white as they hadn't upgraded to a color television. "Don't need a damn color TV when this one works just fine," Father had said when Mother had suggested one just last winter.

"Hmm," Susan looked at the TV. "I don't see it myself, but maybe that's because he's older."

"He is not that old," Mother said. "I think he is only in his late forties."

Susan looked at her mother. "And to me, not yet nineteen, that's older."

"Well, yes," Mother relented, "I suppose it would be."

Susan giggled her response, which made Mother chuckle as she placed a popcorn kernel in her mouth.

Jeopardy! ended and Mother and Susan made themselves a light lunch. When finished, they chatted at the kitchen table over warm cups of coffee until Susan looked at the clock upon the wall and saw the time.

"I should be going now," she said.

Mother sighed. "I suppose you should. Your friends are waiting, and I know how much you would like to be with them right now instead of with little old me for company." She lovingly smiled at her daughter.

"I love being with you, Mom," Susan said. Her mother might have only been jesting, but right now, Susan was not.

"And I love being with you as well. Very much. When I held you in my arms when you were a tiny little baby, I prayed to God that we would one day have the relationship we do now, darling, and I am blessed that my prayer was answered. You have grown into a kind, caring, wonderful young woman, and I am so proud of you."

"Thanks so much, Mom." She sighed. "Tomorrow!"

"Yes," Mother said. "Tomorrow. I cannot believe my baby is going to be a married woman." She reached out hands whose veins had become more pronounced with age, whose skin was dry and brittle from years spent at the kitchen sink. Susan took them in her own.

"Neither can I, really."

"Now you go and have a good time with your girlfriends."

"I will." Susan went to her bedroom to grab an overnight bag, kissed her mother, and walked out the door to Janet's house.

Janet and Bobby had come home for Susan's wedding. They had been across the country in California when Janet had called, and Susan asked if she would consider being her maid of honor. She had clearly heard Janet's elation after the connective pause on the other end of the line.

Susan spent the night in Janet's bedroom talking and giggling with Janet, Betty, and Sandy Speckles. She felt like she was in high school again. She felt carefree and exhilarated.

"Ooh, I'm so excited," Betty said. "Tomorrow you're getting married."

"I am," Susan smiled broadly.

"And to Henry," Betty said.

"I bet you're looking forward to the wedding night, aren't you?" Janet teased, lifting and lowering her eyebrows, widening her eyes.

"Janet!" Betty hissed. She looked at Susan, whose face color now complemented her hair.

"It's okay," Susan said. "I can't believe I'm talking about this, but I have to admit I'm nervous."

"Nothing to be nervous about," Janet said. "Hurts the first couple of times but you get used to it."

"Oh, my gosh, Janet!" Betty trumpeted.

Susan's face was now covered by the palms of her hands. Sandy giggled beside her.

"What?" Janet protested, considering this to be a perfectly typical Friday night conversation for many young women across the country. There had been a women's movement, after all, and had she not just been traveling, meeting various dynamic people, conversing with folks she never would have met or conversed with had she stayed in this sleepy little town? Her friends had to lighten up!

Susan peeked through her fingers and sporadically shook her head. "It's okay, really," she said as she lowered her hands and sat erect on the bed. "I need to know. I've never talked to anyone about this before."

"Never?" Janet was dumbfounded.

"No," Susan admitted. "Can I admit something to you all?" The girls merely looked at her intently, waiting for her to continue. "When I got my period, I was in school. I had no idea what had happened. I was so scared, and when I got home, all my mom did was tell me that I had become a woman and walk with me to the general store."

"You have to be kidding," Sandy said.

"I'm not," said Susan. "These things are just never spoken of in our house. I've never really spoken about them to anyone, really. *We* haven't even had a conversation like this before. I'm a bit uncomfortable." Sandy's hand found its way to Susan's arm, consoling. "But I'm getting married tomorrow. Tomorrow! And I know what sex is. At least, as much as I think I can when I've never done it before. And I'm just... I'm really nervous."

"I get it," Janet said. "I was nervous my first time, too."

"You said it hurts?" Susan asked meekly, a look of agitation on her face.

"A bit. But only the first couple of times. Like I said, you get used to it. And then it just feels good. Feels right. Especially if you're with Henry. Susie, I can't believe he's waited all this time. Usually, guys want to do it way before now."

"He has," Susan admitted sheepishly, "I mean, we almost have. A few times. But I stopped him. I just had to. I knew we were getting married, but in the back of my mind I've always had this little voice telling me I had to wait until the wedding."

"Well, maybe that will make tomorrow really special," Betty offered.

"I hope so," Susan said.

"And you'll be married," Janet said. "You'll have plenty of opportunities to practice!" She laughed.

"Janet!" Betty admonished.

"Susie, I mean this as a compliment, so don't take it the wrong way, but if I had Henry right there, looking at me with those eyes, blinking those long lashes and smiling at me with that mouth of his, I'd be jumping at the chance to lie on my back."

"Holy shit, Janet!" Betty reproached vehemently.

"Ahhh!" Susan brought her knees up to her chest, hid her face on her thighs.

"Oh, my God," Sandy giggled.

"All I'm saying is," Janet continued, "you're one lucky girl. Not only is Henry a great guy who's going to treat you well, he gets more gorgeous every year. Damn, when I saw him the other day... phew!"

"What about Bobby?" Sandy asked.

"I love Bobby, no doubt, but I can still appreciate a nice-looking man, can't I?"

"Jeez, Janet," Betty said. A pause for a moment, and then she lifted her head, mouth open, and let out a burst of laughter. Sandy followed suit, then Janet. Susan eventually lifted her face from her thighs, looked at her friends holding their stomachs, heard the booming convulsions, and couldn't help but laugh herself.

Peep.

Janet's laughter intensified. "Sandy cut the cheese!" she announced and fanned her nose in jest.

Betty hugged her friend, forcing her down upon the bed. The girls continued laughing hysterically, tears dripping down their cheeks. "You're the bomb, Sandy!"

"Because I cut the cheese?" She held her stomach as she laughed, fingers reaching under her glasses to swipe at the tears.

"Yeah," Betty said.

This made Sandy laugh so hard she couldn't breathe.

Peep.

"Sandy, you did it again," Susan laughed.

"Sandy, your new nickname is going to be "Cheesie," Janet teased.

"Cheesie," Betty laughed. She rolled onto her side, black hair splayed upon the pillows.

Eventually, the laughter subsided, although the sides of Susan's stomach ached still.

"I just love you all so much," Susan said.

"Aww," Janet teased, "having a moment?"

"I suppose I am, " Susan admitted with mock haughtiness. "No, but in all honesty," she continued, "I really do love you." Her expression serious, she looked from Sandy to Betty and then rested upon Janet. "I am so lucky to have you as my friends, and tomorrow when I marry Henry, I wouldn't want anyone else by my side."

"Very sentimental, Susie," Janet said, "but we love you, too." She leaned over and hugged her friend. Betty and Sandy joined in, and as Susan sat there on the edge of Janet's bed, the recipient of such an embrace, she knew her life was truly marvelous.

* * *

Saturday dawned and Susan was incredibly pleased to see the sun through Janet's bedroom window. She woke, stretched, and walked to look out at the sky. Blue, only a few clouds. How wonderful!

She called her mother to inform her of her wakeful state, hung up the phone, and picked up a book she had packed for this very possibility that she would rise before her friends. She opened her book where it had been marked, began to read, but soon realized that she was rereading the same paragraph. Today was her wedding day. She was entirely too anxious to read, and that was certainly saying something for Susan!

When the girls had all woken, they packed up their bags and walked next door to Susan's house, Janet, Betty, and Sandy holding their dresses carefully over their arms so as not to get them dirty before the wedding even took place.

Susan walked into her house first, the wonderful, sweet smell of warm syrup hovering in the air. Mother was making homemade waffles and fruit salad.

"Good morning, ladies," Mother said cheerily from the kitchen counter.

"Good morning, Mrs. Dubois"—a chorus of gay girls' voices.

"Morning, Mom," Susan said. "It smells so good."

"It does, does it not?" Mother answered. "I almost ate a waffle while I was cooking, they look so good. These should fill you ladies up so you will not be hungry before we have the wedding meal."

"Thanks, Mom. Where's Father?"

"I think I scared him off when I told him all you girls would be coming over for breakfast and to get ready for the ceremony." She chuckled. "He is in the bedroom, and I believe he may just stay there until it is time for us to go to the church."

Susan smiled. She wasn't surprised. Just like Father. At least it was too early in the morning for him to take the car to one of the local bars he frequented. And she was pleased to see he wasn't out fishing. She needn't worry that he wouldn't make it home in time for them to leave for the ceremony.

The girls deposited their dresses in Susan's room and walked back to the kitchen.

"Mom, is there anything I can help you with?"

"Absolutely not!" Mother exclaimed. "This is your wedding day. It is a day where people do things for *you*."

Breakfast was finished, Mother washed the dishes and the table, and then it was time to prepare for their day.

Amidst giggles and laughter, the girls put their bridesmaid dresses on in Susan's bedroom, soft-flowing material in a baby blue, Susan's favorite color. The necklines were high, the sleeves long and loose. It was June, but still there could be found a chill in the New Hampshire air. Empire waisted, the dresses were beautiful.

Mother knocked on the door, entered. "Oh, how lovely you all look," she said as she moved forward. "Just lovely."

"Wow, so do you, Mom!"

"Why, thank you," she said as she turned slowly in a circle. Her dress was a medium yellow in color, of a thicker material than the bridesmaids' dresses. The neckline was heart-shaped, the sleeves long. It hugged her curves, though not tightly, and ended below the knee. "I think it is your turn now, Susan," Mother said as she walked to Susan's closet. She pulled Susan's dress down and brought it over to the bed.

"It's so beautiful," Betty said, rather appreciatively, hands clasped together upon her chest.

"It is," Susan agreed. "I just love it. We got so lucky. It was just like my prom. It was the first dress I tried on, and Mom and I both loved it straightaway. I tried a few more on because I couldn't believe I'd be so fortunate as to find my dress so quickly, but there it was. There was no mistaking it. I tried on those other dresses and took them right off."

"Okay, okay," Janet said, "let's get it on you!"

"You look stunning," Mother announced with awe once Susan was through.

"You really do," Sandy said. "The dress is just your style."

Susan ran the palms of her hands down along her stomach, felt the smooth material beneath. She beamed, the anticipation of the day churning within. The dress fit her perfectly. With a high neckline and empire waist, it mimicked her bridesmaids' dresses. The sleeves were also long but made from lace, her skin visible beneath the floral designs. Lace was woven under her bosom into a delicate bow, but the dress was otherwise unadorned, simplistic.

Perfect.

"Let us go into my bedroom. We will do your hair and put your veil on. How does that sound?"

"Wonderful," Susan said.

"I will just go tell your father. I imagine he will want to go back to the kitchen."

Once Mother returned, signaling that Father had indeed moved to the kitchen, the girls turned the corner and entered Mother's bedroom, walked to her vanity. It was still in the same place against the wall opposite the foot of the bed, just as it was when Susan had been a young child watching her mother comb her hair and put her makeup on before church services.

Today Susan sat where Mother typically rested, facing the lit mirror. Her pale skin and blue eyes were staring back, her dress shimmering from the lamp's illumination and the sunlight peeking through the windows. Mother stood behind her daughter, hands on Susan's shoulders.

Mother lifted Susan's hair, gently bringing it to the nape of her neck and pinning it into a bun, a few stray curls falling forward to rest upon her cheeks. When done, she leaned back to admire her work. "How is that, darling?"

"I think it looks great," Susan said.

"Okay, now the veil," Mother said. She turned on her heel and took the veil from Janet's extended hands. Mother gently placed the headband on the top of Susan's head, the band wide and satiny. The veil was only slightly uplifted at the back of the band; it otherwise fell straight down her shoulders softly, lightly. It was made of much less material than many other veils she had seen at the bridal shop, and for this she was thankful as it fit her liking very well. The bottom of the veil ended around her waist and was edged with the same lace as her sleeves.

Susan gazed at her reflection.

A deep breath in and a satisfied smile.

Susan stood from the vanity and turned to face her mother, her best friends. Mother had tears upon her cheeks, her friends were all beaming back at her.

She was ready. Ready to head to the church on this, her wedding day.

"Wow," she breathed when she entered the kitchen and saw Father sitting at the table. "You look really handsome." Father was wearing a gray suit—how long had it been since Susan had seen him in a suit?—and a black bow tie on a white shirt. Broken blood vessels lined his cheeks—more each year, it seemed—and his red hair was combed in his typical fashion: parted at the side, pomade stiffening the thinning red strands. But his eyes—his eyes were clear this morning as he looked at his daughter, the sclera white and unclouded. Susan was relieved to find them so, as opposed to the reddish tint they held when he had been drinking heavily.

Father mumbled a response, though Susan couldn't quite decipher his words.

"He does look handsome, does he not?" Mother said. Pride filled her voice.

Mother and Father walked toward their vehicle. As their decrepit station wagon was no longer in use, they had acquired a new car: a white Chrysler Newport. They entered as Susan and her friends walked just next door to Janet's waiting car, Susan careful not to dirty her white dress.

Father pulled into the road first, and Janet followed.

Henry had been quite adamant that he'd rather not be married at St. John's. He wasn't against a church service, but Father Denis's teachings were not in keeping with Henry's beliefs. Having had many a conversation with Charlie, Henry was well aware of the aura within the confines of St. John's, and he wanted his wedding day with Susan to be one of celebration, of delight and merriment. What he did not want was to be in the church of his best friend's childhood, the church that spoke of obedience and domination. Of fear.

Susan could easily admit that she understood her fiancé's apprehension and concurred, but was unable to offer up an alternative. A church service was needed, was it not? A marriage simply had to occur with a priest officiating under the eyes of God in one of God's homes, or so she had been led to believe. When one was taught from birth that something was so, it was difficult at times to stray, was it not?

Then she thought of Ma Tante Alice and the church she attended. She had called Ma Tante Alice and they had spoken for quite some time. With Ma Tante beside them, Susan and Henry had met with Pastor Glenn and took a liking to him immediately. He was personable and kind, and Susan trusted Ma Tante's opinion of him greatly. Where Susan had always felt rather tense and troubled in the presence of Father Denis, here, beside Pastor Glenn, she felt a sense of comfort and tranquility. When Pastor Glenn had shaken Henry's hand and she saw the joviality upon his circular face, saw Henry's easy grin in return, she knew they'd be married here, in the Church of Christ.

When she had announced to her parents that she wouldn't be married in Father Denis's church, Father has seemed unaffected. Apathetic, even. Mother, though, had been greatly disturbed. "Susan," she had said, "you must let Father Denis marry you. He has been your priest your entire life. Surely he is the one who should marry you as well."

Susan remained resolute, though it made her anxious to do so when speaking to her mother. She relied heavily upon Henry to persuade Mother that they had made the right decision for themselves, and she eventually capitulated.

A twenty-minute car ride and they arrived at the Church of Christ, a white building on a less-traveled road, front pillars standing thick and tall.

Susan exited the car and, together with her friends and her mother (Father had already made his way inside), walked up the large steps of the church to the white doors propped open to allow the beautiful June breeze to float within. To the right of the entryway was a small hallway. At the end was a door leading into a room in which Susan could rest while she awaited the beginning of the ceremony. She opened the door, stepped inside, and saw both Ma Tante Alice and Viola had been awaiting her arrival. They sat in chairs by a large window at the right of the room, knees tilted, bodies facing each other, having apparently been in amicable conversation.

They both turned when Susan entered and stood, broad smiles indicating their pleasure.

"Oh, Susan," Ma Tante declared, "you are gorgeous!"

Susan smiled brightly as she walked forward farther into the sunlit room.

"You really are," Viola said. "How do you feel?"

"I'm feeling nervous," Susan replied as she sat in a plush chair. "How does everything seem in there?"

"Oh, perfectly fine," Viola said. "Guests have arrived and seem happy, the organ is playing a bit of soft music so there's a little something in the background, and the flowers look simply beautiful."

"Thank you so much for picking those up this morning, Viola," Mother said.

"It was my pleasure, really. I'm happy to help in any way I can."

The women chatted for a while longer until there was a light rap at the door and Pastor Glenn peeked his head through. "May I come in?"

"Yes, of course," Susan said.

318

Pastor Glenn opened the door fully and stepped inside, closing the door behind him.

"I was just speaking with your soon-to-be husband and your brother, Susan. All is good. Do you think you're ready to begin now?"

Susan stood from her seat and took a large breath. She exhaled, palms on her stomach. "I am," she said.

"Wonderful to hear," Pastor Glenn said.

"Let's do it then," Viola said excitedly. Father Glenn left the room. Viola lifted from a table three small bouquets of flowers and handed one each to Janet, Betty, and Sandy. Baby blue and white carnations interspersed with lilies of the valley lay within a small white basket. A white handle arching from one side to the other produced a handhold. "Look at that," Viola announced. "They match your dresses perfectly."

"I am so happy you are all here with me today." Susan looked from her girlfriends to her mother to Viola and Ma Tante Alice. "I feel so incredibly blessed to have you all in my life." Her eyes began to well, her voice slightly cracking as she spoke. "I just can't believe I'm getting married right now."

"Eeee!" Betty squealed, which made the women in the room laugh.

Her eyes no longer able to contain the liquid flow, a tear fell. Mother quickly took a tissue off the table and lifted it to Susan. "No tears now," she said, though she was crying herself. She dabbed at Susan's cheek, lowered her hand. Susan held her gaze and was cognizant of the love within her mother's crystalline stare.

"My baby is getting married," Mother said.

"I am."

"All right, now, you two," Ma Tante interjected. "Helen, your baby won't be getting married unless we get going here, right?" She gently pulled her sister aside and handed Susan her small bouquet of baby blue and white roses held together with a baby blue ribbon.

Susan lifted her finger to her cheeks and wiped gently at the tears. "Okay," she announced. "I'm ready. Really this time." She looked at her aunt. "Are my eyes okay?"

"Perfect," Ma Tante replied.

"Okay, then," said Susan, "let's do this. Let's get me married."

A cheer from the women in the room. Ma Tante exited first to make her way to her husband and children awaiting her presence in the church. The rest of the party walked through the doorway and into the main hallway. Mother lined the girls up alongside the wall: Sandy, then Betty, Janet last before Susan herself.

Charlie and James appeared in the entryway and extended their arms to both Mother and Viola. Mother turned to Susan and lowered her veil over her face before turning back to the men. Though Susan was pleased that both Charlie and James were here, she couldn't help but mourn Gilbert's absence. She lamented this for a moment, took a deep breath, and watched as Mother disappeared into the nave on her son's arm, the organ's melody playing within.

Sandy walked forward and through the doorway. Betty followed slowly after her. Janet turned to Susan. "This is it," she announced with a smile.

"This is it," Susan echoed.

Janet turned the corner.

She was alone.

Father and Charlie appeared in the doorway, and even though Susan had expected this moment, she was taken aback by their presence together, side by side. Charlie had been just sixteen when Father had bellowed for him to leave his home. As far as Susan was aware, they hadn't seen each other since, unless there had been a spotting at her high school graduation. Charlie was now twenty-two.

She stood there for a moment, looking from Father to Charlie: Father, with his short stature and slight frame; his son beside him, tall and handsome in his black tuxedo and bow tie, the smile upon his face one of pure bliss, even as he stood beside his father. The happiness of his sister and his best friend outweighed any anger or pain he might have felt otherwise standing here with the man who had exerted his self-righteous presumptive superiority over him time and time again.

"Ready?" Charlie asked.

"I am." Though it was unconventional, Susan had been resolute that she be led down the aisle by not only her father but her brother as well. Her father might have sired her, but it was her brother, she had come to realize, who had truly cared for and nurtured her through the years, and she loved him all the more for it. He had been utterly shocked at the notion of walking his sister down the aisle with their father but humbled as well. Once he understood she was adamant in her choice, he agreed readily.

She stood sandwiched between the two men, her bouquet held in her left hand, her father's fingers resting on her elbow. She laced her right hand through her brother's proffered arm as the two men slowly led her around the corner.

She looked in the distance.

Henry.

She saw him well, even from the space that divided them. Black tuxedo, black bow tie, white rose on the lapel of his jacket. She saw his brown hair was styled, waved back from his forehead, the sides and back shorter than the top.

The smile on his face let her know she was loved, wanted. It made it clear that he was waiting for her to take that first step toward him.

So step she did. With Charlie and her father leading her, she slowly walked toward her fiancé. Her eyes didn't waver. Though she had been nervous about the attendees all looking upon her, at this moment she wasn't fully aware of their presence, nor the presence of James and Freddie (Henry's mentor from college) beside Henry at the altar. She looked only at Henry, he only at her.

She stopped. He was there before her.

"Dearly beloved," Pastor Glenn began as the organ stopped its playing, "we are gathered here today in the presence of God and these witnesses to join Henry and Susan in holy matrimony. If any person can show just cause why they should not be married, let them speak now or forever hold their peace."

Pastor Glenn paused momentarily, but Susan heard only a few shufflings of bodies in the pews, her father's heavy breathing, and the beating of her own heart.

"Who gives this woman to be married?"

"I do," Father said.

"And I," Charlie added.

Susan felt her father stiffen beside her as he clung to her elbow.

Charlie lifted her veil gently and kissed her upon the cheek before lowering it again and taking his place beside Henry.

She turned to Father, who lifted her veil again, kissed her dryly on the cheek and lowered it. He took her hand and placed it into Henry's extended palm. Father turned and walked to sit beside Mother in the front row. Susan handed her bouquet to Janet and turned to Henry.

Henry took both of Susan's hands as they stood facing each other in front of Pastor Glenn, both smiles radiant with anticipation.

Pastor Glenn led them all in a short prayer.

"Amen." Susan lifted her head, looked at Pastor Glenn's slight smile, then tilted her head up to look at the man standing beside her, so handsome and proud.

Her heart lifted, a warming sensation spread throughout.

"I would like to invite the mother of the bride up to read a Bible passage of her own choosing to bestow upon the happy couple here today. Helen?"

Mother stood, smoothed her yellow dress with the palms of her hands, and walked to the microphone to the left of Susan. "A reading from Colossians chapter 3, verses 14 to 20," she said, and then paused as she unfolded a small sheet of white paper that had been clenched in her fist. "'And over all these put on love, that is, the bond of perfection. And let the peace of Christ control your hearts, the peace into which you were also called in one body. And be thankful. Let the word of Christ dwell in you richly, as in all wisdom you teach and admonish one another, singing psalms, hymns, and spiritual songs with gratitude in your hearts to God. And whatever you do, in word or deed, do everything in the name of the Lord Jesus, giving thanks to God the Father through him. Wives, be subordinate to your husbands, as is proper in the Lord. Husbands'"— a slight crack in her voice—"'love your wives and avoid any bitterness toward them. Children, obey your parents in everything, for this is pleasing to the Lord.'"

She folded her paper until it fit in the palm of her hand, and she walked to sit beside her husband.

"And now the mother of the groom would like to read a passage of her choosing for Henry and Susan," Pastor Glenn said.

Viola stood from her seat and walked to the front of the microphone.

"I'd just like to say how happy we are that you are all here today. Thank you so much for sharing in this incredibly special day. My reading is from First Corinthians, and while I bet many of us are very familiar with this passage, it speaks volumes to my heart and I find it very fitting for today. Chapter 13 verses 1 to 8." She looked at the faces staring back at her, then down at the sheet of paper she held in her hand. She spoke boldly, with conviction. "'If I speak in human and angelic tongues but have not love, I am a resounding gong or a clashing cymbal. And if I have the gift of prophecy and comprehend all mysteries and all knowledge; if I have all faith so as to move mountains but have not love, I am nothing. If I give away everything I own, and if I hand my body over so that I may boast but do not have love, I gain nothing.'" Viola paused and lifted her head to look at her son and his bride. She spoke her next words from memory, passionately. "'Love is patient, love is kind; it is not jealous, it is not pompous, it is not inflated, it is not rude, it does not seek its own interests, it is not quick-tempered, it does not brood over injury, it does not rejoice over wrongdoing but rejoices with the truth. It bears all things, believes all things, hopes all things, endures all things. Love never fails.'" She paused, her gaze lingering on the young couple before her. She smiled. "I love you both," she said, then walked back to her seat.

"Henry and Susan," Pastor Glenn announced, "it's time for your vows. Are you ready?" His voice was jesting, his smile kind. Susan heard soft laughter from the guests behind her. "Please face each other."

Susan looked up into Henry's hazel eyes through her veil, at his smile. He took her hands in his.

"Henry, repeat after me," Pastor Glenn said. "I, Henry..."

"I, Henry..."

"Take you, Susan..."

"Take you, Susan..."

"To be my wife..."

"To be my wife..." Henry repeated.

"To have and to hold from this day forward..."

"To have and to hold from this day forward..." Henry's voice was firm, carrying through the room.

"For better or for worse..."

"For better or for worse..."

"For richer, for poorer..."

"For richer, for poorer..." Henry said.

"In sickness and in health..."

"In sickness and in health..."

"To love and to cherish..."

"To love and to cherish..."

"From this day forward..."

"From this day forward..." Henry repeated.

"Until death do us part."

"Until death do us part," Henry finished.

"Now, Susan," Pastor Glenn said, turning to look at her. "Repeat after me."

Susan's voice was soft. She had to pause several times to catch her breath as the tears trickled down her cheeks. But she finished her vows and smiled as Henry squeezed her hands in his.

"And now the rings," Pastor Glenn said.

Henry turned to Charlie, who passed on the ring he had been holding to his best friend, still marveling at the fact that it was to his sister this ring was gifted. Susan saw her brother lift his eyebrows, a sly smile on his face before Henry turned back.

"Please place the ring on Susan's finger and repeat after me," Pastor Glenn said.

"I, Henry, give you, Susan..."

"I, Henry, give you, Susan..." he repeated.

"This ring as a symbol of my everlasting love and devotion."

"This ring as a symbol of my everlasting love and devotion." He slipped the golden ring fully onto Susan's bare finger, her engagement ring being within her mother's safekeeping.

"And now for you, Susan," Pastor Glenn said.

Susan turned to Janet behind her, and Janet handed over Henry's ring. She repeated Pastor Glenn's words and placed the ring on Henry's finger. He clasped her hands within his own and smiled, revealing his straight white teeth, the yellow at the center of his eyes seeming to sparkle above his upturned cheeks.

Pastor Glenn looked upon the couple, smiled warmly. "By the power vested in me—" He paused, allowing anticipation to hover in the air around him. "I now pronounce you husband and wife. Henry," he said, "you may kiss your bride."

Henry's lips parted once again in a broad smile as he lifted Susan's veil from her face and slowly bent forward to his new wife, kissing her gently on the lips.

"See?" Henry whispered in her ear. "Short and sweet just as you wanted."

When they parted, the guests cheered their congratulations. Susan heard Janet whooping behind her, the cries of merriment echoing around the room.

Henry and she walked back down the aisle. She held her bouquet as the organ played their exiting tune, her left hand resting in his right. Her feet felt light in her flat white shoes; she felt the thin, soft material of her dress dancing against her legs.

When they arrived outdoors, Henry lifted her in his arms, spun her around. He lowered her and kissed her once again, longer, slower.

The wedding party took photos together; photos were taken also with family members and good friends. David and Mikey had promised to arrive at James and Viola's home before the other guests to ensure all was well before the wedding party arrived at the reception.

When photo taking was done, Susan and Henry climbed into his car and made for his parents' house while the rest of the party followed behind.

They exited the car and walked to the back of the house, where they heard "I Feel the Earth Move" playing on a record player, a microphone held just to the side to intensify the sound.

Susan halted. She was overcome with the transformation that had taken place. White circular tables and chairs had been erected in the grass, thick white tablecloths spread evenly on top. Small white baskets lay at the center of the tables with baby blue and white carnations with lilies of the valley to match the bouquets of both Susan and her bridal party. A beautiful touch. A solitary white circular table stood in the left-hand corner of the yard, the wedding cake in the center, simple white frosting on circular forms. There were three cakes total separated by baby blue columns, each portion descending in size from the bottom to the top. A cake topper adorned the smallest portion, heart-shaped and white with two wedding bells hanging from the center, baby blue ribbons floating in the slight June breeze of the early afternoon.

Viola had insisted on hiring a catering company so that she and Mother would be entirely free to enjoy the festivities, though Susan was adamant that the food remain simple and the staff small. The staff was seen now behind a large rectangular table, finishing food preparations.

Heads turned and cheers erupted as Susan and Henry made their entrance. Susan smiled, looked around the yard at people dancing by the music, others sitting upon chairs at tables. There were David and Mikey, both with dates Susan had never met before. Her cousins Ellie and Elizabeth were there with their families. Walter Wentworth, Betty's boyfriend, was standing next to Janet's boyfriend, Bobby. There were extended family and friends of James and Viola, friends of Henry's from school. There was Carla sitting at a table, Edmond Biladeau by her side, an aide from the nursing home accompanying him.

Susan discarded her veil on a tabletop as Henry took her hand and spun her around. They danced with friends and family surrounding them, ate heartily.

Henry stood, walked to the microphone. He placed a new record upon the machine, looked out into the crowd of friends and family before him. "This one's for my wife," he announced. He placed the needle on the record, set the microphone into its stand, and walked toward Susan.

Sam Cooke's "Cupid" began to play, the song that had been on when Susan had entered Henry's home the day he proposed to her. A song they both adored that now held further sentiment.

She stood as he took her by the hand and led her to the grassy portion of the yard where they had danced before their meal. Wrapping his arms tightly around her back, he held her to his chest, nuzzling her neck with his nose.

He began to sing along.

Susan giggled. "You're a terrible singer, you know."

"Oh, I know." He sang even louder, distancing himself by an arm's length from Susan and twirling her around in a circle while guests finished the last of their food and looked on.

The catering company cleared the tables, and friends and family joined Susan and Henry in dancing.

A commotion behind Susan. Father had fallen over, knocked a few chairs to the ground. Expletives soared through the air to accost Susan's ears. Her dancing halted; she turned. A pull on her arm. Henry had her back by his side, hands holding her against his body. He shook his head.

"He's drunk," Susan said.

"He is. And my dad's got it covered."

Susan looked behind her. James was lifting Father from the ground.

"Look at me," Henry said. Susan obliged. "Everything's okay," he assured her. One last glance over her shoulder found Father sitting in a chair, James by his side.

Susan began to relax in Henry's arms.

Dancing progressed a while longer. "I'm going to the bathroom," Susan said. "I'll be right back."

Susan entered through the back of James and Viola's home, the bathroom just to her left. Charlie was sitting at a small table in the kitchen.

"What are you doing inside?" Susan asked her brother.

"Just needed a break."

"A break?"

"Yeah."

"Charlie, are you okay? You were so happy just a while ago. Now you look quite sad."

"Yeah, I'm okay. I'm just thinking about Gil."

Susan walked to her brother, sat down. "I'm so sorry, Charlie. I should have thought about how you'd feel today."

"Absolutely not," Charlie insisted. "I am happy for you, Susie. You and Henry both. Really. And I'm sorry I'm like this right now. I get like this a lot, but I shouldn't be like this today."

"Of course you should," Susan assured him. "Charlie, it wasn't that long ago that we lost Gilbert, and I understand that it's all been really hard on you. I wish sometimes that you'd open up to me a bit more."

Charlie shook his head. "I'm okay," he said. He paused for a moment as Susan looked into his eyes. He stood. "I'm going home . Lucy probably has to go to the bathroom."

"I imagine she does," Susan relented, regretful that the conversation had ended so quickly.

"I'll be gone when you get there. Sleeping at a friend's house tonight so you and Henry can have the place to yourselves."

"Thanks, Charlie," Susan said. Though grateful for his kindness, she was also disconsolate that he wasn't out with the other guests enjoying the reception as she had hoped.

Charlie turned to leave.

"Charlie?" Susan stood from her chair. He turned to look at her.

"I love you."

"I love you, too."

She reached for him, but he had already turned his head, was walking toward the front door.

* * *

Lucy greeted them with enthusiasm as Henry lifted Susan over the threshold of the home she would now share with him and Charlie.

"Welcome home, Mrs. Beaumont."

"Why, thank you, Mr. Beaumont."

Henry placed her feet on the carpeted floor and Lucy jumped on her legs, small brown tail wagging from side to side.

"Hi, Lucy," Susan said. "I'm home and I'm here to stay this time."

Henry glided his palm over Susan's shoulder, grasped her waist with his other hand. "I'm glad you're here," he whispered.

"Me, too."

He lowered his head, closed his eyes. The kiss was soft, patient at first, then deeper and wanting. Susan circled her arms around his waist, dug into the back of his black suit jacket with her fingers. Henry's hands wandered slowly down her back, her bottom. He lifted her in his arms, her feet dangling as her body pressed against his. He walked toward his bedroom, the bedroom he would now share with his wife.

They entered, and he sat her upon the edge of the bed in the center of the room, the window admitting sunlight, intensifying the auburn of her hair. His eyes bore into hers as he lifted his hand and undid the pins around her bun, allowing her curls to flow freely against her shoulders. Placing the pins aside, he ran his fingers through her hair, brushing it off her cheeks. He leaned down, placed his right knee next to her thigh on the bed, slowly laying her upon the blanket. She scooted her body awkwardly to rest her head against a pillow, Henry hovering over her, brown hair falling to cover the side of his left eye.

"Are you okay?" he asked.

She nodded her head slowly, bit her lip. She was anxious and a bit tense, but as she ran her fingers through the hair of the man she had grown to love so passionately, she found she was able to relax slightly, knew he wouldn't hurt her intentionally. Ever.

She fell asleep in Henry's arms that night, disregarding the fact that she was unclothed. She cared not now that she was in the comfort of her husband's embrace.

TWENTY-THREE

A few weeks passed. Henry picked up hours at a summer internship at the college with Freddie, a groomsman as well as his mentor and a professor of English he emulated. Charlie managed the grocery store, and Mother managed the home that Father was increasingly absent from.

After a day well spent at work, Susan found she was the first to arrive home that evening. Gilbert's car was now her own as his parents weren't in need of another car and sold it to her for a nominal price, and she knew Henry would be late, but she was surprised not to see Charlie's car in the driveway. She entered the house, called his name.

No answer.

She figured he'd be home soon. She said her hellos to a very excited Lucy, took her outside to relieve herself, then rummaged in the refrigerator, hoping to find something to make for dinner.

She pulled out some raw chicken, unwrapped it, and placed it upon a cutting board on the kitchen counter. The soft smell of its meat wafted to her nostrils and she gagged.

What in the world?

She continued to cut, gagged again.

She placed the knife down, washed her hands. She stood in front of the sink for a moment, thinking, breathing, hoping the nausea in her stomach would abate.

Whoa. Wait!

When was her last period? She hadn't had it for her wedding. It had certainly been before then, hadn't it? Yes! Just a couple of weeks prior to her wedding, if she remembered correctly. Yes! She and Henry had been at the movies when she was relieved to find her cramping had dissipated, marking the end for that month. That would put her at... about a week late. Maybe more.

Late?

She was never late.

Oh, dear Lord! She was late.

She wrapped the chicken back up in its plastic wrap, placed it in the fridge. When were Henry and Charlie going to be home? She wished desperately there was a way to detect right now, at this very moment, if she was expecting.

She placed her hand on her belly, looked down.

Lucy barked. She ran to the living room and saw Charlie walking inside.

"Oh, thank goodness," she exclaimed. "Charlie, I need to tell you something!"

Charlie's face looked frightened as his sister led him to the couch to sit down. "What's wrong!?"

"Oh, no, no," Susan assured him hurriedly, "everything's all right. It's just— Charlie, I think I'm pregnant!"

Charlie stared at her for a moment, face expressionless. Then as the information dawned and settled, a smile formed. "A baby?"

"I think so."

"Holy shit," Charlie pronounced in wonderment.

"I know. Charlie, I didn't think it would happen this fast. I'm kind of freaking out here."

"Why?"

"Because it's so soon!" Susan cried.

"Yeah, it's soon. But Susie," Charlie said, "a baby. You and Henry."

Susan took a deep breath in, exhaled. "Yes," she agreed. "I knew this was a possibility for sure, but... oh, my goodness!"

Charlie nodded. "Holy shit," he said again, "I'm going to be an uncle."

"Well, I think so anyway. I could just be late. I may not be pregnant at all."

"Either way, fine. But if you are, Susie, it's a great thing. You and Henry? The two of you will be great parents. What a great way to grow up," he pronounced, "with two parents like yourselves. And I'm going to be an uncle. You're making me an uncle."

"Charlie, you're really happy."

"I am."

"It's just that, well, I haven't seen you happy for a while now."

He shook his head. "I know. It's been rough going. But I'm happy here, right now, with you and my possible unborn niece or nephew."

"I just can't seem to wrap my head around this, Charlie. A baby."

"A baby." He hung his arm over his sister's shoulders, leaned back, and rested his ankle upon his knee as he sat on the couch. "A baby," he said to the air with a large grin on his face.

* * *

Henry arrived home about a half hour after Charlie. When Charlie watched him walk through the door, he chuckled and left the room, closing his bedroom door behind him.

"What was that?" Henry asked. He walked forward and kissed Susan on the cheek.

"He's giving us a minute."

"Why?"

"Because I have something I need to tell you." She began to wring her hands in front of her, anxious as to how he'd respond with the news she was about to convey.

"Suze, are you okay?"

"I am," she said. "Here, come sit down."

"What's going on?"

"Okay," she said as she sat beside him on the couch, "so…" Henry lifted his eyebrows, humor evident upon his countenance. "Okay," she repeated, "Henry, I think I might be pregnant."

His smile faded. "What?"

"I think I might be pregnant…?" she repeated, her voice sounding much like a question instead of the statement she was attempting.

"Pregnant?" he asked.

She nodded her head.

"You're pregnant?" A smile began to form.

"I think so," she said. "I can't be sure just yet—" Henry jumped from the couch and threw his arms in the air.

"Whoo!" he shouted. "We're having a baby! Hey, Charlie," he yelled to the closed door, "we're having a baby!"

Charlie came back into the living room, and Henry pounced on him, lifting his friend off the floor with the force of his embrace.

He turned to Susan, the smile on his face immeasurable. "We're having a baby," he said as he bent his knees and lifted her into the air. She laughed, mouth open, hair flinging with the breeze formed by his rapid movements. "We're having a baby," he repeated in a hushed tone, as he placed her back upon the floor and rested the palm of his hand on her flat stomach.

She smiled. "I think we are."

He hugged her then, the embrace long-lasting as Charlie crossed his left arm over his chest and rested the fingers of his right hand on his grinning lips.

An appointment with a physician a week later confirmed what they already suspected: Susan was pregnant.

* * *

The following day she stopped by Mother's on her way home from work to tell her the good news. She walked up the porch steps and entered through the kitchen door. Father wasn't yet home, and Mother was at the kitchen table.

"Oh, hello, darling."

"Hi, Mom."

"What a nice surprise to have you here."

"Thanks." She walked toward her mother, quite enthusiastic to relay her announcement.

"How was your day at work today?"

"My day was fine, but that's not why I'm here."

"Oh?"

"Mom, I've got some news."

"News?"

"Yes," Susan said. "Some pretty big news that I think you'll like." Her mother looked at her expectantly. "Mom," she continued, "I'm pregnant."

Mother's hand flew to her mouth, and she stood speedily from the chair. "Oh, OH," she said happily. "Oh, Susan!" She bent her knees and bounced slightly up and down on the balls of her feet. "Oh," she exclaimed, "Susan, you are pregnant! I am so very happy for you and Henry. Oh, how wonderful this is!"

"Thanks, Mom," Susan said. "You're going to be a grandmother."

"Oh, my goodness, I am going to be a grandmother!" Her hand covered her mouth once more, shock still evident. "Oh, I could not be happier." She sat back down. "I cannot wait to tell your father; he'll be so pleased."

Susan held her tongue, not wanting to upset her mother with a rebuttal.

* * *

The following weekend, Henry had left in the afternoon to help his friend and coworker Freddie with a home-improvement project and had stated he would be staying through dinner and a social visit as well. Susan had gone to the movies with Betty and Sandy (Janet was in New Mexico with Bobby and friends) and returned to a dark house. Charlie's car was parked in the driveway, so she was confused as to why the lights were off and there was an eerie stillness to the air. Even Lucy hadn't barked or greeted her at the door.

"Charlie?" she called. "Are you home?"

She turned the living room light on and walked forth. She knocked on his bedroom door, and when there was no answer, she opened it a crack and peered inside. Lucy wagged her tail when she saw Susan enter but didn't leave Charlie's side as he sat upon Gilbert's bed and gazed out the dark window into the moonlit night.

"Charlie?" she whispered as she walked forth. He didn't look her way. She sat beside him on the bed, Lucy's little body between them. She patted her puppy's head to appease her and looked at her brother's profile. "Are you all right?"

No answer.

They sat for a time, and Charlie eventually turned to look at his sister, eyes red and bloodshot. His breathing was shallow, slow, and he looked exhausted. Susan placed Lucy gently on the floor and moved closer to her brother. She looked into his eyes, placed her hand on his forearm.

A tear fell from Charlie's eye. Another joined. "I'm fucked up, Susie. So fucked up." He began feverishly scratching the skin on his left arm.

"Charlie," Susan protested, "Charlie, please stop."

He eventually obliged, though she could see plainly, even in the darkened room, that he had broken the skin.

"I'm so fucked up," he repeated as his shoulders began to shake, his face contorted, and his body trembled.

Susan looked at her brother breaking down before her and was frightened. She wrapped her arms around his back and he bent to lean his head on her shoulder, tears streaming to soak her shirt.

"I..." he sobbed. "I can't..." He was heaving, shoulders quaking. "Over there, it was... over there." His speech was broken, and she strained to understand the words he was willing to share. "Sergeant... Sergeant told me to stay. Told me to stay. Walked in... screaming, she was screaming... hurt her... Nothing. I did nothing." His mouth opened as he wailed, drooling on Susan's shoulder. She held him in her arms as he released. "Coward. Woman... baby... grenade. Truck. He... he..." His body shook. "Shots. Scared. I was so scared. Billy's head, so much... so much blood. Gone," he wailed. "Gone." He continued to howl as his head bounced on Susan's shoulder, tears streaming down, intermixed with secretions from his nose and saliva drooling from his mouth.

"Father," he whimpered, "Father... Why? Gilbert. Gil..."

Susan was struggling to comprehend. She sat there holding her brother in her arms until she thought they'd collapse, until her legs prickled with numbness. Until Henry arrived home, saw the scene before him, and removed Charlie from his wife's arms, laying him gently on Gilbert's bed and covering him with a blanket. Charlie closed his eyes and immediately fell asleep, the blanket slowly rising with each inhalation of breath, the only sign of life before them.

* * *

Susan woke beside Henry the following morning, Sunday. Where only a couple of months ago she would have been getting ready for church, this morning she lay beside her husband as the sun seeped through the window, its rays resting upon their figures as they held each other close.

"I'm worried about Charlie," she said.

"I am, too," Henry admitted. "I really don't think he should be alone for the next couple of days."

"I agree. Henry, yesterday was the worst I have ever seen him. When we were small, he'd break down a bit after Father was particularly cruel to him, but as a man? I haven't seen him as bad as last night. Ever. Henry, it wasn't just a breakdown. I could barely understand what he was telling me, and the way he was crying—it was terrible. He scared me."

"One of us can do the grocery shopping today, the other can stay home. I don't know about tomorrow when I'm due at school and you're due at work, but we'll figure something out."

"Okay. Thanks, Henry."

He pressed forward and kissed her gently. When they parted, she rested her head in the crook of his arm. Her eyes closed as she thought about her brother.

* * *

"There's no way you're going into work today," Henry protested as

Charlie dressed the following morning. Susan had already left for the nursing home and was due to return home around the same time Henry was that day.

"I sure am."

"Charlie, you haven't been well, you really should stay home."

"I'm fine, Henry. Really. Getting to work will be good for me, right?"

"Maybe," Henry admitted.

"No maybe about it. I'm heading out soon. I'll see you this afternoon."

"Okay," Henry relented, though hesitantly. Outwardly, Charlie did seem fine, and his motivation to work was a favorable sign, indicative of better health. "I'm glad to see you feeling better. Have yourself a good day and I'll see you when you get home. I think both Susan and I are due before you on Mondays?"

"You are," Charlie affirmed. "See you then."

* * *

Susan was surprised to see Charlie's car in the driveway when she arrived after her shift; Henry had phoned to say he'd gone into work, and she wasn't expecting him so early. And for that matter, she was surprised to see Henry wasn't home just yet. She parked the car and walked up the front walkway, opened the door.

Static. She turned her head to the left and looked down at the record player. She turned the player off, lifted the needle, passed Charlie's guitar resting against the wall.

Lucy was at Charlie's door, sitting on her bottom, whining.

"Hi, Lucy," Susan said. "Why aren't you coming to say hello to me?" She looked around the empty room. "Charlie?" she called out. "Are you home?"

More whining from Lucy. "What's wrong, sweetie?"

Susan walked farther forward, leaned down to pet Lucy on the head and saw a figure in her peripheral vision.

She startled, whipped her head, and let her eyes adjust.

Charlie.

He was on the floor of his bedroom, supine. She hastened to his side.

Blue lips, eyes partly open and glazed over, pupils dilated. His arms were splayed to either side of his body, his legs bent and resting to the side. The putrid smell of vomit permeated forth, some dried to the skin of his cheek and chin, the remains puddled on the carpeted floor.

"Charlie"—pleading, imploring.

She knelt by his side, shook him by the shoulders, the chest, and watched as his body rattled from side to side but his eyes remained unmoving, his body unresponsive.

"Charlie!" she screamed. "Charlie, oh, God, NO! Charlie!"

Tears streaming down her face, her knees in the sickness on the floor, she screamed. Hands upon his cheeks, in his hair.

Wake up, she pleaded silently. *Oh, God, please wake him up!*

"No, no, no, no, no. Oh, God! Charlie, NO!"

A whine, a bark. Henry was by her side, lifting her, forcing her away from her brother's figure. He lifted the lids of Charlie's eyes, examined them, shot his head in Susan's direction. "I called the paramedics, GO!" he yelled. He pounded on Charlie's chest, slapped his face. To no avail.

Susan didn't move.

Henry placed two fingers on Charlie's neck, felt no pulse. His face contorted, anguished. Tears coursed down his cheeks. He looked at his wife, his hands upon his best friend's chest.

He shook his head.

"No," Susan sobbed, "no, no, no." She shook her head vehemently. If she willed it enough, he'd come back to her. He would!

"Charlie," she screamed. "No, no, oh, God! NO!" She lunged forward, and Henry caught her in his arms before she could reach her brother. "Let me go!" she screamed. "Let me go!" Her vision was blurry, secretions from her nose leaking into her mouth as she wailed her protest, her torment. "Let go!" she screamed at her husband as she pounded his chest. "LET GO!"

She wasn't aware when the paramedics arrived or when they hovered over the dead body of her brother. Her eyes were closed as she moaned and whimpered into her husband's broad chest. "Charlie," she lamented. "Charlie." A whisper now, "No, no, no. Not Charlie."

Henry's tears soaked her head as he held her, rocked with her on the floor of Charlie's room.

"Charlie," she pleaded. "Charlie..."

Had she looked up, she would have found two items lying neatly upon Gilbert's bed. The blue handkerchief Susan had gifted Charlie prior to his army induction—now weathered and stained—was on his pillow. Gilbert's Vietnam dog tag was enfolded within.

* * *

A heroin overdose, the coroner's office concluded. They had his body for a week before releasing it to family.

She and Henry had never even realized he was using. He didn't make it to work the morning of his death; had called out sick quite a bit in the last month, they had learned.

Unbeknownst to her, Charlie had written a will prior to his having been inducted into the army for Vietnam. He had altered it when

Gilbert died. Had named Henry as executor of his estate.

The police had arrived after the paramedics informed them of Charlie's death. Susan and Henry were both asked various questions. Susan answered them rotely, dazed. Henry had called both his mother and mother-in-law, and they arrived soon thereafter, before Charlie's body had been removed.

Susan stood aside and watched as her brother's covered body was lifted, watched as he was taken by complete strangers into a waiting ambulance on the street. Watched as they shut him inside.

Her knees gave out and she collapsed in the doorway, heaving and holding her stomach as fresh tears streamed down. When Henry reached her side and took her in his arms, she bent over and vomited on the walkway.

Henry carried his wife to bed while Viola cleaned up the contents of her daughter-in-law's stomach. Mother sat upon the couch in a stupor.

Charlie's body was released to the funeral home after the hospital mortuary was through with their investigation, and Susan and Henry opted out of a family viewing prior to the cremation they had decided upon. Susan thought of Gilbert, of his rubbery skin, the caking of his eyelashes, the stillness and rigidity of his body. She remembered, too, the conversation she and her brother had had, the conversation in which Charlie had made it clear he didn't want her to remember him in such a way should he expire before her. And, if she was being honest with herself, she was scared. Scared to walk into a room, see him lying there before her without the ability to sit up and smile her way. Without the ability to tousle her hair in the big-brotherly way he had always had. Without the ability for her to place her cheek upon his chest and feel his beating heart.

Seeing him splayed out and deceased in his room in a puddle of his own vomit was nightmare enough.

The cremation had taken place, and his ashes were now in an egg-shaped brass urn that rested upon the side table next to the couch in the room his living presence had once filled. Henry had found his wife asleep on their bed the afternoon after Charlie had been returned to them, his urn cradled in her arms, Lucy at her feet. The framed photo of them as children at Stuart's he had gifted her prior to Vietnam rested by her side. Shelly, her childhood doll leaned upon the bed's headrest.

And now, two weeks after his death, they were to have a memorial service for this man they had both dearly loved.

Henry had phoned Pastor Glenn, who had readily offered up his church for Charlie. Henry had made it very clear that they wanted this service to be rather unconventional; that Charlie had been cremated, and instead of Pastor Glenn preaching, they simply wanted friends and family in one central location to reminisce on the life that Charlie had led. Charlie had ceased going to church when he was sixteen years old and evicted from his father's home; they wouldn't force a religious service on him now.

"Are you ready? We should head out, Susie, get there well before everyone else so we can set up."

She sighed and stood. She gently picked up the urn that held her brother's remains, and together they walked out the door, leaving Lucy to continue her rest on Charlie's bed, something she had been doing frequently the past two weeks.

They went to pick Mother up on the way.

Henry sat in the car behind the driver's wheel as Susan walked through the screen door and onto the porch, knocked gently on the front door before opening it to step inside. Mother was standing at the kitchen table. A large box of framed and loose photos of Charlie that she had promised she'd procure from storage and display at his service rested on the table in front of her.

She was crying.

Susan walked to her mother, embraced her as Father sat at the kitchen table, cigarette in hand, leg crossed.

Mother's shoulders shook as her daughter held her close.

"I know," Susan said comfortingly. "I almost couldn't leave the house."

"Oh, Susan," Mother said, "I do not think I can make it through today. I am about to say goodbye to my son for a last, final time, and this just after your father has informed me that he is having an affair with another woman."

"What!?" Susan was incredulous as she turned to stare at her father, a look of apathy on his face as he inhaled a large puff of smoke into his black lungs. "You're having an affair?"

"I am," he affirmed after he exhaled, the smoke wafting to the ceiling toward a yellow-hued circular stain, an accumulation of many years of abuse.

"But," she expostulated, "how could you do that? And why would you tell her this now, of all times? That's horrible!"

Mother sniffed at her side, wiped her nose with a hand. Mascara trickled down with her tears to stain her cheeks.

"How can I do that, you ask?" Father sneered. "I can damn right do as I please. For Christ's sake, I'm the man of this fucking house, aren't I? I'll do whatever the hell I want, when I want to." He inhaled again as Susan looked at him, appalled. After an exhale: "And your mother over there? Just not doing it for me anymore. Used to be pretty, now she's just fat and ugly. A man has needs and I'm not getting them here. Your mother just has to deal."

"To deal?" Susan's voice was raised, exasperated.

"Damn right, girl, and don't you dare raise your voice to me. I'm still your father even if you've gone off and gotten yourself married. You're spreading your legs now, you know the appetite of a man."

Susan's eyes widened as she stood rooted to the floor, so incapable was she to form a retort through this blow.

Father continued to puff on his cigarette, angry red cheeks indenting as he inhaled.

Susan regained control of her body, lifted the box of photos from the table, and ushered Mother out the door and to her husband in the waiting car.

She opened the front door and helped in her broken, shattered mother. Susan climbed into the back seat behind her mother and Henry started the car. He pulled onto North Street, then reached for Mother's hand, holding it within his own until they arrived at the Church of Christ.

Pastor Glenn greeted them at the side door. Mother's tears had dried, though her face was blotchy and red, mascara still clinging to her weathered skin. Susan helped her to the bathroom, where she dabbed at her mother's eyes and took a warm, wet cloth to her cheeks, removing the black stains. Mother brought Susan's hands to her lips and kissed them. "Thank you."

Susan nodded. "Let's get ready," she said.

Susan and Mother left the bathroom and entered the large room where food would be served after the service. Henry had placed the urn upon a table to rest while he unloaded the box Mother had provided with various photos of Charlie. Susan walked to them now, lifting them up one by one.

Charlie as an infant before Susan was even born. A black-and-white photo set within a white border.

Charlie sleeping on the couch as a toddler, brown hair dangling upon an eye, his chubby cheek pressed against the cushion, drool seeping from his mouth.

Charlie holding an infant Susan on the living room couch, Susan bundled in a blanket, Charlie's smile broad and joyful.

Charlie opening a gift on Christmas Day, his excitement uncontained as he stood on his knees peering inside the box.

Charlie frowning as he held a fishing pole as a child, a younger version of their father standing by his side in a form-fitting white T-shirt and brown pants, belt cinched tight on his slight frame, a cigarette dangling from his mouth as he baited the line.

Charlie's arm around a young Susan as they waded in the water at Stuart's Campground, Mother standing beside them. Though the photo was in black and white, Susan vividly remembered the suit her mother was wearing, could picture her in it even now. Emerald green suit, a bright smile on her red lips, auburn hair perfectly waved from her forehead.

Charlie and Henry in the middle of North Street smiling for the camera, each with a baseball cap on his head, gloves in hand.

Charlie and their cousins as boys digging for worms in the backyard.

Charlie in ice skates on the pond, holding a four-or five-year-old Susan by the hand.

Charlie pushing Susan on the swing at Emerson Park, Janet and Betty on either side of them.

Charlie, taller now, in his school uniform in the doorway from the kitchen to the living room of their house.

Charlie in the backyard as a young teenager, plastic cup in hand on a summer day, Henry by his side, extended family in the background.

Charlie and Gilbert on the couch in the living room of their house.

Charlie in his army service uniform.

Charlie and Henry standing at the altar on Susan's wedding day, brilliant smiles on their faces.

She could no longer see through her tears.

She placed the photos down on the table, and Henry helped her spread them out so guests could have the pleasure of looking at them that afternoon.

Mother stood behind her now. "He was always such a happy baby, such a happy little boy," she said. "You should have seen him when I brought you home. He would have been almost four then and he was so thrilled to have you there, his little sister. So many siblings I had known back then fought and resented each other's presence, but not you and Charlie. Never you and Charlie. He loved you dearly, Susan. I hope you know that."

"And he loved you, too," Susan said, wiping her eyes.

"I know," Mother said. "I felt it every day. I will never know how he came to be such a caring, wonderful, loving young man. But I thanked God every day for him and thank Him now that He sent my Charles to me. I know Charles is with God now and that pleases me greatly, though I miss him terribly, Susan. My boy. I have so many regrets in this life, and I have been on my knees so much lately praying that God forgives me, praying to Him for guidance that he may lead me on the right path."

She slipped her hand into Susan's and stood in silence.

When all was set up in the large conference room, they made their way to the main portion of the church, where Pastor Glenn was greeting the first mourners to arrive, and mourn they did. As much as Susan had attempted to make this a celebration of her brother's life, it was truly difficult not to mourn the way in which he had passed, the tribulations he had endured prior to his life ending in such a macabre way.

She, Mother, and Henry stood within the doorway with Pastor Glenn to welcome friends and family. Susan was touched to see so many familiar faces walk through the door and into the church. Grandparents, aunts and uncles, cousins, Gilbert's parents, Janet and Bobby, Betty and Walter, Sandy, David, and Mikey. Mr. Biladeau slowly approached Susan on the arm of a nurse from the home.

"Edmond, I can't believe you're here," she said as she kissed his stubbly, wrinkled cheek.

"Wouldn't miss it," Mr. Biladeau said kindly.

Several of Charlie's coworkers were present, as well as men he had gone to school with, many of whom Susan didn't know.

When she saw both Mercedes Doyle and Tommy Walters approach the entrance, she was stupefied.

"Welcome," Pastor Glenn said, "and thank you for coming."

Mercedes gave a compact smile in return, looked over at Susan, and lowered her eyes meekly as she passed through to sit at a back pew. Tommy's look was impassive when Pastor Glenn greeted him, but he walked to Susan, stood in front of her.

"I'm really sorry." His voice was coarse, though his words were effective and his countenance honest and frank.

"Thank you," Susan replied, still highly astonished at his appearance.

Tommy turned and walked to sit near Mercedes Doyle.

Guests having arrived, it was time to begin. Susan, Mother, and Henry walked down the aisle and sat in the left front row, Pastor Glenn standing before them, ready to address those in attendance. Charlie's urn was in the center of the aisle; a framed photo of his smiling face rested beside it on the small table. Susan could almost lean over and touch it if she so willed.

A microphone had been erected, and it was into this that Pastor Glenn now spoke.

"Hello to you all and thank you for being here with us today. Though we never can quite understand why God calls home a man as young and vibrant as Charlie, we must trust in His plan for us all and take solace in the fact that he was loved by so many. Looking around now, I can see that he has touched many lives." Henry slid his hand into Susan's. "As I would like to honor the wishes of Charlie's family, I ask Susan to take my place here now. Susan?"

Susan stood and walked the few steps to where Pastor Glenn had vacated his position at the microphone. She thought only of her brother in the urn by her side, wishing the situation were different, that he was standing with her, flesh and bone, instead.

"Charlie was my best friend," Susan said, her voice carrying through the large room. "For as long as I can remember, he put me first. He always thought of other people. I know family and friends mourn their loved ones, and they often think of kind things to say after they pass. I mean, they're no longer here; who wants to reminisce on the ugly? But Charlie? I honestly don't think any one of us can say something bad about Charlie. He was just inherently kind." She paused to look out at the sea of faces, then to her husband sitting to her right, a slight, sad grin of commemoration on his face.

"Charlie was just such a wonderful man, and I think Pastor Glenn is right when he said that Charlie has touched so many lives. I'm looking around right now. Some of you I don't even know. But Charlie touched you, or why would you be here?" She paused, thought for a moment. "I think I'm beginning to truly believe that a person comes into your life for a reason. A wise man once told me that." She locked eyes with Mr. Biladeau briefly before breaking contact and continuing to speak. "I think Charlie has come into ours for a reason. I hope you felt his love. My brother was an amazing man; that I know. It hurts so much for me to be standing here right now without him." A tear dripped down her cheek, though her voice didn't quaver. "But he came into my life to show me what love was, what protection was. I have to believe God's got a plan. I just have to. I have to believe my parents moved to North Street for a reason, that Henry Beaumont moved to the street over for a reason. I have to believe that Charlie and Henry met for a reason. I have to believe that I was placed in their lives for a reason, and they in mine. I have to believe that we all *have* a reason. Every one of us. And although I will never, ever understand why my brother isn't still here with us today, I know that his life had a purpose. That his love for me I will always remember. He loved me well." She wiped a tear from her eye.

"He never would have wanted us sitting here and crying on his behalf. I know that now. He would have wanted us to celebrate the life that he had, the life that he was given. And I know how tough it was for him at the end, but we all have so many wonderful memories of Charlie, and I think the best way to show him our love and appreciation for who he was in life is for us to come up here and share our stories. So," Susan said, "I'm going to step down for now and invite anyone up who would like to speak of my brother."

Henry spoke next, embracing Susan before she sat back down. "I've known Henry since I was really small. Honestly, I can't remember a time when he and I weren't friends. Man, we had some good times." Henry shook his head in remembrance. "There was this one time at my folks' house. Mom thought it would be a good idea to teach me how to bake cookies, why I have no idea, but there she was, recipe book out, having me and Charlie find our way through. Now, I've learned to bake a bit, cook a bit, but Charlie? He was never good. That day in my folks' kitchen we burned those damn cookies to a crisp, smoke was everywhere. We had to open all the windows and the doors. And Charlie? All he could do was lie on the kitchen floor laughing so hard he couldn't breathe. I have no idea why that's the memory that I thought of just now with the amount of time we've spent together through the years, but there you go. Just an everyday memory, I suppose. And almost every good memory I have growing up, Charlie's been in it.

"I even remember our first day of school—we were what? Six? We met on the corner of my street, did that for years. He was nervous, I wasn't, but you know who helped a girl up when she stumbled on the steps and began to cry? Charlie. Even when he was scared of something, he still thought of other people. It was just in him.

"And it didn't stop at people, either. Some jerk had tortured a toad at Emerson, left it there to die. Charlie found it, almost stepped on it. I remember him stopping dead in his tracks, then kneeling down on the ground. He lifted that toad up and walked it to the edge of the fence. He dug a hole in the ground with his bare hands and buried that toad. Sat there for a long time afterward, too. I didn't realize until I reached around to see if he was okay that he was crying. So no, not just people. He really cared for every living creature and he was amazing for it.

"We pretty much did everything together that we could. Good times, bad times, we had them both. He was more level-headed than I was when we were younger, talked me out of a lot of crazy ideas I stirred up in my mind. He was just always there," Henry said. "And now he's not." He shook his head. "I'm not going to go there because Susie's right. He'd want us to smile. We need to make this about the good times, the good memories we have of this amazing guy. I'm leaving the mic to anyone else who'd like to come up, but please stay and join us in the conference room afterward. We've got Charlie's favorite foods and favorite music and photos. I'd love to talk to you all about this man that meant so much to me, to us."

He stepped away and Mother took his place.

"Charlie was my son," she said slowly. Her smile was sorrowful but also filled with pride. "A mother could not have asked for a better son. He filled my heart with joy from the moment he was born. He fills my heart still and always will. While I am sad he is no longer with us, I know we will be reunited in Heaven and I yearn for that day. His sorrows are gone as he is with the Lord now, and I am thankful he is in God's capable hands. It pleases me greatly to see so many of you here today to honor my son and the man he was. Thank you so very much."

Many people came to the microphone to speak of Charlie; many wonderful, delightful memories were shared. Tears fell upon Susan's cheeks, but she was smiling through them as more and more people reminisced. She sat there in the first pew of the Church of Christ, listening to these people—some she knew; others she did not—and realized that as much as she thought she knew her brother, there was so much more to learn. Each recollection shared filled her with pride for the brother she had been blessed to have by her side through the first almost nineteen years of her life.

The last person who wanted to share shared, and Susan had a compulsion to look behind her before joining the others to rise and walk in the direction of the conference room. A figure was discreetly peering into the nave.

Was that—Was that Father?

Susan sprinted from her seat and walked quickly down the aisle, dodging the throng of people who had exited their seats. The figure had already moved and was gone when she arrived outside.

Yes! It was Father! He was there, climbing into the Chrysler parked on the street. She stood at the threshold of the church's entrance and watched as he pulled into traffic and drove the car down the road.

She stood for a while longer, astonished not only that he had been here, but at the tear he had wiped from his eye as he opened his car door.

Susan had never before seen her father cry.

TWENTY-FOUR

"Well, hello, foxy mama!" Henry whistled as Susan emerged from their bedroom. He walked forward, wrapped his arms around her upper back. Her swollen belly hindered her from fully encircling his waist. With her compact torso, there was nowhere for her stomach to grow but out. "How's my baby this morning?" He released her from the hug and circled the palm of his hand over her stomach, stooping to kiss the fabric of the dress that covered her expanded girth.

"Active. The baby didn't let me sleep much last night, so I probably look like a zombie."

"Mmm," Henry said. "A sexy zombie, though." Susan gave him an unconvinced smile but laughed as he shimmied his way to her again, gyrating to Sam Cooke on the record player.

"You can't dance," she said with a giggle. "Just like my brother."

"Your brother was better than me," Henry said.

"Yeah," Susan agreed, "I suppose he was." Her smile faded. "Henry, I can't believe this is our first Christmas without him. I almost didn't want to get out of bed this morning and you know how much I like going to your parents' house."

"Yeah, I understand," Henry said. "Charlie was always there with us."

"I thought Gilbert would be with us indefinitely. And Charlie, I was sure he and I would grow old together, that he'd live here with us, see this baby of ours. Hold him or her in his arms. I get these pictures in my head sometimes of him doing just that—I can even see the smile on his face. If I close my eyes, I can see those few freckles on his cheeks, the green of his eyes. I can feel his arm around my shoulder. Henry, I'm so scared that I'm going to lose that, that with time his face is going to fade, his scent, his presence. I'm so scared I'm going to lose him entirely."

Henry held her close to his chest.

They spent that Christmas morning with James and Viola, and though Charlie was not with them and they all missed him sorely, they did have a wonderful time together. James and Viola had become an integral part of Susan's life and she loved them dearly. They were so different than her own parents, their marriage a stark contrast from the marriage she was privy to as a child in her own home. In James and Viola, she could see her husband and his playful nature, his loving demeanor. In James and Viola, she could see the way in which she wanted to raise her child.

After dinner, they parted ways and Henry drove them to Susan's childhood home, where they were to spend some time with her parents. She knocked lightly on the door before walking inside.

Father was at his seat at the kitchen table, the exact place she'd expected to find him. An almost empty glass of whiskey rested by his side (what number was this?), a wad of tobacco balled in his left cheek. He had recently acquired this new habit in addition to the cigarettes he still smoked most fervently. An empty can of Campbell's tomato soup was in his hand. He lifted it to his mouth and spat a dark tobacco-infused mass of liquid into the hollow steel container.

"Father," Susan said by way of greeting.

"Susan," her father replied.

"Merry Christmas, Sir," Henry said amiably.

355

"Mmm."

"Where's Mom?"

"Bedroom."

She turned to Henry. "I'll be right back."

Susan walked into the living room and past her old bedroom, straight to the door of Mother's room. She knocked.

"Oh," her mother's voice from within, hoarse but pleasant, "come on in."

Susan opened the door and found her mother seated at her vanity. Every light in her room was on, illuminating her exaggerated clown-like appearance in the mirror before her.

The strong smell of lavender accosted her nostrils and she winced.

"Mom? What's going on?" Susan asked with hesitation.

"Oh, darling, it is you. Come here, come here," Mother said gaily. Her face was almost comical as it was irradiated by the lights. Her mascara was clumpy, her blusher overly done and pronounced upon the whole of her cheeks. Her lips were bright red, and she had failed at outlining their true form as lipstick was smudged upon her upper lip and the corners of her mouth. "I am so happy you came to be with me again this morning, darling. Come stand by me. You know how I love my little girl helping me to get ready for church." She fiddled with the strand of imitation pearls around her neck.

Church?

She continued to mark her lips, the tube of red lipstick held firmly in her trembling hands.

Susan walked forward, stood by her mother.

Mother placed the tube on the vanity desk and turned to look at Susan. She began to hum. Susan knew the tune well. She and her mother spent many minutes with Paul Anka's "Put Your Head on My Shoulder" in this very spot when she was a young girl.

She took Susan's hand. "Sing with me now, darling. Oh, how we love to sing together."

A tear trickled down Susan's cheek, but she obliged.

Mother turned to gaze at her reflection, ran her fingers through her graying hair as she finished the song.

She turned to her daughter, held her hands as she sat on her cushioned chair. "I wonder what Father Denis will speak of today," she said. "Susan, darling, would you be a lamb and go make sure your father and brother are almost ready to go? And oh, just to think: tomorrow we are on vacation. Oh, how I adore our summers together. Now, run along, darling. I will join you in a moment."

Susan turned on her heel, tears coursing to her bosom. In her haste to exit the room, she didn't notice the hand-drawn picture she had sent to the floor with the breeze produced by her body. A little girl's depiction of the baby Jesus in a manger, juvenile stick figure people and angels as well as fluffy scribbled sheep surrounding him. She was just a young child on a jolly Christmas morning when she had gifted that to her mother.

"How long has she been like that?" she demanded of her father when she entered the kitchen.

Her father grumbled.

"How long?" Susan yelled.

"Don't you yell at me, girl! I'm your father! Show some respect!"

"Yes, and what a great father you've been," Susan retorted with loathing in her voice. "How long?"

Father stood abruptly from his chair and wobbled in his stance. "How dare you speak to me like that, you little bitch!"

Henry's chair fell backward to the floor with the force of his legs rocketing out beneath him. "Whoa, Gerald, there's no need—"

"And you shut your mouth," Father bellowed, cheek extended and voice muffled with the substance in its pouch. "This is my goddamn house you're both in."

"Listen, *Dad*," Father's eyes widened in surprise with the mocking, informal use of his name ejaculated from his typically meek and obedient daughter's lips.

"Gerald, Gerald," Henry said hurriedly, "sit back down for just a minute, let's sort this out." He extended his arm across the table, motioning for Father to retreat.

"How long?" Susan demanded again.

"Been like that a couple times," Father said as he sat back down on his chair and spit the entire wad of tobacco into his soup can. "Comes and goes. If she's not like this, then she's brooding. I like her more like this. When she's not, she just sits around or sleeps, doesn't get off her fat, lazy ass to clean my house or make my meals."

"Whoa," Susan said, outraged. She didn't know if it was the pregnancy, the hormones. She didn't know if it was the fact that she had met and married a man who had given her a life that transcended the boundaries of the home she had been born into, or if it was simply the fact that she had finally had enough and had boiled over, but she found in this very moment, standing upon the linoleum floor of her childhood, glaring upon the father who had become progressively more demonic with each passing year, that she no longer cared. He could say whatever he wanted to her. She was indifferent, immune to his abuse.

Never did she imagine she'd be in this position.

She felt indestructible in her outrage.

She looked to her husband, the husband who gave her strength.

She felt her brother's hands upon her shoulders.

"She needs help," Susan said. "And you're going to get it for her."

"To hell I —"

"You *will* get it for her," Susan interrupted. "You want that clean house? You want some meals in that refrigerator of yours? You want me around to do it? Then you *will* get her help. And you *will* treat her well. She is your wife."

A grumble from her father.

"I'll come. I'll come and help around here."

"About time, too. You go off and marry this guy, forget about your family."

"Henry is my family now. This baby is my family. I'm not doing this for you. I'm doing this for my mother. *She* is my family." She paused, her blue eyes boring into those of her father, bloodshot and droopy. "And you get help, too. The drinking needs to stop."

"Fuck that!"

"No? Then show me you can treat her well even through the booze."

Father made no comment. Lit a cigarette and pulled.

Susan turned to Henry. "I'll be right back." She walked to check on her mother. She remained seated at her vanity, but the smile had faded from her face. She gazed at her reflection before her, unseeing. She was elsewhere.

"Mom?" Susan whispered.

Her mother didn't answer.

Susan helped her mother to stand, walked her to the bathroom. She wet a cloth with warm water and soap and gently scrubbed the makeup from her face. She patted her skin dry with a towel. Henry emerged from the kitchen and helped Susan guide her mother back to her bedroom, where they laid her down on her bed and pulled the blanket to her neck.

They remained by her side until she fell asleep.

"What happens when she wakes up?" Susan asked her father when she returned to the kitchen.

"She'll be fine. Just mopey."

"I'll be back tomorrow," Susan told him.

"Whatever." He dismissed his daughter with a slight wave of his hand, smoke billowing upward.

Henry held her hand as he drove the short distance home.

"Henry, she needs to come live with us."

"I had thought about that, too. But Suze? She's a woman with her own convictions, her own beliefs. I'm not sure she'll leave your father, no matter how shitty he is to her."

Susan shook her head in agitated wonderment. "After all this time, he's only getting worse. I know she sees it. I think he's a big part of the reason she's so unwell. Henry," she turned to look at her husband, "she's scaring me."

* * *

Susan's plan proved futile, for Henry's prediction was right. Mother refused to leave her husband even with the acknowledgment of his irrefutable faults: his supposed affair, his abuse, his apathy.

Susan was then determined to be there for her as much as her schedule permitted, and was adamant that she would ensure Father procured intervention for her well-being. If he refused, then she'd do it herself, and damn him!

TWENTY-FIVE

I t was March 22, 1973, a Thursday. Susan's due date had come and gone two days ago, and both she and Henry had taken time off work for the impending birth of their baby. Henry stood next to the muddy edge of the pond she and Henry frequented for ice-skating in the winters, leisurely walks in the spring, summer, and fall.

"This one's hungry," he said as he threw a large chunk of white bread to the ducks splashing toward him, beaks extended as they fought one another for the morsels of food splattering the water beside them.

Susan sat watching the dark water ripple, the metal seat cold against her bottom. Her jacket clung tightly to her chest, buttons open to reveal her bulging belly in Henry's burnt-orange sweater.

She hadn't felt well that morning. Her stomach had been clenching, and she was rather nauseated.

The baby stirred within. She placed her hand on her stomach, watched as a body part pushed her skin forward, moved from her right side to her left. What a strange sensation this still was to her. She was awestruck every day by the fact that there was this human life inside of her, that she could feel its movements, its beginnings.

"Henry, I really don't feel well. My stomach is just so tight and my body is achy all over."

Henry turned to look at his wife, the ducks quacking and splashing before him. "Okay," he said as he threw the last of the bread their way, "I'll take you home. Maybe you need some rest."

He walked to Susan, threw the plastic bag in the waste receptacle by the side of the bench. "Ready?" He offered his hands and she grasped on, straining as he helped to lift her. She found it incredibly difficult to stand from a sitting position without the ability to bend her back more than a few inches, her stomach pushing upward and lifting her breasts. She had to admit that however nervous she was for this baby to come, she'd be happy when it did and she could have her body back to herself instead of sharing it with a cohabitant who produced intolerable discomfort and forced her to use the bathroom every hour.

"Oof," she grunted as she stood.

A slight trickle from between her legs, her panties now damp.

Ugh! Had she urinated? It wouldn't be the first time, she had to admit. She had trickled a few times when she was in a rather precarious position with no bathroom in sight.

She took her first step, and her stomach cramped up again, this time a bit more intense than it had been all that morning thus far. "We need to get me home," she said to Henry. "I'm really not feeling well."

"Do you think you're all right?" He looked down at her with a concerned expression.

"Yeah, I'll be fine, I'm sure. I haven't been well for the past few days. This baby's really taking a lot out of me."

"Okay," he said. "Here." He offered his arm and Susan took hold.

More liquid trickled as she took further steps to the car. *Please stop,* she pleaded with exasperation. *Just wait until you get home, please! Henry doesn't need to see you peeing yourself.*

She held her stomach as it clenched again, but didn't halt her steps. Henry helped her down and into the car, and she sat with legs splayed to the sides, making room for her belly to rest upon the edge of her thighs.

They arrived home and Henry helped her inside. She immediately walked to the bathroom to relieve her bladder. She wiped and saw a minute smearing of blood.

Blood!?

She stood from the cool seat and felt more liquid trickle down her legs.

Wait... this couldn't be...

Her stomach clenched again, and she inhaled a bit with the pain, held her breath until it dissipated.

Susan lifted her panties, then her pants, walked to the living room. When she didn't see her husband, she called out. "Henry?" He emerged from the kitchen, biting into an apple slice, a knife in hand.

He looked at his wife, saw the anxiety on her face.

"What's wrong?" he asked, chewing his bite slowly, swallowing.

"I think," she began. "I think—" She grimaced as her stomach tightened once again.

"Holy shit!" Henry said. "Susan, are you having the baby?"

"Yeah," she said, "I think so."

"Oh, shit, shit!" Henry threw his apple on the couch, Lucy jumping up to inspect. "I just took the dog out; she's good. Let's go!"

"Henry, my mom. Call my mom? And Viola?"

"Yeah, yeah," Henry said as he ran his fingers through his hair in agitation. "I forgot. Yeah, I'll call them now. Do you want to sit down for a minute?" He reached for her.

"No." She shook her head.

She heard him on the kitchen telephone. "Helen, I'm so glad you're home. No, no, we're okay. It's time. Yeah... yes, we're going now. You have a ride? Okay, see you there." A pause and then, "Mom! Susan's in labor! Yeah... no, I can get her there. Yeah, meet you there. Bye."

He walked back to his wife, took her by the hand. "Holy shit!" he repeated.

"Yeah," Susan smirked, thrilled but nervous. "Mom seemed okay?"

"She did, yes. I think it's a good day for her, thank God. I think He knew she needed to be there with us today."

Susan visibly relaxed a bit. "Okay, Henry, I'm ready." Her face contorted as another contraction took hold.

"It hurts?"

"Yeah, it's been hurting for a little while now. I just didn't realize..."

"It's okay, Suze. How would you? You've never done this before."

He helped Susan back into the car and drove to the hospital about thirty minutes away from their home. There were two hospitals local to them, and Susan was adamant that she wanted Henry in the labor and delivery rooms with her. One hospital would allow him to be there; the other would not. Their decision was an easy one to make.

They arrived, and Henry parked the car at the main entrance, pocketed the keys, and opened the door for Susan. She was wincing in pain. He stood there powerless until she opened her eyes again and he helped her out of the car. They walked through the door of the hospital and into the main reception area within the foyer.

"Maternity!" Henry demanded with panic as he held his wife under her shoulder.

"Second floor," the receptionist said. "Would you like a wheelchair?"

"Suze?" Henry looked to his wife.

"No, no, I'm okay." She walked a few steps to the white wall next to the entrance, placed her arms against it to the elbows, and rested her forehead on her hands, breathing deeply as another contraction spread a painful sensation within.

It passed, and together they walked to the elevator, taking it to the second floor. They checked in at the maternity ward, and Susan was whisked to a labor room as the nurses on duty could plainly see that her time might be close.

Susan was asked to strip herself of all clothes and put a maternity gown on her body.

"How long have you been in labor, hon?" This woman had introduced herself as Blanche, and was young and portly with a kind, round face mirrored by curly brown hair.

"I don't know exactly," Susan said. She was now in her gown and stood standing in the middle of the laboring room, Henry tying the gown closed at her back so her bare bottom wasn't exposed, though her pain was intense enough now that she didn't care.

"When did you start feeling a bit of pain?"

"Early this morning," Susan said. "It woke me up, but it didn't hurt. It just felt different. But I've been feeling like that for a few days now."

"Yes," Blanche said, "many women do. It's your body's way of preparing for childbirth, and completely normal. If you've been feeling like this since earlier this morning then you've been in labor for, what—six or seven hours now? Maybe more."

Susan's jaw clenched, and her eyes shut tightly as she clung to Henry's shoulders in an attempt to hold herself up as her contraction hit its peak, then dissolved. "Yeah, probably," she breathed in response. "Maybe more because it was pretty early I was woken up."

"Well, now," Blanche said. "I'd like to get the doctor in here to check your progress, Susan. Dad, if you'd get her to lie on the bed, that would help."

"Nine centimeters," the doctor said after the examination. "Hook her up. Delivery room soon."

"Okay, hon," Blanche said, "I'm going to hook you and your baby up to some monitors, make sure the heartbeat is steady and the baby's doing well. You'll even see your contractions on there. I'll have the doctor check on you again soon, then we'll wheel you on over to the delivery room. Sound good?"

Susan nodded. She felt another contraction coming on, the sensation beginning softly, then intensifying rapidly until her eyes were forced to shut tightly once again and she yelled out in pain.

It felt like an eternity before it relented and let go, but was probably less than a minute in reality. The entire time Henry gazed upon the face of his wife, feeling utterly useless and incredibly distressed.

Susan looked intensely into Henry's hazel eyes. "Oh," she moaned, "it hurts so much." A tear fell. "It just hurts so much."

Blanche was beside her, hooking her stomach up to be monitored. Susan could hear her baby's heartbeat and smiled. It was there. Everything seemed to be okay. She looked at Henry. He stared affectionately into her blue eyes, a look of thanksgiving upon his face.

"Sounds great," Blanche announced. "Nice and strong."

"OH!" Susan exclaimed. "Here it comes again." She writhed in pain as she maimed Henry's hand with the intensity of her squeeze, his knuckles pressing together.

"You're doing a great job, Susan," Blanche said when Susan had taken a deep breath and relaxed her body.

"It hurts so, so much. Is it supposed to hurt *this* much? I don't know if I can keep doing this!"

"Yes, hon," Blanche said, "it's supposed to hurt this much. And yes, you can certainly do this."

"You can," Henry confirmed. "You are such a strong woman, Suze. You can do this."

Susan was soon wheeled out of the room she had labored in, and into the hallway, accompanied by the fetal heart rate monitor that was also on wheels for easy portability. The maternity waiting room was directly down the hallway, and Mother, Viola, and James rushed toward Susan and Henry as they approached.

"Oh, Susan," Mother exclaimed. "Are you well?"

"I'm—" Susan clenched her jaw and scrunched her face as the pain began again.

"Oh, oh… is she all right?" Mother asked.

"She's fine, Helen," Viola said reassuringly. "The baby's just ready to come out is all."

"Dad"— Henry looked at his father—"I wasn't expecting you here." His voice was surely pleased.

"And miss the birth of my first grandchild?" James said. "Of course I'm here!"

"We really need to get her into delivery," Blanche said kindly, though forcefully.

"Of course, of course," Viola said.

Susan watched the three figures of her family fade in the distance, Viola and James beaming, Mother clenching her fists together as her face contorted in a look of perturbation.

They turned a corner—Henry continuously holding her hand—and entered a room on their right. The doctor was readying himself for the impending birth. Another nurse was present, setting up a metal tray of various birthing devices.

Both nurses helped Susan to stand and transfer onto the birthing bed.

"OH!" she exclaimed, "Ow, ow, ow… Henry! Henry, it hurts so much," she screamed.

Henry moved to her side, placed his fingers on her forehead, smoothed the stray hair away from her face as she clung to the side of the bed, knuckles turning white. "I know, Suze," he said soothingly, "I know. I think we're almost there."

"Okay, Susan," Blanche announced, "we're ready. Baby's looking good. With this next contraction, I want you to push down as hard as you can, okay?"

"Oh, oh…" Susan moaned. Henry placed his hand on his wife's

upper back in support as she bore down and pushed. "OW!" she screamed.

"That's it, hon, that's it. Keep pushing until I tell you to stop. Dad, just stay right there by her head."

Henry had no intention of moving as he saw blood on the doctor's gloved hand as he lifted it into the air.

Susan continued to push, to bear down with all her might during each concurrent contraction. She pushed for approximately thirty-five minutes, sweat pooling on her forehead, body pained and exhausted.

"I see hair," Blanche announced, "and lots of it. Another big push, Susan."

Susan's face turned red with the force of the pressure she was exerting on her body.

"Okay," Blanche said. "Okay, Susan. Good job. Head's out. Don't push just yet... hold still..." She looked to the doctor. He nodded his consent. "Okay, Susan, now. One last big push for me, hon."

"Eeeeee..." Susan pushed with every last ounce of energy she had left. She felt immense pressure between her legs and then a great release as the pressure disappeared, leaving only a throbbing sensation in its stead.

She opened her eyes, heard a high-pitched cry, looked down.

"It's a boy," the doctor announced.

"A boy! Susie, did you hear that?" Henry exclaimed. "It's a boy! We have a son!"

Susan, despite her exhaustion, smiled at her husband and sobbed as her baby was lifted and placed in her waiting arms.

Susan looked down at the newborn son she held to her chest. His eyes were open, though squinting from the sudden light he had never before seen. His small, perfect lips pursed, and he moved his arms to his face. Susan was so incredibly overwhelmed with emotion. She attempted to see through her blurry vision. She wiped her eyes with her fingers, but the tears continued to come.

"Henry," she said with awe, "Henry, he's so beautiful."

"Sure is," Henry said.

Susan sat there staring at her infant son; she simply couldn't look away. She was oblivious to the doctor stitching the skin he had cut during the stealthy episiotomy he had given her; paid no attention, either, as he delivered the afterbirth and deposited it in the waste.

"Can I hold him?" Henry asked by her side.

"Oh, my gosh. Of course. I'm so sorry, Henry." She lifted their son, and Henry took hold, bringing him to rest upon his chest, his arms crossed under his tiny body. He looked so minuscule in her husband's embrace. From head to bottom he didn't even fill an entire forearm.

Susan looked at her husband's expression as he held their son. At the tears that dropped from his eyes, and the smile of pure love that was molded by his lips. Never had she thought her love for her husband could be intensified, but at this very moment, she had been proven wrong.

"Okay, hon," Blanche said, "we really need to take him to get washed up and set up in the nursery. You can go and see him as soon as you're ready."

"Oh, Blanche," Susan protested, "can't he just stay here with us?"

"Sorry, Susan. Hospital protocol. Mary will take him now, and I'm going to help get you cleaned up a bit. You can both go see him soon. In fact, Dad can take any family waiting as soon as we have the go-ahead."

"Suze, do you think you're okay for a minute? I just want to go tell everyone that he's here."

"Yeah, of course. Go ahead."

Clean and with a new gown on, Susan was eventually allowed to leave the birthing room. Blanche wheeled her to see her son through the glass of the nursery before she was moved to the recovery room in which she would remain for the next five days.

"She's here!" It was Viola who saw her first. She was outside the nursery with Henry, Mother, and James. Ma Tante Alice and Memere Richard were present as well, apparently having arrived after she had been taken to the delivery room.

A cry of cheers as Susan was wheeled over.

"How are you feeling, dear?" Memere asked.

"I'm all right," Susan said, offering no further information. She wasn't comfortable in divulging various small details of her birthing experience to her family just now.

"She's probably over the moon," James supplied.

"I really am," Susan said through her smile. "Where is he?"

"He's right there," Henry said, pointing through the window. He nodded his head at Mary, who picked their swaddled son up in her arms.

Susan leaned forward in the wheelchair to peer through the window. Mary held him facing forward, and she looked upon his sleeping face. Fresh tears welled in her eyes.

This was her son. She and Henry had created this beautiful boy together.

"Okay," Viola said, "I'm kind of dying to know now. What's his name?"

Susan and Henry exchanged a look. Susan's smile widened as she looked at her surrounding family members. Her heart beat strongly in her chest. "We've decided," she confirmed. "It really wasn't hard at all to pick a boy's name." She paused, looked from her husband to her son still held aloft in Mary's arms, then rested on Mother standing before her.

"His name is Charles Gilbert Beaumont." She watched her mother's lips tremble, and the tears course down her cheeks.

TWENTY-SIX

"Where's Mom?" Father was sitting at the kitchen table, spitting tobacco liquid into his Campbell's soup can. Susan had been home with baby Charlie for two days now, and this was her first visit with Henry to her parents' house with their son in tow. Henry had gone back to his internship at the college just yesterday, though he was able to keep his hours minimal to help Susan out at home at least for the next week until she had settled in a bit more, and for this, she was extremely grateful.

"In the bedroom," Father said.

Susan handed Charlie to her husband and walked through the living room and into her parents' bedroom. Mother was asleep, breathing softly.

"Mom," Susan whispered as she bent down to hover over her. "Mom?"

Mother slowly opened her eyes. "Oh, Susan," she said sleepily. "Did I fall asleep?"

"You did."

"I am sorry," she said. "I was just so tired. Give me a moment, please, and I will sit up."

She heaved her body into a sitting position, rubbed her drooping eyes. Susan helped her to stand and led her to the couch.

"I brought Charlie, Mom. You rest here and I'll go get him." Susan

371

walked to the doorway to the kitchen, motioned for Henry to come to the living room. Susan took their son from her husband and gently placed him on her mother's chest, watching as her mother's arms encircled his tiny, six-pound-twelve-ounce body.

"Oh, my," Mother breathed. "Oh, Susan, he's so beautiful."

"Yeah," Susan agreed, "he really is." Pride and love swelled within.

Mother held her grandson for quite some time as she chatted with Susan and Henry. Father chose to remain in the kitchen, which was perfectly fine by Susan.

"Oh," Mother said after a while, "I almost forgot. Here, Henry can you take the baby for a moment?"

"Sure can." Henry leaned over and picked up his sleeping son.

"Susan," Mother said as she slowly stood from the couch, "come to the bedroom." She walked forward and through her bedroom door. "I was going through storage the other day, and I came upon a bunch of photographs that I did not even remember I had. I would like to keep many of them, but I thought perhaps you would like some as well. I placed them just in this shoebox for you. Would you like them?"

"I'd love them," Susan said appreciatively. "Thanks so much, Mom."

"You are welcome," Mother said. "I had forgotten how many photographs I had taken through the years. It appears I went a little overboard." She chuckled.

Susan took the box from her hands, and together they walked back to the living room.

Susan and Henry visited for a while longer and then took their leave to get back home directly after a large feeding. "He should be happy for a while," Susan said.

They opened their front door and greeted Lucy, who was standing at the threshold, wagging her little tail and barking her joy at their arrival.

"Henry, I'm taking these to the bedroom to look at," Susan said as she motioned to the shoebox in her hands.

"Okay," he said as he placed Charlie down in his bassinet on the living room floor and went in the direction of the kitchen to grab a snack for himself.

Susan closed the bedroom door behind her and sat on the edge of the quilted bed. She opened the box and placed the top aside. Reaching in, she removed a large bundle of photos and began looking at them one by one. A couple of pictures she was familiar with as she had seen them at Charlie's memorial service: Charlie as an infant, Charlie and she at Stuart's, Charlie in uniform.

She continued to gaze at each photograph she held.

Susan as a very chunky baby sitting on the living room carpet of their home in a rumpled lace dress, a drooling, gummy smile for the person behind the camera.

Charlie, Susan, and Henry playing catch with a baseball in the backyard as children.

Mother in a housedress and bare feet smiling at the kitchen sink.

Susan, Janet, and Betty in the middle of a snow igloo in the backyard, Charlie and Henry smiling at the camera on either side of the girls.

The family posing for the camera in the cold snow, Father holding a new found Christmas tree aloft, his chin lifted and expression proud.

Dinner with her grandparents, Ma Tante Alice sticking her tongue out at the camera.

Charlie and Henry in heavy jackets, arms around each other's shoulders, ice-skating at the pond as young children.

Susan's graduation from high school, eyes shining as she posed with Janet, Betty, David, and Mikey.

Gilbert about to take a bite of whoopie pie.

Susan posing with Henry, Charlie, and Gil directly after Henry had proposed, red, white, and pink balloons filling the air around them.

She continued to rummage through the photos, a few tears trickling down. She wiped them with her sleeve and placed the pictures back in the shoebox. She put the cover back on top of the box and lifted it.

A picture fell, apparently having landed on the side of the box when Susan had initially taken the photos out. She picked it up, looked down at the image in her hands.

Baby Charlie began to cry, his voice lifting from the living room to carry through the closed bedroom door.

"Aww, what's wrong, buddy?" Henry said to his son. "Daddy's here."

It had been almost a year since she had seen Father Denis, yet she recognized him immediately. He wasn't wearing his priestly white robe; instead, he wore a black shirt and black pants with a white clerical collar. He stood outside his church, his face the face she remembered from her youth. He was middle-aged then, not yet the older man he was now. Weathered skin, graying black hair, clean-shaven. She looked at his crooked teeth through the photograph as he smiled, his incisors sharp. She stared at his beady, narrow eyes. He had one arm around her brother, and his other arm around… That was Tommy Walters. Charlie was looking at the ground, though his head was still held aloft, his shoulders slightly drooped as Father Denis possessively clutched his shoulder. Tommy Walters was looking directly into the camera, daring, bold, his lips curled into a grimace, his jaw clenched.

Father Denis had the expression of one at the height of achievement. His smile was confident, mischievous even.

Susan's hand trembled, and she lost her hold on the photograph. It floated and landed on the floor.

She placed one hand on her stomach, the other on her quivering lips.

EPILOGUE

He splashed in the water of the lake, this handsome young boy. He was perhaps four years of age, the chubbiness of his toddler self now in the past, though he still held the look of a young child, face round, eyes large. His sparse eyelashes were like his mother's, the curls, too, though hers were tighter. His were looser, finer. Mommy refused to cut them short, though Daddy said they'd have to go sometime; he was continuously brushing them off his forehead and snotty cheeks.

Daddy grabbed Mommy and pulled her to him, kissed her. He didn't so much like it when they did this. Cooties, his friend Grace always said.

He splashed them both, and they pulled apart laughing. Daddy chased him farther into the water, and he lifted his little legs in an attempt to outpace him. He was grabbed from behind, whisked into the air, and spun around, much to his delight. He giggled gleefully, and then Mommy came to him and tickled him on the thighs, what she called his "magic spot." He wriggled in Daddy's arms, laughing uncontrollably. His small dog yapped happily from the water's edge.

"Serves you right, you little booger," Mommy teased. Her belly was big now, bigger than it was before. She had told him she had a baby brother or sister growing in there. Daddy was always touching it, touching her. Just like Grammy and Grandpa Beaumont. Ew.

She stopped her tickling, and his laughing diminished to a slight chortle. Daddy put him back down in the water, and he continued to play as Mommy and Daddy sat in the sand. Daddy sat with his legs crossed, Mommy with her knees bent and her feet just barely in the water, her pink toenail polish shimmering in the summer sunlight.

He picked the water up with his small metal bucket, poured it out onto his chest, and watched it cascade down his tummy and onto his legs, splashing into the water beneath him.

A sudden inkling. He looked up.

They were behind Mommy and Daddy, two ethereal figures, barely visible. His innocent young child's eyes could discern them well enough, though. He had seen their pictures plenty of times in his new house; Mommy even had a picture of herself right at this lake when she and one of the men were younger. That man stood staring at him now. The man Mommy had said was "an angel standing by, waiting up in Heaven for us." Just like he was waiting for Mommy's friend Mr. Biladeau, who went to Heaven last year. And Grand-Pepere Richard—Mommy's pepere with the cane— before him. Mommy said Grand-Pepere's heart was unhealthy and stopped working.

The man had a tear running down his cheek. Just one, but the boy could see it glimmer in the sunlight. He had hair the color of his own, though it was shorter. Mommy always said the boy had his green eyes as well. "Such a handsome, lovely man," Mommy claimed, sounding to the boy like his mommy's mommy when she said it.

Behind him was another figure, a man. He was a bit shorter in height than the first, though his shoulders were broader. His hair was darker. Longer and wavy. His cheeks were high, his jaw pronounced. He had thick, dark eyebrows and lashes. He was embracing the first man, his arms around his chest. The first man held onto those arms with his fingers.

The second man rested his cheek against that of the first.

376

Both were smiling, faces wistful yet contented as they focused on the boy in the water.

"Hi, uncles!" The boy called with the ingenuousness of the young child he was. He waved jovially their way before steadying his gaze back to the water in his bucket, concentrating intently on the ripples spreading on its surface. He marveled at the fact that his little finger was able to affect a change to something that was otherwise smooth of appearance, and visually unaltered.

About the Author

Amy Fillion graduated from the University of New Hampshire with a degree in Psychology. She worked in the field of Early Intervention before making the decision to leave and stay home with her growing children. When she's not voraciously reading or writing, you can find her spending time with her husband and three boys. She is proud to call New Hampshire her home. This is her first novel.

Find her at www.amyfillion.com

Made in the USA
Middletown, DE
20 November 2019

79093663R10229